✔ KU-262-738

WEARING HIS RING TILL CHRISTMAS

NINA SINGH

CROWNING HIS SECRET PRINCESS

KATE HARDY

MILLS & BOON

First published in Great Britain 2022
by Mills & Boon, an imprint of HarperCollins*Publishers* Ltd,
1 London Bridge Street, London, SE1 9GF

www.harpercollins.co.uk

HarperCollins*Publishers*
1st Floor, Watermarque Building,
Ringsend Road, Dublin 4, Ireland

Wearing His Ring till Christmas © 2022 Harlequin Enterprises ULC

Special thanks and acknowledgement are given to Nina Singh
for her contribution to A Five-Star Family Reunion miniseries.

Crowning His Secret Princess © 2022 Pamela Brooks

ISBN: 978-0-263-30227-1

10/22

MIX
Paper from
responsible sources
FSC® C007454

WEARING HIS RING TILL CHRISTMAS

NINA SINGH

MILLS & BOON

To all my fellow wanderers out there.
Keep roaming and exploring.

CHAPTER ONE

SHE HAD TO get her act together already. Chiara Pearson plopped down on the bed she'd made—and if that wasn't a metaphor, she didn't know what was—then slid her cell phone into her maid uniform pocket. Lately, as much as she loved him, speaking with her dad left her apprehensive and anxious afterward.

The call she'd just disconnected had been no different.

Of course, it was her own fault. No fault of Joshua Pearson's whatsoever that their long- distance conversations recently left her shaky and guilt ridden. After all, she was the one lying to her own parent. Well, perhaps lying was a bit harsh. She was merely fibbing a bit, telling the old man what he wanted to hear. And that would be that Chiara was all set to travel in a few weeks to be with him and her brother at Christmas. But the truth was she had no idea how she might pull that off.

She was beyond broke. Barely covering the expense of living in Bali. Luckily, her job at the Garden Beach Hotel afforded her a couple meals throughout the day. Anything left over after the buffet-style meals served to guests was fair game once the event was over. She refused to think of them as leftover scraps. Because that thought was just too demeaning. Not that she could think of a better way to describe what it was.

But she had even less clue about how to break the news to her parent that she had little to no money with which to pay for a trip home. Her father would give her more money, no question about it. He wouldn't even hesitate. If it weren't for her pride, she'd be tempted to ask him to do just that.

He would be absolutely devastated if she broke her word about being there for Christmas this year.

Her phone vibrated in her pocket and Chiara hesitated to pull it out to see who the caller might be. If it was Dad calling her back for some reason, she might very well break down and admit her failings, admit that she'd lied to him about how well she was doing and how solvent she was.

Guilt had her hesitation ending just before the call went to voice mail.

With a sigh, she pulled the device out to look at the screen. Not her father, thank goodness. But only a slightly better scenario that the caller happened to be her brother, Marco. She clicked the answer icon.

"Hey, sis. Been trying to call you. Where've you been?"

Despite the situation, Chiara couldn't help the warm affection that spread through her chest. Marco and her father were the only immediate family she had now, and she cherished them. As she did the memory of her mother. They'd always been a very close unit. One that was now irreparably fractured.

"Hey yourself," she replied. "I was on the phone with Pa. You know how long those calls can be." Their father was definitely not the strong, silent type when it came to conversations with his kids.

Marco chuckled. "Let me guess. He wanted to go over all the Christmas plans. Over and over and over again."

Chiara tried to squelch down the panic bubbling through her chest at the mention of Christmas. Time to come clean.

But Marco didn't give her a chance. Before she'd taken her next breath, he continued speaking. And his words crumbled her already fragile resolve. "I've never seen him so excited for the holidays, sis. Keeps talking about how we'll finally all be together again."

Perhaps not all of us, Chiara thought, the sting of tears behind her eyes. "He does?"

"Oh, yeah." He paused a beat. "And if I'm being honest, I have to admit to being pretty excited myself. It has been a while, hasn't it?"

Something twisted in the area around her chest. Now her brother was talking up the holiday season. As if hearing Dad's hearty excitement earlier wasn't bad enough. Of course, she wanted to be with them in December. But fate didn't seem to be on her side these days.

Not that she wouldn't make the same decisions all over again if given the chance. How could she have turned down a friend who needed her money more than she did?

"Um... I have to go Marco. Rooms to clean and all that."

"I understand," he answered. Chiara could see the smile he'd spoken through clearly in her mind's eye. "Call me later."

"I will." She'd have to. After she'd built up enough courage through the day, she'd have to call her brother and let him know once and for all that she most likely wouldn't be able to make it back to the States for the holidays, after all. Despite all her assurances and promises earlier in the year that she wouldn't miss it for the world.

Telling Marco could serve as a practice run for the dreaded conversation she would have to have with her father. It would give her a nice preview of the lecture she'd receive. About how she was too spontaneous for her own good. Or how she never thought things through about what her decisions would mean long-term.

Chiara walked over to the glass doors of the balcony to stare at the misty gray sky outside. Bali was such a gorgeous location. Full of culture and national spirit. But Decembers were often rainy and wet most days. Today was no exception. And it fit her mood perfectly.

She couldn't dwell on her melancholy right now. There was a full day's worth of work that awaited her. The last thing she needed was to jeopardize her job. Cleaning rooms at a luxurious beachside hotel wasn't the most glamorous of duties. But she desperately needed the money. Especially now that she'd given away the money Papa had sent her. The savings she'd been putting away painstakingly for the past several weeks simply wouldn't be enough to cover what she needed.

What in the world was she going to do?

Giving her head a shake, she turned away from the view and went to her utility cart. She had plenty of time to fret over her predicament as she scrubbed and wiped for the next several hours.

Not that she had any hope of coming up with any kind of solution.

Evan Kim stared at the crisp white envelope he held in his hands and bit out a curse. He didn't need to open it to know what it was. An invitation to the wedding of the century. As far as those in his former circle were concerned, anyway. Especially his parents.

That thought made him wince.

Not that he wasn't happy for Louis. He really was. His friend was one of the most genuine and generous people Evan knew. He deserved all the good fortune the universe seemed to be bestowing upon him at the moment.

No, the issue Evan had about his friend's upcoming nuptials had nothing to do with the groom nor the bride—a lovely woman who was currently taking the music world by storm as a classical violinist.

The problem Evan had was completely about the wedding itself, as well as the ceremony. And all those who would be in attendance. Every instinct he possessed screamed at him to send his regrets.

But that would be the coward's way out. Evan had many faults. But being a coward was certainly not one of them.

Of course, he wouldn't send his regrets. Besides, he had too much respect for Louis to be a no-show at the man's wedding. They'd been as close as brothers growing up. It was bad enough Evan had missed the week-long excursions in Hong Kong for the bachelor party activities. No, Evan would go of course. And he'd endure the pain and awkwardness that would ensue as soon as he came across his parents.

Evan sighed and tossed the envelope onto the still-unmade bed. Walking over to the window overlooking the water, he ran a frustrated hand through the hair at his crown.

To make matters worse, he'd be attending the wedding sans a plus-one. His mother was sure to comment on that. Right after she reminded him what a disappointment he was as a son. His father would simply nod in agreement.

Most peoples' parents would have been impressed with him as a son. But not his.

All his success. Everything he'd accomplished on his own. None of it mattered as far as his mother and father were concerned. All they cared about was that he'd turned away from the family business. Hence, he'd turned away from *them*.

Same story for years now. One would think Evan would be past the point of having any of it affect him. But it wasn't in his nature to be comfortable with failure. And when it came to his parents, he'd indeed failed them. Apparently, nothing he did would ever be enough. In his parents eyes, his betrayal was absolute because he'd turned down the family business. The ultimate sin for the only Kim heir.

Well, it wouldn't do him any good to dwell on it now. He had a lot to deal with at the moment. He'd rushed back to Bali for a technology convention being held right here in the hotel he called home. The convention would finally grant him the opportunity to meet with the Italian AI company he'd been courting for several months now. Between that and the latest rollout of his gaming app, he had plenty on his plate without drama from the past intruding on his focus.

He strode to the corner desk and reached for his laptop just as the ding of a direct message appeared on the screen. His assistant back in the US with an ominous question.

Have you been online yet today?

He had not. And he could think of only one reason Emily might be asking. Some tawdry website had done yet another hit piece on him. He hammered out a quick reply before calling up a browser to check.

Yep. Bingo.

He was trending. Again. For all the wrong reasons. Nothing to do with the popular game app he'd developed or any of his latest investments. No. Someone had found and posted several photos of Evan partying on a yacht surrounded by scantily clad laughing women.

The film festival he'd attended last month. He'd just been trying to let off some steam after weeks of tense negotiations around a new development deal. Clearly, he should have been more careful about the wayward cell phone camera that had captured in him in full party mode.

Evan bit out another curse and slammed the laptop cover closed. The timing couldn't have been worse. He had to convince the Italian businessmen tomorrow that he was a serious and competent professional who would do well on their board. But his reputation as a ruckus-raising partier seemed to follow him and pop up at the most inopportune times.

His cell phone vibrated with a call. Emily.

"Please tell me you're calling to say you've already rolled out some damage control."

"I'm working on it."

"Isn't there some feel-good story we can have our media team push to replace some of these hashtags?"

"Hmm. Unfortunately not. But there does seem to be a developing story about that one influencer and her rocker ex-husband fighting about a custody dispute."

Evan scoffed. "Marriage. What a scam, right?" The very idea of matrimony made Evan shudder. His own parents were still together but Evan couldn't recall a time he'd witnessed any kind of display of affection between them.

Emily didn't respond to that. Instead, Evan heard a deep sigh from the other end of the line. "I'm not calling about the photos, boss. I'm afraid I have some more bad news."

Evan pinched the bridge of his nose. "Let me hear it."

"The Italian translator just canceled. Some type of family emergency."

Great. Just great. Was anything going to go right today? Anything at all? This technology convention in Bali was Evan's best chance to meet face-to-face with Roma AI and convince them he was a sure investment. Now he wouldn't even be able to communicate effectively.

"Thanks for the update, Em," he replied before disconnecting.

He needed to get some air.

Not bothering with a jacket, he strode to the door and rode the elevator from the penthouse level to the first floor. He'd seen a beachside restaurant/bar adjacent to the hotel on his way in earlier this afternoon and he hadn't eaten all day.

A heady cocktail and the view of the sunset over the water might help to clear out some of the frustration currently riding through his system. He just needed to step back and gather his thoughts.

Something had to go his way tonight.

Maybe she could pick up an extra shift or two. Chiara grunted as soon as the thought occurred to her. A measly added shift wasn't going to come close to covering her airfare back to the States. She didn't regret giving Jess the money. Of course not. The woman had needed it much more than she did. But it had brought her to this current precarious position.

There was nothing for it. Only two choices. Chiara had to either figure out a way to get the money or she had to come clean to her dad and tell him she wasn't going to make it, after all. And break his heart in the process. The thought of that crushed her. She'd made him a promise. The burn of fresh tears stung her eyes, but she refused to let them fall. She was done feeling sorry for herself.

Hanging up her uniform in one of the closets in the housekeeping quarters, she undid her ponytail and let her hair fall loose. It felt good to be in her own clothes. Though still desperate for some kind of solution, at least she felt a little better.

Now all she needed was a meal and refreshing swim. Not necessarily in that order. She always kept a spare swimsuit in her tote bag. Being in the water never failed to help soothe her nerves. If only temporarily.

Chiara wasted little time making her way to the hotel's beachside restaurant and bar. Clive, the bartender on call this time of day, was one of her favorites. He'd been one of the first people she'd met when she arrived in Bali two months ago and landed the housekeeping job at the hotel. He was generous with a smile, and he was always good for a laugh.

The complimentary meal he usually sent her way helped, too.

But when she got to the bar area, Clive looked as flustered and harried as she felt. The place was packed. Every table was full, every stool occupied.

"Some kind of technology convention," Clive explained when she approached him.

"Can I help?" So much for relaxing for a few minutes. But the bar staff was clearly swamped. And she still harbored some nervous energy she could work off.

"You're an angel for offering." He handed her a tray. "Here. Table fourteen. I appreciate it."

Dropping her tote bag behind the bar, Chiara took the loaded tray and turned on her heel.

Then slammed into what had to be a solid wall. "Oh!"

One of the bottles slid off the tray and she waited for the inevitable spray of cold beer to splash her lower legs and shoes. But it never came.

It took a minute for her to get her bearings. The object she'd collided with wasn't a wall at all. It was a man. And said man was currently stabilizing her with one hand on her upper arm even as he'd caught the falling bottle with the other. Some impressive reflexes. She started to tell him so and stopped short. Even in her frazzled state, her breath caught when she looked up at him.

For a fraction of a second, Chiara thought she must be imagining just how handsome he was. He sported just a hint of a five o'clock shadow over a strong jawline. Soulful dark eyes a woman could easily lose herself in. Jet-black hair the color of midnight. He looked like he could have stepped out of an ad for a yacht or cologne.

And her skin tingled where he still touched her.

Somehow, Evan managed to catch the frosty beer bottle before it hit the ground, only a minimal amount of liquid escaping the narrow mouth and hitting the sand by his feet. And he didn't know exactly what the young woman had muttered in her alarm but his rudimentary knowledge of the language told him it was most definitely Italian.

Huh. Maybe his luck was about to change, after all.

A pair of sapphire-blue eyes blinked up at him in clear gratitude. "Uh, thanks."

He felt as if someone had just landed a gut punch when his gaze landed on her face. She was stunning in a way he'd be hard-pressed to describe. Tanned skin, long wavy hair that fell past her shoulders. Her eyes reminded him of the color of morning sky over an ocean.

Since when had he become so poetic?

"I'm so terribly sorry," she said, straightening and balancing the tray. "I guess I wasn't watching where I was going. I'm a little distracted," she added almost as an afterthought, as if she were talking to herself more than to him.

It took Evan a moment to find his voice. "My fault," he finally managed. "I was staring at my phone. Walking and scrolling. Bad combo." A habit he typically abhorred when he witnessed it in others. But he'd been checking that blasted hashtag to see if he was still trending in the top-twenty topics.

She answered him with a small smile. "We all do it."

The accent clearly said American. Maybe he'd simply been hearing what he wanted to hear when he thought she'd spoken Italian earlier.

Several moments passed in awkward silence. For the life of him, Evan couldn't come up with a single word to say. When was the last time that had ever happened to him?

Never. The answer was never.

Somehow this waitress had rendered him dumbstruck. Finally, she lifted the tray ever so slightly. "Well, I should deliver these."

"Of course," he said, stepping out of her way.

By the time he'd found an empty stool at the bar and sat down, she'd delivered her load and come back for more. Evan ordered the nightly special and a strong brandy. All thoughts of gossip websites and AI meetings seemed to have slipped his mind. His focus remained squarely on the pretty waitress who quickly and efficiently served the crowded bar and cleaned and wiped tables in between orders.

He could hardly take his eyes off her.

CHAPTER TWO

AN HOUR LATER, the crowd in the bar was finally starting to thin out. Evan realized with surprise that he'd barely touched his food, despite having found it delicious. And his drink remained full in his glass. He'd slipped into hyper-focus mode at some point. It must have happened when he'd finally managed to pull his gaze away from the pretty waitress he'd almost barreled over upon arrival. In front of him on the table sat a napkin scribbled full with notes and ideas, all the things he wanted to go over with at the meeting tomorrow night. If he could somehow get past the language barrier.

His eye automatically roamed the bar area until he found her. She'd finally sat down at one of the smaller tables, holding a glass of wine and picking at a plate of food. Had he or had he not heard her utter an Italian word earlier?

Only one way to find out.

Hah. He wasn't fooling himself. It was an excuse to go talk to her. He did owe her a real apology, after all. He'd been practically tongue-tied when he'd tried to say sorry before. Rising out of his chair, he grabbed his drink and made his way over to where she sat.

His pulse quickened and he felt his mouth go dry. He was actually nervous! How utterly surprising. He'd never had any sort of problem approaching women before. Though it didn't happen often—usually *they* approached *him*.

Halfway to his destination, she suddenly looked up. Evan's heart skipped a beat as their eyes caught. Too late to back out now. She was watching him. Her lips curved into a small smile. He was going to go ahead and take that as an invitation.

"Hello again," he said when he reached her table, then immediately cringed at his words.

That's it, fella. Dazzle her with some charming and witty conversation-opener.

How lame could he be?

"Hi."

"I just wanted to come over and offer another apology. I'm so sorry that I almost knocked you over."

The smile widened. "That's very nice of you. But not necessary. You did catch my fall, after all. Plus, I wasn't paying attention to where I was headed. Like you, I was a little distracted myself."

A tightness settled over her face as she made the admission.

"Oh?" There was clearly a story there. Why did he want to hear about it so badly? It shocked him how curious he was about her given that he'd just laid eyes on the woman and any story she might have was really none of his business.

"Do you want to talk about it?" Again. Very original line. *Not.*

She gave a small shake of her head. "I wouldn't want to bore you."

"Please, you'd be taking my mind off my own woes." Woes? Had he really just said he had woes? Why was he acting so uncharacteristically around this woman?

She shrugged. "Sure. Why not?"

He clasped a hand to his chest in mock horror. "Your lack of enthusiasm is downright wounding."

She chuckled. "I'm sorry. What I meant to say was I'd be delighted and could use the company."

He returned her smile. "That's so much better. Thanks."

"You're welcome."

Pointing at her, Evan remarked. "You don't have a name tag." Unlike the other servers, she wasn't wearing one.

"That's because I'm not technically here."

"I have quite the imagination, then."

She chuckled at that. "I only came down after my cleaning shift for a bite to eat. But I saw they needed help. I'm Chiara."

"Evan. You work here at the hotel?"

She nodded.

"So, Chiara. Do you live here in Bali, then?"

She shook her head in answer. "Well, yes. And no. I'm here temporarily but long-term."

"I see. Business or pleasure?"

"Both, I guess. I'm here mainly to sightsee but working to support my travel habit."

He nodded. "That can be an expensive habit."

"You would know firsthand, I'm guessing."

"I do get around. You're right. Bali is my long-term home at the moment. I'm here now for this technology convention. But more for an important meeting it's taken me weeks to set up. Only it might be a bust now."

She took a sip of her wine. "How so?"

"I need a translator but the one I hired canceled at the last minute. So now I don't know how much I'm going to be able to even get across to the folks I'll be meeting with."

"I'm sorry to hear that."

He leaned toward. "I have a confession I should make to you."

Her eyes grew wide. "A confession?"

"That's right. For a second back there, when we ran into each other, I thought I heard you say something in Italian."

A rosy blush spread across her cheeks. "Oh, I do that sometimes. Hopefully, no one around here understands Italian. It wasn't a very nice term I called out."

So he'd been right. Evan resisted the urge to pump his fist in the air in triumph. Maybe this dreadful day might end in a stroke of luck. "You're not gonna believe this, Chiara, but you might be the answer to all my current problems." Realizing how close those words came to sounding like a cheesy pickup line, he immediately added, "In a completely professional way."

She blinked at him. "How so?"

"The translator I need happens to be for Italian. Any chance you're free tomorrow evening? Of course, you'll be comp—"

She held up her hands before he could go any further. "Whoa, let's slow down a bit here. I don't claim to be anywhere near fluent."

"Can you carry a conversation?"

She shrugged. "I suppose so. My mom spoke Italian to me and my brother sparingly growing up. We were much more comfortable with English. And I certainly don't know any technical terms. Probably wouldn't know those in English for that matter."

He chuckled. "Leave that part up to me. Coding

and AI is universal. I need you for the conversational pieces."

She crossed her arms in front of her chest. "I don't know…"

That wasn't a *no*.

"Where is this meeting to be held exactly?" she asked, eyeing him.

"Right here in the hotel. Your territory. A dinner meeting."

"I could definitely use the funds," she said under her breath, as if thinking out loud. Evan didn't the think the comment was meant for him. "I'm supposed to travel back to the States to spend Christmas in Vermont with my brother and father. Only I'm a little short on funds at the moment."

"If your father wants you there badly enough, won't he just give you the funds?"

She ducked her head with a sheepish motion. "He already did. I gave it away. I can't bring myself to ask for more."

"You gave it away?"

She nodded. "To one of the boarders at the hostel I've been staying at. She was here on a backpacking trip, too. Came to Bali after her boyfriend proposed to her because she wasn't sure about saying yes. Needed time away from him to process and make a decision."

"I see."

"Anyway, the boyfriend was in a horrible motor-cycle accident a couple of weeks ago. The scare told her everything she needed to know about how much she loved him. She was frantic, had to get back to the States right away."

"That's terrible. But what does that have to do with you giving away your—" Evan didn't have to finish the question as the answer came to him. This lovely person sitting before him had given away her travel money to someone she'd just met. "You paid for her to go back to the States, didn't you? To go back to her boyfriend?"

She nodded slowly. "How could I not?"

Many people would not have. In fact, most wouldn't.

Chiara released a heavy sigh. "You know what? Why not? I'll do it."

Evan felt a surge of relief flow through him along with something else he didn't want to examine too closely. He couldn't deny, language assistance aside, the fact that he'd be seeing her again held its own appeal.

He leaned closer to her over the table. "Then name your price, Miss Pearson."

How in the world had she ended up here?

I hope that spontaneity trait of yours doesn't get you in trouble one day. Her father's voice echoed in her head.

Her mother's followed immediately behind, however. *Don't waste any opportunity, Chiara. You will most often live to regret it.*

Chiara sighed. She'd long ago accepted the warring voices in her head borne of both parents' warnings over the years. Her mother's usually won out, for better or worse. It convinced her to make the most of her life in a way that her mother couldn't.

Besides, the question was more of a figurative one. Because the answer was clear. She was in this predicament because she needed the extra cash. It wouldn't cover the full cost of travel back to the States. But it was going to make a good dent. She must have lowballed herself when Evan had asked her price because he'd scoffed at the number, then said he'd pay three times the amount.

Chiara smoothed a hand down her midriff and studied herself in the mirror. Not bad for a girl who'd worked eighteen out of the past twenty-four hours. The silk red dress she'd borrowed from one of the lounge singers luckily fit her well and flattered her curves in all the right ways, if she did say so herself.

So she looked all right, she supposed. But was she really about to play translator for an international businessman she'd literally met the day before? What if she couldn't pull it off?

An ill-formed whistling sound echoed through the air behind her. Nuri bounced into the room and took her shoulders from behind.

"You look fabulous, Chi! Those businessmen we'll be unable to tear their eyes off you."

Chiara smiled at her friend in the mirror. "Never mind that. I just hope they understand me. It's been a decade since I had a conversation in Italian. And that was a very basic one talking about the weather with my mom."

Nuri gave her shoulders a squeeze. "You'll do great." After a pause, she added. "You miss her, don't you?"

"My mom?"

Nuri nodded. "Your voice hitches ever so slightly whenever you mention her."

No one had said that to her before. No one had ever noticed. Chiara wasn't surprised. Nuri had come to know her better than most of her friends back home. Though they'd only met a few weeks back, when Chiara had just arrived in Bali, Chiara felt closer to her than anyone she could name. Besides Marco. But sibling closeness was an entirely different matter. In Nuri, she'd found the closest thing to a sister she'd ever had.

"I talk to her all the time," she admitted. "In my head. I swear I can hear her respond. Her sweet gentle voice, reassuring me, encouraging me."

Nuri gave her shoulders another affectionate squeeze in silence.

Chiara fought back a tear and sniffled on a small laugh. "I'm not quite sure what she'd say about what I'm about to do here tonight, though. I'm guessing she'd tell me to go for it. As she often did when she was still here."

Nuri chuckled. "She'd also say you were brave and smart and clever. Because all those things are true."

"Thanks, Nuri. Helps to hear that."

The other woman glanced at the smart watch on her wrist. "You are also not great with time. You're running late again."

"Oh, no!"

Nuri gave her a gentle nudge. "If you hurry and the elevator cooperates, you'll make it to his penthouse in the nick of time."

Five minutes later, Chiara released a sigh of relief that her friend had been right. Right on the dot, she was punching in the code Evan had given her that would grant her entrance to his penthouse suite. The rush of adrenaline to make it here on time did nothing to soothe her frazzled nerves, however.

What if she made a fool of herself? Or used the wrong word? Worse, what if she made a terrible faux pas and inadvertently insulted one of the gentlemen? She was debating whether to turn around and send Evan her regrets when he rounded the corner of the hallway. He appeared to be adjusting his cufflinks. He stopped in his tracks when he saw her. His eyes grew wide.

Chiara tried to stamp down on her panic. Why did he look surprised? She was here at the time he'd told her. And why did this man make her so nervous and unsettled? He'd been nothing but friendly and congenial with her since they'd met. A complete gentleman in every way.

A small voice in her head answered her question. *Because you see him as an attractive virile man and not a gentle man at all.*

She cleared her throat. "Sorry, I should have announced myself. But I just arrived seconds ago."

He blinked at her. "No. Don't apologize. It's just… you look…spectacular."

Oh, no! She'd overdressed. This was supposed to be a business dinner meeting, after all. But he wasn't exactly clad in casual attire, either. The dark navy suit he had on had to have been tailored for him. A crisp white shirt and burgundy tie completed an outfit that screamed wealthy, sophisticated, successful businessman. To describe him as handsome would be too simplistic. Plus, he had the most kissable lips. The man probably had women trailing him everywhere he went.

Still. He appeared rather stunned the way he was looking at her. "If there's enough time, I can go change," she stammered out the words. Already she'd made a big mistake, it appeared.

Evan's reply was quick, almost brisk. "Don't you dare."

Okay. Chiara motioned to her midsection. "So, this is okay, then?"

He nodded once. "More than okay. Way to impress them immediately upon entry."

Her shoulders sagged with relief. Phew. "Oh. Thank

you. It's just, the way you were looking at me, I couldn't be sure if I'd met the dress code."

He smiled at her. "My apologies. I didn't mean to alarm you. Trust me. What you have on is perfect."

Thank heavens for that. Chiara had no idea what she might have replaced the dress with if he'd asked her to change. It wasn't as if she had a full wardrobe. Traveling the world backpacking and working odd jobs didn't exactly accommodate for the latest fashions.

Which reminded her just how utterly out of place she was going to feel at a business dinner. Too late now, though.

Evan held his arm out to her. "Shall we?"

As she went to place her hand in the crook of his elbow, he appeared to give her another once-over. Something flickered behind his eyes. Huh. If she didn't know better, she might think he was showing genuine male interest.

Right. She had to push that thought aside this very minute. Men like Evan Kim didn't often fall for hotel housemaids. She would do well not to forget that over the course of tonight.

Within minutes, they were walking into the main dining room of the hotel. Chiara felt a strange sensation of altered reality, like none of this was real. As if she were an actress in a movie or a play. She'd never entered this room without a cleaning cart. Now, she was about to dine here, sitting at a table with international titans of the tech industry. As the guest of one of those titans who also happened to be one of the most handsome men she'd ever laid eyes on.

Don't go there, Chiara.

Was that her voice in her head or her mom's? Either way, it was sound advice.

Evan must have sensed her discomfort. "You all right?" he asked, giving her arm an ever so slight squeeze.

She nodded. "Yes. I guess. Just feel a little out of place. Even though I've been in this room countless times." *To clean it*, she added silently to herself.

"Believe it or not, so do I."

"I don't. Believe it, that is."

His response was a soft chuckle.

"Well, for someone who doesn't think she fits in, you sure seem to be turning a lot of heads."

She didn't really believe that, either. If anything, Evan was the one most likely garnering all the attention. Especially among the females in attendance. More than a few were outright staring in their direction. Their attention most definitely didn't seem focused on her.

Evan glanced around the room. "I don't see them. They must be running late." He led her toward the bar. "How about a drink while we wait?"

She immediately shook her head. "I shouldn't. Not if I want to keep my wits about me."

He lifted an eyebrow. "You sure? It might help to calm your nerves a bit. Though I want to assure you, you have no reason to be nervous whatsoever." He leaned over onto the bar. "I'm the one who should be apprehensive here."

Chiara studied his chiseled profile. Steely determination was clear in his expression. Evan Kim was not a man accustomed to losing out on what he pursued.

"This deal means a lot to you."

He motioned for the bartender. "It does, indeed."

"Why exactly? If you don't mind my asking."

He shrugged. "AI is where the industry is headed. I want to be in front of the game."

That was no doubt his surface reason. Something told her his personal reasons ran much deeper. She found herself very curious about what they might be. Maybe she'd even get a chance to ask him sometime tonight.

Then again, why would he bother to tell her anything personal about himself? She was merely here to help him with a business meeting. Technically, she was his employee. Strictly professional. By this time tomorrow, they'd both be on their separate ways with Evan hopefully richer with a business deal and her richer with some much-needed extra cash. She might not ever lay eyes on him again.

She had no business feeling the sense of sadness that washed over her at that thought. "On second thought, I think I will have a glass of wine, after all," she told him when the bartender arrived.

"You got it."

He ordered a straight bourbon for himself and something that sounded very French for her. When their glasses arrived, Evan scanned the dining area once more. His eyes landed on a pair of gentlemen just entering through the doorway. "There they are."

Chiara followed his gaze to where two middle-aged gentlemen in expensive-looking suits stood, scanning the restaurant.

"Showtime," Evan said in her ear. He took her free hand in his and led her toward the two men. The warmth of his palm against her skin sent tingles down her spine. Wow. She really had to get a grip here. In her defense, she hadn't felt a man's touch in close to two years now. That had to be why she was reacting this way to one she'd barely just met.

She didn't have time to reflect on that thought much longer as they approached the two gentlemen.

"*Buonasera*," she offered when they reached their side. In somewhat broken Italian, she explained who she was and why she was there.

By the time they were seated at their table, Chiara felt relaxed enough that her pulse had slowed somewhat. The businessmen were very friendly and full of laughter. And her Italian seemed to be passable enough to move the conversation forward. When things got technical, Evan was able to take over with the necessary terms.

But then one of the men asked her a question. For the life of her she couldn't understand what he'd said. She stared at him blankly for several seconds. A cold wave of panic washed over her as she scrambled to decipher what he'd been asking. Suddenly, she felt Evan's warm hand on her knee under the table. He gave her a small squeeze of encouragement. Darned if it didn't work. Chiara mentally worked through the words she recognized and filled in the rest. The man had been asking about Evan's supply chain contacts.

She interpreted the question to Evan who told her what to say in response.

Crisis averted, the conversation resumed smoothly once more. All in all, she would have called the evening a success. By the look on his face, Evan seemed to be thinking along the same lines. Chiara had to acknowledge the sense of pride coursing through her at the moment. She'd done it!

Thanks for the early language lessons, Mama.

If only she could have told her mother how she'd been able to put it to use.

CHAPTER THREE

EVAN HAD TO resist the urge to grab Chiara about the waist and spin her around in circles. It was hard to keep a lid on his glee.

"Well, what did you think?" she asked. "How'd it go?"

"I think you've earned every penny of your fee. In fact, I think your performance deserves a bonus on top of what we agreed to."

She smiled widely even as she lifted her hands in protest. "I can't accept any kind of bonus. You're already paying me too much as it is."

She was right, of course. He'd doubled the amount he was to have paid the original translator, even when taking into account travel and lodging expenses. Chiara didn't need to know that, however.

"Nonsense. I'll wire the funds into your account as soon as we get back to the suite."

She cleared her throat. "We?"

Maybe he was being presumptuous, but he couldn't seem to help himself. "I have a bottle of fine Cristal chilling up there in an ice bucket. And I'm inviting you to come celebrate with me."

"You were expecting things to go well, then? A true optimist."

Ha! He chuckled out loud at that. If she only knew how wrong she was. "Let's just say I had a lot of faith in my newly found Italian-American assistant."

She bit her lip, a look of concern washing over her features. "Um... Not to be a killjoy or anything..."

He knew what she was getting at. "You're thinking how nothing has actually been confirmed."

She nodded once. "That's exactly what I was thinking. I didn't hear anything, in Italian or English, that sounded like any kind of confirmation, Evan. No one mentioned signing on the dotted line just yet. Only that you could expect to hear from them."

He had to agree. She was absolutely right. Still, the evening had gone off swimmingly. And he'd take victories when he could. Even the small ones.

He held his hand out to her. "There's still reason to celebrate, though, isn't there? They were clearly impressed by you, and I didn't hear them say no."

She bit her lip again. Despite seeming a bit on the spontaneous side, Chiara Pearson was also clearly a worrier. "I suppose..."

"Come on." He gently took her by the elbow and began to guide her out of the room. "Help me enjoy that champagne. We'll worry about the next step when we hear back."

Evan found he'd timed it all well when they got back to the penthouse. The champagne was perfectly chilled. He uncorked the bottle and poured some into one of the flutes on the food service cart, then handed it to Chiara before pouring for himself. "To you and your language skills, Ms. Pearson."

She performed a small bow before taking a sip. Her

eyes grew wide as she swallowed. "Wow, this is delicious. And I thought I might be too full after that dinner."

"I find there's always room for good champagne. Though one should sip slowly," he added with a chuckle after she'd taken something of a gulp.

Several minutes of comfortable silence passed before she spoke. "I've never been up here before. Not even to clean."

"Oh?"

She shook her head, studied the room. "They give the penthouse to the more experienced housekeeping staff." After a pause, she added, "I'm still considered a newbie here. Even though I grew up in the hotel business."

"You did?"

She nodded. "My family owns the Grand York Hotel in Manhattan."

He'd certainly heard of it. If he was recalling correctly, The Grand York was known for classic luxury.

She walked over to the glass wall overlooking the beach and sea beyond it. "What a breathtaking view."

He had to admit he hadn't really noticed. Now, as if seeing it through her eyes, he saw what she meant. The scene before them was rather extraordinary. Water huts dotted the crystal blue water. Silvery moonlight bathed the sand and ocean, glittering upon every surface.

"Good thing they don't send me up here to clean," Chiara said.

"Why is that?"

"I could spend hours up here just staring outside."

Before he could answer, his phone vibrated in his pocket. A call from overseas he had to take. "Excuse me for a moment, please."

When he returned a few minutes later, Chiara was seated on the couch, slumped in her spot, her head resting back against the cushion behind her. Her eyes weren't completely closed but close enough to it.

He cleared his throat softly so as not to startle her. Despite his attempt, she jolted upright at the sound.

"I'm so sorry," she said, straightening and glancing around her as if disoriented and not sure where she was. "I'm just so tired."

He surprised himself with his next words. "Then stay."

She gasped and turned to look at him.

"Just relax for a bit tonight," he quickly added. "You've earned yourself some downtime, I'd say. If my calculations are correct, you've been working in some way or another for about eighteen hours."

She gave a brisk shake of her head and stood up rather slowly. "I'm afraid I can't. It's late enough as it is." She didn't meet his eyes, her gaze focused wholly on her feet.

Great. He'd rattled her with his clumsy invitation. Setting his own flute down, he stepped closer to her. He could smell the fruity scent of her shampoo, the sweet bubbly on her breath. "Chiara, it is indeed late. There's plenty of room here. The sofa is a pullout and it appears quite comfortable. There's no need to venture out at this hour. Just spend the night."

This time her gasp was downright loud.

He gave her a reassuring smile. "You can stay in the main bedroom. It locks from the inside," he told her. "You won't even have to see me until the morning."

"I'd hate to make you sleep on a pullout bed."

"After what you accomplished for me at dinner, it's the least I can do. And trust me, I've slept in worse."

She looked skeptical but she wasn't saying no. She glanced over her shoulder in the direction of the master room. "The bed is large and soft," he nudged.

"It's not so much the bed."

"Then what?"

She closed her eyes and released a sigh. "It's just— It's been so long since I've been in any kind of private shower stall. The hostel I'm staying at has three shared ones. There's always a wait. And the water is always cold."

Evan could hear clear longing in her voice. About a shower. Sometimes he took the privileges in his life for granted. Chiara reminded him just how much. "I see." He leaned over closer and winked at her. "The shower head has five different settings. Oh, and there's also a full-size Jacuzzi tub in there."

Her mouth formed a small *o*. "That is tempting, I must admit."

Tempting was an adequate word. For his mind had just traveled to all sorts of forbidden places when he'd mentioned the Jacuzzi. He pictured Chiara submerged in the water surrounded by thick white bubbles. Naked, in the very next room.

He gave a slight shake of his head to clear it. The woman just wanted to bathe. "That settles it, then."

"I don't know, Evan."

He took her by the shoulders, gave them a slight squeeze. "Stay. Take a shower. Or a bath. Do both."

She laughed in response.

"You'd be doing me a favor," he told her. "Again."

She lifted an eyebrow. "How so?"

"Simple. If you insist on leaving, I'll have no choice but to walk you to your place. Then I'll have to walk all the way back."

"I wouldn't make you walk me."

"What kind of gentleman would I be if I didn't insist on doing so?"

She glanced toward the master once more. Finally, with a resigned sigh, she nodded in agreement. "Sure. I'll stay, then. Thank you."

The pleasure that rushed through him at her acceptance was immediate and rather surprising. It made no sense. He had to chalk it up to appreciating the good fortune of finding someone like her when he needed it most. Someone who spoke Italian and needed extra money so she could travel for the holidays. He'd almost forgotten how much importance others gave to the Christmas season. All the traditions, the celebrations. None of it mattered to him. Christmas was just another day. One he'd spent mostly alone in his room while growing up, on the latest computer his parents had gifted him. His mom and dad were never around during the holidays, preferring to travel to exotic locations rather than spend it at home with their only child.

"I have a large T-shirt you can sleep in and some sports shorts with a drawstring waist," he offered, turning back to the topic at hand.

His offer was simply the act of a savvy businessman, Evan tried to tell himself. It might even be considered a bonus for the fine work she'd done for him tonight. Or what if the Italians had further questions and he needed her to translate once more? Evan needed her to be rested and ready in that case. And that was all he needed from her.

He sighed as those thoughts were immediately shut down by a critical voice in his head. He was making excuses. Truth be told, Evan wasn't sure why he wanted her to stay so badly. He only knew he wasn't quite ready to say goodbye to her just yet.

She slept like a baby. Chiara couldn't even remember the last time she'd slumbered so soundly. Definitely not

38   WEARING HIS RING TILL CHRISTMAS

since she'd left home. Maybe even before that. And she had Evan to thank for it.

With a yawn and a stretch, she slowly made herself get out of bed. The shirt he'd given her was several sizes too big and hung on her curves like a sack. She hadn't bothered with the shorts. Aside from a restful night of sleep, she felt clean and refreshed. In fact, it was a wonder her skin wasn't pruned and wrinkly all over. After spending a good amount of time in the Jacuzzi, she'd then taken a long hot shower. She didn't regret it the slightest bit. When was the next time she'd get a chance to enjoy such indulgence?

In fact, she was going to go take another long shower before venturing out of the room and heading back to her regular non-luxurious life.

A wave of sadness washed over her. After today, she'd probably never get a chance to come back into this room. Not even as an employee.

She also wouldn't see Evan again. That, she had to admit to herself, was the real reason for the doldrum. The chances of meeting someone like him ever again were slim to none.

Thinking back to the meeting last night, she recalled how utterly in his element he was. Despite not speaking the language of his potential investors, Evan was fully in control throughout the entire night. He drove the conversation and made sure all his points were clearly communicated. It wasn't hard to see why he was so successful at such a young age. She had no doubt he would not only strive but reach even higher heights.

Charming. Successful. Charismatic. Devilishly handsome—the man looked like something out of a magazine cologne ad for heaven's sake.

Maybe she should run the shower cold. A giggle

bubbled up her throat. *As if.* She was going to take the longest shower with the hottest water she could stand while she had the chance.

Half an hour later, she had to accept the reality. It was time to unwrap the thick Turkish towel and put last night's dress back on, then make her exit. She couldn't exactly walk out of here wearing Evan's T-shirt and gym shorts.

And it was time to thank the man who had made her night of excitement and luxury possible. Then say goodbye to him.

A lump formed at the bottom of her throat, and she had to swallow it down.

Best to just get it over with. It was time to bid the man adieu and get back to her own mundane life. One where she still had to figure out how to earn some more of the cash she needed to travel back home. What Evan paid her last night would help, of course. But she still had a ways to go.

The upside was she'd discovered last night that she had yet another option in terms of earning her way. Maybe she could segue this translation ability into a regular gig of some sort.

She had Evan to thank for that new idea as well. And thank him she would. Right now.

But when she left the master bedroom and ventured out in the main living area, he was nowhere to be found.

Huh. Maybe he'd had an early morning meeting. But he hadn't mentioned it last night.

It felt wrong to leave without saying goodbye. *Right. As if that's why you're hesitant to leave while he's gone. Just admit you want to see him again.*

Oh, dear. She had to face the facts. She'd grown overly fond of the man. In the short period of time since she'd smacked into him with a serving tray, she'd developed unexplainable and inconvenient feelings she had no business entertaining. He'd hired her for a simple purpose, and she'd done the job.

Now it was all over.

The truth of that hit her like a ton of bricks. Especially when she heard the door click open and heard him enter the suite. He'd apparently gone for a run. Dressed in a tight sleeveless shirt and running shorts, his skin glowed with the sheen of sweat. He was breathing heavy, wiping at his forehead with the back of his hand. Something shifted in the vicinity of her heart. If she thought he'd looked handsome in a suit, she didn't have the words for the magnitude of sex appeal he exuded at this moment. It took her breath away, the sheer pleasure that slammed into her when he entered the room and walked toward her.

But then she got a look at his expression. Something was terribly wrong. Evan Kim appeared to be furious.

The run hadn't done much to improve his mood. He could have run for miles, though, and it wouldn't have made a difference.

The meeting last night seemed to have gone so well. But not well enough judging by the email Evan had woken up to.

He walked into the suite absentmindedly pulling his sweaty shirt off to find a startled Chiara gaping at him. He must look a mess. Between the sand chafing his shins and the effects of the punishing run he'd just pushed himself through, it was no wonder Chiara appeared to be keeping her distance.

By contrast, she looked beautiful and refreshed, despite wearing last night's dress.

"Uh, good morning?" she said in a gentle voice, then added, "Or is it?"

"How'd you guess?"

"Well, for one, you're scowling. And for another, most people look much less tense after a run."

Evan rubbed his forehead. He had to tell her what had happened. He had to let her know that despite all her charm and competence with Italian, despite all their efforts last night, they had failed.

She didn't give him chance. "Oh, no," she said, covering her mouth with her hand. Sharp cookie. She'd figured it out without him having to say a word.

"So you guessed, I take it," he added, bundling his shirt and tossing it onto the sofa in frustration.

"The Italians said no."

That wasn't entirely accurate but close enough. "They said they need more time to decide. They have to think it over some more."

She blinked at him, color creeping into her cheeks and her jaw hardening. If he didn't know any better, he'd say she was as upset as he was.

"Tell me exactly what they said."

He reached for his smart phone in his back pocket and called up the email. "See for yourself."

As he watched her read the screen, the message came back to him and reignited his frustration and disappointment.

Very impressed with all you've accomplished. Need to decide about your professionalism. Looking for maturity and stability in our business partners.

And more along those lines.

Chiara's breath had quickened and her eyes narrowed. She was obviously rereading the email more than once. Finally, she handed back his phone.

"I don't understand. Why are they saying these things about you?"

He sighed with resignation. Now, he would have to explain to this sweet accommodating woman all the ways in which his reputation preceded him. Or maybe he could show her.

Calling up the most intrusive of the websites, he clicked on the appropriate link and handed the device back to her. "Here. See for yourself. This is what they're referring to in that email."

She eyed him up and down before taking back the phone and looking at it. Several seconds of awkward silence went past before she finally gave it back to him.

"Well, you seem to have your share of fun."

He scoffed at that. "Trust me, it's all highly exaggerated. They take a well-timed photo and embellish the circumstances. And their readers eat it up."

She crossed her arms in front of her chest. "So, are you like famous or something?"

Despite his ire, he couldn't help but chuckle at her tone. It held utter horror and maybe even some disdain. "Hardly. Only those in very specific circles will even see these hit pieces. Unfortunately, the investors we met with last night would be included in such a group."

"Huh. So now what?"

"Now I have to regroup and somehow figure out how to change their minds."

Her lips tightened in concentration. "You'll have to start by convincing them you're not some sort of party animal."

Evan sighed. "And I have no idea how to do that. My

professional accomplishments should speak for themselves. In a perfect world, they would."

"But all they see is that you're a jet-setting, high-living bachelor," Chiara supplied.

He grunted in frustration. "Well, it's not like I'll be able to acquire a wife and family overnight. I'm not even in any kind of committed relationship at the moment."

At his words, Chiara did that thing where her gaze fell to the direction of the floor. She was probably wondering why he was keeping her here, getting into all of this. She probably had things to do. She was still in last night's dress for heaven's sake. He had no right to impose on her further. It wasn't as if there was anything she could do about any of this.

As much as he hated to see her leave, there really wasn't any reason for her to stay. And he had to figure out where to go from here.

He rammed his fingers through the hair at his crown. "I'm sorry. You probably want to get going. And I could use a shower." He started making his way toward the master bedroom, picking up his discarded T-shirt along the way. "Feel free to order room service. There's an automated coffee bar in the kitchen area."

He sincerely hoped she would take him up on the breakfast and coffee offer and maybe still be here when he exited the shower. For some odd reason, he wasn't quite ready to see her go. Again, strictly business he tried to tell himself. If there was any way Chiara could help him talk some sense into the Italians, he might still need her.

In any case, he certainly couldn't ask her to stick around any longer. He'd imposed on her long enough.

Besides, he had work to do. He also had to figure

out how to appear less like the high-living bachelor the websites described him as. Not that he had any kind of clue how to go about doing that.

And, like he'd just told Chiara, he wasn't even seeing anyone at the moment. No one even came to mind when he considered dating; he hadn't met anyone who'd interested him romantically for quite some time now. In fact, Chiara was the only female who he'd even come close to spending any amount of time with him alone over the past several months.

It hit him as he turned the water on and waited for it to heat up. *Chiara.* Maybe there was, indeed, a way she might be able to help him out with all this.

Sure, it was a harebrained and far-fetched idea that had just sprung into his head. But it just might work. A way to address all his problems. His reputation as far as potential business partners. Attending the wedding. The unwanted attention from the tabloid sites.

Chiara could be the answer to it all.

CHAPTER FOUR

SHE COULDN'T HAVE heard him correctly. Chiara had just made her way to the coffee machine for a much-needed jolt of caffeine when Evan rushed back out of the bedroom. He was still shirtless by the way. So maybe she hadn't been exactly concentrating fully when he said what he did.

She gave her head a brisk shake to try to clear it. "I'm sorry. I could have sworn you just said something to the affect that you and I should tell people we're engaged."

He nodded once. "Uh-huh. That's pretty much what I said."

A giggle burst out of her, and she put her empty cup down before she could drop it. "Evan. What in the world are you talking about?"

Darned if she knew for sure. She was having trouble concentrating. Would it be too awkward to ask him to put his shirt on? The site of his chiseled muscular chest and tanned sweaty skin wasn't making it any easier to focus here. "Did you hit your head on the side of the tub or something?"

"No. I had what you Americans might call a light-bulb moment."

She didn't even know if he was joking. He seemed lucid enough. "Here." He lifted the coffee cup and stepped to the machine. "I'll make you a cup of coffee and we can talk. You have some time?"

Okay. "I guess so. I'm not scheduled until noon."

"Great. How do like your coffee?"

"Lots of cream. Lots of sugar."

"You got it."

"Thanks. But, Evan, just one thing."

"What's that?"

"Could you maybe get dressed first?" She didn't even care how her request sounded. She really couldn't stare at his bare chest any longer, especially not if he was going to try to explain whatever this lightbulb idea of his was.

He gave her a sheepish grin. "Sure thing. Go have a seat. I'll be right back."

Less than five minutes later, he was back after taking what had to be the fastest shower in the history of running water. And thank the heavens above, he'd put on a fresh shirt and khaki shorts. Now maybe he would stop talking nonsense about the two of them pretending to be engaged. Hard to believe that's what he'd really said. How preposterous.

Only, the look of determination on his face had her second-guessing about him backtracking in any way, preposterous or not. He sat across from her at the coffee table and braced his forearms on his knees. "Just hear me out before you say anything. Deal?"

She nodded but her mouth had gone dry. Evan Kim seemed very determined to convince her of whatever he was about to say. Something told her he didn't hear the word *no* often. Well, he was going to have to learn to accept it coming from her. This was beyond ridiculous.

"You said you needed money to get back home in time for Christmas."

He certainly had that right. "Uh-huh."

"And I need to convince several people that I'm on the path of settling down and giving up the life of a freewheeling bachelor."

Well, that statement certainly begged a question. Who else besides the Italian businessmen did he need to convince? She'd have to hold her tongue, though. She'd just promised to hear him out before saying anything. Easier said than done.

"I think we can help each other out."

"How exactly?"

He leaned closer. His breath felt warm on her cheeks. Freshly scrubbed from his shower, she could smell the minty lemon scent of his aftershave. His jet-black hair glistened with dampness. How would it feel to fun her fingers through it? Then she might lower her hand down his cheek and over that chiseled jawline.

Focus! This was important.

"I know this is going to sound crazy," he said now. "But I think it may just work. To pretend we've gotten engaged."

"You're right."

He blinked. "You really think so?"

"About it sounding crazy."

"Just hear me out. All we have to do is pretend we've fallen for each other. At first sight. And we've decided to get married. We knew right away we were meant to be."

He made it sound like some kind of romance novel. "Come again?"

"We met and it was immediate. Chemistry and all that."

Did he even hear himself? Wow, when she'd thought he was driven and determined before, she hadn't even grasped the full extent of his tenacity. She'd never seen anything like it.

"At first sight?" she repeated, hoping he heard how ridiculous such a notion sounded.

He nodded. "Kismet."

"How might it possibly work?" she asked against her better judgment, more out of curiosity than anything else.

He took both her hands in his—absentmindedly, she was sure, whereas she had to make sure to hide her reaction to his touch. Ignore the fact that her heart rate went up a notch. Or how heat seemed to curl in her belly.

Oh, dear. The way she was starting to feel, it was almost as if Evan's words about love at first sight were in fact reality. For her, anyway.

Or it might be more like lust. The man was stunningly alluring.

"I have three high-profile events coming up. You just accompany me to each event as my significant other. We let the cameras snap away while we pose as the besotted couple on the verge of tying the knot."

"Huh."

"Of course, I'd be compensating you for your time. Handsomely. Which solves your problem of travel expenses to America. While in turn solving mine with my reputation."

But why her? "Why would you ask me to do this? There has to be other women who would make more sense to be your fiancée," she stuttered as she said it. No doubt, Evan had countless women in his contact list who would jump at the chance to accompany him around the world, acting lovesick. In fact, they probably wouldn't even need to act. How many women were pining for him right this minute? Why that thought had her muscles clenching, Chiara didn't want to examine. "There must be someone else," she reiterated, resenting how true that statement had to be. Not that it was any of her business. But Evan probably had countless women on speed dial. Women who were probably savvier, prettier, more accomplished, more successful. A bitter taste burned the back of her throat before she swallowed it down and admonished herself. She had no business feeling any kind of way about Evan's history with the opposite sex. "I'm sure there's someone else you can ask this of."

His lips tightened into a thin line. "No. There is no one. Besides, my previous romantic ties all reinforce the image of me I'm trying to erase. Those ladies are no strangers to the party scene themselves. You're the only one."

Heavens, those last few words sent a rush of heat to her cheeks. She knew he didn't mean it in any significant sense, but to hear him say such a thing had her heart thumping.

But he was right about one thing. The entire plan did, indeed, sound crazy. "You can't be serious. This has to be some kind of joke. You're playing with me."

He shook his head in answer. "No joke. No playing. Dead serious."

How could that be? What he was suggesting sounded downright ludicrous. To pretend they were engaged after falling for each other upon meeting?

Even from a practical standpoint, he had to see how little sense he was making with this suggestion. Even if she decided to humor him for a moment. "All the absurdity aside, what you're describing sounds like some kind of acting gig. I have no thespian experience whatsoever. Aside from playing a dancing girl for a middle school production. How would I possibly pull this off?"

"You don't need experience. Just smile for the cameras and follow my lead during conversations."

He made it sound so simple. But the smallest misstep could mean catastrophic embarrassment. Especially for him. She would feel horrible if she messed up at any point along the way. Still…he definitely had a point about her needing the money. "Tell me more about these events."

Chiara's apprehension grew with each word he uttered as he explained. "You're saying I'd be traveling across the world with you."

His smile faltered. "A wedding in Singapore. Beijing for an investor meeting. And Switzerland for a final business meeting with the Italian AI executive." He dropped her hands and pulled back a bit. "I've got to say, I thought you'd be more excited about that part. Sightseeing at all those places."

She couldn't deny that it sounded like the opportunity of a lifetime. Those were all spots she had on her bucket list. Particularly Beijing. But the circumstances were just so…unconventional.

Don't turn away from opportunities when they present themselves.

Chiara pushed the thought, sounding in her mother's voice, out of her head. Spontaneity was one thing. Insanity was something else.

And that's what this idea was. Insanity. Wasn't it?

She stood up and walked several steps away toward the glass wall. The close proximity wasn't helping. "I'm sorry, Evan. As exciting as this all sounds—"

He held up his hands and interrupted before she could continue. "Don't answer just yet. I have another forty-eight hours before I depart Bali. Just think about it."

She swallowed. "If you insist. Though I don't think time is going to make a difference."

He shrugged. "Maybe, maybe not. I'm just asking you to give it a think. And think about all those places you'll get to visit. All the sights you'll see."

Wow, he really was playing hard here. Playing to win. He had to know she might never get a chance to visit all those places on her own.

"Chiara, just a few hours to mull it over. That's all I'm asking."

That sounded reasonable enough. Though she wasn't sure how more time was going to make any of this sound any more feasible. Traveling the world with a man she'd just met. Acting as if they were engaged. Pretending to be in love with him.

She nodded silently in answer. Though she knew she was just delaying the inevitable. Just putting off telling in "no". In no uncertain terms.

There was absolutely no way she could accept his offer. Not for any amount of money.

She had to get it over with. Just tell him her answer already that she would be turning him down. The sooner the better. No reason to drag this out any longer than necessary. Then Evan could move on to plan B.

He'd be able come up with a plan B. Wouldn't he?

He wasn't exactly making it easy, however.

She wasn't surprised, of course. Evan Kim was clearly a man who pursued his goals with determination and grit. Since she'd left his penthouse, he'd texted her no less than half a dozen pictures of the luxurious hotel where the wedding would be held as well as majestic scenes from the Great Wall in China. Surely, breathtaking photos of the Swiss Alps would be following in no time. No

sooner had she completed the thought than her phone
pinged with an attachment message. She ignored it. Not
like he was tempting her with breathtaking photos. She
was already tempted. A lack of desire to see those sights
firsthand was hardly the problem. How many times had
her mother mentioned wanting to see the Great Wall?

Mama had never gotten the chance.

Chiara let the sadness at the memory of her mother
wash over her as she let herself into her apartment.
She'd learned years ago that there was no use fighting
it. But she never let herself wallow for too long. That
was a slippery slope that she had to avoid for her sanity.

The drab surroundings of the hostel room posed
quite a contrast to the suite she'd just spent the night
in. That shower and tub had felt like a piece of heaven.

The hotel in Singapore probably had really nice tubs.
And a Jacuzzi pool just like the one she'd enjoyed last night.

She could find out for herself in a few short days.

Chiara squeezed her eyes shut and fell onto the mattress. Why was she even going down this road mentally?
Her mind was already made up. She would find another
way to get the money. And Evan would find another way
to convince his investors. He was adept and resolute and
talented. He would figure this out without her. She had
no reason to feel guilty that she was letting him down.

Another ping on her phone made her groan out loud.
Fully expecting to open a file to a scene of a snowy
mountaintop, she was surprised to find a message from
her friend instead.

Early lunch? Just made *bakso*. Come by. Lots to share.

Even as she read the note, her stomach grumbled.
She loved Nuri's *bakso*. And she could certainly use the

company. Nuri wasn't going to believe any of it when Chiara got around to telling her about last night. Or the bombshell proposal Evan had made to her this morning.

Changing and freshening up with haste, she replied on her way out the door that Nuri could expect her as soon as she could get there. Within minutes, she was seated at Nuri's round wooden table, the aroma of pungent spices and seasoned meat wafting through the air.

They ate in comfortable silence. The warmth of the dish along with the comfort of Nuri's company finally had the knot in her stomach loosening. Nuri leaned back in her chair and popped a piece of bread in her mouth. After swallowing, she shot Chiara a friendly smile. "So, tell me all about last night. How did you do translating?"

Chiara put down her spoon and inhaled deeply. Where to begin answering her friend's question?

"Translating was the easy part. It's the rest that you're not going to believe."

Nuri's eyebrows lifted with curiosity. "Oh? Do tell."

Releasing her breath, Chiara let loose with a torrent of words she could only hope made some semblance of sense. She began by explaining how well she and Evan had thought the meeting had gone, only to be disappointed by the email that morning. Then she told her about spending the night in Evan's suite locked away in the master bedroom. Her friend's eyes grew wide at that part, but she remained silent, listening intently.

"Wow. That's a lot. Will he contact you again, you think? How did you two say goodbye?"

Chiara bit her bottom lip. "That's just it. We might not have."

Amusement mixed in with mild surprise washed over her friend's face. "You didn't? Please explain."

As she told Nuri about Evan's proposal, Chiara realized exactly how harebrained it all sounded when spoken aloud in her own voice. Nuri's eyebrows had lifted practically to her hairline when she was done.

"I don't know, Nuri. On the surface, the answer seems clear. I can't accept such an offer." She rubbed her forehead, deep in thought. "I mean, I just met the man. He seems to be an upstanding person of character. If not a bit of a partier."

"And?"

"And how would I even begin to explain it to my brother or Papa if they ever got wind of any of this?"

"So, you've made your decision, then?"

Chiara's silence was answer enough for her friend.

"Beneath the surface, you're torn," her friend said. "More than a little, it seems."

Chiara puffed out a frustrated breath. "I guess I am. I can't help but keep remembering all the times my mom told me about wanting to travel to all these places. Particularly the Great Wall in Beijing. And she loved the mountains and snow. I know she would have jumped at the chance to visit the Swiss Alps."

Chiara pulled out her cell phone and called up the photo she looked at daily. A picture of a piece of notebook paper; the original was safely tucked away in a drawer at home in New York. The paper was wrinkled and faded from constant handling. Hence, the need for the snapshot. Not that there really was a need at all. She practically had the words on the screen memorized.

"Is that the list?" Nuri asked, emphasizing the last two words as if she referred to a sacred item. In many ways, it was just that. Sacred.

"Yes. The bucket list my mom helped me write of all the places I wanted to visit and the things I wanted to do as soon as I became an adult."

The memories came rushing back as she recalled the afternoon. Sitting down and writing in a notebook was the last thing she'd wanted to do. She would have rather ran upstairs and cried into her pillow after what had happened earlier that day. But her mother wouldn't hear of it. As usual, she'd been right. "Did I ever tell you how the list came about?" she asked her friend rhetorically, as she already knew the answer. Chiara would have remembered sharing such a memory with her friend.

Nuri leaned closer. "Tell me."

"I'd just gotten rejected by my high school crush. I'd planned an elaborate way to ask him to the main event of high school."

"Oh?"

She nodded. "A prom. I planned it for weeks, the perfect prom-posal."

"Prom-posal?"

"An elaborate way to ask someone to the prom. The last major dance in high school before graduation. A really big deal."

"And you wanted to ask this boy to take you."

"Oh, yes. Not just any boy. The star running back on the football team. Popular and handsome. I didn't really think it through."

"What happened?"

She cringed as she called up the memory. "I dressed up in a fancy gown, did my hair and makeup. And waited outside the locker-room door with a big sign for him to exit with the rest of the football team."

Nuri visibly winced. "Uh-oh. I think I can guess what happened."

"He turned me down flat. In front of all his team-mates and buddies. They all started laughing. At me." Chiara actually laughed as she explained. Funny how she could laugh about the incident now. At the time, it had seemed so tragic to her teenage psyche.

"Ouch."

"Yeah, it hurt. Afterward, all I wanted to do was wallow in my room and cry. I told my mom in no uncertain terms that I would never take a chance again. No more risks. It was too painful."

"Your mom had other ideas."

Chiara nodded. "She sure did. She told me I had so many more adventures ahead of me. And that we would sit down and start planning some of them right that very minute." A rock formed at the base of her throat as she spoke, and tears stung her eyes. Her mom had known exactly how to combat her sadness and come up with the perfect way to get her focused on the future instead of one boy's rejection. Hence, the bucket list. It mostly consisted of traveling to several exotic locations.

She'd already checked off Bali. And Mexico, thanks to a class trip senior year. A couple of spots in central Europe when she first started backpacking. But there were so many boxes left. So many more places she wanted to see while she had the chance.

Evan was giving her a once-in-a-lifetime chance to check off some of those boxes. All expenses paid.

Nuri braced her hand on her chin over the table. "Hmm. What do you think your mom would say to all this? What would she advise you to do?"

Chiara glanced once more at the screenshot on her phone. The answer was all too clear.

CHAPTER FIVE

CHIARA WAS STILL ruminating on that question ninety minutes later as she packed her cleaning cart. In some ways, she felt as if her mother was always with her, guiding her spiritually. But how could Chiara possibly say what Gabriela Pearson may have said about her daughter's current predicament?

She could guess what Papa and Marco would say if they ever got wind of all this. A resounding *no* from both.

As if she'd summoned it, her phone began to vibrate in her pocket, then sounded her brother's ringtone. Darn, she usually texted him before her shift, but she'd been too preoccupied this afternoon. Marco had a tendency to worry. In some ways, it was as if she had two fathers.

She picked up before it could go to voice mail. He was just going to keep calling if he didn't talk to her live. "Hey, sis. Haven't heard from you. How're things down in paradise?"

Paradise wasn't quite what she'd call this supply room with its metal shelves and scrub mops hanging on the walls. "Oh, you know. Living a fantasy."

He chuckled at that. "Just think, you'll be home in a few short weeks to tell us all about it."

Chiara felt the now-familiar tightness in the pit of her stomach every time the subject of traveling back home came up. She did her best to ignore it. "I'll give you all the juicy details as soon as I set eyes on you."

"Waiting with bated breath." Was it her imagination or did Marco sound off? Distracted?

No doubt, it was just the upcoming holidays he had on his mind. She had her own issues.

For a split second, she wanted to just give in to what felt so natural and confide in her big brother. He'd always been there for her while they'd been growing up. Even before Mama was gone. Her current predicament was made all that much harder because she couldn't lean on him emotionally. Because then she'd have to tell him that she spent all the money she'd earned and given away what their father had sent her to cover her travel expenses.

The only thing that might come close to having her father disappointed in her would be for her brother to feel that way. But it pained her on such a deep level. She could really use his feedback right now.

Except maybe there was some small way he could provide it. Between his studies and his hospitality experience, Marco had a lot of contacts. She might be able to pick his brain, after all.

"Hey, I have a question for my big brother," she began.

"Shoot."

"Between the hotel and your school buddies, would you happen to know anything about a young entrepreneur by the name of Evan Kim? I thought maybe you may know who he is."

"Hmm," he answered. "Name's not ringing a bell. Why are you asking about him?"

"There's some sort of tech convention here at the hotel in Bali. He's one of the names being tossed around as an up-and-comer in the field. Has done so much at such a young age...yada yada." Everything she'd just said was the absolute truth.

Her brother chuckled. "We do have one regular guest who's a titan in the industry. I also consider him a friend. I have his contact info. I could drop him an email and see what he knows about the guy."

Knowing more about the man would certainly help. Basic research. She was considering a job offer, after all. Though it was a rather unorthodox one. "Thanks, Marco. I'm just curious. And you know how I can get when I'm curious about something."

He laughed again. "You're the ultimate researcher." She knew the part he wasn't voicing out loud. Neither her brother nor her father could understand why she hadn't put her curiosity and research skills to use by finishing her university studies.

"I'll call you as soon as he gets back to me," Marco said, then bid her goodbye.

As it happened, that didn't take long. Chiara was in between rooms about an hour later when her brother's ringtone sounded again from her pocket.

"That was fast," she answered after clicking on the call.

"My friend replied fast. Caught him waiting on a delayed flight so he had some time. He had a lot to say about the name you gave me."

Chiara's heart fluttered in her chest. No matter what she decided to do about his proposal, she didn't want to hear anything untoward about Evan. Why that was, she wasn't ready to examine just yet. "And? Was it good?"

"All good. Described him as a wunderkind who developed his own app at the ripe old age of nineteen. That's just how he made his first couple million. He's had his hands in various technological ventures ever since."

What about his personal life? Chiara didn't voice the question out loud. "Is that it?"

"For the most part. Lately he's been labeled as something of a partier. But I was told that seems to be a lot of hype. A way to get clicks from a certain crowd who follows this stuff."

Overhyped or not, the rumors were certainly problematic when it came to convincing investors.

"So, to rest your curiosity," her brother continued, "he appears to be a stand-up guy."

Relief washed over her in waves. "Well, it sounds like Evan Kim is on the up and up."

Someone behind her in the hallway loudly cleared their throat. Chiara froze where she stood. The sting of embarrassment burned her cheeks. She didn't have to turn around to know who was right behind her and had just heard every word.

Closing her eyes with a resigned sigh, she turned over her shoulder before opening them again. Yep. She'd been right. Evan.

He leveled a steady gaze on her face. Chiara willed for the ground to open under her feet and dropped her several floors below. Did Bali ever suffer earthquakes? She wouldn't mind a mild one right about now. No such luck.

Evan crossed his arms in front of his chest. "Sounds like you're checking up on me, Ms. Pearson."

Evan stifled a chuckle at the look of utter horror on Chiara's face when she turned to find him standing in the hallway. When he hadn't heard from her, he'd begun to grow restless, even though she had ample time before she owed him an answer. Still, it'd been hard to focus on anything else. He hadn't been looking for her just now per se. He'd describe it more as wandering around in the hope she would show up where he was.

And it had worked.

Though Chiara was looking at him as she if she wished she were anywhere else. He held up both hands, palms up. "Look, I don't blame you for looking into who I am. In fact, you'd be remiss if you didn't."

Her features relaxed as he spoke. "It was the most basic of inquiries."

"Did I pass?"

"A minus, give or take."

He clutched his chest in mock horror. "Less than an A plus. My former tutors would be beside themselves to hear it."

"It can be our secret."

"What about our other prospective secret?"

"You mean the secretly fake engagement?"

He nodded. "You're clearly asking around about me. Does that mean you've given it any more thought?"

She ignored his question, throwing out one of her own. "What are you doing here, anyway? On this floor?"

He pointed a playful finger at her. "You're good at avoiding answering questions."

She tilted her head. "Really? You just did that exact same thing."

Evan pinched the bridge of his nose. They were going around in circles here. "Give me another chance to continue trying to convince you."

She leaned back against the wall, crossed her ankles.

Evan had an urge to brace his hands on either side of her head where she rested against the wall. She had her hair up in some kind of haphazard ponytail that left curly tendrils around her face. Her uniform clung to her in all the right places.

Something had to be wrong with him. There was nothing particularly enticing about a housekeeping uniform. Except the way Chiara wore it.

"I'm listening. What do you have in mind?" she prompted.

He returned to the matter at hand "I'm extending you an invitation. One I hope you'll accept."

She scrunched her nose. "Like a business meeting or something? Listen, Evan, we can go over numbers until sunset. I know you're willing to pay handsomely. Numbers are not the issue."

He shook his head. "That's not it. No business. Just some pleasure."

Just some pleasure.

Chiara's heart thudded in her chest at his words. Made all the worse when he continued, "Can you come by around seven? We can grab a bite to eat and go from there."

She shrugged, feigning an indifference she didn't feel. "Sure. Why not? I have nothing going on tonight." Or any other night in the foreseeable future. Unless, of course, she went globetrotting around the world with Evan.

Dear saints. Was she really thinking about saying yes? When exactly had that tide turned?

"Bring a swimsuit and a change of clothes," Evan said, distracting her.

"A swimsuit?"

He winked at her. "Trust me."

If he only knew, Chiara thought, watching him walk away. It appeared she was beginning to do just that. For she had every intention of heading to his suite at the end of her shift.

Which couldn't come soon enough.

Hours later, by the time she rolled her cart back into the supply room, Chiara was more than ready to find out exactly what Evan had in mind with his latest *invitation*.

Within half an hour of clocking out, she was in the elevator that led to the penthouse suite with her swimsuit and a towel tucked in a tote bag hung over her shoulder. She'd changed into a loose-fitting top that looped into a bow at the side of her waist over a pair of slim-fitting capri pants.

She hadn't thought to ask about any kind of dress code for dinner. What if Evan had something more formal in mind? So she was relieved when the elevator doors opened to find him dressed just as casual in khaki shorts and a form-fitting white T-shirt that accented every inch of his muscled chest and arms. For a successful app-and-code developer, the man certainly must have made time for regular workouts. Or maybe he was just naturally chiseled.

"Right on time," he greeted her with a wide smile. But instead of inviting her in, he stepped into the lift with her and keyed the button for the lobby floor.

"Are we eating on the beach, then?"

He shook his head, watching the elevator panel. "Nope."

"Then where?"

"You'll see." He pointed to her tote bag. "Did you bring a swimsuit?"

"Uh-huh."

"Good. I was thinking we might swim first. Depending on how hungry you are. I'll let you decide."

Where was he taking her? "If we're not eating on the beach, then how would we swim?"

He gave her another wink. "Patience, Ms. Pearson. Like I said, you'll see."

There was a car and driver waiting for them when they left the lobby and stepped outside.

"It's not far," he explained as he helped her in the back seat, then settled in next to her.

Unlike her, the driver must have been told in advance where they were going. He slipped into the chaotic, noisy traffic and moved them along until they reached a Lagoon Villa Chiara knew to be one of the most exclusive tourist attractions in the area.

She was speechless as he escorted her out of the car and along the wooden pathway leading to one of the larger bungalows sitting atop the water.

A private table had been set up for them and the satay was sizzling on an open flame pit. Platters of vegetable and exotic fruit had already been set out.

"Wow," was all she could come up with to say.

"This is one of my favorite spots in Bali. I come here as often as I can."

She took in the scene before her. The jade color of the water, the tiki torches lit up with flames leading up the wooden pathways. "I don't blame you."

"So, did you want to eat first?" he asked.

Here stomach answered for her with a loud grumble.

Evan threw his head back with a laugh. "Dinner it is."

The satay was some of the best she'd ever tasted. Seasoned skewers of chicken and lamb served on a bed of *nasi goreng*, Indonesia's national dish of specialty fried rice. With a side of crisp grilled vegetables, it all made for a scrumptious meal her taste buds wouldn't soon forget.

"What brought you to Bali, anyway?" Evan suddenly asked between bites of fried rice. "I'm guessing it wasn't to work in a touristy hotel down here?"

She shrugged. "I got bit by the travel bug about a decade ago. Bali was one of the places on the list."

Evan didn't need to know that it was more her mother's list, and her mother's bug for that matter. Chiara had promised Mama just before losing her that she would do all she could to travel to as many of the spots her mother had wanted to see before illness robbed her of the opportunity.

No, she didn't want to get into any of that with Evan right now.

Even a decade later, the wound was too fresh, the loss too deep. She might completely fall apart if she tried to talk about it. The same as always.

He lifted his glass up toward her in salute. "Well, I'm glad you decided to come to Bali. Now."

Come to think of it, so was she. No matter what tomorrow held, this night was sure to become a cherished memory. One for the journals to tell the grandchildren about.

Though she would leave out the part about how attracted she was to her dinner companion. Or how he was trying to convince to fake marry him.

Just when Chiara thought she couldn't take another bite, the server arrived with a tray of cassava cakes. Spongy and syrupy, they made her mouth water despite how full she already felt. "How well do you know this chef?" she asked in a teasing voice even as she reached for one. "I heard cassava can be dangerous, poisonous even, when not cooked properly."

He playfully pulled the dish away before she could reach one of the pieces. "Then I won't have you risk it. I need you too much."

Wow. The man certainly knew what he was doing, didn't he? As if the setting and this romantic dinner wasn't enough to sway her decision, now he was tempting her with his words. Had anyone ever come out and explicitly said they'd *needed* her before? Growing up in the family she had, it was implied as a matter of fact. But when had it ever been acknowledged with words to her directly?

She couldn't recall.

"Here." Evan grabbed a cake off the tray. "I'll go first." He popped the entire morsel in his mouth at once.

"My taste tester?"

He gave her a wide smile and a wink. "We might be on the verge of insulting the chef here," he warned. "Hopefully, he's not listening."

She pulled the tray over to her side of the table. "If he is, our only means of atonement is to finish every last piece."

It didn't take long before nothing but crumbs remained. Chiara was certain she'd eaten at least two pieces more than Evan had. Oh, well, it wasn't often a girl was treated to a gourmet dinner in a bungalow sitting in a pretty lagoon.

Evan took a sip of his water. "There's a changing area around the back if you want to go put your suit on. If you still want to swim, that is."

She nodded with enthusiasm. "Yes. I can't believe it hasn't rained at all the past few days. You better believe I'm going to take advantage."

He was already in the water when she returned. Not normally shy while wearing a swimsuit, something felt different about this time. Evan tore his gaze away a little too quickly; he appeared to be looking at anything except in her direction. Was he simply being a gentleman until she could get into the water? Or was there another reason he was avoiding looking at her at all costs?

"Are you going to get in or not?" he asked after several beats had passed.

There was something to be said for jumping straight out of a bungalow where you'd just had dinner into a refreshing body of water. Another experience she wouldn't soon forget.

Taking a couple steps back to get a running start, she performed what her brother would have called a bomb cannonball and jumped in.

Sometimes you just have to jump right in and not overthink. Mama hadn't been talking about swimming so much as life in general.

As Chiara submerged completely below the surface, she felt the cooling water soothe her nerves and let it relieve some of the tension and anxiety of the past several days. Ever since she'd given away her travel money.

Chiara envied the fish that could stay down here indefinitely. In an environment so peaceful and serene. The noiselessness beneath was like a balm to her soul. Her mind hadn't been silent in so long. It was so very silent down here under the water. Silent enough that answers became clearer. All the background noise and warnings had faded.

She had her answer. She was going to jump right in, as she had just now into the water. Calmness settled over her. She'd been offered a solution—why in the world would she turn it down?

She held her breath for as long as she could, relishing in the newfound relief that came with her decision.

Finally, her lungs began to scream out in complaint. She thrust herself upward with a sputter.

"You were under a long time," Evan said when she resurfaced. "I was about to come down there to see if you needed rescuing."

Maybe she did. As strong and independent as she'd always prided herself on being, maybe at this point in her life, being rescued was exactly what she needed.

CHAPTER SIX

One week later

HE OFFICIALLY HAD a fiancée.

How exactly was an engaged man supposed to behave, anyway? How did a man carry off the experience of being happily committed to someone?

Darned if he knew, Evan thought as he tipped the bellman who had escorted them to their suite, then closed the door behind the young man.

Louis certainly seemed to have gotten the hang of fiancé-ing. The man had been wearing a smile and look of utter contentment since he'd met his bride-to-be. Maybe he could ask him for some pointers. Of course, Evan's particular disadvantage here was that his engagement was a farce. No proposal. No wedding at the end. Just a means to serve a purpose.

No matter. He just needed it to appear real. Just for a few short weeks.

Chiara definitely looked the part. And she would even more so by tomorrow after a visit from a personal shopper in about an hour.

"This view is breathtaking," she said now, staring at the skyline outside the glass balcony doors.

If he were her real intended, he would acknowledge

her comment by walking up behind her, wrapping his arms around her waist and pulling her tight against him, back to chest, as they admired the view together.

"I'm glad you like it," he said instead. "We'll be staying here until the wedding."

He saw her visibly tense at the last word. The urge to go to her grew exponentially, simply in comfort. "No need to be nervous, Chiara. Everyone will love you."

That might have been a bit of a fib. He didn't even know what pleased his parents anymore. Or if they would even make the effort to meet her. Telling Chiara any of that wasn't going to help her nerves, however. He'd somehow managed to dodge her questions about his family during the plane ride by focusing on the code on his laptop while she read a newsmagazine. But he could only dodge for so long.

"I'm just a little anxious about meeting your friends and family, that's all." She bit her bottom lip. "It's so much more nerve-racking than translating for a meeting."

"You'll be fine. Have faith in yourself."

She sighed. "I'll try. Could we maybe go over some details about your family and your friends? Maybe over dinner?"

Evan fought not to visibly shudder at the idea. "I'm afraid I have some things to do tonight. Some deliverables for an international investor."

Her shoulders drooped. "I see."

"Take a look at the room service menu. The hotel restaurant employs a world-renowned chef. Or you can order in from one of the five-star restaurants in the area."

"It's too bad you'll be busy. I was hoping to see a bit of the city the first night."

Before he had a chance to respond to that, the door sounded with the buzz of an arrival.

"Excuse me," Evan said. "That would be the shopper."

The same bellhop was back with the woman and together they hauled in several cases and two full racks of garments.

"What is all this?" Chiara asked, walking over to the racks and fingering a blue silk top.

Was he imagining it or did she sound irked?

She dropped the fabric and turned to him. "I thought I was just being fitted for a dress for the wedding."

Yep. She was definitely annoyed. For the life of him, he couldn't figure out why.

"That's the primary intent," he told her. "But you need other things as well for the next several weeks."

"I had no idea I would be having a full wardrobe fitting. You never mentioned it."

He shrugged. "I said a personal shopper would stop by because you needed a dress for the ceremony, because that was the most important item."

The shopper stood glancing at one of them, then the other, tension clear in her expression. After several seconds of silence, she excused herself and hastily made her way in the direction of the hallway.

"Chiara," he began as soon as he heard the hallway bathroom door shut. "This is only to get you some garments so that you look the part."

Something shifted behind her eyes and her lips tightened into a slim line.

"But I can't afford this, Evan. Any of it. And I certainly don't expect you to purchase me a whole new wardrobe."

What was she talking about? He didn't understand

the issue. She seemed to be making one out of nothing. "How is this any different than how the Bali hotel provided you with a housekeeping uniform?" he asked.

She lifted a red silky scarf and held it out to him. "This is very different than a cheap maid's uniform."

"Only in that it's more expensive."

Her eyes grew wide with astonishment at his words. "How do you not hear how that sounds?"

Evan pinched the bridge of his nose and summoned up all his patience. Being in Singapore for Louis's nuptials had him on edge as it was. Everyone from his past life was going to be at this wedding. People he hadn't seen or spoken to in years, including his mother and father.

Perhaps that's why he wasn't handling this well and addressing her objections about the clothing. But it was just clothing, for heaven's sake.

"Look, if it makes you feel better, don't keep the clothes." Though he had no idea what he would do with them. Maybe his assistant would be more enthused about a new wardrobe than Chiara seemed to be. As she looked to be the opposite of enthused. In fact, she appeared downright insulted.

"I just need you to wear them for the duration of this bargain between us. So you can—"

"Right." She held a hand up before he could continue. "So I can look the part. I get it."

Then she turned her back to him to stare out the window once more.

What had she done?

This whole thing had been a mistake. She'd fallen for Evan's charm and the lure of easy money and committed herself to a deal she now had no way out of.

Now that she was on board, it was clear that she was nothing but a business partner to Evan. He'd been cold and aloof with her on his private jet.

And the clothes! How humiliating. He hadn't even seen much of her wardrobe but had already decided it wouldn't be suitable for the likes of his friends and kin.

Chiara was nothing but a Pygmalion project to help him achieve his latest goal.

Well, she had no one but herself to blame. She should have never expected anything more. It was only three weeks. Then she'd be on her way to see her own family and spend Christmas with those she loved most.

Evan Kim would be a distant memory in no time once she made it back home. A tiny voice in her head mocked that thought and she felt a tug in the vicinity of her chest.

"I'd ask that the items be donated to charity once we are done."

He nodded once. "Of course. That can certainly be arranged."

"Maybe an international women's charity. Or an auction where the proceeds will be used for such a cause."

"Of course. I'll send my assistant a note right away to find a suitable recipient."

With perfect timing, the personal shopper reappeared in the doorway.

"Let's begin then, shall we?" Chiara asked her with the widest, fakest smile she could muster.

The woman's shoulders sagged in relief, which made Chiara feel a tug of guilt that she and Evan had made her uncomfortable. She strode over to her with her hand extended. "I'm Chiara. Thank you so much for coming today."

She returned the smile and took her hand. "I'm Trina."

"I'll leave you ladies to it, then," Evan said, Chiara couldn't quite bring herself to look at him. "I'll just be in the study, if you need anything."

"Thank you, Evan," she said, keeping her gaze focused squarely on Trina's expression of relief.

He walked away silently.

Chiara walked over to the rack with the more casual outfits. "Where do we begin?"

"Anywhere you'd like." She clenched her hands together. "If you're sure you'd still like to. I can always come back another time." Everything in her voice told Chiara she'd much rather not do that.

"Absolutely not. I just wasn't aware of exactly what Evan had in mind. Just a bit of a shock to see so many items, that's all."

Trina barked out a laugh. "I totally understand. Boyfriends can be so clueless."

"Oh, he's not my boyfriend," Chiara quickly corrected, then remembered why she was here. She and Evan were, indeed, supposed to be romantically involved. That was the whole point, wasn't it?

"Oh?" Trina appeared confused.

"He's actually my fiancé." Close one. Though she wasn't even sure if they were supposed to be announcing it just yet. It wasn't like Evan had given her any kind of guidance. In fact, he'd been downright stone-faced since she'd signed on the dotted line of his contract.

Trina clasped her hands together. "Congratulations!" Her eyes fell to her left hand. Drat. They hadn't even talked about a ring. She might have to say something to him about it.

She cringed when she thought about how uncomfortable that conversation was sure to be. Never in a million years would she have thought she'd be put in the awkward spot of asking after her own engagement ring. A ring that would be the gesture of a complete farce.

"Have you two been together long, then?"

Stick to the story. "No, actually. We just met. You know what they say, about instant attraction and love at first sight."

Trina's smile widened. "Oh! How romantic. Getting engaged so soon after meeting."

Chiara shrugged. "Thanks. Some might call it impulsive. My father always said I'm too spontaneous at times." That was the absolute truth. Though she shuddered to think what her father would say if he saw her now.

She looked up to find Trina watching her with a curious look. Chiara clapped her hands in front of her chest, feigning the excitement of a bride-to-be about to attend her first few events with her intended. "Right. Let's go ahead and get started, then."

For the next hour and a half, Chiara played dress-up. She probably shouldn't admit it to Evan but trying on fancy clothes was more fun than she would have realized. Despite knowing that she wouldn't actually come to own any of it for herself. She pretended she was a fashion model about to walk the runway or sit for a glamorous magazine shoot.

After showing her casual outfits to wear during the day, Trina pulled the rack of dresses over. How in the world would she be able to pick just one? They were all lovely pieces of art that had to be one of a kind.

Finally, she settled on a sapphire-blue silky number that Trina said brought out the hue of her eyes.

They made small talk while Chiara tried on clothing, walking back and forth to the restroom with each new outfit. She didn't think Evan would come back out to the sitting area anytime soon. But Chiara wasn't going to risk being mistaken on that front and have him catch her in a state of mid-dress.

"So, is this your first time in Singapore?" Trina asked. Her delightful accent sounded like poetry to Chiara's ears.

"Yes, I'm looking forward to seeing the city." *When we finally get around to it*, she added silently. Or *if*.

"There's a new place in town. Really good sushi and wontons." She supplied the name of the restaurant and emphasized that Chiara and Evan just had to try it.

"I'll be sure to let my fiancé know." She wasn't going to get used to saying that word anytime soon. If ever.

The other woman surprised her by giving her a mischievous wink and taking her by the hand. "I also want to show you these. They might come in handy for a newly engaged woman."

She lifted the top of a wooden chest to reveal a stash of lingerie folded neatly in a stack, then held up a pantie and bra set made of nothing but lace. Chiara tried to hide her gasp of surprise. She definitely wouldn't be needing those over the next few weeks. But she couldn't help several unwanted images playing in her head. A masculine hand lowering the thin strap off her shoulder, heavy-lidded eyes taking in the picture of her wearing such a thing, his breath warm on her cheek.

Heaven help her, the man in all those images was Evan Kim.

Oh, dear. She had it bad. For a man who wasn't even taking the time to eat dinner with her their first night in one of the most exciting cities on the planet.

Just to get it over with, without having to divulge too much to Trina, she lifted a slip of a negligee and studied it. "I'll take this one."

"That's all?" Trina asked.

She could only nod.

Trina giggled. "Silly me. Of course, a woman like you must have made sure to pack plenty of things like these."

Chiara swallowed her gulp of laughter. If Trina only knew. Her delicates consisted mostly of sports bras and boy shorts made for comfort and nothing else.

Finally, after she'd made her final decisions on which were the most flattering pieces, Trina bid her goodbye. Chiara guessed Evan must have worked out a payment process with her in advance.

The same way he'd done with Chiara for that matter.

Well, she had no right to feel any kind of way about that dismal thought. After all, she was merely an employee fulfilling a contract, too.

After seeing Trina to the door, Chiara couldn't help but pick up the negligee and hold it up to admire its delicate beauty. Too bad no one would ever see her in it save for herself. It felt soft as tissue in her hand. Luxurious and featherlight. She held it up to her body, imagining what it would feel like to wear as she snuggled under the covers in the middle of the night. A sigh escaped her lips at the image.

Evan picked that moment to stride into the room.

Evan was totally unprepared for the sight that greeted him when he walked into the sitting area to find Chiara holding what could only be described as temptation incarnate. He couldn't make himself look away.

He knew he should have stayed in his study.

She quickly dropped the item onto the couch behind her, but it was too late. His mind had already processed what it was taking in and proceeded to all sorts of thoughts he had no business thinking.

Like how Chiara would look actually wearing the thing. And how it would feel to take it off her.

Steady there, fella. She's just here on an assignment you hired her for.

Right. He was essentially her boss. He tried to come up with something to say but his mouth had gone dry. Finally, he managed a dry, "Hello."

That's it. Dazzle her with witty conversation to get past the highly awkward moment.

Chiara gave him a smile that was much too tight to be real. "Um…hi. Trina just left."

"Trina?"

"The shopper."

Right. He'd forgotten the woman's name. Heck, he'd come darn close to forgetting his own name. The blasted images still hadn't left his mind's eye.

Evan cleared his throat. "Um, I should have explained exactly why she was here. I didn't mean to throw you a curveball about the clothing."

"It's okay. I overreacted. But I'll still feel better if the clothes are donated…when we're done."

"Of course. As you wish." More awkward silence ensued after that rather useless exchange. What was wrong with him? He'd been with plenty of women, and he'd seen his fair share of racy nightwear. She hadn't even had it on, for heaven's sake. The sight of it really shouldn't have conjured up the wanton images and turned his brain to mush the way it had.

"Trina was lovely," Chiara supplied, clearly looking for ways to keep the conversation going.

"My assistant found her. Through a friend."

"She mentioned a new restaurant nearby. I know you said the hotel chef is world-renowned, but I thought we might try her suggestion instead tonight."

"Whatever you want."

"Great. Thanks."

"You're welcome." For the life of him, he couldn't come up with anything else to say. How lame.

"Well, I should let you get back to work." She pulled her cell phone from her pocket. "I'll see if I can locate the place Trina suggested and see if they'll deliver."

Suddenly, it occurred to him that work was the last thing he wanted to do at the moment. He wanted to enjoy the city, in the company of the woman who had dropped everything to travel the world with him. He'd been so selfish to ask her to stay in their first night. She was probably dying to get out there and take it all in. And he had come close to denying her the chance to do so.

You're selfish, Evan. You only ever think of yourself.

Evan forced the unwanted memory away and made himself focus on the present.

Though, in a way, he supposed he was still being somewhat selfish. For what he said next was just as much for his own sake as for Chiara's.

"You know what? I think we should go out and have that meal at the restaurant."

Her eyes lit up. "You do?"

"Yes. We'll even make a couple stops along the way."

"Oh, Evan, I would love that." Her brows furrowed. "But I thought you had things to do."

He shrugged. "I've just decided it can wait."

Months from now, when Chiara was out of his life,

he didn't want to regret any of the decisions he'd made when it came to her.

The work would still be there, more of it in fact. But Chiara would not.

So, for tonight at least, everything else could wait.

And his decision had nothing whatsoever to do with Chiara's new nightwear.

CHAPTER SEVEN

CHIARA COULDN'T GUESS what might have made Evan change his mind. She was just so very happy that he had. She'd been itching to explore the city, probably would have ventured out on her own at some point. She'd been backpacking across several countries for the past two years. Sightseeing alone wouldn't be a new experience for her.

But it was so much more enjoyable with company. Evan's company in particular.

Apparently, she wasn't hiding her excitement very well.

"You look downright giddy, Ms. Pearson," Evan chuckled as they walked out of the hotel lobby and onto the sidewalk.

"Guess it's pretty obvious."

"Are you up to walking?" he asked as they stepped into the cool evening air. "The weather seems mild enough."

She nodded with all the enthusiasm she felt. "I'd love to. I want to see as much of the city as I can."

Chiara knew she sounded like a little girl on her first trip to Disneyland. But she didn't care. It was exactly how she felt. Singapore was alive around them. Towers that seemed to reach higher than the sky were lit up like neon monoliths. The water of the marina in the distance glistened like liquid diamonds.

Christmas decorations and lights adorned the street. As if Santa's wonderland had moved to a warmer, much more exotic locale. The sights took her breath away.

Within minutes, they had reached the restaurant and were seated at a booth.

The dining area looked like a cross between an old-fashioned American diner and a Michelin-starred restaurant. Chiara gasped as covered bowls of food sped past her ear on some kind of conveyor belt.

Evan chuckled at her reaction just as another bowl flew by.

"I take it you haven't had *kaitenzushi* before."

"Does that mean flying sushi? If so, then yes, you would be correct. I've never had the pleasure."

He laughed at that. "The best translation would be conveyor belt sushi. Various pieces go by—you can pick one you want or special order using the screen." He pointed to a mounted tablet above their table. It was playing some kind of anime cartoon on the screen.

"Here, let's try this one." He opened the bowl that happened to be passing. Two pieces of rolled sushi sat on the plate and they each took one. Chiara popped it in her mouth and began to chew. A burst of flavor exploded over her tongue—delicate fish, a tangy sauce and another subtle taste she couldn't quite place.

"Oh, wow. This is delicious." She took out the next plate without bothering to ask. This dish was just as tasty as the last one. When they were done with the latest rolls, Evan grabbed the two empty plates and slipped them into an open slot at the side of the table.

"How often have you had *kayta*…?" She gave up. There was no use trying to pronounce what he'd called it. "How often have you had conveyor belt sushi?" she asked. She wouldn't have even thought to push the empty plates through the slot, had barely even noticed it was there.

"In Tokyo a few times. The concept originated in Japan. One restaurant on Shibuya Street has three floors with different kitchens and belt systems."

Tokyo. It was one of the cities her mom had talked about visiting. Then again, there weren't that many capitals her mom hadn't been interested in. "I'd like to get to Tokyo someday," she admitted.

He reached across the table to take her hand in his. The warmth of his touch spread from her fingers, through her core and down to her toes. "I have no doubt you'll get to Tokyo, Chiara. You'll love it."

Just as Mama would have.

"My mom and I talked about going there together someday. Before she got sick." Her words came as a shock to her own ears. She hardly ever talked about her mom. Not even to her closest friends. And most definitely not with her brother and father. Speaking about their loss only served to amplify the pain for all three of them. "I really miss her," she found herself confiding.

"When did you lose her?" Evan asked in a gentle voice. He gave her hand a reassuring squeeze.

"About ten years ago." The burn of tears stung behind her eyes, and she swiped them with her free hand before they could fall.

"You were barely more than a teenager."

She nodded, gulping against the lump that had formed at the base of her throat. "It still feels like it happened just yesterday."

"I'm really sorry. I know there are no words that can adequately address the pain of that kind of loss."

"You must feel so happy that you're going to get to see both your parents in a couple of days at your friend's wedding."

Something shifted behind his eyes. He let go of her hand, then looked down at the table. "I haven't seen them in quite some time," he finally said, not really confirming her earlier statement.

Interesting.

They sat in silence for several minutes as he gave her time to wrangle her emotions under control. Chiara appreciated it, she really did, but at the same time she wanted badly to have him divulge a part of him the way she just had.

Eventually, it became clear that just wasn't going to happen. Not tonight, anyway. She forced a smile on her face and popped open the next passing bowl. "This looks good," she commented as she set it down between them on the table.

He pointed at her. "You sure? That's one of the spiciest rolls on the menu."

With a fortifying breath, she picked up one of the pieces. "I guess I'm living dangerously."

He wasn't kidding. Her mouth was burning by the time she swallowed. For his part, Evan appeared barely affected after swallowing his share in one bite.

"I tried to warn you."

"You didn't try very hard," she countered with a grimace as the pain of her burning tongue started to slowly subside.

Evan signaled for more water and soon she was ready to try again.

"How many plates has that been?" she asked, beginning to feel rather full. "Dozens?"

He laughed, lifting the latest empty one. "This is

number twenty." He slipped it into the slot. "Watch this."

The anime cartoon on the tablet above them began to dance and sing. Then an array of fireworks played on the screen. A clear plastic tube by the side of the table started to vibrate. Then a small plastic round ball dropped through it and into Evan's hand where he held it below the tube.

He handed it to her. "For you. In honor of your first *kaitenzushi*."

"A prize?"

"Yep. Diners get rewarded after every twenty plates."

Chiara was ridiculously amused. She felt like a child who'd just managed to snag something out of one of those arcade claw machines. With a laugh, she took the ball and twisted it open. Inside was a small plastic Christmas tree ornament meant to be a wrapped present. "Perfect!" she squealed in delight, loud enough to earn a smile from the older couple at the table next to them. "I will cherish it forever."

Evan threw his head back with a peal of laughter. "You're into the finer things in life, I see."

"Oh, yes. Tiny plastic Christmas ornament. I collect them."

He lifted an eyebrow. "Want to try for another? We only need to eat twenty more plates of sushi."

As much as she'd enjoyed the meal, her stomach groaned in protest at the thought. "I'm happy with my winnings for the night," she said and pocketed her tiny present. "Plus, I'm very full."

Evan keyed in a request for the check when Chiara noticed something heading toward them on the conveyor belt that most definitely didn't belong there. She pointed at it. "That's not sushi?"

Evan followed the direction of her finger. "No. It's not. That would be a cell phone."

Huh. That was curious. "Why in the world would someone put their cell phone on the belt?"

"To take video as it goes around."

What a novel idea. Still, it seemed rather risky.

"I've seen it in Japan," Evan said. "Kids like to record video and post it on their social media accounts." He leaned forward over the table. "We'll be polite and give a wave."

She met him in the middle, their heads touching. Both smiled for the camera as the device glided by. Was it her imagination or did Evan linger near her just a bit longer after the cell phone had gone past them and reached the next table? He'd grown some stubble on his chin since this morning, the five o'clock shadow lending a casual ruggedness to his handsome face. For an insane moment, she wanted to turn her head to face him directly, wanted to look straight in his eyes to see what she might find there.

The moment was over before she could decide either way, leaving her to wonder whether she would have been bold enough. And where exactly such boldness may have led.

Within minutes, they'd paid the bill and were back outside. The night had grown darker but no less busy. Crowds of people lined the sidewalk where long lines had formed in front of street food vendors. Bouncy pop music in a language she didn't recognize rang through the air. She found herself bopping her head to the beat as they began to walk.

"I thought the hotel was the other way?" she asked.

"It is. I thought we might do some sightseeing. If you're up for it, that is."

Oh, she most definitely was. She clapped her hands together in front of her chest. "I would adore that."

He chuckled. "Now, why did I know that would be your answer?"

Which said a lot, didn't it? Somehow this man knew her better than most other people on earth, despite them having met only days ago.

Soon, Chiara found herself approaching what could only be described as a holiday wonderland.

"Oh, my heavens."

Evan paused, letting her just take in the spectacular view.

"What is this place?" she asked, her breath hitching.

"Come on. I'll show you."

He led her by the hand down a path toward the activity. A bridge done up in what had to be thousands of tiny lights served as the entrance. A gondola sat floating beneath, and seated inside was a waving elf and a woman costumed as a princess.

Chiara took her cell phone out to take a video, but she knew there was no way to capture the magic before her digitally. "Wait till Nuri sees these pictures."

"Hope you have a full battery," Evan said. "The Gardens by the Bay Christmas Wonderland goes on for at least a mile."

They walked past the bridge into a kaleidoscope of colorful lights beyond. The towering city buildings above the gardens served as a frame for the overall picture. A Christmas tree in the center of the square sat amidst dozens of tall columns lit up with circular designs atop that reminded her of elaborate dream catchers.

Beyond the square, a merry-go-round turned with children and adults alike riding the statue animals. A portly Santa walked through the surrounding crowd, handing out wrapped presents and treats.

"What do you think so far?" Evan asked as she snapped more photos.

"I don't think I have the right words to answer."

"Does it compare to the holiday season in New York City?"

"Most definitely. But it's very different as well."

He lifted an eyebrow. "Oh? I've been to New York, of course. Several times. But I'd like a native's point of view for comparison's sake."

Chiara tried to gather her thoughts. Christmas in New York was just something she'd taken for granted growing up. It was her home city, and the holidays was only one of the ways the city changed dynamically through different times. Now that the subject had come up, it surprised her just how much she'd missed being there during the holiday season.

"And this is different?" he asked, gesturing with his chin at the scene before them. "Tell me, what might we be doing if we were in New York right now?"

So many possible answers came to mind. "Maybe watching *The Nutcracker* at the Met. Or taking in all the decorations in Times Square. Or we might attend a Broadway show like *A Christmas Carol*. And there's Rockefeller Center if you wanted to do some ice skating."

She turned to find Evan staring at her with an expression that sent a shiver through her spine. His eyes hooded, his lips slightly pouted.

"Maybe you could show me all that someday."

Her heart skipped a beat. This was the first time he'd so much as hinted at the two of them staying in touch once this AI business was taken care of.

"I'd like that, Evan," she said in a soft voice that sounded foreign to her own ears. But he'd already turned away, as if he regretted the words that had come out of his mouth and wanted to move on quickly.

Their earlier easy and comfortable conversation seemed to have dissipated. Chiara wanted badly to get it back. Waving her arm around at their surroundings, she tried again to answer his earlier question. "This is like if somehow somebody had figured out a way to walk through an array of active fireworks as they lit up the sky. Right amongst the stars."

He laughed at that for some reason. "Then I know exactly where to go next." He draped an arm over her shoulders and began to lead her to the right. It was a casual gesture, Chiara knew. Friendly. Nothing more. But having Evan's arm around her had her blood thrumming through her veins.

"Where?" she asked with fake nonchalance, trying to ignore the electricity that seemed to be crackling between them.

"To walk amongst the stars," he answered.

A few minutes later, Chiara understood what he'd meant. He'd taken her to an open-air tunnel glowing with tiny blue lights shaped like stars. The pathway beneath their feet leading into and through the tunnel was lit up the same way.

As they began to move through the tunnel, Chiara felt as if she'd somehow been lifted into the sky during a starlit night. Evan still held her about the shoulders.

This was going to be a moment she'd remember and cherish forever. Such experiences seemed to be adding up. The thought was bittersweet. For she had no idea what it was going to mean for her psyche long-term. Or her relationships for that matter. What man was ever going to be able to compete when he tried to show her a good time?

A small child brushed past them, giggling and skipping through the tunnel, and pulled Chiara out of her thoughts.

Here and now. She would focus on the moment at hand and not let one second of it go to waste.

When they reached the end of the tunnel, Evan gave her a knowing look. She didn't even need to say anything. He knew exactly what she was thinking. "You want to go through it again, don't you?" he asked.

They walked through the tunnel twice more before she was ready to move on.

An enticing aroma tempted her nose as they walked back toward the square. Something sugary sweet and fruity. Again, Evan seemed to read her mind.

"I know you said you were full after dinner, but there's a row of food vendors that way. Lots of them serve dessert."

Chiara patted her middle. "I always have room for dessert."

The choices were plentiful when they reached the food area. Each one more tempting than the last. The longest line seemed to be at the ice-cream hut. Chiara figured that was as good a way as any to make the decision.

Once they'd gotten their ice cream, Evan found them an empty bench to sit. As much as she wanted to keep snapping pictures to send to Nuri, Chiara desired more to simply take in all the views before her. And to enjoy Evan's company undistracted. Ha. She could laugh at that. As if she could forget for even one instant who she was seated with and the growing effect he seemed to be having on her emotions.

An older couple walking past smiled at them, then paused directly in front of their bench. Evan's response was a respectful nod with a slight bow. Chiara had no idea what to do so she followed his lead and mimicked the action.

But they didn't move on.

The woman pointed to the top of the pole behind the bench and said something Chiara didn't understand. Then she nodded enthusiastically. Chiara shrugged her shoulders and gave the woman a smile in return. Why hadn't she thought to learn a few words of greeting in Mandarin before coming to Singapore? Most of Singapore spoke English but it couldn't have hurt to learn a bit of the second most popular language here. Things had just moved so quickly after she'd yes to Evan's offer. In fact, time seemed to be speeding by since the day she'd met him. She leaned sideways in Evan's direction. "What's she saying?"

He turned to her. Their faces were inches apart. "She's pointing out that we happen to be sitting under some mistletoe."

Oh, dear. The couple was still staring at them expectedly. Chiara froze in her spot, at a complete loss as to what to do.

But then Evan lifted her chin with one finger. Suddenly, despite the chaotic fun and boisterous noise surrounding them, Chiara's entire focus narrowed to just the two of them. She gripped the cone in her hand so tight it was a wonder it didn't break.

And she almost dropped it when she felt Evan's lips on hers. Soft yet firm, gentle yet somehow demanding in equal measure. She had no idea if he'd meant to deliver a small peck on the lips in response to a stranger's prompting, but this kiss was quickly turning into so much more than that. Heat and desire curled through her stomach as his mouth remained on hers. Every cell of her being vibrated with desire.

When she finally made herself pull away, she had to take a deep breath to try to regain some of her senses. The older couple wasn't even there any longer.

At some point, their fake kiss had become all too real. For her, anyway. Maybe even for Evan.

CHAPTER EIGHT

WHAT HAD HE been thinking?

It was midnight by the time they made it back to their hotel suite, but Evan was still silently cursing himself.

He hadn't been thinking at all. That was the problem. Kissing Chiara should have never been in the cards. How many times had he reminded himself throughout the night that he had to ignore his attraction to her?

In his defense, that had become increasingly difficult as the evening wore on. He couldn't recall the last time he'd enjoyed himself quite so much in the company of a woman. The way she'd enjoyed herself at the sushi restaurant. Her utter delight at her prize of a tiny piece of plastic. Her excitement at the Christmas Wonderland. He'd been growing more and more intrigued by her sheer magnitude for enjoying life.

Still, he'd managed to hold strong for the most part by reminding himself repeatedly that she was essentially only here as his employee. Until fate had intervened in the form of an older observant couple, as well as a sprig of mistletoe. The woman must have thought he and Chiara were together.

None of it could excuse kissing her. Now he had to try to rectify the situation. He had to somehow regain his sense of camaraderie and easy friendship they'd been enjoying until the ill-fated kiss.

And he had to do it before Louis's wedding. The two of them had to be absolutely convincing at the ceremony and following celebration. At some point, they would have to clear the air about the way he'd kissed her. But it was going to have to wait until the morning.

Because right now he had another awkward scenario to address. When his assistant had booked this stay for him weeks ago, there'd been no need to ask for an extra room or a suite with more than one bed.

Chances of there being any empty units in a hotel like this at Christmas time were slim to none. More poor planning on his part.

Plus, how would he explain that if it ever came up later?

There was nothing for it—he would have to sleep on the couch.

As if on cue, Chiara covered her mouth with her hand to suppress a wide breathy yawn. "I think I'm ready to call it a day. Is it okay to grab the extra blanket and pillow from the bedroom?"

Confusion washed through him. Was she seriously assuming that she'd be the one sleeping out here? What kind of a guy did she think he was?

"What do you mean?" he asked.

She chuckled at the question. "I mean I'm ready to go to bed. Aren't you?" She gasped and squeezed her eyes shut. "I mean, in your bedroom. You, that is," she quickly corrected. "I'd be out here, of course." She motioned to the couch. "If I could just grab that pillow and blanket."

Before she could take more than one step in the direction of the bedroom, Evan stopped her with a hand to her arm.

"I'll get them." She blinked up at him in confusion. He hadn't meant to sound so brisk. He was just so thrown off by her unquestioning assumption that she'd be the one to sleep on the couch.

She gave her head a vehement shake. "Oh, no. Absolutely not. This is your suite. You're paying for it. I can't be the one to take the only room."

Her voice was hard and determined. She sounded offended, as if he'd insulted her. Well, they were at a bit of a standoff, then. Because he felt rather offended at the idea that he'd let her sleep on a lumpy couch. As expensive and posh as it was, it was no mattress.

"Listen, Chiara. I've slept on much worse."

She held up her hands before he could continue. Then, before he could guess what she was doing, she walked to the center of the room, plopped down on the couch and lay back. "I refuse to leave this sofa," she declared. Grabbing one of the furry cushions, she placed it under her head. "Perfect. I could use a blanket, though."

"Chiara, I can't—"

In a dramatic gesture that bordered on comical, she turned her head and closed her eyes. Then she pretended to snore. Loudly.

Evan fought between laughing at his predicament and swearing out loud. The woman was as stubborn as the black tabby cat he'd had as a child. The one who refused to eat unless it was hand fed, no matter how hungry it got.

He pinched the bridge of his nose, then went to retrieve the blanket and a real pillow. Chiara's eyes were still closed when he came back. He nudged the pillow under her head and removed the cushion, then draped the blanket over her. The obstinate woman didn't so much as open her eyes to look at him. Several beats passed where he just looked at her. Of course, she hadn't fallen asleep this quickly. She had to know he was staring. But he couldn't turn away. Partly to wait her out to see if she might change her mind. And partly because he enjoyed just looking at her.

Delicate cheekbones beneath thick dark lashes. Her wavy hair disheveled and loose after the busy day they'd had. She was beautiful in a way he wouldn't have normally described beauty. If he were a man who wrote poetry rather than code, he could write verses and verses about Chiara Pearson.

Wow. That was a rather fanciful thought.

As much as he hated leaving her out here, he had to walk away.

"Thank you," she called out to his retrieving back when he finally turned in the direction of the bedroom.

Two hours later, it wasn't any kind of surprise that he couldn't sleep. He'd been tossing and turning for most of that time.

This was ridiculous. He just couldn't do it. It wasn't in his DNA to leave Chiara out there while he slumbered in a massive, luxurious bed under a thick down comforter.

Walking back out to the lounge area, he approached the sofa where Chiara lay breathing steadily. She'd kicked off her covers and he could see she'd changed into a tank and a loose pair of running shorts. He didn't want to startle her, so he whispered her name. She roused just enough to offer a sleepy "Hmm?" in response.

"It's just me," he told her, his voice low. Slowly, gently, he picked her up and carried her to the bed. After settling her on the mattress and covering her with the blanket, he turned to make his way to the empty couch.

She grabbed his hand before he could take a step. "Stay."

Evan stood frozen with indecision. Her word was clear, but she was also barely awake. He didn't want to make any kind of presumptuous error here.

"Evan, please. It's a very big bed. There's no need for you to leave."

She had a point. The bed was ginormous. They didn't even need to so much as come in physical contact with each other. And he could definitely use the rest before the spectacle of the big wedding tomorrow. With a sigh, he walked to the other side of the mattress and crawled in. See, no problem. There was at least three feet of mattress between them.

But when he awoke the next morning, Chiara was snuggled tight against his chest, sound asleep, his arms wrapped around her waist.

Chiara awoke with a start as soon as she felt Evan shift next to her. Thing was, she shouldn't have felt him at all. Somehow, they'd ended up not only side by side, but she was actually wrapped in his arms.

Slowly opening her eyes, she took in her surroundings. She wasn't on the side of the bed he'd placed her in last night. So she'd been the one who'd breached the distance and moved over towards him in her sleep.

How utterly mortifying. Was he awake? If not, maybe she could salvage what was left of her pride and sneak out without him any the wiser about their proximity to each other. And which of them had most likely initiated the closeness. But how in the world was she going to remove herself from his arms?

For one insane moment, she wanted to pretend she hadn't woken up, either. To have an excuse to remain exactly where she was, cocooned in Evan's warmth, his bare chest tight against her back and his strong arms wrapped loosely around her. His hot breath at the bottom of her neck.

Moot point. No such luck. She heard him clear his throat before he spoke. "Chiara? You awake?"

The temptation to lie almost won over. Almost. "Just woke up. Good morning," she added, though it sounded like a question.

"Good morning," he answered and then, in what had to be the most awkward three or four seconds of her life, unwrapped his arms from around her waist. "I'll go order us some breakfast. We'll have to get ready in a few short hours. Pastries okay?"

She could only nod and stare at him where he stood, wearing only loose-fitting pajama bottoms that looked like they'd been tailored for him. It had never occurred to her that pajamas could be custom-made.

"Pastries sound great. Coffee, too, please."

"That's a given," he threw over his shoulder before walking out of the room.

Huh. Was that it, then?

Between the mind-blowing kiss last night, then waking up like a honeymooning couple, maybe they needed to talk. But she certainly wasn't going to be the one to broach the subject. She wouldn't even know where to start.

Chiara took her time lingering in bed under the covers. Not only because this had to be the most comfortable bed she'd ever lain in, but also to try and assemble her jumbling mess of emotions into some sort of sensical order. She and Evan were clearly attracted to each other. It was going to be a long two weeks if they didn't somehow acknowledge that reality. In fact, she felt more drawn to him than any other man she'd ever encountered.

A disquieting thought slithered into her brain. What if the attraction was completely one-sided? Maybe that's why Evan had hightailed it out of the bedroom just now. Because she'd made him uncomfortable by scooching over to his side. She threw her forearm over her eyes.

But the kiss. She certainly hadn't been the one to trigger that. Evan had been the one to kiss her. He'd had a legitimate reason, an annoying voice told her in her mind's ear. He was simply humoring a sweet older couple who'd noticed they were sitting under mistletoe. The kiss might not have even gone past a peck if she hadn't responded as enthusiastically as she had.

Chiara groaned with mortification and took several steadying breaths. Finally, the smell of freshly brewed coffee had her tempted enough to summon the fortitude to go face Evan.

She found him at the dining counter setting up breakfast. At least he wasn't shirtless this time. She couldn't guess when he'd done so, but at some point he'd put on a tight-fitting cotton T-shirt that looked whiter than first snow.

Too bad it was only slightly helpful that he was fully dressed. The contours of his muscular chest and upper arms were still prominent enough to be distracting. She'd been nestled up tight against those muscles just a few short minutes ago.

"Perfect timing," he told her. "Room service delivery just left." He pointed to one of the dishes. "I know we said pastries, but I took the liberty of ordering you soft-cooked eggs and toast."

She inhaled deeply the savory aromas wafting through the air. "Smells scrumptious. Thank you." The man knew what she wanted better than she did.

He poured her steaming coffee and handed her the mug while she settled onto one of the stools.

After a large gulp of coffee to help summon her nerve, she cleared her throat. "Um...and thank you also for...uh, you know, sharing your bed." Dear saints, could she possibly sound more awkward?

He shrugged. "You were right. It's a large bed. We're both adults."

"Still. It was nice of you to come get me."

Evan grabbed a fork and started in on his own food. "You're welcome."

Now came the hard part. "I just wanted to explain. I'm something of a snuggler."

He swallowed and stared at her. "Snuggler?"

"When I sleep. I like to snuggle with something. At home, I sleep with a really large teddy bear."

He lifted one eyebrow. "Huh?"

"So that's what happened last night," she finished abruptly.

"I see."

An uncomfortable silence hung in the air. Great. In her effort to explain herself, she'd only made things more awkward. She had to change the subject.

"I'm very excited to meet your friends at the wedding." That wasn't entirely true. Actually, the statement was mostly a lie. *Excited* was definitely not the right word to describe the way she felt about the wedding. *Anxious. Terrified. Nervous.* Those were more appropriate.

"And your parents," she added. Another lie.

The way Evan's facial features tightened gave her the impression the change of subject hadn't helped the former awkwardness. In fact, it had somehow intensified. The space between them now practically crackled with tension.

"Look," he began, cramming his fingers through his hair. "There's something you should know."

The muscles above her stomach clenched with dread. What hadn't he told her?

"The truth is my parents and I haven't spoken much over the past few years."

That's it? She could certainly relate. Her desire to travel had kept her from seeing her father or brother for over two years. But she'd spoken to one or both of them nearly daily. She got the impression Evan couldn't say the same about his mother or father. If he had any siblings, she had to think he would have mentioned them by now.

"Oh. Is it because you were too busy launching your app and companies?"

He swallowed with a nod. "Something like that."

"You must be looking forward to seeing them, then."

Evan remained silent.

"Right?" she prodded.

Still no answer. Instead, he glanced at his watch. "I've gotten used to not seeing my parents. They haven't been in my life for several years now."

Chiara couldn't imagine what he was describing. How did anyone grow estranged from their parents to such a degree? She longed for so much as another hour with her mother.

"Did something happen to cause the rift?" Perhaps it was none of her business, but as his faux fiancée, she had to know a few details. What was she supposed to say if the subject came up?

He shrugged. "We were never particularly close to begin with."

"Not even when you were a little boy?"

A flinch of pain seemed to cross his features before he shook his head. "No. I was mostly tended to by nannies and other caretakers." His answers were so matter of fact, as if he were just rattling off data of some sort. But her heart was breaking for the small boy who'd had to grow up with such cold and distant parents.

The wedding was in a few short hours. She really didn't want to walk into something like that, blind about the social dynamics.

"But that's the overall gist of the situation. There's really not much more to explain," he assured her. Something told her that couldn't be quite true. There had to be more there. Evan just didn't seem to want to talk about it. "You're all caught up," he added.

Maybe. But would she have enough time to prepare herself to act accordingly? It sounded like there was some kind of unresolved issue between Evan and his parents. That was sure to make for some uncomfortable encounters between them.

And she'd be right there in the middle.

Evan glanced at his watch, clearly indicating the conversation was over as far as he was concerned. "Anyway, I have an appointment. I'm just going to hop in the shower, then it's all yours. Enjoy your breakfast."

"Thanks. I will," she said as he strode to the bedroom without so much as a glance behind. Yet another lie. As she seemed to have lost her appetite.

She'd compared him to a teddy bear.

Evan left the revolving door of the hotel lobby and walked out onto the sidewalk. He wasn't sure how his ego was supposed to take that, being compared to a large stuffed animal. When he'd awakened last night to find Chiara had moved over to his side of the bed and nestled herself up against his length, his first reaction wasn't one he was proud of.

He'd been ready to leave the room to go sleep on the couch like he'd first intended. But then she'd tucked her head under his chin, shimmied closer against his body. And suddenly there was more than temptation running through his blood. Comfort. Complete and total comfort.

He couldn't recall the last time he'd felt that way. Not since losing his beloved amah at the age of eleven. The memory of that volatile day sent a shudder through him before the familiar wave of sadness he always felt when he thought of her. He usually avoided such travels down memory lane. But the conversation earlier with Chiara about his parents had brought all sorts of buried ghosts to the surface.

A few feet away from his intended destination, his cell phone vibrated in his pocket. A smile creased his lips when he saw the contact photo on his screen.

Stopping mid-stride, he clicked to answer. "This is quite an honor," he said into the tiny speaker. "To have a man call you on the day of his wedding... Shouldn't you be rehearsing your vows or something?"

He heard Louis chuckle before answering. "Just thought I'd check in. You know you would have been my best man if I didn't have a twin brother."

"And I would have been honored. Sorry about missing the bachelor parties. There's a lot going on."

"No worries. But you know I'm going to have you make that up to me."

"Name the time and place," Evan said with a laugh.

He'd expected nothing less. "How's your beautiful bride? Any last-minute jitters?"

"Who? Gemma? No way. The woman performs for thousands of people on a regular basis. This will be a walk in the park for her."

"You're a lucky man."

"Don't I know it. She mentioned you just last night."

"Oh, yeah? How so?"

"Her manager's daughter will be at the wedding. Solo. We thought—"

"Hold on right there, brother," Evan interrupted before Louis wasted any kind of effort explaining a potential setup for him.

Louis's laugh sounded through the phone. "Let me finish. You can't stay a bachelor forever."

"That's not it, man." Things had moved so fast he hadn't had a chance to update Louis about bringing a plus-one to the wedding. Besides, his friend was rather busy with his upcoming nuptials. He could only hope Louis would be convinced when Evan delivered the news. It wasn't going to be easy; the other man knew him too well. "There's something I need to tell you."

CHAPTER NINE

DID SHE LOOK the part?

Chiara studied herself in the mirror and took a deep breath to calm her shredded nerves. The delicate silk dress with lace trim clung to her in all the right places. The color seemed to flatter her skin tone. She'd done her hair up in a loose bun that was just formal enough for a high-society wedding outdoors. She hoped so, anyway.

Did she portray what she'd be pretending at later? Is this what the fiancée of a world-renowned tech pioneer might look like at a wedding?

A knock on the bedroom door told her it was much too late to second-guess any of it now. It was time.

"Yes?" she answered. Evan poked his head through the partially open door. "Can I come in? If you're ready?"

She spread her arms out wide. "As ready as I'm going to be."

He walked in and she sucked in a breath at the sight of him. Clad in a tailored tuxedo, he looked like something out of a spy movie. Only he was real. And devastatingly handsome. The dark color of the tux brought out the ebony-black of his eyes. Cleanly shaved, his hair so dark it nearly shimmered, he looked every bit the international success that he was.

Looking into those eyes now, the expression in them as he studied her had her breath hitching in her throat.

"Wow," he finally said after several tense moments. "You look stunning."

Those words combined with the look in his eyes had her stomach clenching in a knot. She may not have had much experience with the opposite sex, but she knew male appreciation when she saw it. Whatever it was that was between them at the moment, she wouldn't have even been able to try to define it. But she had no doubt that if she made any kind of move right now, acted on her attraction in any way, Evan would respond in kind.

The mere thought had heat rushing to her cheeks.

For his part, Evan continued to stare at her, without so much as a blink. For an insane moment, her temptation had her thinking all sorts of impossible thoughts. Like maybe she should act on her desires? Would it be so bad if she stepped toward him, lifted her head up to meet his? Would he kiss her?

Finally, he cleared his throat and looked down. The moment had passed. Relief and disappointment warred within her. She had no idea if she might have gone through with it.

"So, the reason I ran out earlier was to get this," Evan interrupted her confusing thoughts and reached in the pocket of his pants. He pulled out a small black velvet box. "We are engaged, after all."

Her breath caught in her throat as her brain processed what was about to happen. A man was about to give her an engagement ring. But it was all fake. Phony. She wasn't really Evan's fiancée. The moment meant nothing. Not to Evan, anyway.

Still, her breath hitched when he popped open the lid. On a bed of white silk fabric sat a delicate platinum band and a large emerald cut diamond nestled between a pair of blue-sapphire gems. It was the absolute most beautiful piece of jewelry she'd ever laid eyes.

"Might be a little tight," Evan said. "I figured I'd err on the side of too small."

Her voice seemed to have left her. For several moments, she could do nothing but stare at the work of art he'd just presented her with.

"That was smart," she finally replied, hardly hearing her own words over the pounding in her head. "But how?" When had he managed to order a custom ring?

He shrugged. "I asked to have it made ASAP. As soon as you said yes back in Bali."

He must have paid a fortune. Not only for the ring but for the timing. Silently, Evan reached for her left hand and lifted it. Her mind narrowed to the scene before her. Nothing else matter. Evan slipping the ring on her finger, the way his large masculine hand looked holding her smaller one, the glimmer of the three stones. If she allowed her mind to leap, she could easily convince herself that this was all really happening. That this dynamic, exciting, handsome man had really proposed to her, and they were about to embark on a life together as a married couple. That he was, indeed, in love with her. As much as she was with him.

Dear saints, she had it bad, didn't she?

Chiara gave her head a brisk shake. She had to snap out of it. Evan had simply presented her with a piece of a costume. Sure, he'd put some thought into what he'd asked for, considering the color of her eyes. But in the end, it was simply another smart decision made by a very smart man in order to further sell the facade.

"We should go," he told her, guiding her gently by the hand. "The helicopter should be on the roof waiting."

Helicopter?

"You might want to grab a scarf," he said, pointing at her head. "For your hair. It can get windy in those things."

"We're flying to the wedding?"

He gave her mischievous smile. "We can't very well swim there."

She tilted her head. "Evan."

The smile grew. "Oh, didn't I tell you? The ceremony and celebration are being held on a small island off the coast, a few miles away."

Sure enough, when they reached the top of the building, she could hear the loud roar of an engine. A short flight of stairs led them to the roof where a sleek-looking, shiny black helicopter awaited them.

Chiara felt like she could be filming a scene from a spy movie.

Evan handed her a pair of large ear protectors as they climbed aboard. He said something she didn't understand to the pilot and soon they were rising into the air.

Chiara clung to the seat, excitement sending adrenaline shooting through her blood stream. Soaring above the hotel and the other towering buildings, she couldn't even decide where to focus her gaze. The view below her looked like some kind of dynamic painting. To her left, she could the Christmas Wonderland they'd visited just yesterday. Soon, they were above the lion-head statue majestically sprouting a heavy stream of water. The Singapore Flyer observation wheel made for an imposing figure that towered over everything else. She'd have to ask Evan if they might visit the attraction at some point so she could take in the view from the sky just once more before leaving the city.

The water shimmered like painted glass when they reached the air above the shore.

She glanced over where he was seated across from her to see if he was as enchanted by the sights as she was. To her surprise, he wasn't looking down. Rather he was staring right at *her* instead. And heaven help her, the look in in his eyes reminded her of the way he'd looked at her earlier in the bedroom. She had to remind herself to breath.

He lifted his hand and made a motion that mimicked taking a picture. It was too loud to try to explain that she wasn't going to bother, there was no need to pull her cell phone out to try and capture the moment.

She'd been taking so many pictures and videos because she hadn't wanted to risk forgetting even one small detail about this trip. But she'd never forget any bit of this.

Years after she and Evan bid their goodbyes and she returned to her familiar life back in New York, this memory would be a highlight of her life that stayed with her forever.

He couldn't seem to take his eyes off her.

Evan realized he wasn't the only one as they made their way from the beach toward the crowd that had already formed in front of a tall waterfall surrounded by tropical trees and shrubs. The helicopter had landed about a half mile away from where the ceremony would be held. A two-person buggy driven by a tuxedoed driver had taken them the rest of the way.

Louis and Gemma had gone all out. He would have to take notes for when—

Whoa. Where had that thought come from? He wasn't going to need notes about any kind of wedding reception anytime soon. He just wasn't meant for any sort of real relationship. He couldn't even make peace with the two people who had brought him into the world. The only other person he'd ever grown close to... Well, she was gone for good.

He liked his solitary life just fine. He just had to pretend otherwise until he got the signatures on the dotted line.

First, though, he had to get through this wedding. And he had to play the part of a besotted man in love. Glancing at Chiara walking beside him, he had to admit the act might be easier than he would have expected. He hadn't been exaggerating when he'd told her she looked stunning. The silky wrap dress she wore brought out the dazzling color of her eyes. The fabric clung to her in all the right places. Her hair was done up in some complicated style that somehow looked both elegant and loose. His fingers itched to loosen the ribbon tie and run his fingers down every strand. Then he could proceed to slip the thin straps off her shoulders and lower her dress.

Just. Stop.

He certainly sounded besotted, didn't he?

He couldn't begin to explain what might be wrong with him. It had to be the unusual circumstances he and Chiara were in that had him behaving so uncharacteristically. Slipping an engagement ring on a woman's finger before accompanying her to a romantic wedding would have a disarming effect on any man.

He was only human, after all.

They were approaching the seating area with chairs set up in front of a small waterfall when he heard his name called out from behind. He knew that voice well.

If it wasn't the groom himself.

He turned to find Louis striding toward them. The other man reached their side in seconds and Evan couldn't even be sure which one of them initiated the hug.

"Don't you have somewhere to be?" Evan asked, teasing his dearest friend. "What are you doing out here?"

"I had to see for myself who finally managed to pull this man away from his computer servers." He leaned toward Chiara and jokingly spoke in a quiet voice, his hand hiding both their faces. "You sure you know what you're getting into?"

Chiara answered with a laugh and reached her hand out. "I think so. It's very nice to meet you, Louis. Congratulations."

"Thanks for coming. I hope you enjoy yourself." He gave Evan a useless shove on the shoulder. "You, too. And I want to hear all about how you managed to snare this fine lady."

"Hey, don't go putting doubts in her head now. Also, don't you have to be somewhere? Like the altar?"

"I had to come out here and see for myself. But you're right." He pointed with finger guns at Evan's chest. "We are absolutely catching up during the reception. You two will be at the head table."

With that, Louis turned on his heel and hurried back in the direction he'd come from.

"That was clearly a display of nervous energy just now," Evan said, watching his friend's retreating back. "Don't let his casual demeanor fool you. He's nervous as...well, as a man about to say his vows in front of hundreds of people. He needed a distraction."

"You certainly provided him with one. Bringing an unknown fiancée to his wedding."

Evan chuckled. "I guess I did."

"You know him pretty well."

Better than most anyone else. Evan didn't know what he would have done without Louis's friendship over the years. He'd have to tell Chiara about it someday, all their shenanigans and troublemaking during uni. The time they'd set off unsanctioned fireworks on the roof of their dorm building.

"Known him since we were tots," he answered, then led her toward the seating area, greeting several acquaintances along the way with an acknowledging nod. Not surprisingly, he found his name printed on placards on two wooden chairs in the front row, close to the waterfall.

"Oh, my," Chiara said breathlessly next to him. "What an absolute beautiful setting for a wedding."

"Gemma is the one responsible, I'm guessing. Louis would have been happy to elope in Maui or even Vegas, I'm sure." Though Louis's parents would have been horrified if their son had taken that route. So his friend hadn't even considered that option. Louis was the prodigal son in every way. Unlike Evan himself.

Speaking of which, Evan tensed where he sat in his seat. He felt their presence before he saw them. The very air he was breathing seemed to change and grow thicker, a heaviness settling around his shoulders.

His eyes found them immediately, taking their seats in the first row at the opposite end to where he and Chiara sat.

His mother and father had just arrived.

Chiara felt Evan's whole body go stiff sitting next to her.

In one instant, he had gone from relaxed and carefree to rigid and tense. She wasn't going to get a chance to ask him about it, though, because a string quartet standing next to the podium began to play.

Evan's friend Louis appeared with another man who looked remarkably like him except he'd dyed the tips of his hair to a blonder color. Together, they stood to the side of the podium.

Chiara studied the area around the pond, trying to determine exactly where the bride would appear. There didn't seem to be any kind of pathway on either side of the waterfall. How would anyone, let alone a bride in any kind of gown or heels be able to walk through all that sand?

Then she saw it.

Chiara's jaw fell open when she noticed the vertical haze of white behind the waterfall. A moment later, the very water itself parted down the middle, like stage curtains drawing to the sides. The crowd erupted in applause and a chorus of oohs and aahs. The bride stepped forward, holding the hand of an older gentleman with silver hair wearing a white tuxedo. Together, they stepped out of the cave behind the waterfall and walked down slabs of stone. A rock pathway led them to the podium. There, Louis nodded to the older gentleman and took the bride's hand.

"Wow," Chiara whispered in Evan's ear. "I've never seen anything like that. It must have taken meticulous planning." And cost a fortune, she added to herself. Suddenly, she felt odd and out of place. What was she doing here? These people who surrounded her now had the type of wealth and resources to manipulate actual waterfalls. Her family had been successful enough back in New York. But this was a completely different stratosphere.

Chiara mentally hit pause and took a deep breath.

She could do this. She could play the part she'd been hired to play. Not like she could turn back now in any case.

The ceremony was heartfelt and touching. Despite being the center of attention, Louis and his bride seemed to have eyes for only each other. The love they shared glowed like a tangible aura between their bodies. Chiara felt herself sigh. Would she ever have that? A love that was clearly all-encompassing? Would a man ever look at her the way Louis was looking at his now-wife?

Did she even want it, though? She thought of how heartbroken and shattered her father had been after he'd lost the love of his life. There'd been days when she'd been convinced he might never recover. Did she want to risk that kind of heartbreak for herself?

Her gaze slowly shifted to Evan sitting next to her. His facial features were much softer, some of the tension seemed to have left his shoulders, and he'd shifted lower in his seat. Whatever had caused the earlier tenseness she'd sensed in him appeared to have been lessened somewhat. The ceremony must have had some kind of effect on him also.

What kind of wedding vows might Evan come up with to say to his beloved?

She squeezed her eyes shut and pushed the question out of her mind. She had no business wondering such things about the man. Hadn't she just seen proof of how mismatched they were in terms of economic status? Evan was nothing more than a temporary blip in her life. A man who had simply come up with a way to help her make it back home for the holidays.

Once she handed the ring on her finger back to him in a few short weeks, she'd best forget he even existed.

Right. As if Evan Kim was a man who could be easily forgotten, if at all.

When she reopened her eyes, it startled her to find Evan staring at her. A flush of heat crept into her cheeks. Had he somehow guessed where her mind had led her just now? It was a mortifying thought and she made herself look away before she could meet his eyes fully.

To her further surprise, he reached for her hand and pulled it onto his lap. Chiara's breath caught in her throat at his unexpected touch. Heat shimmied up her spine. Evan tilted his head to the right, indicating the woman sitting a few seats away, gawking at them.

Chiara wanted to kick herself for her foolishness. The way she'd reacted to his touch just now was down-right silly. The gesture to hold her hand was just that, a gesture. Merely for show. Whoever this woman was, Evan wanted to convince her he had a fiancée.

She'd been a fool to think otherwise for even a moment.

CHAPTER TEN

CHIARA CLAPPED AND cheered as loud as everyone else around her as the couple kissed after their vows.

She felt like she'd just watched something out of a fairytale. In fact, she felt as if she'd somehow stepped into a fairy tale.

Evan gently nudged her shoulder with his own. "Come on. Now, we eat. I'm starved."

The woman who'd been staring at them during the ceremony approached before they got past the seating area. "Evan. It's been so long. How have you been, dear?" She didn't wait for an answer before turning to Chiara. "And who might this be?" she asked.

Evan greeted the woman with a large smile. "Nice to see you, Marylin. Allow me to introduce my fiancée. This is Chiara Pearson. From New York City."

If the other woman was taken aback at all by the announcement, she didn't show it. Marylin shook her hand, somehow barely touching it to do so.

"Pleasure to meet you," Chiara said politely.

"Congratulations," she addressed both of them. "I'm so happy for you."

Chiara had no idea how genuine the statement was. The woman was impossible to read.

"Marylin is head of global acquisitions for Fruit-land," Evan explained.

Whoa. That was a major platform to download prac-tically every app in existence. No wonder Evan had pulled the little handholding act back there. The peo-ple Evan was hoping to convince were here and they had noticed.

Time to put her game face on.

"Chiara's family owns the Grand York hotel chain, which is based in New York. We met when she served as a translator for me during a business meeting."

Of course, he would introduce her that way. And not as the hotel housekeeper he'd met only days ago. But rather as some kind of hotel heiress. Which, techni-cally, she supposed she was. The truth was she hadn't really been active or involved with the family business. It had hurt too much after the loss of her mother. Just walking into the Grand York's lobby brought back too many memories of the days they'd spent there together as a family.

Marylin congratulated them once more before mov-ing on. Evan was then stopped by several other people as they made their way through the crowd and Chiara's face muscles started to grow strained from all the smil-ing as he introduced her to everyone who approached. Shock at the news of his engagement seemed to be the general reaction.

Finally, they reached the head table where the bride and groom had just begun to take their seats. Louis im-mediately abandoned his chair and reached their side.

"Chiara, come let me introduce you to my bride," he said, taking her lower arm and leading her to the center of the table. Evan followed close on her heels.

After he made the introductions, Chiara reached for

the woman's hand to shake but found herself in a tight hug instead. "That was quite an entrance!"

Gemma clasped a hand to her chest. "Do you think it was too much?"

Chiara had to laugh at the concern in her voice. "Absolutely not. A girl should be able to make a grand entrance at her own wedding."

Gemma giggled. "I debated and agonized over going through with it." She glanced downward. "I just wanted to take his breath away."

Goal achieved, then. Chiara's own breath had left her at the sight of the bride and her father walking through a waterfall, then over the pond to her intended. "I have no doubt you would have done that no matter how you entered."

The other woman reached for her hand then and took it in hers, giving it a squeeze. "I think we're going to get along marvelously, Chiara Pearson."

A lump formed in her throat. Genuine sentiment shone in the other woman's eyes. Suddenly, she felt small and unworthy. If Gemma only knew that at this very moment Chiara was betraying her with a blatant lie...

And though Chiara had only just met the other woman mere moments ago, it shamed her that she'd already betrayed her trust. She could only hope when all this was over, Gemma and Louis would understand and forgive her.

Not that she would ever know. The chances of her running into a real estate mogul and his classical pianist wife afterward were slim to none. Chiara didn't exactly run in the same circles. That thought only served to escalate her sadness.

Maybe they'd stay at the Grand York someday. And

she could try to explain herself. Chiara would love to get the chance at some point.

A chance to clear her name would mean so much.

Evan watched as various couples gradually made their way to the wooden dance floor built near the water. This was as good a time as any to ramp up their act. A man had to dance with his fiancée, didn't he?

He waited while Chiara took another bite of her crab and shrimp curry. She took her times chewing and swallowing, as if savoring every morsel. The woman certainly seemed to enjoy good food. In fact, it was doing strange things to his libido to watch her eat.

Wasn't that a sorry state of affairs?

In his defense, the way she made a soft moaning sound with each swallow would tempt any man, for more than just food. He had to look away before she took another bite.

Finally, she set her fork down and he leaned toward her and spoke just loud enough in her ear over the loud hip-hop beat of the song the band was playing. Though *band* wasn't quite the right word. Mini orchestra was probably more like it. In addition to the quartet for the ceremony, Louis and Gemma had commissioned another group for the celebration afterward.

"Ready to dance?" he asked.

Her eyes grew wide. For a split second, he thought she was going to turn him down. Instead, she bounced out of her seat. "I thought you'd never ask. They're playing some of my favorite songs."

Evan chuckled at her reaction, then led her off the dining platform and toward the action on the beach.

"I've never seen such a large band at a wedding,"

Chiara remarked, following behind him to the dance floor, her hand still clutched in his.

"Gemma knows quite a few musicians, given her line of work."

Her pace faltered a step. "Right. I'd almost forgotten. The bride is a world-renowned classical musician barely in her twenties and one of the guests is the CEO of a major media platform. I'm guessing all the other guests are just as accomplished."

Evan couldn't guess what she was getting at. But he thought better of mentioning the two diplomats in attendance. Not to mention the global status of his own parents.

"Come on," he encouraged her instead as they joined the throngs on the dance floor. "Let me show you my moves."

He playfully twirled her around three times before they started shuffling together to the bouncy music. Chiara's laughter was contagious. He couldn't remember the last time he'd actually enjoyed dancing. If ever.

She leaned in closer. "You know, for a techie, you're not so bad on your feet."

He gave her a mini bow. "I accept your compliment. You're not so bad yourself."

Suddenly, without announcement, the band slipped into a much slower love song, one full of suggestive lyrics. Chiara's eyes darted around the dance floor, then found his, silently asking him what to do. Without thinking, Evan pulled her close to his chest, wrapped his hands above her hips. She stood frozen for the briefest second. Then her arms found their way around his shoulders. For several moments, they simply swayed together.

"This is working great," he whispered in her ear,

simply to have something to say. "We've definitely got the right people's attention. And letting Marylin Tamin know we're engaged will go a long way."

For the second time that night, he felt Chiara's steps falter. She stiffened in his arms and pulled away a fraction of an inch. "I'm glad it's working," she said into his shoulder after staying silent so long it surprised him when she spoke.

Half a song later, she stepped out of his arms. "I think that's enough dancing for me, right now. I'm feeling a little thirsty."

Was it his imagination or had her voice hardened somewhat? Probably just tired after all the dancing. He wrapped his arm around her waist. "Let's get you something to drink, then. There are cocktail fountains somewhere."

She shook head. "Maybe just some water for now. I had a couple of glasses of wine with dinner earlier. I usually pace myself better."

"Don't be too hard on yourself. Louis's dad owns several vineyards in the Loire Valley region in France. That was some of the finest wine bottled within the last century."

Chiara's hand flew to her mouth. "And I gulped it down like cheap bubbly from the corner store. You should have told me."

"Told you to stop drinking your wine with dinner?"

"No. But you might have mentioned how expensive it was. I wouldn't have had so much."

Evan chuckled as he led her away. "Chiara, you need to relax a bit. You're doing great. Everyone thinks we're head over heels—"

He swallowed the last word when the woman appeared in front of him. Dressed in an off-gray silk gown that had to have cost a fortune, she remained silent. Surprising as it was, she hadn't really changed at all since the last time he'd seen her all those years ago, though a few more wrinkles framed her eyes and lips. Hardly noticeable ones. The woman had always been meticulous about taking care of herself with a skin-care routine that could best be described as militant.

Evan blew out a sigh and cursed the timing that had caught him off guard. He wasn't prepared. Had been too preoccupied by the way Chiara had felt in his arms as they danced together. But it was just as well. It wasn't as if he was going to be able to avoid them the whole wedding. May as well get it over with.

"Hello, Mother," he said, fully meeting her gaze. Chiara's gasp was clearly audible next to him.

"Chiara, this is my mother, Luann Kim."

Chiara immediately stepped forward with her hand outstretched. The other woman took it for less than a second before pulling her arm away.

"Mother, this is Chiara Pearson. My fiancée."

"So I've heard."

Chiara felt zero warmth emanating from this woman. None. It was like speaking to an icebox. What was wrong with her? Evan said they hadn't even seen each other for years. And here he was introducing her to his *fiancée*, albeit a fake one. But she didn't know that. Yet, his mother was utterly, astonishingly unmoved in any way.

"I congratulate you on your engagement, then," she added, not sounding congratulatory at all.

"Thank you," Chiara and Evan replied in unison.

"You feel ready to be married then, son." She said

it in a way that sounded like it could be both statement and question.

Evan simply nodded once.

"I hope it works out," Luann said, with a quick glance in Chiara's direction. Chiara could only hope the woman really meant it.

Her next words gave her some kind of clue about how genuine she was. "You certainly don't need to add a failed marriage to your list of life disappointments."

Chiara couldn't believe her ears. What kind of statement was that? To her own son? Barely realizing what she intended, she took a small step forward, partially standing between Luann and Evan. "With all due respect, ma'am, everyone has disappointments and failures. Very few men accomplish all that Evan has at such a young age." Chiara knew she should stop there. But her mouth didn't seem to want to listen to her better judgment. "Most mothers would be proud of all he's done," she added.

For several beats, an awkward silence hung there with only the background noise of the wedding. Oh, dear.

"Hmm… You're from New York, yes?" The words sounded like some sort of accusation.

What was she getting at? "Yes, that's right. Though I'm not sure I understand what that has to do with anything."

Luann lifted her shoulders in a mini shrug "I've heard those from New York are prone to speak their mind. Even things better left unsaid," his mother uttered as her eyes ran the length of Chiara.

"I'm sorry," Chiara repeated, not really meaning it this time. "But I don't agree with that." Some things did, indeed, have to be said.

"I'm sure you don't," the other woman replied. Without so much as another glance, she turned on her heel and walked away.

Chiara's blood ran cold. Her first encounter with Evan's mom and the conversation had not gone well. Maybe Mrs. Kim was right. She should have never said what she had, should have found a way to keep her mouth shut. To make matters worse, there was no doubt there'd been at least a couple people who'd played audience to the display. And she was certain at least one of them had snapped a picture.

What had she been thinking?

Chiara was horrified at what she'd just done. Only, she hadn't been thinking at all, had she? She should have just smiled politely and expressed her pleasure at meeting Evan's mother. She had no excuse. Except that her nerves had just been so frazzled after that slow dance with Evan. The way he had been holding her, swaying with her to the soft melody. The smell of him surrounding her, the warmth of his body against hers. Then to have him throw cold water over her when he'd explained exactly what he was doing.

Playing at the charade he was paying her for.

This was a calamity. The wine probably hadn't helped matters.

She risked a glance at Evan once his mom had walked away. A muscle twitched along his jaw. His chin was set in a rigid hard line, his lips tight.

Probably not a good sign.

She clenched her hands together, willing for him to say something. Anything to let her know how big of a faux pas she'd just committed and if there was anything she could do to rectify it somehow. Should she be chasing his mom down, pleading an apology?

Evan remained silent so long Chiara was close to panic. She would have welcomed the random opening of a sinkhole right where she stood so the earth could swallow her whole.

Finally, when she was certain she wouldn't be able to take another moment, he pivoted on his heel.

"Come on," he said to her over his shoulder. "Let's go get you that water. And I could use a drink myself."

Chiara blinked at his retreating back. That was it? He wasn't going to even acknowledge what had just happened? He answered that question a moment later when she caught up to him at one of the four bars set behind the stage.

"Let's take a walk," he told her, handing her a sweaty glass bottle of water from a standing ice bucket near the bar, then reaching for a small tumbler half full of amber liquid the server handed him.

Great. This was probably going to be worse than the silent treatment she'd been so worried about just moments ago. Evan was about to read her the riot act. Estranged or not, Chiara had just somehow offended his mother. In front of witnesses. Something told her that sort of thing didn't sit well, particularly in this part of the world.

Evan led them to a couple of wooden Adirondack chairs near the water and deposited his tuxedo jacket over the back of one. Chiara kicked her shoes off, tucking her legs under her as she sat.

"Look, Evan," she began before he could say anything, arguing in advance in her defense. "I know I overstepped back there, and I shouldn't have said what I said, but I want you to know that I meant it all."

He took a generous sip of his drink, his eyes never leaving the horizon. "Chiara, there wasn't any kind of need for you to say anything. We're here portraying an engaged couple so I can finalize a business deal."

Ouch. Pretty matter-of-fact summary. It stung more than she would have liked, enough that she felt the burning of tears behind her eyes. He was telling her to stay out of his personal life. "I see. In other words, I just need to play my little role and not cause any waves."

"That's not what I said."

Maybe not. But it was what he meant. Suddenly, she felt no small amount of anger herself. She was thoroughly out of her element here. She could have used some advanced knowledge of the rift between Evan and his parents before attending the same wedding and coming face-to-face with one of them.

"Maybe you should give me a script so there isn't any more instances of overstepping on my part."

When he finally looked at her, his eyes were hard and cold. Chiara sucked in a deep breath. Despite his relatively mild tone of voice, Evan Kim was beyond annoyed. She might even venture to guess that he was angry.

Yep, she must have really stepped in it this time. No one had probably ever spoken to Mrs. Kim like that in her lifetime. Chiara had really been out of line. She would have to apologize. Evan would have to guide her on the best way to do that.

Only, Evan's steely profile didn't give her the impression he was ready to talk just yet.

What was she even doing here? The whole situation was surreal. For the first time since they'd left Bali, real doubt and trepidation rose like an evil serpent in the back of her mind. The reality was she had no idea what she was doing.

Damn it. She was not going to cry. The tears would

stay unshed no matter how hard she had to fight them. But she couldn't suppress an errant sniffle, which was just loud enough that Evan turned to her. Shock washed over his features, and he cursed out loud.

In an instant, he'd set his tumbler down on the armrest of his chair and he was in front of her.

"Oh, God. Chiara, please don't cry."

His reaction only made her feel worse. She didn't mean to guilt him. It was why she'd tried so hard not to give in to the urge to say something in the first place.

"I'm not crying," she argued.

He swallowed. "That's pretty damn close." He forced his fingers through the hair at his crown. "Look, if it makes you feel better, your delivery was wrong, and you went about it terribly…"

"How is any of that supposed to make me feel better?"

"Because, despite how you went about it, no one's ever stuck up for me like that before. Well, not since several years ago. And then I was just a child."

Chiara sniffled despite herself, dabbed at her eyes with the back of her hand. "Tell me."

"I had a nanny when I was little. She was the one who looked after me as a child. She actually stood up to my parents on my behalf. More than once."

"Do you still stay in touch with her?"

"She's gone. I lost her years ago."

"I'm sorry."

Before he could respond, a group of guests ran onto the beach only a few feet away from where they sat. They had some kind of small rubber ball and started playing an impromptu mini volleyball game without a net. Or the right-sized ball. Dressed in glamorous gowns and tuxes. Despite herself, Chiara found herself distracted and laughing at the sight.

Evan didn't seem as amused. He stood and held his hand out to her. "Come on, let's find a more private spot where we can talk."

She bent forward for her shoes in the sand, but Evan beat her to it and picked them up. As he stood, he reached for her, tucking a strand of wayward hair behind her ear.

Is that real? she couldn't help but think. Was he simply putting on a show for the volleyballers on the beach? Or did he really want to touch her that way? And what did it mean for her that she had to know for the sake of her heart?

Leading her by the hand, he walked them down yet another stone pathway behind the line of shrubbery. To her surprise, once they cleared the greenery, there appeared rows and rows of small huts. "What is this?" she asked.

"For guests who want to spend the night. Anyone who wants to celebrate into the wee hours."

"Huh." It was all she could think of to say.

"They're equipped with everything. From a complimentary change of clothing to generator electricity."

This was certainly unlike any other wedding she'd ever attended. The ultra-wealthy certainly lived in an entirely different world, didn't they? Fully functional housing huts on the beach for those guests who didn't feel like flying back to shore in private helicopters.

The ever-present question was highlighted yet again. What was she doing here amongst such people?

"We can talk privately in one of them." He took her inside the closest hut and shut the wooden door behind them.

Chiara had to blink to believe her eyes. A fully made bed sat in the center of the single room. Two robes and various clothing hung on a rack against the wall. A wicker door led to a small restroom on the opposite wall. The place was bigger than her hostel room back in Bali. "This is unbelievable."

"They've been planning this wedding for close to two years," Evan explained, then crossed his arms in front of his chest. "Look, it's my fault what happened out there. I should have warned you to say as little as possible to either of my parents."

Did he really think that was the problem?

"I didn't mean to make you feel uncomfortable at any point during this arrangement we have," he continued.

For several beats, Chiara could only stare, slack-jawed. Then she finally found her voice. "Do you really think that any of those things I said to your mother back there has anything to do with our arrangement? That I might have been playacting or something of the sort?"

He swallowed and nodded, though his expression appeared much less certain than it had seconds ago when he'd made his comment.

"I see. What you really think is that I stuck my nose in where it doesn't belong. That it's really none of my business. Is that right?"

His lips tightened before he spoke. "Chiara."

"Maybe I made it my business because I've grown to care about you!" Chiara actually stomped her foot, and didn't care that it might look like a childish tantrum. "Though, at this moment, I can't exactly say why." She hated that the last word came out in a hiccup. But she was way past her boiling point now.

Suddenly, the very air in the room seemed to have

shifted, grown heavy. Evan's eyes darkened. He took a step toward her. "What did you just say?"

Despite his ominous tone, or what it might mean, Chiara decided to hold her ground. She'd made an admission because it was the truth. She would stick with it, not about to backtrack in any way. Heaven help her if that decision proved to be a mistake. "I've grown to care about you, Evan." She pushed her hair off her forehead, not caring that it might mess up her meticulous updo. "I don't even know when it happened. But I hated hearing those things your mother said. Hated that *you* had to hear them."

He reached her in two strides. Before she knew what was happening, his lips were on hers. Her body's response was immediate and fierce. Heat exploded deep in her belly, her blood pounded through her veins, her skin felt aflame from head to toe. Chiara wrapped her arms around his neck and succumbed fully to his kiss, tasting him, inhaling his scent, feeling his warmth.

She'd wondered all her life and now she knew. *This* was what true passion felt like, true desire. The way she wanted this man made her feel alive in ways she couldn't define. She'd felt that desire from that moment on that Bali beach when they'd collided. How in the world had she fought it so long? No more. She'd admitted it now. Both to herself and to Evan. Regret would not enter the picture in any way. No matter what came next.

Evan's hands moved down to her hips, and he pulled her tighter against him. A feminine rush of pleasure washed through her entire being at the contact. He continued the delicious onslaught against her lips. Chiara wanted to melt into him, nothing in the world existed except the man who held her in her arms.

Without warning, he suddenly pulled away, panting and leaving her downright breathless.

"Tell me if you think we should go back to the wedding, Chiara. Right now."

It took several moments for her mind to come back to earth and process what he was asking. Evan was making sure she knew it was her decision.

"Or would you like to stay here. In this cabin?" he asked.

Try to live your life as fully as you can, my dearest. Don't let any moment of happiness pass you by.

Her mom's voice echoed through her head yet again. Surely, this would be one of those moments she must have been referring to.

"I'd like to stay." Her voice sounded thick to her own ears.

Evan closed his eyes tight, tilted his head back. "Chiara, I need to be sure what you're saying here. I don't want to misconstrue anything only to find out I'm terribly wrong."

The man really needed everything laid out in black-and-white, didn't he? Zeros and ones.

Chiara reclaimed the distance between them. She ran her hands along his shoulders until he'd reopened his eyes and focused them back on her face. "I'd like to stay," she repeated. "And seeing as we've already taken over this cabin, I'd like to stay all night."

His enthusiastic response told her just how much he wanted the very same thing.

CHAPTER ELEVEN

Three days later

WELL, THE PLAN was working. It hadn't even taken very long. Evan tossed his tablet onto the sofa and rubbed his eyes. Just as he'd expected, the gossip sites and magazines had taken the bait. He and Chiara were the talk of the tech world. Which meant the private social grapevines were most likely raging with countless messages back and forth about the big mystery surrounding Evan Kim's sudden engagement.

Even their photo from the sushi place in Bali had somehow been found and published. The headline above it read *Tech Wunderkind to Tie the Knot.* With the subheading *Rumor Has it They're Traveling to Beijing Together Next!*

Exactly what he'd intended when he'd made Chiara the offer all those days ago. Now the only question was what exactly was real and what was pretend. So many lines had been blurred the night of Louis and Gemma's wedding. He had to wonder if a few major ones had been crossed.

One thing was certain, he had to try to keep his distance from Chiara as best he could until he figured it all out. Which wasn't going to be easy. Close proxim-

ity aside, his attraction to her tempted him like no other
woman had before. He'd always prided himself on his
unwavering discipline and the strength of his sheer will.
Both those traits were taking a serious hit because of
Chiara Pearson's effect on him.

The object of his thoughts strode into the room at that
very moment, fresh from a long shower. The woman
sure enjoyed bathing. That thought had all sorts of
unbidden images that he had to push away. She was
dressed in dark wool pants and a thick knitted sweater.
She wrapped a winter scarf around her neck as she
walked past where he sat on the couch.

"Good morning, Evan."

"Morning." Evan stood. "Are you going out?"

She flashed him a brilliant smile full of excitement.
"I called the concierge earlier. She mentioned some
tours I can join."

"Tours?"

She nodded with enthusiasm. "To see the Great
Wall."

Huh. "You want to play tourist?"

She tilted her head. "I've wanted to see it since I was
a little girl. My mom used to read me a picture book
about an adventurous crow who tried to fly the wall
from end to end." Some of the light seemed to fade from
her eyes as she spoke. She clasped her hand together.
"Anyway, you said you'd be much too busy prepping for
your meetings to do any kind of sightseeing."

He had said that, hadn't he? On the flight here to
Beijing, he'd made sure to emphasize to her that he
wouldn't be able to spend much time with her or away
from his desk. He'd almost convinced himself it was
really because he had work to do. And not due to the

self- preservation instinct that had kicked in after their night together.

"So I looked into ways I could venture out myself," Chiara said.

It made no sense whatsoever, given that the situation was of his own doing, but a sliver of hurt settled in his chest that she hadn't asked him to take her.

Evan thrust his hands into his pants pockets. How silly of him. He should be happy. Chiara was resourceful enough that she'd found a way to entertain herself. Plus, she'd be with a tour group, so he didn't have to worry about her safety out there in an unfamiliar city where she didn't know the language.

So why was he dreading having her walk out the door? Suddenly, the thought of spending hours and hours here, alone in a hotel room without her company, going over line after line of code, had him tempted to hurl his laptop out the window.

While she was out there taking in the sight of the majestic wall for the first time. He could picture her gasping at its beauty while she shivered in the cold. Maybe there'd be a solo American businessman there on the tour with her. Doing some sightseeing himself. He might offer her his scarf. They'd get to talking...

Just stop.

A trail of guilt crept into his chest. Despite the intimate night they'd spent together, he had no claim to her. In fact, he'd been downright insensitive to her wishes. She wanted to see the Great Wall because of a memory tied to her mother. Instead of offering to accompany her to one of the true wonders in the world, he'd shot down the idea before it had even come up.

She studied his face and bit her top lip with her bottom teeth. Why did the woman look so damn sexy when she did that? "Unless… Do you want me to stay here for some reason?"

Evan puffed out a breath. What a loaded question that was. The answer couldn't be denied. He did want her here. With him. And selfish or not, the thought of her being approached by another man made him queasy.

"Evan?" she prompted after several seconds in silence. She glanced at the digital clock above the flat screen. "The tours are due to leave in a short while. I need to get down there if I'm going to hop on to one."

A much too loud voice in his head screamed at him to tell her that her leaving now was the last thing he wanted. The words were on the tip of his tongue.

I want to be the one you see the Great Wall with. I want to hold your hand as you take in the sights. I want to see your expression when you first lay eyes on wonder that attracts millions of people. Instead of random strangers and a monotone tour guide, I want to be the one to tell you about its history. I want to tell you about the many times I visited it myself as a child.

But the words never left his mouth. Instead, he uttered ones he didn't mean. "Yeah. You should definitely get down there before it's too late."

Her shoulders dropped, whether in relief or some other reaction he couldn't be sure of and didn't want to guess.

"Have fun," he said to her retreating back as she grabbed her gear and walked out the door without another word to him.

She couldn't bring herself to do it. Chiara settled into one of the plush velvet chairs in the lobby and watched the group of tourists follow the smiling guide outside to a sleek, shiny black van. She'd made it all the way downstairs and to the concierge desk and gotten into line before she turned on her heel. As much as she wanted to see the Great Wall, she wasn't sure she could do it surrounded by people she'd never laid eyes on before.

The memory of her mother was already bubbling to the surface of her emotions. Being there without her mom was sure to bring her to tears at some point and she didn't want to be around strangers when that happened. For one insane second upstairs, she thought maybe Evan would change his mind about staying in and offer to accompany her. Instead, he'd practically pushed her out the door. He was probably glad to be rid of her.

And if she thought spending one night in his arms made that unlikely, she should have known better. They'd simply succumbed to their desires. Plus, she'd practically thrown herself at him. Not many men turn down such offers. She'd obviously made more of their intimacy than he had. He'd been nothing but cold and distant since. No wonder he wanted her gone.

Now, she just had to figure out what she was going to do with herself for the day.

Two pots of jasmine tea later, no ideas had materialized. Any kind of tour the hotel offered had already embarked and she was in no mood to wander the streets alone. She also didn't have any kind of money to shop.

One thing was certain, she couldn't drink another drop of tea, as delicious as it was. And she certainly couldn't sit here for hours shuffling through her phone, staring at pictures of an attraction she could have physically visited if only she could have been strong enough to bring herself to do it alone.

Her phone lit up and vibrated where she'd placed it

facedown on the coffee table in front of her chair. Her heart leaped with hope. But when she grabbed the device and glanced at the screen, it wasn't Evan's contact icon that greeted her.

Her brother's goofy picture she used as his avatar photo popped up on her screen instead. She hadn't called him in days after telling him she would. She had to answer. Besides, it would kill at least a few minutes.

"Hello—" She'd hardly gotten the word out before Marco interrupted her.

"Hey, sis. Long time, no talk."

"Yeah, sorry about that. I've been kind of busy."

She heard her brother suck in a breath. "Yeah, about that. Anything you want to tell me?"

A queasy feeling curled at the top of her stomach. What was he getting at? "Uh…about?"

Several seconds passed without an answer. She pulled the phone from her ear to see if they'd somehow lost the connection. Marco was still on the line.

"I don't know," he finally said. "Maybe you can explain why my tech friend just called to congratulate me on your upcoming nuptials. He saw a picture of you on some website. It was taken in a restaurant in Singapore. You're seated with a tech world wunderkind billionaire."

Oh, no. She should have been better prepared for this. Marco and Evan may not travel in the same circles, but her brother was a hotelier who knew all sorts of people from various backgrounds and fields of work. Things with Evan had just moved so fast, Chiara hadn't even had time to give much thought to how she'd explain her 'engagement' once word of it reached her sibling. Truth be told, she hadn't expected Marco to catch wind of it quite so soon. She gripped the phone tight in her hand, trying to come up with a response.

Marco continued, "I called up the photo for myself. Unless you have a doppelgänger, the mystery lady rumored to be engaged to this software mogul appears to be you."

"Marco. Things are…complicated in my life right now." The explanation was so much less than he deserved. But right now, it was all she could give him.

She heard him sigh. "Are you safe? I have contacts all over the world who can be at your side in no time if you need."

An ocean of love and gratitude blossomed in her chest at his concern. She hastened to assuage it. "I'm fine. Really. You absolutely don't need to worry."

"Are you sure?" he pressed.

"Yes. In fact, I'm enjoying tea in the busy lounge of a five-star hotel as we speak. I'll send you a snapshot."

She could almost feel his relief through the tiny phone speaker. "Okay. Then tell me what's going on."

"I can't, Marco. I'm sorry."

"Chiara—"

She didn't let him finish. "Can you just trust me, big bro? I'll explain everything as soon as I can. I know it's a lot to ask."

He uttered a mild curse. "It really is, sis. You're not making things easy on me here."

She closed her eyes and thought what her own reaction would be if the roles were reversed. No doubt, Chiara would demand to know every detail. But Marco was unlike her in so many ways, despite their shared DNA.

"And please don't say anything to Dad," she pleaded, horrified at the mere thought of her father finding out.

"Dad seems kind of…"

"What?" Chiara asked at the hesitation, panic sprouting in her core.

"He's fine," Marco reassured. "Just seems distracted for some reason."

She allowed herself the moment of relief. "Please don't say anything to him. I'll explain to you as soon as I can," she repeated, willing him to understand.

"The sooner the better."

Chiara released the breath she'd been holding and thanked him profusely before hanging up. At least she'd bought herself some time. But she was much too frazzled now to continue sitting around in a lounge any longer. The unexpected conversation with Marco had taken up the last reserves of her emotional strength.

Time to head back upstairs. There was nothing for it. Maybe she'd catch a break and Evan would be locked away working in the suite office. If so, he might not even notice her coming back in.

No such luck.

Evan was exactly where she'd left him. He gave her a questioning look when she walked in and shut the door behind her.

"I was too late, it turns out. Didn't get down there in time. The tour must have left a little early."

He merely lifted an eyebrow at her explanation, seemingly convinced. "That's too bad."

She was getting really good at this fibbing thing. She'd have to make several trips to the confessional and shore up some volunteer days at the local shelter as soon as she got back to the States to try to rebalance her karma scales. "I'll try again tomorrow."

"What were you doing all this time?"

Drinking too much tea and trying to convince my brother not to fly across the world in his concern that I might elope with some stranger.

"Just looking into other options as to how to spend my day." That part was true enough. "Nothing came to mind," she added, heading toward the other room to wallow in her boredom.

Evan touched her arm as she walked by him, stopping her in her tracks. Her gaze fell to where he touched her. He had barely lifted a finger in her direction since that night in the hut at the wedding. Neither of them had so much as mentioned it aside from an awkward conversation the next morning about how they'd both gotten carried away by the romantic mood of the wedding. Chiara braced herself against the onslaught of desire that ran through her veins at the mere feel of his hand on her skin.

"Yes?" she asked, eager to move away before she did something to embarrass herself. Like step farther into his arms and ask him to kiss her again, the way she so desperately wanted to.

Evan dropped his hand to his side. "It just so happens I was more productive than I'd hoped to be this morning."

Well, that seemed hard to believe. He was still sitting right where she'd left him this morning. Seemed they both might be doing some fibbing. Then it dawned on her what he might be implying. Was he possibly saying he had some free time?

"What does that mean?" Chiara asked, not daring to hope.

He executed a mini bow that made her laugh. "If you would allow me, I'd be honored to play tour guide for the rest of the day."

Try as she might, Chiara couldn't help the squeal of delight that escaped her. "Really?"

He nodded with a smile that warmed her soul. "Really. It'll be fun. Let me just make a couple calls, then we can be on our way."

"Then go make those calls," she urged, giving him a weak shove before he could change his mind.

The smile on Chiara's face as they made their way out of the lobby to a waiting limo made the lie worthwhile. The truth was he hadn't gotten much done at all after she'd left. His usually laser sharp focus had completely abandoned him. It was hard to drown out the annoying voice. The one in his head that had nagged at him all morning. Telling him he'd been a fool to let Chiara leave without him. When she reappeared, it began to scream that he couldn't waste the second chance he'd been presented with.

She paused and turned to him halfway to the vehicle. "Is that for us?" she asked, pointing to the car.

"That would be why the driver is holding the door open as we approach."

She blinked up at him. "Got it. We're taking a limo to the Great Wall."

"It's over an hour's drive from here. May as well be comfortable."

Still, she didn't move. "You didn't have to do all this, Evan. I would have been happy to take a bus or something. Just as long as you…" But she didn't finish her sentence.

Evan was tempted to press, ask her exactly what she was about to say. But now the driver was staring at them in confusion.

"Come on." He gently nudged her with a hand at her waist. "It's not a big deal. This is how I usually travel long distances in Beijing."

With clear reluctance, she finally moved, and he

helped her into the back, then sat on the opposite bench. The driver reappeared with a steaming pot of tea and a bamboo basket and placed the items on the table between them before settling into the driver's seat.

"Early lunch," he told her and lifted the lid of the basket to reveal several dumplings. He handed her a set of wooden chopsticks.

"No tea for me, thanks," Chiara said, taking the chopsticks and plucking up one of the dumplings.

"You sure? You'll appreciate the warm-up once we get there. This is the coldest time of year to visit the Great Wall."

She nodded. "I'm sure. I had my fill earlier in the lounge of the hotel." She licked her lips after a bite of food and Evan lost his focus for a moment. Her next words brought him back to the present. "I have a confession," she began.

Interesting. And curious. "Oh?"

She set down her chopsticks and leveled her eyes on his. "I didn't really miss the tour group earlier."

"What happened?"

"The truth is I didn't want to go by myself. Or with a group of strangers."

Now he really felt like a heel. He should have just asked her to go with him from the get-go. Such a mistake on his part. What she said next didn't make him feel any better.

"So I feel a little guilty that you went through all this trouble," she said, waving her hands around the car. "Arranging for a limo. One that serves lunch."

Evan leaned toward her over the table. "If we're confessing, I have to come clean about something, too."

"What's that?"

"I lied to you about how much work I got done this

morning. In fact, I barely accomplished anything after you left."

She chuckled at his admission. "Why would you lie about that?"

"To give me an excuse to spend the day with you."

CHAPTER TWELVE

HER MOTHER'S CHAPTER books had not prepared her for the view before her. Nor had all the websites and travel guides she'd browsed over the years. Chiara let Evan guide her down the stone pathway, stopping every few feet just to take in the scenery. She couldn't blame the photographers. There was no earthly way to capture the majesty and grandeur that was the Great Wall of China. Godlike mountains as far as her eyes could see, now dusted with a layer of snow just thin enough to have the greenery below peak through. A blue-gray sky framed the horizon. Thick puffy clouds roamed the sky like grand ships

It was also very cold. Skin-numbing, bone-numbing cold. Despite her thick coat and clothing, Chiara felt the chill clear to her center.

Evan must have noticed her shivering. "Too bad we're not here during a summer month," he said. "The weather is much more pleasant for one. And you might have witnessed a traditional Chinese wedding."

"Couples get married here?"

He nodded. "Just not in December."

Another chill ran through her. "I don't blame them." But what a stunning and unforgettable location for a wedding. To be surrounded by this view as you commit yourself to the love of your life. Chiara could just imagine how sacred and beautiful a ceremony held here would be. "What a wonderful way for a couple to begin their life together."

"The only wedding venue visible from space."

They walked toward the closest tower. She could only guess what the view might look like from that height. In her haste, she clumsily stepped on a patch of slick snow and her foot slipped out from beneath her. She braced herself for the inevitable impact of hard stone against her knee and prayed fervently to be spared a broken bone. A miracle spared her just before the tumble, though, as a set of sturdy arms suddenly wrapped around her waist.

Not a miracle but Evan.

"Whoa, steady there." She straightened to thank him. But the words caught in her throat. His face was a mere inch or so from his. The fog of their breath intermingled between them. His now-familiar scent, masculine and woodsy, tickled her nose and sent longing surging through her core. As if in slow motion, he tilted his head closer. The world simply stopped.

Kiss me. Please.

She wanted so badly to say the words aloud. Or to just do it herself, spare him from making the decision by simply reaching for him. Settling her mouth over his and tasting him.

The sound of footsteps nearing them barely registered in her ears. But Evan suddenly straightened and balanced her back on her feet. Then he let her go. A family of three stepped around them with polite smiles. The loss of his nearness had her shaking where she stood. It had nothing to do with the cold this time. The moment was lost, disintegrated like smoke as if it had never happened.

"Let's get to that tower," he said, guiding her gently by the elbow.

The air got cooler and cooler as they climbed up the stone steps. Chiara could hardly bother to notice when they reached the top, however. She felt like she could be flying, like the crow from the book her mother read to her all those years ago.

The view from up here was even more breathtaking. Spiritual even. "I've never felt such a connection to the planet." She hadn't even meant to say it out loud.

The look that passed over Evan's face gave her pause. "You must think I'm being silly," she said with a soft chuckle. "Waxing poetic."

He shook his head in a slow, steady motion. "Actually, I was thinking that was pretty much the exact thought I had the first time I climbed up one of these towers."

"Really?"

"Really."

"How old were you?"

"About ten. My ahma brought me here to visit."

"Your ahma?"

His lips tightened. "She's like a nanny. Or caregiver to a child."

"The one you said was the only person to ever stand up for you as a child."

He swallowed and turned away but not before she saw his features wash over with tenderness. "That's right. She brought me to the Wall for the very first time. Once when it was just this cold. If not colder."

So, not his parents, then. Chiara got the feeling Evan didn't have many memories that involved his parents.

Just how distant and cold had they been to their son? If the confrontation with his mother at the wedding was any clue, he hadn't grown up in the warmest environment.

She was trying to figure out a way to ask him that very thing when a cold gust of wind gushed through the tower, her teeth actually chattered hard enough to be heard. She could stay up here simply taking in the scene all day, even longer. But her body was beginning to protest the elements.

Evan unbuttoned his topcoat and unwrapped the scarf from around his neck. He held it out to her. Chiara immediately protested with a shake of her head. The man wasn't even wearing a hat, for heaven's sake. She wasn't about to take his scarf.

He didn't wait for permission, instead draping the scarf around her shoulders and tucking it under her chin.

"Thank you. But how are you not even cold?"

"I've come up here in the winter before. It's not new for me."

The scarf had to be cashmere, soft as air yet rugged enough to protect her from the cold. The description reminded her of the man she was with. Wearing the scarf resurfaced vivid memories of the night they'd spent together back in Singapore. The passion that had combusted between them, her body's heady and strong reaction. And the way she'd felt afterward, encased in his arms, surrounded by the smell of him. His warmth seeping through her skin.

Heaven help her, she wanted badly for it to all happen again.

Chiara's cheeks were the color of a Bengal rose by the time they made it back to the limo. Evan wanted nothing more than to gather her in his arms in the back seat. Then he'd take her lips with his own and kiss her until she was so far from cold she was burning for him.

Instead, he reached for the pot of steaming hot tea the driver had ready for them and poured her a generous cup. "This will warm you up in no time," he assured, still wishing badly he could do it himself.

Then he could ask the driver to rush them back to the hotel and join her in one of those steamy showers she enjoyed so much. Apparently, the cold hadn't done much to tamper his libido at all.

He recalled the way she'd fallen against him on the way to the watchtower. If that family hadn't walked past them, she would probably be in his arms right now with the divider to the front seat raised for privacy.

Studying her now as she slowly sipped her tea, he vividly remembered the way she'd tasted the last time he'd kissed her. He really shouldn't be heading down that path.

Evan turned his head from her sparkling eyes and rose-red cheeks to stare out the window. This thing with Chiara was never supposed to become a distraction. The only reason she was here was to help him land a business deal.

How had things gotten so complicated between the two of them?

Maybe heading back to the hotel right now wasn't the wisest move. Not if he wanted to try to keep his hands off her. And he absolutely had to keep his hands off her. He had two important meetings coming up that he had to focus on. The tension between them here and now was practically tangible. He knew exactly where it would lead as soon as they were alone together back at the hotel suite.

He cleared his throat before turning back to her. "If you think you're warm enough now to handle another outdoor activity, there is one more stop I'd like to show you."

She narrowed her eyes at him. If he didn't know better, he'd say Chiara had guessed exactly where his thoughts had just traveled and why he was suggesting a detour. "What kind of stop?"

"You mentioned ice skating at Rockefeller Center back in New York."

"You want to go ice skating? Now?"

He nodded once. "Something like that."

About a half hour ride later, Chiara found herself standing in front of a stadium unlike any she'd encountered in the States. Or anywhere else she'd visited for that matter. The place was colossal. With steel lattice beams around the entire structure.

She uttered the only word that came to mind as they approached one of the many entrances. "Wow."

"It's called the Bird's Nest and it was built for the Olympics," Evan explained. "But now it's used for all sorts of activities. And in the winter months, the entire place hosts the Ice and Snow Festival."

Festival was hardly an apt word to describe what they walked into once they entered the building. Massive ice sculptures depicting various cartoons she remembered from her childhood. Brightly decorated Christmas trees. Evan led her through the crowds and into what could only be described as an actual life-sized city sculpted entirely out of ice, complete with a castle and forts surrounded by a circular wall. Chiara felt as if she might have walked into some medieval frozen planet.

"And here I thought we would just be skating."

He winked at her. "Oh, we're going to do that, too. Only, it's not the kind of ice skating you're thinking of."

What other type of skating was there on ice? Chiara got her answer a few minutes later.

Ice cycling. That's what Evan had meant. Chiara Pearson, who thought she'd heard and seen everything as a life-long resident of New York City, who'd been backpacking across the globe for the last seven years, was about to try a sport she hadn't even known existed an hour ago.

It certainly seemed popular. The rink was crowded with all manner of skaters. From small children to elderly grandparents and everything in between. Everyone seemed to be having a grand time. Laughter echoed from every direction.

Once they were on the ice, Evan hopped on the main seat and had her sit behind him. The bike was small. Try as she might to maintain even a sliver of distance, it was no use. Chiara's upper thighs cradled Evan's hips, snug and tight. She had to squeeze her eyes shut and try to ignore the heady sensations rushing through her at the intimate contact.

"You nice and secure back there?" he asked over his shoulder.

If he only knew. "Ready to go," she answered.

He took off before she'd barely gotten the last word out. They moved so fast she had to wrap her arms around Evan's waist for fear of toppling off her seat. How he maneuvered the bike through the crowded rink at such a high speed had to be some sort of learned skill. Or maybe Evan was the type of man who just happened to be good at everything he did.

Oh, dear. That certainly sounded like she'd become rather keen on him.

Stop overanalyzing.

She made herself focus on Evan's joyous laugh instead. He was thoroughly enjoying himself. Chiara found herself chuckling at the mere joy radiating from Evan as he accelerated and turned on a sharp angle. They came to a stop when he reached the edge of the ice. A teenage couple pulled up alongside them and both gave a friendly smile. The boy motioned with his hands at Evan.

"They're challenging us to a race," he told her. "You up for it?"

A race? With all these other skaters in the way? It seemed rather hazardous. Evan took her pause as an affirmative answer.

A moment later, they were shooting across the ice, skirting around other bikes and skaters. There were so many close calls Chiara squeezed her eyes shut and awaited the inevitable impact more than once. Somehow, Evan avoided colliding with anyone else. He had fast reflexes and animal-like agility. Still, the close encounters were enough to send adrenaline pumping through her body. Or maybe that was due to Evan's proximity. When they finally came to a stop at the opposite end of the rink, Chiara was sure her heart was galloping at the speed of stampeding horses. They'd won the so-called race by several seconds. But the teenagers were smiling good-naturedly when they reached their side. They both gave Evan a small respectful bow, then turned around and rode off.

"That was impressive," she told him.

"Want to try?"

"Sure, why not?" She'd ridden bikes before; how different could it be to ride one on the ice?

But when they reversed positions, this time it was Evan's strong, muscular legs around her hips. His chin sitting on her right shoulder. His breath felt warm on her cheek. His arms wrapped around her waist. Chiara had to remind herself to breath.

Slowly, she began to move the bike forward, their pace much slower than when Evan had had command of the vehicle. She was certain Evan must have been bored out of his mind given how much slower she was going. But he leaned and spoke into her ear. "Take your time. You're doing great."

Silly as it was, she felt a surge of pleasure at his compliment. When had it become so important to her that Evan be pleased with her? In fact, her feelings for him were growing more complicated by the minute. And darned if she knew what to do about it.

It took several minutes, but they finally reached the entrance after doing a half circle around the rink. Evan assisted her off the bike. "Well done, Ms. Pearson."

She performed a mini bow. "Thank you. Though I won't be winning any impromptu ice bike races any time soon as you did."

"Still, I'd say you deserve a warm drink."

Within minutes, Evan had turned the bike in and they were seated at a wooden bench with steaming cups of coconut milk and a plate of delicate biscuits. Chiara watched the skaters on the ice, taking note of one small girl who repeatedly slipped and fell, stubbornly refusing help from her mom and giggling with each topple. The image brought forth a storm of memories from her own childhood of all the times her mother had taken her skating at Rockefeller Center. She'd been just as stubborn. Her mother had been patient as a saint with her.

"What has you smiling so fondly?" Evan asked.

She took a sip of her drink before answering. "Just remembering all the times my mother took me skating at Rockefeller Center as a child."

"Explains why you're such a natural on the ice."

She had to chuckle at that. "Trust me, those first few times I remember spending more time on my bottom than upright on the skates. My mom would just patiently wait for me to get up because I refused any help."

"Sounds like she was very indulgent with you."

"My dad would certainly say she was. Too much so." She sighed with deep sadness. "I wish you could have met her." Whoa. Where had that come from? But now that the words were out, Chiara realized just how true they were.

Her mother would have been beyond impressed with Evan Kim, had she known him. He was exactly the type of man Mama would have been proud of if she'd had another son. Or son-in-law. Chiara gave her head a shake. Another wayward thought she had no business thinking.

Evan surprised her with his next words when he responded. "I wish it, too, Chiara," he said, then took her hand in his.

Hours later, after they'd left the dinner meeting and made it back to their hotel suite, Evan was still thinking about the admission he'd made to Chiara. He should have never told her he would have liked to meet her mother. It was personal, implied a personal intimacy he had no business acknowledging out loud.

Chiara turned to him with a bright smile, unpinning her hair and shaking it loose. "That went well, didn't it?"

He nodded. "We played our parts perfectly. Everyone there is convinced we're a legitimate couple."

She took two hesitant steps toward him. Evan kept his feet firmly planted where he stood. He knew what was to come next. They'd been heading to this conclusion all night. But the next move had to be hers. The decision had to be hers and hers alone. "I didn't have to do much pretending, Evan."

Seemed it was the day for honest admissions. She took another shaky breath before she spoke again. "And I'd like very much to stop pretending tonight."

Evan did the only thing he could think to do. Spreading his arms wide, he beckoned her to him. Chiara reached him within seconds, tight against his length. Then his lips found hers.

No more words needed to be spoken. They both knew what the other wanted. There'd be no denying. Somehow, when he wasn't looking or paying attention, he'd begun to care for her in a way that felt utterly new and foreign. He wasn't sure what that meant for him. But there'd be time to examine all that later. Right now, she was here.

Silently, gently, he broke the kiss and led her by the hand to the bedroom. A nagging voice whispering in his head told him that he needed to examine this, whatever was happening between them. Too many lines were being blurred, too many boundaries crossed. But in this moment, Evan knew couldn't take his next breath if he made himself turn away from her. Later, he would have to come to terms with what it all meant for him. With what Chiara might mean to him. But not now. Now there was only the two of them. They had all night together.

It was near dawn when he felt her awaken in his arms, rousing him as well.

"Ready to do some skiing in a couple days? By this time tomorrow we'll be in Switzerland."

"I know. To be seen on the slopes as the happy couple."

"That's right. St. Moritz is a magnet for celebrities, so it always draws a lot of international paparazzi. I figure we'll stop there first and spend a few days skiing and enjoying the mountain air. It will give us one last chance to be seen and maybe photographed together before the final meeting with the Italian AI executives."

"Got it." She executed a mini stretch, never leaving his arms. "I hope I don't embarrass you with my skills. It's been ages since I've been on the slopes."

"I'm sure it's a lot like riding a bike. Once you learn, you don't forget."

"Hmm. I hope so." A chuckle escaped her lips. "I'll have you know that once, at the immature age of seven, I went skiing in a full pirate's outfit over my ski suit. Complete with plastic sword and patterned bandanna under my helmet."

Evan had to laugh at the image.

"You did?"

She nodded against his bare chest. "Yep. I decided I was going to be the only skiing pirate on the slopes that day and my mother obliged. Went to the costume store and found me everything I needed to become a bandit of the seas. To wear in the snowy mountains."

"You must have made quite the picture."

"Marco thought so. He was both amused and horrified to be seen with his swashbuckling sister. My dad just shook his head."

She turned to face him, bracing her forearms on his chest as she spoke. "See, Dad thought Mom was too permissive when I asked to do such things. Said she never told me no. But he always said it with a rather indulgent smile on his face as well," she added, then rested her head on his chest. "It's funny."

"What is?"

"I don't typically talk about my mother this much. It's too painful. But with you, I can't seem to keep my mouth shut about her."

Evan stroked her hair, touched that she could confide in him about the loving parent she'd lost. She said she'd been indulged as a child. He couldn't think of a single time he might have used that word to describe himself. Even his ahma, as affectionate as she was, had been strict about his schedule and his studies.

He and Chiara had drastically different childhoods. In fact, they didn't have very much in common at all. For one, Chiara belonged to a loving and devoted family. She always had.

The way Chiara spoke of her parents and brother was both touching and bittersweet. Despite the devastating loss of her mother, there was nothing but love echoed in her recollection of her childhood whenever she spoke of it. Her voice filled with tenderness in each word.

A faint curl of envy swirled in his chest, then grew to a low ache. He would never have that. The comfort of a loving and devoted family. Hell, if anything ever happened to him, it wouldn't even make a difference in anyone's life. What a devastatingly brutal truth that was. Besides Louis, would anyone even care if he were gone?

Without thought, he dropped a peck of a kiss atop Chiara's head. She shifted in his arms and nestled her back closer against his chest. In about a week or so, she would be out of his life as well. Back home to the loving arms of her father and brother to spend the holidays in a welcoming home she'd grown up in. While he'd be back in Singapore. Or maybe he'd return home to Bali. Alone. Spending Christmas like any other day. A hollowness settled in his chest at the thought.

It was for the best. He did better on his own. The one time he'd grown close to anyone, she'd been tragically taken from him with no other source of comfort to help him deal with the loss. He'd had to mourn her on his own. Evan didn't need that kind of pain again.

Look how successful he was. How far he'd come. He would have never accomplished so much in such a short period of time if there'd been any emotional distractions in his life.

No reason to change what had worked so well for him up until now. Not even for Chiara Pearson.

CHAPTER THIRTEEN

St. Moritz, Switzerland

CHIARA HAD NO idea how it had happened, but somehow the last couple of weeks had flown past in the blink of an eye. In just a few short days, it would be Christmas, and she'd be back in the States to make her pilgrimage to the house in Vermont and finally see her family. And Evan would be on his way somewhere else, back to his old life.

They'd literally and figuratively be going their separate ways. Who knew when she might see him again, if ever?

One day, one moment, at a time. It was the only way she was going to get through this. Staring at the large glass window overlooking the snow-peaked alpine mountains, she heard Evan walk into the room. He was fully dressed in a casual sports jacket and pressed khakis.

"Are you going out?"

He nodded once. "I have a brief lunch meeting with the woman who runs my charity organization."

"Your charity?"

"Yeah. I donate to various causes, mostly children's issues and some refugee organizations. At one point, it

just became easier to form a foundation. And put someone else in charge of running it."

Huh. She'd had no idea. As close as they'd become,
there was so much about this man she still didn't know.
So much he hadn't revealed. He'd founded his own charity. As if there wasn't enough about the man she admired already.

"It just so happens that the president resides in Switzerland. Priya offered to take the train and meet me here
to catch up on the latest."

Priya. An image popped into Chiara's mind of a long-
legged, statuesque beauty with thick ebony hair and
doe-like eyes.

He hadn't thought to invite her to this breakfast
meeting. And she had no reason to feel slighted in any
way by that. In fact, she was no different than this president he was about to meet with. She was merely an employee, after all.

A nagging curl of doubt nevertheless crept into her
brain. So far, Evan had taken her to every meeting and
function. Why was this one different? Was it because
he was meeting with a woman? Had they shared some
kind of intimacy in the past?

She gave her head a brief shake. None of her business. She had no claim to him whatsoever.

He must have read the direction of her thoughts. "Did
you want to come along? I just figured you'd want some
time to rest up after our long flight and before we hit
the slopes later today."

She did. So very much. But for all the wrong reasons. Reasons she had to squelch and bury deep, never
to be uncovered again.

She shook her head in response. "No. You're right.
I could use some downtime before hitting the slopes."

He reached her in two strides. Took her hand and kissed the inside of her palm. A fairly innocent gesture. Still, it sent a flush of heat rushing through her center and out toward her limbs.

"Good. I want you fresh and rested for that final meeting with the Italians."

"Right." Though how she was supposed to pull off the facade of happy fiancée when all she could think about was how they'd be parting ways so soon afterward, she had no idea. "No pressure."

He dropped her hand. "It's our final shot to convince them to take a chance and invest in my expansion."

Chiara could only offer a weak smile in response. Here she was, practically woeful at spending the morning without him as he had breakfast with a female associate. While Evan's sole focus remained his business goals and the part Chiara was here to play to help him achieve them. The only reason she was here, really.

That made her all kinds of a fool.

Evan guided Chiara to the bottom of the hill and helped her hop onto the moving gondola car, then quickly joined her in the seat. "No pirate costume this time?"

She smiled at him. "I guess I forgot to pack it."

"Just as well. I would have had to draw the line at the eye patch."

He'd been right about Chiara's ability to ski. It only took a couple of runs down the mountain for her to get her bearings and ski like someone who'd learned as a child.

Costume or not, Chiara looked beyond enticing in the form-fitting ski suit and parka. Even dressed in layers of fleece and down, she posed the sexiest, most fetching picture. Not for the first time that day, he wanted to whisk her off the mountain and rush them back to the hotel where he could proceed to slowly peel all those layers off her and warm her chilled skin.

Stop it. They were only here in the hopes of having one or two snaps of them taken for one final hit on a gossip website. He was in the final stretch, about to grasp all that he'd been reaching for professionally for the past several months.

Yet, all he could think of was holding Chiara in his arms.

He had to snap out of it. Now was not the time to let his hormones run the show. He had to stop thinking about her in such lurid ways. And he absolutely had to keep his distance.

Fate seemed to have a different plan.

They'd reached the top of the ride when a loud grinding noise echoed through the air and their car came to a gradual stop. Great. They were stuck. Evan knew from past experience that it could take some time to get the lifts moving again. The small speaker below the seat came to life to explain that there'd been a minor glitch in need of repair, first in Swiss, then translated to English, followed by several other languages. So much for keeping his distance. How was he to keep his hands off her when they were stuck up here alone for who knew how long?

"Huh," Chiara said next to him, leaning slightly over the edge of the gondola to look down. "We're rather high up." Her words were followed by a full body shiver.

She was either cold or frightened. Or both. He was only human, for heaven's sake. He couldn't very well just let her sit there, shaking. He wrapped his arm around her shoulders and pulled her close against his side.

"It's okay. This happens often here. They'll have us

moving in no time," he assured, hoping he wasn't lying to her yet again.

The tension in her shoulders relaxed and she leaned into him, resting her head on his shoulder.

"Try to focus on the view," he advised. "It's beautiful up here." That statement was most definitely not a lie. Snow-capped mountains as far as the eye could see, a bright, light blue sky and tiny snowflakes had begun to fall in the few short seconds they'd been up there.

"All the same, I'd rather be looking at it from the glass wall of the hotel suite," Chiara said. Another shudder racked through her body.

Evan tilted her chin up to his face with one finger. "Hey, it's okay. We'll be moving in no time."

She nodded, her eyes far from convinced. "I've been stuck in a lift before. Just never this high up." Her bottom lip quivered, and the small motion led to Evan's undoing. All thoughts of keeping his distance fled his mind. Instead, he shifted her onto his lap, held her tight. When she reached for his lips with her own, he didn't have the strength to deny her. He took her mouth with his own in a deep lingering kiss. Now, it was his turn to shiver, for entirely different reasons.

He'd been fooling himself to think he could stay away from her. Despite the mounds of clothing between them, Evan felt every inch of her against his body. Her warmth seemed to seep through her clothing straight to his bones. He couldn't get enough of the taste of her. When she moaned against his mouth, he could only kiss her deeper. He wanted to hear her moan for him every day for the rest of his life.

Mercifully, in that moment, their gondola car jerked to life.

Evan made himself pull away, took several deep

breaths before he could get his mouth to work. "See, we're moving already."

Shifting in the seat, he moved out from under her until she was no longer in his lap. Dazed, Chiara looked up at him, her eyes confused.

Well, he was pretty confused himself. He'd only meant to comfort her. But it had turned into so much more.

"There's something I've been putting off."

Chiara finally found the nerve to go interrupt Evan at the dining room table of their hotel suite. He'd been working all morning. They were to ski again later that afternoon, but she had a more pressing errand she needed to run.

"What's that?" he asked her absentmindedly in response to her statement, barely glancing up from the laptop screen.

She pulled out the chair next to him, moved it closer to his side and sat down. Perhaps she was being too forward, but surely the man didn't have to work quite so much. It was the holiday season, after all. Most of the world had slowed down their productivity. Surely, Evan could do so as well. "It's not so much that I've been putting it off exactly," she answered him. "But I didn't really have the money. Not until very recently."

"Money for what?"

"I need to do some shopping."

"What kind of shopping? I thought the personal shopper secured everything you needed."

"Not presents."

She watched as he typed some more, then pounded on the backspace button.

"Presents?"

Chiara blew out an exasperated breath. Honestly, for such a brilliant mind, he could be quite clueless at times. "It's Christmas in a few short days, Evan."

Releasing a sigh, he turned away from the laptop at last. Finally, she had his full attention.

"And?"

Oh, come now. Was he honestly not seeing the direction she was headed in? "And I'd like to go find some presents. For my father and brother. And a couple of other people back in the States."

"Why didn't you just say so? There's a major shopping center about a mile away. With several top fashion house boutiques. I can call a car for you."

"Don't you have people you want to shop for? What about Louis? Or any of your employees?"

He narrowed his eyes on her. "Of course. My assistant takes care of it for me. She's already done so."

Chiara's exasperation was replaced with a resounding sadness. Christmas for Evan was such a cold and practical experience in his life. "Don't you want to pick anything out yourself to give them? It would make the gift so much more personal."

"Are you asking me to come shopping with you?"

"I think it would do you good," Chiara answered and meant it. "To experience a little Christmas cheer."

Evan practically rolled his eyes at her, an indication of what he felt about that idea. He tapped her playfully on the nose. "I think you just want my company. Admit it."

"I admit it."

The smile he gave her had her blood pressure rising and she had to force her focus back on the conversation at hand.

"Fine. If it's that important to you," Evan said, closing the lid of his laptop.

She nodded once. "It is."

He pulled out his cell phone. "I'll call for a car."

Chiara glanced at the crystal blue sky outside the glass balcony door. The bright rays of the sun kissed the snow-topped mountains. She reached for Evan's hand before he could dial. From what she'd seen of the town so far since arriving, it was decked out and festively decorated for the season. "I think we should walk."

How had he gotten roped into this? Evan couldn't remember the last time he'd gone shopping for anything. He'd always had people who were paid to do it for him.

One glance at Chiara and he had the answer to his question. The smile she wore lit up her entire face. She was practically skipping next to him as they made their way to the shopping plaza. He'd never seen anyone so excited to get things for other people.

"Have you thought any more about what you might get Louis?" she asked.

He had not. "I'm hoping I know it when I see it."

She aimed the full force of that brilliant smile in his direction. "That could work. I've found more than one gift that way."

A few minutes later, they approached the palatial structure that housed some of the most luxe stores in Switzerland. Evan turned toward the entrance but realized Chiara had stopped a few feet behind him. She was focused on several booths set up across the street. A number of craftsmen had set up tables and displays with their various wares. Not unusual for this time of year.

"Can we go there first?" she asked.

He'd barely gotten the words out before she'd already

begun to cross the street. He followed her to the first table. It held several trays of blown glass ornaments. "Oh, these are beautiful." She pointed to one shaped as some sort of complicated icicle. "I'll take that one please." The vendor flashed her a smile and began wrapping the item.

"Don't you want one? For your tree?"

"I don't really see one I like." He wasn't going to tell her that he never even bothered with a tree. Someone like Chiara, who placed such an importance on the holidays, wouldn't be able to understand but Evan never bothered to decorate for Christmas in any way. What was the point?

In fact, he wasn't even sure why he was bothering with this trip other than to humor Chiara. But much to his surprise, within minutes Evan found himself purchasing several boxes of homemade candy at one of the booths for his employees. At yet another, he found a hand-sewn necktie that he purchased for Louis along with a matching scarf for his new wife.

Go figure. He was actually Christmas shopping.

For her part, Chiara was armed with several shopping bags holding gifts, including a hand-knitted wool scarf for her brother that bore the likeness of a goofy cartoon yeti. For her father, she'd picked out a hand-crafted leather wallet. Costume jewelry for a couple of girlfriends in New York rounded out her purchases. And somehow, she was carrying another small bag with an item Evan hadn't even seen her purchase. He had no idea what it could be, but he wasn't going to ask. If she'd wanted him to know, she would have told him.

"Are you ready to go into some real stores now?" he asked.

Chiara turned her focus toward the building that had

once been a chateau for a Swiss count but had long since been converted to a luxe shopping center. "No, thank you." She lifted her bags. "I have everything I came for."

She really was something else. Most women he knew would have made a beeline for the boutiques. Or the designer handbag store.

Between them, they'd spent a fraction of the figure Evan might have guessed they'd spend. Yet, somehow, Chiara had gotten her family and friends the perfect gifts.

He hadn't done so bad himself.

When Evan had told her they'd be dining on a train, Chiara couldn't have imagined such a glamorous setting. The meal car reminded her of one of the grander ballrooms in the Grandview Hotel. Walls lined with thick velvet, mahogany tables, rich upholstered chairs.

She and Evan were taking the train to Liechtenstein where they would meet with the executives one final time before a decision was made. One of the Italian gentlemen owned a villa in that city and was there for the holidays. They'd been welcomed to spend the night, then travel back to their hotel in St. Moritz in the morning. All in all, a dizzying twenty-four hours. Such was the life of a jet-setter like Evan Kim, she supposed. A life that would definitely take some getting used to. Not that she had to worry about it.

A tuxedoed server handed them two flutes of champagne as they made their way to their reserved table. To think, she'd thought she might be overdressed in her satin burgundy wraparound dress and high-heeled black suede boots. Everyone on board was just as swanky. A lot of jewelry donned the necks and wrists of their fellow travelers. For his part, Evan looked beyond dashing in a dark navy suit that brought out the dark ebony highlights of his hair and a crisp shirt the color of the sky.

Did she even fit in amongst these people?

And how would she do tonight as she faced the final test?

She had to be on her toes, no mistakes or all their efforts these past few weeks would be for naught. Evan would be so disappointed. In her.

Distracted by the stunning view that greeted her, her worries found a back seat as they took their seats at the table and the train began to move. A large window by their table afforded her an unobstructed look at the majestic mountains that surrounded them.

"Quite the scene, huh?" Evan asked, unbuttoning his suit jacket.

"It's magnificent."

"I think beautiful would be a more apt description." But he wasn't looking out the window as he spoke; he was looking directly at her. Her heart did a funny little jump in her chest. Before she could think of any kind of response that didn't have her sounding like a giddy schoolgirl with a crush, a waiter appeared with a sweaty bottle of champagne to refill their glasses. He was immediately followed by another who placed a fondue set on the table between them and lit the bottom burner. A blue flame began to glow beneath the pot. Yet another server then arrived with a tray of cheese squares, crusty bread pieces and a dozen silver skewers. With a friendly smile, she dropped the cheese into the pot and poured some kind of alcohol out of a tall glass bottle, then stirred the contents.

"Enjoy," she told them with a slight accent, when

the concoction had reached the consistency of thick, rich cheesy sauce.

Chiara had no doubt that she would. The smell of the melting cheese had her mouth watering. Following Evan's lead, she stabbed one of the bread pieces with a skewer and dipped it into the cheese. The gooey warm flavor exploded on her tongue when she began to eat.

"This is unlike any cheese fondue I've ever had," she told him, helping herself to another piece.

"I'm glad you like it."

Several minutes passed and she allowed herself to indulge. But Evan seemed to have slowed. He'd barely eaten more than a few bites. "Do you? Like it?" she asked.

He blinked at her. She pointed to the fondue. "Oh. Yeah. It's delicious," he finally replied after several beats. "I guess I'm just not that hungry today."

Either that or he was distracted. She reached across the table and took his hand, gave it a gentle squeeze of reassurance. "Evan, tonight will go great. You know they're impressed with your accomplishments. And we'll be proving to them that you're a stable, reliable businessman who's ready to settle down and get married." Her words held an inflection of confidence she didn't really feel. In fact, Evan's nervousness was only serving to heighten hers.

He placed his free hand on top of hers, sandwiching her small fingers between his own. "You're right. Of course."

She gave him a bright smile. "Of course I am. Now, eat some cheese. Or I'll be the only one having it and will arrive at this gentleman's house bloated and much too full."

The afternoon gradually started to grow darker as

Chiara watched the view outside turn from one majestic scene to another. They reached an arched bridge that towered over the ravine below and she could swear they were suspended in midair and flying between the mountains.

Just when she thought she couldn't eat another bite, the cheese fondue set was removed to be replaced with another one, this time filled with chunks of chocolate. Again, a bottom burner was lit and the delicacy slowly began to melt. Another tray then appeared, piled high with colorful fruit—berries, melons, kiwi and bright citrus. Chiara picked the plumpest strawberry she could find and skewered it, then dipped it into the rich, creamy chocolate sauce. The combination of ripe fruit and sweet candy tasted like a treat from the gods.

Heaven help her, she couldn't escape the moan of pleasure that escaped her lips.

She looked up to find Evan staring at her, a blend of amusement and…yes, desire showing clearly in his eyes. Without thinking, she skewered another piece of fruit, dipped it, then reached it over. Evan leaned in and took the offering, chewing slowly, his eyes never leaving hers.

It all came crashing down on her, then. There was no denying. As she sat here, hand-feeding Evan Kim dessert in a speeding train car across the Swiss mountains, Chiara had to admit what she'd been brushing away for several days now.

She was wholly, desperately and undoubtedly head over heels in love with the man.

CHAPTER FOURTEEN

THE MEETING SEEMED to be going really well. Everything Chiara translated so far sounded positive for Evan. Almost as if the deal were already done and they were just discussing the specifics. By the time they walked out of the chalet tomorrow morning, Chiara had no doubt Evan's deal would be signed and sealed.

They'd done it!

She could finally relax some of the tension that had gripped her since this morning and start to breathe a bit easier. About this meeting, anyway. As for the rest, she had no idea what she was going to do. How would he react if she just told him how she felt about him? What would he say if she were to admit that she was in no way ready to say goodbye?

He had to see what was so obvious—they couldn't just walk away from this after all that had happened, not after everything they'd shared. What they'd come to mean to each other.

Chiara puffed out a deep breath, watching as the men began with the paperwork.

But what exactly did Chiara and Evan mean to each other? She couldn't define it. All she was certain of was that she wasn't ready to turn her back on it.

But she had no idea if Evan felt at all the same way. She

was still working up the courage and thinking of a way to ask him when they were led to the suite in the chalet they'd be spending the night in. A celebratory bottle of chilled Chasselas sat waiting for them on the center coffee table. With deft motions, Evan uncorked the bottle and poured into the two goblets by the bottle. He handed one to her.

"Thank you."

He took a sip of his wine. "No, thank you. You're the reason I've gotten this deal. It would have never worked without you by my side."

Chiara tried not to let the swell of disappointment at his words crush her too deeply. Of course, he was excited about his business expansion. She could give him that. It didn't mean that was the only reason he was happy to have her by her side at the moment.

He walked over to the balcony doors and pulled them wide open, then stepped out onto the concrete. Turning, he held his glass up in a salute to her, his smile as bright as the crescent moon above. If only she could return that smile with one of her own. If only she could pretend she wasn't falling apart inside, that he still hadn't said anything about a change in plans.

She had to get some answers. She had to know. About where he stood. How he felt now that their official mission was accomplished. With heavy feet, Chiara walked over to meet him outside.

The first thing he said to her gave her a slight clue, and it wasn't encouraging in the least. "I'll wire the funds to your account tonight. You've more than earned every penny. And your plane ticket back to New York is on me. Consider it a bonus."

Earned. Bonus. Evan was all business. While inside, her heart was shattering in her chest.

Now or never. She had to take the chance. Without giving herself the opportunity to second-guess, she blurted out the question that had been haunting her for several days now. "Would you want to come with me? To New York. Then to my family's place in Vermont?"

He lowered his glass, his smile fading. He cleared his throat before he spoke. "Chiara, I can't. Thank you for the invitation. But I just can't."

Every last shred of hope she'd been harboring disintegrated into confetti. He wasn't even going to pretend to take her up on her offer. "It's not that you can't. It's that you don't want to. Why Evan?"

He thrust his free hand into his pants pocket, tilted his head. "It's not that simple of an answer."

"It is from where I'm standing. Please, tell me why you would rather spend the holidays alone in your penthouse in Bali rather than spend that time with me."

"Chiara, it's not fair of you to ask me such things. That was never part of the deal."

She lifted her chin, ignoring the arrow of pain he'd just pierced her heart with. "I know that's how things started with us. But you can't tell me things aren't different now."

At his silence, she pressed on. "Evan, I don't know how to explain the feelings I've developed for you." Yep, she was definitely all in now. No turning back. "Except to say that I feel as if I've known you my whole life. Like we met eons ago and just lost touch for some reason."

His shoulders lifted in a mini shrug. "I'm flattered, Chiara. Really. Thank you."

That was it? His response to what she'd admitted was to thank her? This couldn't be happening.

"It's so easy for you to abandon people, isn't it? You walked away from your parents never to look back, after all." If the stricken expression on Evan's face was anything to go by, she had gone too far. But it was too late to turn back now. "If you'll take some unsolicited advice, I think you should try to reconcile with them. You never know when it might be too late."

His eyes narrowed on her face. "Advice, is it? Because you lost your mom."

She could only nod.

He tossed the contents of his goblet over the railing. "That's not advice. And it isn't about you," he said without a trace of kindness in his voice. "You can't compare what you lost with something I never had."

A gust of wind blew through the air and brought goose bumps to the surface of her skin. Even now, in her utter hurt and humiliation, a part of her wanted Evan to step over to her and warm her up in his arms. He took a step in her direction and a surge of hope shot through her. But it was short-lived as he brushed past her instead to walk back inside.

Chiara sucked in a much-needed breath and turned to join him. He was shrugging out of his suit jacket and grabbing his toiletries when she stepped inside the bedroom. The set of his shoulders told her everything she needed to know. The conversation was over. So much had been said between them, yet so much left unsaid. And it appeared it would stay that way.

"We should get some sleep," he told her. "We have a long day of travel in front of us tomorrow."

Chiara swallowed past the lump of pain that had settled like a brick at the base of her throat. They'd be traveling in entirely different directions. Wordlessly, she made her way to the bathroom.

When she emerged from the shower, Evan had already settled himself on the sofa and appeared to be asleep. So that was it, then. No more discussion. He'd made it very clear what he wanted. And that was to have nothing more to do with her. She grabbed the thick afghan draped over the loveseat and softly covered him with it. Evan didn't so much as stir.

Chiara crawled under the covers, too tired and broken to argue with him about sleeping on an uncomfortable couch.

She spent most of the night willing the tears not to fall.

Who knew he had such convincing thespian skills? Or strength of will for that matter. It had taken all he had not to take hold of Chiara's wrists and pull her down with him on the sofa when she'd draped the afghan over him. Instead, he'd somehow managed to keep his eyes shut, feigning sleep.

He should have seen this coming. He should have known Chiara wasn't the kind of woman who could surrender her heart and then just walk away. Part of him had known, he had to admit. He just hadn't wanted to face it until he had to.

He had meant to talk to her, had every intention of telling her on the drive back to St. Moritz tomorrow morning that, although he would cherish what they'd shared these past few weeks, he was in no position to entertain anything long-term. It just wasn't in his DNA to commit to someone. Anyone.

The only time he'd felt close to another human being the end result had been tragic and sudden, leaving him scarred. With no one to turn to, to help him process or grieve.

But he hadn't had the chance to tell Chiara any of that. She'd taken him by surprise with her invitation. Now, it was too late to tell her much of anything.

He listened to her soft, steady breathing just a few

feet away. He would wager she wasn't sleeping, either. What a sorry state of affairs. If only they could do the whole night over. Not that anything fundamental would change. They'd still be going their separate ways. But he might have been able to spare her some of the hurt and pain that had been so clear in her eyes.

He might have explained it all better. Explained how he had no business intruding on her family unit. Pretending to be part of something he could never be part of. During Christmas of all times.

He might have tried harder to help her better understand. Maybe he'd try first thing tomorrow morning to tell her the honest truth. That he never went where he didn't belong.

Chiara was gone when he awoke the next morning, the bed empty and meticulously made. Evan wasn't sure when or how, but somehow he'd managed to fall asleep before the light of dawn and hadn't even heard her leave.

He was about to run out and search the main house when he eyed the engagement ring and a piece of ivory paper sitting atop the duvet in the center of the bed. It served to confirm what he already knew in his soul. She was gone.

With heavy feet, he walked over to read the note.

Evan,
Forgive me. But I couldn't bear the thought of traveling back together after last night. I've taken what I had with me and have decided to go straight to the airport to make my way back home. I've told the housing staff to thank our hosts on my behalf and explain that I was eager to start my day while you prefer to sleep in. Please for-

*ward my belongings to the Grand York Hotel in
New York. Only my belongings. Nothing more.*

The next few words were written in a much shak-
ier hand, as if she were uncertain she wanted to print
the words.

*I will cherish every moment of the past few
weeks and wish you all the success you hope to
achieve. Love, C.*

Evan reread every word, unblinking until the letters
began to swim before his eyes. He'd really made a mess
of things. Chiara was gone.

Biting out a curse, he crumpled the paper in his fist
and slammed the wall hard enough to disturb an oil
painting of the Alps hanging inches above. He caught
it before it could fall and haphazardly rehung it, not caring that it now hung askew.

His gaze fell back to the bed. He'd been so focused
on the ring and the note that he'd almost missed it—a
rectangular white cardboard box with a red satin ribbon
sat in the center of the pillow. His name was scrawled in
calligraphy on the lid. With shaky fingers, he unwrapped
the ribbon and lifted the top. Inside the box sat a wooden
sculpture whittled in the shape of a Christmas tree. A tag
attached to the stump read *a tree of your own.*

Evan's breath caught as he handled the small work
of art. Chiara must have gotten this for him the day
they'd gone Christmas shopping, when he hadn't been
paying attention.

So she'd seen right through his lie about not buying one of the glass ornaments because he didn't like
them. Why was he surprised? In just a few short weeks,

Chiara Pearson had somehow come to know him better than anyone else he could name. She'd also grown to care deeply about him. And he'd thrown that back in her face when she'd told him so.

His phone vibrated in his pocket. A surge of hope shot through his chest.

Chiara.

But it wasn't her who appeared on his phone screen when he fished the device out.

"Hey, man, why are you calling me? You're supposed to be on your honeymoon." Evan knew he sounded overly curt. Right this moment, he didn't much care.

Louis's response was a hearty chuckle. "Had to. After seeing you and your lovely fiancée's pictures all over my tablet on your ski trip in Switzerland. How's the wedding planning going, anyway?"

Evan just couldn't do it; he didn't have it in him to lie anymore. Not to his best friend. Before he knew what he intended, he blurted out the whole convoluted story, ending with the fact that his temporary fiancée hadn't even wanted to say goodbye to him before leaving at the crack of dawn.

A long pause followed his diatribe. Evan heard nothing but his friend's shallow breaths as he took it all in. "So, you're saying none of it was real?"

Evan swallowed back the bile that had gathered at the back of his throat. "That's right. I'm sorry I lied to you, man. I would have come clean sooner, but you had other things going on."

"No apology needed," Louis said without any hesitation. "It's just funny."

"What is?"

"It all looked pretty real to me."

Huh. Evan wasn't sure how to respond to that. His

friend didn't give him a chance to try to come up with a way as he continued, "Evan, you're a fool if you don't try to figure out just how real it was."

Maybe she'd been impulsive, leaving the chalet. But Chiara knew it would have destroyed her to have to spend one more minute with Evan, knowing he cared less for her than she did for him.

If he even cared for her at all.

How could she have read him so wrong? All those times he'd touched her, caressed her, loved her—none of it had meant anything to him. Maybe he just figured it was an added benefit of the bargain they'd struck up that first day. She'd certainly been a willing participant. Evan had never once suggested there was anything emotionally relevant between them. She'd gone ahead and given her heart, anyway.

Her hired car pulled up to the departure area of Lugano Airport and she dabbed at her eyes before exiting. Tossing her two bags over her shoulder, she made her way to the entrance.

Her solo backpacking adventure had come to an end. She didn't know yet what was in store for her back in the States, but her jaunts to various exotic cities abroad were over. She could only hope she'd done her mom proud by visiting enough of the locations Gabriella Pearson would have loved to see herself.

The terminal was bright and cheery, decorated with wreaths and festive, colorful ribbons. Artificial Christmas trees lit up every corner. A Swiss version of "The First Noel" blared through a network of speakers that followed her as she walked to the ticket gate. The Swiss certainly knew how to decorate for Christmas. The airport was almost as festively geared up as their hotel had been. It was also very, very crowded. Perhaps hopping in a taxi and beelining to the airport before so much as buying a ticket wasn't the wisest thing she might have done. But she had her passport and a debit card, which now actually had sufficient funds behind it. What more did she need to make it back home?

But when Chiara reached the gate, the answer to that question wasn't a terribly welcome one. A ticker flashing across every screen announced that all flights back to La Guardia were canceled. Apparently, a major snowstorm was wreaking havoc on half the hemisphere.

The tears she'd somehow managed to hold back all this time were finally unstoppable. This was it. She had nowhere to go. After all she'd been through, all the silly endeavors and playing at being engaged just to get the money to travel back, she wasn't going to make it back home, after all.

All of it had been for naught.

Here she was. Stuck in an airport, unable to go back to the hotel to face Evan. And unable to board a plane that would have taken her to the loving embrace of her family.

With shaky fingers and her eyes blurry from tears, she pulled her phone out of her pocket to deliver the bad news to her father. It immediately slipped out of her hand and fell to the floor. Chiara could only watch helplessly as the screen cracked down the center. Great. Now she would have to replace her phone, too. Though relieved to find it still appeared functional, Chiara couldn't bring herself to call her father. She just couldn't do it. Not yet. Papa would understand—there wasn't much she could do about the weather and he knew that—but he was going to be, oh, so disappointed. She'd promised him she'd be there for Christmas, after three long years of spending the holidays apart.

She needed air. Suddenly, the cheery and festive decorations and the blaring Christmas carol only served to mock her predicament. Alone in an airport three days before Christmas.

Clutching her cracked phone to her chest and wiping away yet another tear with her sleeve, Chiara ran out the doors as fast as her legs could carry her, barely waiting for the sliding glass doors to fully open.

Finding an empty bench by the road, she dropped her bag and purse onto the ground and sat, slumping into the cold wood. She had to pull herself together. She was safe, in a public place, and as soon as the snow cleared, she would begin to make her way home finally. The delayed flight was just a minor glitch.

So why did she feel like sobbing?

As much as she wanted to talk to someone, she didn't have the heart to call her father or brother just yet to announce that she was going to be at least a day late. Another familiar choice came to mind. Quickly calculating the time difference, she pulled up the contact she had in mind. Nuri would have just finished her shift and arrived back home. Her friend picked up on the first ring.

"Hey, *teman*. Nice to hear from you. Been seeing you in some of the society sites. I want to hear all about it."

If she only knew. When Chiara didn't answer right away, her friend immediately picked up that something was wrong. "Are you all right? Where are you, Chiara?"

"I'm fine. Really. It's just, I needed to hear a friendly voice."

"Tell me. All of it."

Where to begin. Chiara filled in as much of the story as she could without succumbing to more tears. When she was done, she heard Nuri's gasp of astonishment. "All that matters is that you're all right."

Chiara hadn't even realized how much she'd missed the other woman until hearing her voice. That thought just sent another wave of sadness rushing through her chest. She should have stayed in Bali and found another way to earn the money home. That way at least her heart would still be intact.

"But, Chiara, do you mean to tell me that you just left? The very next morning after your argument?"

Chiara sniffled and wiped away another tear. "I'd say it qualified as more than a minor argument, Nuri."

"Maybe so. But I don't recall you being the type to run. From anything. Why did you do so this time?"

The words pounded through Chiara's head. Did Nuri have a point? Instead of seeing things through with Evan, had she taken the easy way out by running off with her tail between her legs? After giving her friend a half-hearted nonanswer, Chiara clicked off the call.

As hurt as she was, she at least owed Evan a call to say goodbye, didn't she? She stared at her phone screen, debating calling him to do just that when the screen started glitching. The fall onto hard floor earlier must have taken some kind of toll. Instead of her usual wallpaper picture of the Grand York, various images and old photos from years ago started scrolling by one after another; snapshots that brought up memories of days long past. It finally stalled on a photo of her and her mother smiling at the camera in front of the doors of the Grand York Hotel that last Christmas they'd had together.

Did a dropped phone even glitch like that? Or was some Christmas miracle trying to send her a message?

Chiara gave her head a brisk shake. Now she was just being fanciful and silly. Her phone was back to its normal screen when she looked at it again.

Her imagination had to be playing tricks on her.

CHAPTER FIFTEEN

HE WAS TOO LATE. Evan stared at the screen on his tablet and bit out a vicious curse. All flights were grounded. No aircraft would be flying in or out for the next several hours. He'd missed her. Chiara was gone. All because he'd been too blind and scared to realize how lucky he was to have ever found her.

As if to match his mood, a torrent of snow seemed to suddenly fall from the sky, accompanied by a sharp wind that shook the car. Evan leaned over the divider to tell the driver to pull over as soon as he could. There was no way the man could see more than a foot in front of him with the thick snow that seemed to have come out of nowhere.

The other man obliged with a grateful word of thanks. Great. Now he was stuck in a car in one of the lanes leading away from the airport.

Then he saw her.

Evan thought he had to be imagining it. That the murky visibility was showing him what he wanted to see. But upon closer inspection, he had no doubt. A familiar figure stood up from a bench near the entrance and gathered two small bags sitting on the ground. Evan was out of the car and running to her side in a flash.

"Chiara."

She paused, frozen in place. Finally, she turned to face him and the emotion he saw in her eyes nearly had his knees buckling.

"Evan?"

He reached her in two strides and took both her hands in his. "Hello, sweetheart."

"I was about to call you."

Her words sounded like a sweet melody. The knowledge that she couldn't bring herself to leave without saying goodbye had hope blossoming in his chest. But he couldn't get ahead of himself. He had one heck of an apology to deliver. Followed by a fair amount of groveling.

"What are you doing here?" she asked, still clearly dazed.

"I had to come catch you before you left for the States."

She blinked up at him, thick snowflakes falling on her dark lashes and ruddy cheeks. "You did?"

He nodded once. "You left in such a hurry that you left a couple of things behind. I had to make sure you took them with you before you left."

"What things?"

He reached into his pocket and removed the item he'd made a quick stop to pick up on the way.

"An ornament."

Hand crafted out of the finest crystal, encrusted with colorful gems and platinum carvings. He smiled at her. "To replace the novelty prize you won that day at the *kaitenzushi*."

She huffed a laugh. "This is a bit more elegant than the tiny plastic toy I won." Gently, she lifted the glass globe to eye level. "It's beautiful, Evan. Thank you. But you didn't need to get me a parting gift."

He shrugged. "Maybe not. I also wanted to give you this," he said, holding out the engagement ring.

She immediately shook her head, took a tiny step, backing away from him. "I can't. I didn't mind wearing it temporarily, but a woman shouldn't accept an engagement ring as her own unless she's actually getting engaged."

He reached for her, taking her hand in his. "I agree. That's why I'm giving it back to you." Despite the wet snow, Evan had no hesitation in doing what he did next. Dropping to one knee, he slipped the ring back on her finger. "No pretending this time."

Her jaw dropped. She blinked once, then again. Her eyes questioningly narrowing at him. "Evan? I…uh… I don't know what to say."

"Say yes."

She squeezed her eyes shut. "I need to know this is what you really want, Evan. Last night—"

He cut her off before she could say more. Standing back up, he pulled her closer. "Last night I was being a ridiculous, thoughtless fool. I know that now."

"You do?"

He nodded at her. "Chiara, you're the missing piece I never knew I needed in my life."

"I am?"

He chuckled. "Yes! You give away money that you desperately need so that someone you barely know can go see her injured boyfriend. You stick up for a man you just met to his imposing, hypercritical mother. You are absolutely extraordinary. You don't even know how special you are. It's no wonder I've fallen hopelessly in love with you."

She cupped a hand to her mouth. "Oh, Evan. I've fallen in love with you, too." Her eyes were glistening as she admitted what he'd known deep in his soul for days now. And full of love. For him. He winced inside to think he might have let someone who actually loved him walk out of his life for good. Some lucky twist of fate had saved him from that terrible mistake. For that, he'd be forever grateful. And he'd do whatever it took to make it up to her, for the way he'd behaved last night and all the things he'd said.

If she would only give him the chance.

Chiara still wasn't sure if she was, in fact, imagining things. It had all started with the strange scrolling pictures on her phone, some she hadn't even called up in ages. Then masses of snow had fallen from above as the skies opened up. And through the wall of white flakes, Evan Kim had somehow materialized and approached her. He stood before her now. Asking her to marry him.

It couldn't be real. Could it?

Until she figured it all out, Chiara reminded herself she had to be strong. She was holding her own, fighting the urge to throw herself into Evan's arms and admit how much she'd missed him, how despondent she'd felt when she thought they'd never see each other again. Even when he'd presented her with the handcrafted work of art ornament, she'd held strong. But the ring could very well lead to her undoing, to a complete shattering of her resolve. He'd slipped it back on her finger literally on bended knee.

But it behooved her to remain cautions and guard her heart. Because to lose Evan Kim twice in one lifetime would absolutely crush that said heart permanently and beyond repair.

"But what made you change your mind?" she asked,

adding silently, *And how do I know you won't change it again?*

"The thought of going back home without you had me rethinking everything." He paused to take a deep breath. "I came to a realization."

"What was that?"

"I've been on my own most of my life, but you leaving was the first time I've ever *felt* alone. Even the new business deal didn't matter anymore." He stepped closer, gripped her hand tighter in his. "All that mattered was finding you. And never letting you out of my sight again."

Chiara had to remind herself to breathe. He was certainly saying everything she wanted to hear. How in the world was she supposed to resist such strong words of endearment? He was saying he loved her. She believed him with every fiber of her being. She loved him just as much. The last of her self-control crumbled to dust.

Flinging herself into his arms, she nestled against his chest, reveling in the sensation of being held by him again.

She sniffled, found a way to make her mouth work somehow. "I guess if I have to miss Christmas in Vermont, I'm glad I'll be able to at least spend it here with you."

Tilting her chin up with his finger, he narrowed his eyes at her. "Miss Christmas at home? Why on earth would I allow you to do that?"

She pointed to the sky, then motioned to the flakes that had already formed a thick layer of white over their hair and shoulders. And every other surface for that matter. "In case you haven't noticed, we're in the middle of a massive snowstorm. Every flight out of this place has been grounded for the foreseeable future."

"Maybe those flights have been grounded indefinitely, but I have a private jet that can be at your service as soon as the snow lightens and we get clearance."

"We?"

"I'd love to accompany you to Vermont. That's if the invitation still stands."

"You want to come home with me?"

"If you'll still have me. But I know I have no right to ask. I can come meet them later at some other time. Whatever you'd prefer."

Another sniffle escaped her. "I'd prefer it very much if you would come to Vermont with me to meet my father and brother. So that I can introduce them to the man I plan to marry."

As the thick white snowflakes fell like magical pixie dust around them, his answer was to gather her in his arms and claim her mouth the way she'd so badly wanted him to since he'd found her again.

"We should be landing in just a few minutes." Evan gave Chiara's hand a gentle squeeze. He couldn't seem to stop touching her. His jet and pilot had been readied for takeoff as soon as they'd gotten clearance. Now, Evan was taking his fiancée—his real wife-to-be—back to her home for the holidays.

"I can't wait to get to the cottage." Excitement rang in Chiara's voice as she looked out the window as the aircraft began its final descent. Usually while flying, Evan would be spending the time in the air trying to get some work done. Now, instead, he was simply letting himself enjoy the downtime. Then again, now that he had her back, he wanted to enjoy every moment he was in Chiara's company.

What a fool he'd been to think he could simply give

that up after experiencing it. If it weren't for Chiara, he'd be heading back to his penthouse in Bali right now. By himself. The most enticing part of his days back home would be going over spreadsheets and de-bugging code. The worst of it was he would have never even known all that he was missing out on.

Chiara continued, "They probably cut down the Christmas tree already. We do that every year. But maybe you and I can take a walk to the woods behind the cottage, find another smaller tree to call our own. There've been plenty of years where we had two trees. Did I tell you that already?"

Evan chuckled. She most certainly had. "You might have mentioned it once or twice. But I want to hear it all again. Tell me more."

"Really?"

He nodded. "Absolutely."

The smile she sent his way was like a shot of sero-tonin straight into his core. He'd never get enough of her smiling at him, was looking forward to indulging in that smile every day for the rest of his life.

Chiara went on. "Well, we spend the evening watch-ing classic holiday movies—Marco and I share the same favorites—with Christmas cookies, of course. It's not as glamorous as what you're used to in an international hot spot city like Singapore or Bali but—"

She stopped mid-sentence, then laughed softly. "I'm probably boring you, aren't I? You're just being sweet, pretending to be interested in all the ways we Pearsons spend Christmas."

He had to laugh at that assessment. When in his life-time had he ever been described as sweet? He couldn't think of one example. "You could never bore me, sweet-heart." The weeks they'd spent together since he'd met could be described as anything but boring. In fact, Evan had had no idea what a drab and flat life he'd been leading until she came along. She'd awoken a part of him he'd forgotten had even existed. A part he'd shut down after losing his ahma when he was eleven years old. The part that knew how to love.

He had Chiara to thank for bringing that part of him back to life.

"I'm just so excited to finally be going home," she continued. "And to be able to share it all with you."

He leaned over the seat to kiss her softly on the cheek. "For the record, I'm excited to be going home with you, too."

She had no idea how true a statement that was. Thanks to Chiara, for the first time in his life, he'd be spending the holidays as part of a true family.

* * * * *

CROWNING HIS
SECRET PRINCESS

KATE HARDY

MILLS & BOON

For Gerard—
one day we'll get back to the Mediterranean…

PROLOGUE

'SÉBASTIEN, DO YOU have a few minutes?'

No, he didn't. He was wrestling his way through the paperwork surrounding the latest trade negotiations. But Séb noted the grim look on his PA's face. Pascal wouldn't have interrupted him if it wasn't important. 'Of course, Pascal. Problem?'

'Perhaps. I had a visit from the chief archivist, a couple of hours ago.'

The palace archivists usually made an appointment to see the King or the Queen, not Séb's office. This was odd. He frowned. 'What is it?'

'The team found something in Prince Louis' papers. I promised to bring it to you.'

The papers were from a box that had been shelved temporarily and then forgotten about after the Prince's death, more than a quarter of a century before—until a fortnight ago, when a leaking pipe had caused a minor flood in the archives, and the box had come to light again. Since then, Séb knew that the archivists had been working through the papers, carefully logging them.

Pascal handed Séb a cardboard wallet marked with the name of a high street photographic developer.

Séb opened the wallet and took out the thin sheaf of photographs. The first one was of Prince Louis, the only child of King Henri IV and Queen Marguerite of Charlmoux, who was standing with his arm around a pretty blonde woman Séb didn't recognise; there was confetti around their feet. The second photograph was of the two of them outside the city clerk's office in Manhattan. The third made Séb's eyes widen: the woman was holding a bridal bouquet. Was she a bridesmaid, holding it for the bride? Or maybe a wedding guest, who'd caught the bouquet the bride had just thrown?

The fourth photograph made the situation clear: she and Louis were both posed with their left hands displaying their wedding rings, and they both looked deliriously happy.

'I thought Prince Louis died unmarried,' Séb said quietly. 'These photos would suggest otherwise.'

'Indeed,' Pascal agreed.

'Are there negatives? Or any papers in that box that could shed light on what's actually happening here?'

'According to the chief archivist, no. So I did a little discreet research. I wanted to bring you answers, not questions. Except… Well, you can see for yourself.' Pascal took a piece of paper from the file. 'This is a print from a digital copy which I'll forward to you. A notarised print copy is being sent here by special delivery from New York.'

Séb's spine prickled with unease as he took the document. He studied it carefully. It was the marriage certificate of Louis Gallet—using his family surname, Séb noted, rather than his royal title—to English ballet dancer Catherine Wilson, in New York, dated a month before his death. Louis had given his occupation as 'statesman' rather than 'Prince of Charlmoux'.

'So he did get married.'

'And the marriage is legitimate. I've checked. Using

his family name is as valid as if he'd signed it as Prince Louis,' Pascal said.

'Is the marriage legally recognised here in Charlmoux?'

'Yes,' Pascal confirmed. 'I also looked up some newspaper archives online, and there were a few press photographs of Louis and Catherine together that summer. Some of the gossip columns speculated that the Prince might be secretly dating the ballerina.'

'If the paparazzi were following them, then how did they manage to keep the actual marriage secret?' Séb asked.

Pascal shrugged. 'I assume it was a bit easier to do things quietly in the days before the internet. Before everyone had a camera on their phone and could send pictures across the world in seconds. And it was easier to avoid the paps back then, too.'

'Even so.' Séb frowned. 'Why would the Prince of Charlmoux have married someone at a register office in New York, rather than having a state wedding in the cathedral here? It doesn't add up.' Or, rather, it added up to something that was potentially political dynamite. Had Henri forbidden the wedding and then Louis had eloped and married the woman he loved anyway, without his father's permission? Even though Pascal had confirmed that the marriage was legally recognised here, there could still be a scandal. Plus the King's health was becoming frailer. If he had no idea about the marriage, the shock might be too great for him. 'Does the King know?'

'About the contents of the box, or the marriage?'

'Both.'

'I don't know,' Pascal said, 'but I assured the archivist that you would be delighted with his discretion and would wish that to continue, and that you would prefer him to speak to you about the matter for the time being rather than bother the King.'

'Thank you.' And Séb was grateful, too, that his PA had checked the facts discreetly. 'Did you find anything else?'

'I did some more searching, on a hunch. It was the way Louis was standing that made me wonder.' Pascal indicated the photograph where Louis' hand seemed to hover protectively over Catherine's abdomen, then handed over another document. 'Again, it's a print from a digital copy, and a notarised print copy is on its way from England.'

This time, it was a birth certificate. The birth of Louisa Veronica Gallet to Catherine Gallet, in London; the birth was dated seven months after the marriage. Clearly Catherine had been pregnant at the time of the wedding. This time, Catherine's occupation was shown as 'ballet teacher' rather than 'prima ballerina'; it looked as though she'd stopped performing after Louis' death and had chosen a job that would fit more easily around a baby, which made perfect sense to Séb. She'd named Louis on the birth certificate as the deceased father of her daughter.

Séb sat back and stared at his PA, stunned. 'This changes things.'

Prince Louis had had a child. A daughter who was the legal heir to the throne. The Act of Parliament naming Sébastien Moreau as the heir to the throne of Charlmoux would be null and void. So when Henri IV abdicated at the end of the summer, as planned, there might be a completely different person on the throne...

'We don't have proof that Louis was actually the child's father,' Pascal said.

Séb winced, not liking the implication. The woman in the photograph looked completely in love with her new husband, and he looked just as besotted with her. 'Catherine was married to him. Legally.' Even if the wedding had taken place in another country. 'And he's named as the father on the birth certificate.'

'It's all on paper, Séb. I know it's highly likely that Louisa Gallet is his child, but she can't be formally recognised as the daughter of Prince Louis without a DNA test,' Pascal said. 'We need the physical genetic proof.'

That felt harsh; but Séb had to acknowledge that it was a valid point.

If Louisa really was Louis' child, that would change everything.

Séb had spent nearly a third of his life at the palace, as a king in training. He wasn't actually related to the royal family; his parents came from a long line of farmers. But Séb hadn't wanted to be a farmer. He'd wanted to change the world—or, at least, to change Charlmoux. To become a lawyer and work his way up the justice system so he could make sure a miscarriage of justice like the one that had wrecked his best friend Marcel's life couldn't happen again. The headmaster of his secondary school had spotted that Séb was academically gifted and had persuaded his family to let him go to university to study law instead of joining the family business. Séb had won a scholarship to the top-ranking university in Charlmoux, and he'd worked hard to show that he didn't take either his place or his scholarship for granted. He knew his plans wouldn't bring Marcel's dad back, but at least he could help put in the checks and balances to make sure that what had happened to his best friend's family wouldn't happen to someone else.

In Séb's final year at university, the head of the faculty had suggested that Séb should apply for the role of a special advisor at the palace, rather than taking the usual route of qualifying as a solicitor or barrister. Séb had had to sign the Official Secrets Act before he'd even been able to apply for the role, and then he'd discovered that it wasn't just any old advisory role. The job was to take over from Henri IV, who had no legal heir following the death of his son. To be first in line to the throne. To be a king in training, by a royal decree ratified by an Act of Parliament.

Which meant he'd *really* have the power to make a difference to people's lives. To make things fairer. To stop things going wrong. To highlight the importance of mental health and how everyone needed access to proper treatment.

How could he turn down an opportunity like that?

The interview panel had liked the quiet, earnest young man and offered him the job. Séb had discussed it with his girlfriend, Elodie, and his family—as far as he could, around the restrictions of the Official Secrets Act—and accepted. He'd applied himself to the job, earned the trust of the King, and had taken on more and more of the older man's duties as Henri's health had declined.

Though now it looked as if everything he'd worked so hard for might vanish overnight: because it seemed there was someone who had a better claim to the throne than he did.

'I assume, from what you said earlier,' Séb said, 'that you've also done some research regarding Louisa Gallet.'

Pascal inclined his head. 'Firstly, her mother. Catherine. She didn't remarry. She died when Louisa was sixteen.' He handed over the death certificate.

Séb read it and winced. Cancer. Catherine had been only forty-one. How sad. He felt a wave of sympathy for both of them: for the young woman cut off in her prime and for the child who'd been bereaved during her teens. 'Being sixteen is hard enough, let alone losing your only parent.' And it struck a particular chord with him: he remembered the summer when he'd turned sixteen, and learned that his best friend's father had died. Marcel's family had moved to the other side of the country, two years before; all Séb had been able to do in support was write letters, make phone calls, and promise to visit Marcel in the school holidays.

He'd kept his promises, but it hadn't been nearly enough. It hadn't stopped his best friend taking drugs to blot out the misery and shame, then needing months of rehab.

Though this wasn't about what had happened to his best friend. It was about Louisa Gallet and his own future.

'So what do we know about Louisa Gallet?' he asked.

'She took a degree in textile management. She works part-time for her family's bridalwear business, and part-time for a heritage organisation, restoring textiles,' Pascal told him.

So far, so respectable. 'Married? Significant other?'

'It seems not. Though I'm sure you'd prefer to see for yourself.' Pascal passed his phone to Séb, with the screen open on the internet. 'There's a tab for each of her social media sites.'

Séb scrolled through them quickly. They were completely unremarkable. No wild parties, no shots of Louisa looking drunk or out of control, no scandal or gossip. No signs of any boyfriend—or girlfriend. Most of the pictures she posted seemed to be of textiles, or the occasional photograph of herself with her cousins. There were plenty of messages on the bridalwear studio's website from grateful brides and teenagers, thrilled with the dresses Louisa had made them. She'd reposted a few scholarly articles about textile heritage; Regency shoes, dresses and bonnets seemed to be among her favourites, along with Renaissance tapestries.

There weren't many photographs of Louisa herself. The most recent one, on the bridalwear studio's website, showed that she had her mother's fine facial features and Prince Louis' colouring. Her brown eyes were wide, and she wore her dark hair in a messy updo. She looked quite serious; Séb had to stop himself wondering what she'd look like when she laughed, and whether her smile would light up a room. How ridiculous. He needed to concentrate on the task in hand. Her smile had absolutely nothing to do with her suitability as a future monarch.

'So she loves history and she's dedicated to her work,' Séb remarked. Two things that would probably endear her to the people of Charlmoux—and to her grandparents. 'But surely,' he said, 'King Henri and Queen Marguerite know of her existence?' In which case, why on earth had the King insisted on the Act of Parliament to make Séb his heir?

Pascal spread his hands. 'I've made some very, very discreet enquiries with Emil—' the King's PA '—who has also agreed to refer the matter to you. It's very likely that they don't know. All I know for definite is that Prince Louis died in London and it broke his mother's heart.' He paused. 'There's no record of a Catherine Wilson or a Catherine Gallet being at the funeral or having signed the official book of condolence.'

So Louisa Gallet was a secret.

For now.

But if Pascal had been able to find out all this in the space of a couple of hours, so could the media. Rumours could do a huge amount of damage to the country's stability. Séb needed to find out the truth—and do it quickly.

'I assume you have a contact number for her?'

'Yes.' Pascal handed over the rest of the file. 'I guessed you'd want to talk to her and ask her to do the DNA test.'

'Yes. Thank you, Pascal. You've done an excellent job.' Séb's PA was reliable, discreet and they worked well together. Séb knew that Emil, the King's PA, intended to retire when the King stepped down, and Séb would have no hesitation in promoting Pascal when he took over from Henri.

'Let me know whether you need me to make arrangements for you to go to London, or for her to come here,' Pascal said.

'Thank you. I will.'

Once the door had closed behind his PA, Séb stared at the file in front of him.

The situation left him in a quandary. On paper, it looked as if Louisa Gallet could be Henri IV's rightful heir, meaning that she was the next in line to the throne of Charlmoux. Morally, Séb knew he should step aside for the legitimate heir.

Except he didn't want to.

Becoming king meant that he had a chance to make a real difference—and that was important to him. Growing up, he'd been best friends with Marcel, the youngest son of the family who ran the village shop, which was part of a national chain of small shops. When they were fourteen, the chain had accused Marcel's father of embezzlement, sacked him, and taken him to court. Marcel's father had always protested his innocence, but he'd been sentenced to two years in prison. Marcel's family had moved to the other side of the country to avoid the shame and scandal; Séb's own family had stuck up for them, but he knew there had been a lot of spiteful gossip in the village. The mud had stuck and was impossible to scrub off. Moving away had been their only option.

The week after Marcel's father had been released from prison, he'd died. It had taken Marcel another year to tell Séb that his father's death hadn't been an accident; his father had been depressed and taken an overdose, miserable with the shame of having been in prison—even though he hadn't embezzled a single centime. A year after that, it had come out that there was a major problem with the convenience store chain's new computer system. The discrepancies at the shop had all been due to computer error. Marcel's father's name was finally cleared: but it was too late.

Séb had burned with the injustice and had wanted to do something to stop anyone else's family losing someone they loved very much, their home and their livelihood, all because of someone else's incompetence. It was one of the reasons why he'd wanted to study law, and he'd originally planned to work his way up the justice system until he had the opportunity to make changes to the law, to ensure that miscarriages of justice like this couldn't happen again. The chance to become King meant that he could make even more of a difference, and he wasn't prepared to let that go.

He'd worked hard to prove that he deserved the opportunity he'd been given, and he'd prepared fully for the role. Was it all to be for nothing? And how could

Louisa—assuming that Louis really was her biological father—possibly take over from Henri IV, when she'd never had anything to do with Charlmoux and had no experience of life as a royal? If she didn't have the right temperament to rule, there was no way Séb was just handing everything over to her.

Or maybe he didn't have to?

Maybe there was a way for her to be the heir but for him to run the country? As the new queen, she'd need a consort. Who better than the man who'd trained for years for the role of king?

But he was getting ahead of himself. The first thing to sort out was the DNA test. Once the results were back, he'd know exactly what the situation was and he'd work out how he was going to manage it. He'd start by setting up a meeting in London so he could talk to her.

He picked up the phone and dialled the number of Wilson & Granddaughters Bridal and Prom.

CHAPTER ONE

'OH, LOUISA. It's amazing. The perfect dream of a dress.' Jess, the bride-to-be, gazed at herself in the mirror. 'I mean, I know I came here last week with my shoes for the final fitting, so you could check the hem and everything, and it looked amazing then, but with the veil on as well, I look…' She stopped, clearly lost for words.

'My baby.' Her mother brushed away the tear that slid down her face. 'You look like a princess. Your dad's definitely going to cry when he sees you, and Kev's going to be knocked off his feet.'

Job done, Louisa thought, smiling at both of them. This was her very favourite part of the job: where the client tried on her dress after the final tweaks, ready for her wedding or the prom. This particular dress had been fiddly; Louisa had hand-made the lace on the bodice and sewn on the seed pearls, as well as edging the veil with pearls. But, with the happiness shining from Jess's face so brightly that Louisa practically needed sunglasses, all the hard work had definitely been worth it.

'You look gorgeous,' she said. 'Now, if you don't mind me taking a picture for our website first, you can take the dress off again and I'll box it up for you. But I advise you not to take the dress out of the box and hang it up when you get home; the beading's heavy and you'll

risk tearing the material,' she warned. 'I know you'll
be dying to show it to your dad and your bridesmaids,
but you're best off leaving your dress in the box until
Saturday morning.'

'But won't it crease if I don't hang it up?' Jess asked.

Louisa shook her head. 'Not the way I pack it,' she
said with a smile, and took several snaps of Jess in the
dress. 'We won't put these on the website until after
your wedding,' she said. 'But I'll send you one now, so
that way you've got something to show your dad and
your friends before the day.'

'But *not* Kev,' Jess's mum cut in. 'It's bad luck for the
groom to see you in your dress before the day.'

'Plus you'd lose the impact,' Louisa said. 'Actually,
if I were in your shoes, I'd save it so you hear everyone's gasp echoing round the church when they all see
you for the first time.'

Jess nodded. 'I'll do that.'

Once Louisa had boxed the dress, folding it expertly
and rolling it in acid-free paper so it wouldn't crease,
and sent Jess and her mum on their way, she checked
her watch. There were forty-five minutes until her next
appointment: though this time it wouldn't be a bride.
When he'd phoned her yesterday, Sébastien Moreau
had said something about heritage. She was slightly
surprised that he hadn't made an appointment to see
her at the Heritage Centre where she worked two days
a week; but she could never resist the lure of working with old fabric. Even though her schedule meant
that she should've been working on the detailing of the
next wedding dress on her list, she reasoned that she
could always catch up with that this evening. It wasn't
as if she had a gaggle of men lining up to take her out
somewhere.

She set up the table that she and her cousins used when they had an initial meeting with a client, ready to make notes and sketches that she'd transfer to her computer later. Pencil and paper might look a bit old-school, but she always felt her creativity channelled better with a pencil than with a keyboard. Then she headed into their tiny kitchen area, shook coffee grounds into the cafetière, filled the kettle and set out two mugs.

A quick glance at her watch told her she had half an hour. It wasn't really enough time to work on any of the three dresses she was working on: the seed pearls and lace she was adding to the one that was due for a final fitting next week, working on the seams of the one she'd cut out to sew next, or spreading the bolt of organza across her cutting table and pinning the pattern on for the dress after that. Her restoration work was all done at the Heritage Centre, so there was nothing she could work on from that side of her job at the bridal workshop. Her cousins—the other members of Wilson & Granddaughters—were both out, Sam at a bridal exhibition and Milly at the wholesaler's: so she couldn't help them with any of their projects, either.

Louisa hated wasting time. She was always happiest when she was busy. Maybe she could add a bit more to the piece she was making for her best friend's birthday: Nina's favourite Shakespeare sonnet, back-stitched in flowing script, within a border of embroidered violets.

She'd completely lost track of time when her doorbell rang. Swiftly, she loosened the hoop from the fabric, slid the needle back into its case, put the whole lot into her project box and slipped it into her work bag before answering the door.

'Mr Moreau?' She smiled at the man on the doorstep. He was younger than she'd expected—maybe a couple of years older than she was—and he was the epitome of tall, dark and handsome. With short dark hair, soulful dark eyes, a beautiful mouth and a complexion that hinted at a Mediterranean heritage, he'd be perfect as the model for a groom in an upmarket wedding magazine. Whoever he was, his suit was beautifully cut, and the material was expensive; Louisa had to suppress the urge to ask him if he'd mind taking his jacket off so she could take a quick look at the lining and the seams, knowing that it might come across as rude to someone who didn't share her love of textiles. And she also needed to damp down that immediate flare of attraction. A man as gorgeous as Sébastien Moreau definitely wouldn't be unattached. Better to assume he was off limits. 'Do come in,' she said instead. 'May I offer you some coffee?'

'Thank you, Miss Gallet. Black, no sugar, please.'

'Please have a seat.' She indicated the two chairs by her table. 'I'll be back in a moment, and then we can discuss your project.'

The photographs really hadn't done Louisa justice, Séb thought. Wearing plain black trousers, a black strappy top and with her hair piled up on the top of her head, she managed to look both professional and creative at the same time. Her smile answered his earlier question: it really did light up the room, and she exuded a warmth and sweetness he hadn't expected. Then again, he supposed that someone who worked with brides and teenagers needed to be warm and sweet, to be able to deal with nervous clients or difficult parents. Given that Louisa looked so much like her mother, he could quite see how Prince Louis' head had been turned by Catherine Wilson.

He glanced round the small but exceptionally tidy room. There was a chaise-longue covered in teal velvet in one corner, with a small coffee table beside it, clearly for the bride or prom-goer's family; a large cubicle with a curtain where he assumed the client would change; this table, with four chairs, where he assumed she'd show sketches to clients; and a small pedestal desk which had a laptop, a desk lamp and what looked like a photograph frame on top of it. There were no untidy heaps of paperwork or scraps of fabric lying around; although he knew that she worked with her cousins, neither of them were on the premises, so her organisational skills appeared to be excellent.

There were no dresses on display; then again, they were all made to measure, so he wasn't that surprised. There were photographs on the wall: all brides and prom-goers, he noticed. It was a fair assumption that the images were of happy clients.

Unable to resist, he stood up and took a look at the photograph on the desk. It showed five women standing under an arch of roses with their arms round each other. Louisa was in the middle, wearing a prom dress, so she must've been about sixteen: not long before her mother had died, then. Catherine was next to her, still recognisable as the beauty from the New York wedding photo, but looking tired and a little gaunt, with a silk scarf tied round her head. Presumably post-chemo hair loss, he thought. On Louisa's other side was an older woman who looked so much like the others that she had to be Veronica Wilson, Catherine's mother. The other two women had similar features to Louisa but were blonde; Séb assumed they were the cousins who worked with her at Wilson & Granddaughters.

The photograph must've been taken during Catherine's last summer. Séb was glad that she had at least had the time to share Louisa's prom. He shook himself. There wasn't any room for sentiment, here. This was business. The whole aim of this meeting was to persuade Louisa Gallet to do a DNA test under medical supervision, so the results would be legally admissible. And then, if the results came back showing that she was indeed Louis' daughter, he'd decided to persuade her to marry him.

He'd just replaced the photograph on the desk and sat down again when she came back into the room, carrying two mugs. 'I apologise for not offering you a biscuit,' she said. 'We don't tend to have them here because crumbs *really* don't mix well with fabric.' She gave him another of those smiles that made him feel weirdly hot all over, and placed a mug on the table in front of him. 'You mentioned heritage on the phone, Mr Moreau. I'm a bit surprised you called me here rather than at the Heritage Centre.'

Séb knew he'd been vague on the phone, and he'd known perfectly well how she'd interpret his words; but this was something that needed to be done face to face. 'It's not actually about textiles,' he said. 'It's about your heritage.'

Her heritage?

Louisa didn't quite understand.

Then again, Sébastien Moreau's surname was French, as was the very faint trace of his accent. And hadn't the father she'd never had the chance to meet been French?

Now she thought about it, Sébastien Moreau was dressed like a lawyer. An expensive lawyer. He had that air about him: quality tailoring, properly shined shoes, briefcase. It looked as if maybe her father's family had despatched him to deal with her rather than sullying their hands with her themselves.

'I don't think so,' she said. 'My mother's estate was settled a decade ago.' And, oh, how she still missed her mother. 'My grandparents are both alive. I think you might be here under some kind of mistake.'

'There's no mistake,' he said, and confirmed her suspicions by adding, 'It's your father's side of the family.'

'Given that you look like a lawyer,' she said, 'I assume you were properly briefed. So you'll know that my father was killed in a car accident, a couple of weeks after my parents' honeymoon.' She pushed the flare of anger back down. It wasn't this man's fault that her father's family was completely heartless, so she wasn't going to take it out on him. 'There has been no contact between his family and my mother's since before I was born. I don't wish for any sort of contact—' not with the kind of people who had not only refused to acknowledge her mother, they'd whisked her father's body back to France and hadn't helped Catherine with her visa difficulties so she could attend the funeral '— so I'm afraid they've wasted your time.'

'There's a matter of heritage that I need to discuss with you, Miss Gallet.'

Louisa straightened her back, lifted her chin, and looked him straight in the eye. 'Let me make it very clear, Mr Moreau. I'm not interested in anything my father's family have to say. I've managed without them for my entire life. If someone has died and left me something, then please feel free to donate it to an appropriate charity. I don't need it and I definitely don't want it.' Any money they might have left her would feel tainted. Blood money. She absolutely couldn't accept it.

'Nobody has died,' he said.

Apart from both her parents. But Louisa knew it wasn't worth making the comment. 'I'm sorry you've had a wasted journey, but I can't see that we have anything to discuss.' She gave him a speaking look. 'If you'd told me this on the phone yesterday instead of pretending that you wanted to consult me about a heritage textile project, it would have saved us both some time.'

'I understand that you have strong feelings regarding your father's family, Miss Gallet,' he said, 'but it really is important. I need a sample of your DNA. That's why I came here in person. It will take only a few seconds to rub a swab on the inside of your cheek.'

'No,' she said.

For a moment, before he masked it, the shock was visible on his face. Clearly he wasn't used to people not doing his bidding. 'You're refusing,' he said.

'I'm refusing,' she confirmed. 'If you need something in legal terms, then I suggest you contact my family lawyer. Though it really isn't worth the effort, because the answer will still be no.'

Séb was pretty sure that if he told her the rest of it—that she was potentially the heir to the throne of Charlmoux—her reaction would be the same. She clearly wanted nothing to do with her father's family.

Which kind of solved his problem. If she dismissed her claim to the throne, then it would be back to business as usual and he could take over from Henri at the end of the year, as planned.

But.

If Louisa really was Louis' daughter, her claim to the throne was much more legitimate than his own. He didn't want to pretend she didn't exist and rule Charlmoux under false pretences. He wanted to be a fair, just and honourable ruler, and he wanted to make his country a better place. How could he possibly do that if he started his reign with such a huge lie—especially when a miscarriage of justice had wrecked his best friend's life and taught Séb just how important the truth was? He didn't want to be responsible for another miscarriage of justice.

On the other hand, how could someone who knew nothing of her father's country and hadn't grown up with a royal lifestyle—and whose educational background didn't even begin to touch on the things she'd need to know as a future monarch, the way his had—possibly make a good queen?

But those were all steps he could deal with in the future. He needed to deal with the here and now. She'd told him herself what the barrier was to taking this DNA test. So he'd face it head on.

'Miss Gallet,' he said, 'tell me about your mother.'

She folded her arms—not a good sign, because her body language was all about being closed to communication and shoring up her defences—and looked him in the eye. 'I assume you have a dossier on my family. So why don't you tell me what you know about my mother?'

Séb realised he'd underestimated his opponent. Badly. Cross with himself for not doing his research more thoroughly before meeting her, he said, 'Your mother was a ballet dancer.'

'She was a prima ballerina,' Louisa corrected. 'Do you know what that means, Mr Moreau?'

'That she danced the most important role in the performance.'

'Exactly. She was at the top of her profession. To

be a prima ballerina, Mr Moreau, you need more than talent. You need to work hard. You practise. You practise over and over and over. You practise until your feet bleed. And then you practise some more.'

He flinched at the image.

'You learn routines,' she continued. 'Sometimes they're solo, and sometimes they're a *pas de deux* so you have to know exactly what your partner's moves are and where he'll be in relation to you on the stage at any given second. You can't get a single step wrong because it will show. Everything has to be crisp. It isn't randomly tiptoeing across a stage, flapping your arms up and down. Every movement is precise. You need to know the techniques upside down and backwards until you're flawless.'

'Got it,' he said.

'No, I don't think you do,' she said. 'Because on top of flawless technique you need heart and soul. You're telling a story to the audience, but you're telling them without the benefit of words and you need them to feel it and live it with you. They need to see the Sugar Plum Fairy as the Queen, showing her strength and grace. Or Giselle dancing her soul away to save Duke Albrecht from the Queen of the Wilis, because she loves him more than life—even though personally I think she should've kicked him into touch for being a lying cheat. Or Odette, falling in love with Siegfried. It's the music, the movements, the whole thing. You need to dance well enough to break someone's heart and mend it again. That's why my dad fell in love with my mum. She broke his heart when she danced the dying swan— and then she put him back together again.'

Séb shifted in his seat. Since he'd split up with Elodie, he hadn't dated seriously. He'd fallen in love with the quiet lawyer when they'd been students, and he'd planned to ask her to marry him; but everything had fallen apart within six months of him starting his new role as heir to the throne of Charlmoux. Elodie had wanted to become a family lawyer, but the constant press attention had got in the way of her training and her job. She'd hated all the protocol that came with a royal lifestyle, and she'd hated having so little time with him.

'I love you, Séb, and you're a good man,' she'd said, that last night. 'I know you've got a lot on your plate, and I want to support you. But I hardly ever see you—and, when I do, the press are always there. I can't live in a goldfish bowl like this. You need someone who can cope with this way of life and give you the support you deserve.' She'd kissed him for the last time. 'I'm sorry, but I can't do it.'

Love or duty: that was his choice.

He'd asked her for a day to think it through. And he'd realised that he didn't love her enough to give up his chance to make a difference. He'd picked duty. Eventually there would be a royal bride, chosen on the grounds of political alliances and suitability; love wouldn't come into it. And he'd accepted that.

But even Elodie hadn't made him feel the way Louisa was describing. Not even close. It had never bothered him before; so why, now, was it making him suddenly feel as if something was missing from his life?

'My dad first saw her dance in London, and he came to see every show she performed on a Tuesday night,' Louisa continued.

Tuesday being a quiet day, when the paparazzi were less likely to spot the Prince, Séb thought.

'When the company toured *Swan Lake* worldwide,' she said, 'he followed her. He saw her dance in Paris and

Rome and Moscow. When the company went to New York at the end of the tour, he proposed to my mum at the top of the Empire State Building. They got married that same week in Manhattan.'

A marriage, Séb thought, that Louis' family very probably hadn't known about.

'They had a week's honeymoon in New York, then came back to live in his flat in London. They were so happy,' she finished softly.

Séb had seen the wedding snaps, the shared look of love and closeness between Louis and Catherine, and knew that she was telling the truth.

Would the King and Queen have become reconciled to the marriage, had Louis lived?

But there hadn't been enough time for that to happen. 'And then your father was killed in the accident.'

'A month after they married. They were back in London; my mum was doing the dress rehearsal for a new show, and my dad was coming to meet her at the theatre afterwards,' she confirmed. 'Except the police arrived instead, and told her what had happened. My mother was distraught. Obviously she contacted his family to let them know he'd been killed—but then they took over,' she said. 'They flew his body back to France, and there were various admin problems that meant she couldn't get there for the funeral. She asked for their help, but they didn't act in time.'

'Maybe they didn't get the message,' Séb said, his skin suddenly feeling too tight.

'Or maybe they did,' she said quietly, 'but they didn't want her there, so they didn't lift a finger to help her when she really needed them.'

It was beginning to seem as if the King had known about the marriage. Had Henri been furious that his son had married without his permission, blamed Louis' new wife for his son's death, and instructed his team to put the admin problems in the way in the first place? Right at that moment, Séb didn't know the facts, but what Louisa was telling him added up to something potentially heartbreaking. 'People react in ways they otherwise might not, when they're grieving,' he said, thinking of how Marcel had dropped out of sixth form and gone into a spiral of drink and drugs to blot out the pain of loss, after his father's death. It had taken months of rehab before Marcel had dried out; then Séb had persuaded his family to offer Marcel a job to help support him.

'My mum was grieving, too,' Louisa pointed out. 'My dad was the love of her life. She never found anyone who matched up to him. She never even *dated* anyone, after he died. And I should've been able to bury her next to my dad, instead of having to bury her in a different country.'

And now Séb felt guilty on behalf of his country. It looked as if the royal family of Charlmoux hadn't treated Catherine Wilson well at all. 'I'm sorry,' he said.

'So am I,' she said grimly.

But why had Catherine kept Louisa's existence secret from Louis' family? 'She didn't tell them about you,' he said.

'Given the circumstances, are you surprised?' she asked.

He decided to answer her question with one of his own. 'Don't you think Louis would have wanted them to know about you?'

'Maybe his family would've behaved differently towards my mum if he hadn't been killed.' She looked at him, her brown eyes cool. 'Or maybe they wouldn't.

I don't actually know exactly where he's buried. I've worked out that his family must be rich, because Mum once told me they buried him in a family chapel behind a locked gate. She couldn't even visit my dad's grave, let alone put flowers on it.'

Séb suppressed the insidious flood of guilt. None of that had been his decision. He couldn't apologise on behalf of the royal family, because he had no idea how the King and Queen felt about what had happened. He was completely in the dark. But he couldn't ignore the pain in Louisa's expression, and he wouldn't rub salt in her wounds by refusing to acknowledge her feelings. 'I'm sorry,' he said again.

'It's not your fault,' she said. 'You don't look that much older than I am, so you must have been a toddler when it all happened.' Her eyes narrowed. 'I'm assuming you work for them rather than being one of them.'

Séb knew his position was unusual. Although he had no blood connection to the royal family, he would be one of them at the end of this year—depending on whether or not the woman sitting opposite him was actually Prince Louis' daughter. But it felt way too complicated to explain.

'I work for them,' he said. Which was true, up to a point: just not the whole truth.

'I'm not going to shoot the messenger,' she said. 'But you can tell them from me that I don't want whatever they intended to leave me.'

Even if it was a kingdom? 'Miss Gallet, I understand that you don't want your legacy, but I'd be failing in my duty if I didn't ask you to take the DNA test. If it turns out you're not your father's daughter—'

Louisa stood up, looking outraged. 'So *that's* what they're saying about my mum, now? She was a dancer on a stage, so that means she was obviously a bit too free with her sexual favours and my father could've been absolutely anyone?' She shook her head in disgust. 'For pity's sake. That sounds like something out of the nineteenth century. I never thought France was such a backward country.'

'It isn't, and nobody's casting aspersions on your mother's character or her fidelity,' he said. 'And, for the record, your father's country isn't France.'

'It isn't?' She stared at him in surprise.

'It's Charlmoux. It's a small country on the coast between France and Italy, and we speak French,' he said.

She frowned. 'Mum always said Dad was French.'

'Not *quite*,' Séb said.

'What's this all about, really?' Louisa asked.

'You did say you weren't going to shoot the messenger,' he reminded her.

'I might have changed my mind about that,' she said, sitting down again but still looking cross.

He blew out a breath. 'I'm sorry. I've made a complete hash of this. There isn't an easy way to put this.'

'Then tell me straight,' she said.

'Louis Gallet was the heir to the throne of Charlmoux.'

'What?' She stared at him, those gorgeous brown eyes wide with shock. 'You're telling me my father was a *prince*?'

'The man who married your mother and was named on your birth certificate as your father—Louis Gallet—was the Prince of Charlmoux,' he said, wanting to be accurate.

'*Named* as my father,' she repeated. 'That's insinuating that my mother was lying.'

'A biological mother is never in doubt,' he said. 'Whereas a father could be.'

She folded her arms. 'You're saying my mum was a tart.'

'No. Absolutely not. I'd like to state categorically that I'm casting no aspersions whatsoever on your mother's character. You need to take the emotion out of this and look at the facts.' Which was what he'd been trained to do, over the last nine years. He'd become very, very good at suppressing his emotions. 'This isn't just a family business: it's the throne of a country. We need DNA evidence to prove that what's on your birth certificate is the absolute truth and that you really are Princess Louisa of Charlmoux.'

'I'm not a princess, I've never even heard of Charlmoux, and I don't want the throne,' she said.

His throne. Séb was very aware of the tension between what was morally the right thing to do, and what he wanted to do. Of course he should cede the throne to the rightful heir; but would she make a difference to the country, the way he planned to do? He'd spent years training for the role, whereas she was a complete novice. He'd grown up in Charlmoux and understood its history and its people, whereas she'd grown up in a different country and knew absolutely nothing about Charlmoux. It was obvious who would make the better ruler.

Except he might not be the legitimate heir, any more.

And that made all the difference in the world.

He reminded himself that he had a job to do. 'Actually, you might be a princess. And you can't legally renounce the throne, Miss Gallet, unless you're proven to be the heir.' Even then, she might not be able to renounce the throne. The Act of Parliament that had made him Henri's heir had no provisions for this situation, because nobody had known about Louisa.

'Can't you just pretend I don't exist?' she asked.

It was tempting, but it would lead to a lot more complications. 'No. If I can find you, so can anyone in the press. And certain parts of the media aren't fussy about how they spin a story, as long as it sells.'

Her eyes held a touch of fear. Weirdly, Séb found himself not only feeling guilty about putting that fear in her eyes—even though he'd only told her the truth—but also wanting to protect her. From what he'd seen on the website, Louisa Gallet was a talented dressmaker and clearly had what it took to run a successful business with her cousins and her grandmother; she was perfectly capable of looking after herself. But he still had this weird urge to protect her. He couldn't understand it, because he'd never reacted towards anyone like that before.

'I know it's a lot to think about,' he said. 'Why don't you discuss it with someone you trust—your grandparents, say—then meet me for dinner tonight and we can talk about it further?'

'Dinner,' she said.

'I have a suite.' He named an upmarket Mayfair hotel.

She rolled her eyes. 'Of course you do.'

'That wasn't intended to be boastful,' he said. 'I simply wanted to reassure you that it's a safe place. Discreet. Perhaps we could have dinner in my suite; we'll be able to talk frankly without anyone overhearing our conversation and putting either of us in an awkward position in the media. I'll send a car to pick you up. And your grandparents, if you'd like them to come with you—or a chaperone of your choice.' He took a business card from his briefcase. 'You can reach me on this number. I assume I'll see you for dinner at seven, unless you tell me otherwise. Thank you for your time, Miss Gallet.' He reached a hand out to shake hers.

When she took it, his skin actually tingled. He'd never experienced that before, either.

What was it about Louisa Gallet that affected him like this? And what was he going to do about it, given that they were on opposite sides of a quandary?

'I'll talk it over with my grandparents,' she said. 'I'll confirm our attendance or otherwise by five.'

'Thank you,' he said. 'I'll see myself out.'

CHAPTER TWO

WHEN SÉBASTIEN HAD LEFT, Louisa called her grandmother. 'Nan, I know it's your day at the café—' her grandmother met up with her old backstage friends for afternoon tea every Wednesday '—but I've just had the weirdest meeting and I really need to talk to you about Mum and Dad.'

'Come straight over. I'll text Shanice and tell her I might be late or I might need to give it a miss today,' Veronica said immediately.

'Thank you. I was really hoping you'd say that,' Louisa said gratefully. 'See you in a bit.'

It still felt like some weird kind of parallel universe. How could her father possibly have been the Prince of a country she'd never even heard of? Why didn't she know anything about it? How much had her grandparents kept from her? What other secrets were there?

The bridalwear studio made dresses to measure, rather than keeping a stock of ready-to-wear outfits, so they didn't tend to have walk-in clients. There were no appointments in the book for the rest of the day, so Louisa texted her cousins to let know something had come up and she'd be out for the afternoon, locked up the studio and headed for her grandparents' home. The second that Veronica opened the door, she enfolded

Louisa in a hug, and Louisa could smell something wonderful baking in the oven as she followed her grandmother into the kitchen.

'Tea's brewing,' Veronica said, 'and the cheese
scones will be out of the oven in five minutes. Your
granddad's at the allotment, but I can call him.'

'I love you, Nan,' Louisa said. 'Don't worry Granddad for now. I'm pretty sure you'll have all the answers.'

The routine of setting the table with plates, knives
and two large mugs made her feel more settled. And,
once she was sitting across the table from her grandmother, fortified with a mug of tea and a fresh scone,
hot from the oven and with butter melting on it, she
explained what Sébastien Moreau had told her about
her father.

'He said to talk it over with someone I trust and
then meet him again to discuss it, but I'm sure he's
barking up the wrong tree,' she said. 'My dad wasn't a
prince—was he?'

Then she noticed the expression on her grandmother's face.

'Oh, my God. Are you saying he was telling the truth
and my father really *was* a prince?' She stared at Veronica in shock. 'So how come today's the first time I've
heard anything about it—*and* from a stranger, too? Why
didn't Mum tell me, years ago? Why didn't *you* tell me?'

'It's complicated,' Veronica said. 'Your mum did
what she thought was best, and I agreed with her.'

'Nan, I...' Feeling overwhelmed and not knowing
what to say, Louisa shook her head and took a gulp
of tea.

'Lou, we all love you very much. Your mum loved
you to bits and she was the love of your dad's life, just
as he was the love of hers. Don't ever doubt that. And

I know you're probably angry right now that we kept this from you—'

'*We?* Who else knows?' Louisa interrupted, aghast.

'Just your granddad and me. That's it,' Veronica reassured her. 'The rest of the family only know what we told them. And it's the truth, as far as it goes: your dad's family were posh and they didn't approve of him marrying your mum, which is why your parents got married in New York instead of having a family wedding in London. And there were some, um, difficulties, so your mum couldn't get to his funeral.'

'This is really hard to take in,' Louisa said. 'Was he really killed in a car accident?'

'In London. Yes,' Veronica said. 'Your mum was in bits, especially when his family took his body back to France.'

'Charlmoux,' Louisa corrected dryly. 'When did Mum find out he was a prince?'

'Pretty much right at the start. Your granddad and I didn't know, at least not until after the wedding,' Veronica said. 'It was obvious Louis came from money— otherwise he could never have afforded tickets for the best seats in the house every week, let alone the flights and hotel rooms when he went to see your mum on tour, and he lived in that beautiful flat overlooking the Thames. But when they came back from honeymoon and told us who he really was… Well, once we got over the shock, we could understand why they did it. Your dad just wanted to marry your mum, without all the red tape and the nonsense.' She sighed. 'I wish we'd been at the wedding. I always thought I'd make your mum's wedding dress and your granddad would walk her down the aisle of the church where we got married. But getting married in New York was easier for him. They really loved each other and they wanted to be together, so the register office in New York it was.' She bit her lip. 'I would've given anything for them to grow old together, the way me and your granddad have.'

'Mum always said she wished you and Granddad had been at the wedding, and she'd worn a dress you made—they were her only regrets,' Louisa said, feeling tears prick the back of her eyelids. 'So why didn't she go to my dad's funeral? And I mean *really*, not just what she told me?'

'She tried. There were visa problems.'

'What sort of problems?' Louisa asked.

'I don't know, love. I don't think she ever found out, either. But they took her into a little room and made her wait. Kept her there for hours. Every time she asked what was going on, they said they were waiting to hear. She kept asking if someone would call the King's private secretary or the ambassador, but they kept telling her to wait. In the end, by the time they decided she could leave, it was too late for her to get to the funeral.'

Louisa had a nasty feeling about this. 'Did they arrange that?'

'We don't actually know that for sure,' Veronica said. 'But, I admit, I always thought that was the most likely reason.' She shook her head. 'I could never understand the Queen. I mean, when your uncles fell in love, I couldn't wait to meet the girls they were courting and welcome them to the family.' She shrugged. 'I guess it's different if you're a queen.'

'A few of our clients at the Heritage Centre are minor royals,' Louisa said, 'and they seem normal enough. So I think a queen would probably feel the same way that you did.' She paused. 'If Mum couldn't go to the funeral, how did she find out where my dad was buried?'

'She went to Charlmoux to try to see his family, once she'd got over the morning sickness. I went with her, because I wasn't leaving her to face them on her own. We looked round the cathedral, because she knew Louis had been christened there, and we got talking to one of the guides. He told us the royal family was all buried there; and showed us one of the private chapels; he said Prince Louis had been buried there a couple of months before. We could see his grave through the ironwork of the locked grille, but that was as close as we could get.'

'They wouldn't even unlock the door for his *wife*?' Louisa stared at her grandmother, shocked.

'The royal family didn't accept her as his wife, even though they were legally married. They refused to see her,' Veronica said quietly. 'Cathy tried, but they wouldn't even let her talk to one of the ladies in waiting or what have you. That's when she decided not to tell them about you. She thought they wouldn't believe her—or, worse, that they'd take her to court and take you away from her and she'd never see you again. Just like the way they made her leave the flat she lived in with Louis, because it belonged to the royal family and not to Louis himself.' Her expression hardened. 'I wrote to the King when your mum died, but I never got an answer. Though I didn't tell him about you, because I knew how your mum felt.'

Her father's family had refused to acknowledge her mother, made it impossible for her to attend his funeral, evicted her from the flat she'd shared with Louis and refused to let her visit his grave. These definitely weren't the sort of people Louisa wanted to be involved with, and she could understand why her mother and grandparents had kept her a secret from her father's family.

But.

They'd kept the secret from Louisa, too. And that was what hurt. Why hadn't they trusted her?

'Mum could've told me when I was old enough to understand,' Louisa said, softly. 'I wish she'd told me herself, before she died. This makes me feel as if I'm a dirty little secret.'

'Of course you're not!' Veronica protested. 'Louis would've adored you, just as he adored your mother. He knew your mum was pregnant and he couldn't wait to be a dad. But, after the way his family treated her, she didn't trust them not to hurt you. She didn't want them to slam a door in your face and refuse to acknowledge you.'

Put that way, Louisa could understand her mother's logic.

'But now they've found out about me, Nan. They want me to do a DNA test, when it's completely obvious whose child I am. I look like my mum, and I have my dad's colouring. All they have to do is look at the wedding photos and they'd know.' She clenched her hands for a moment. 'I'm so *angry* that anyone could think my mum was lying.'

'Maybe that's not quite their thinking,' Veronica said. 'If they're saying you're the heir to the country, I imagine they need to tick all the official boxes—and they also have to be *seen* to tick them.' She paused. 'Have you looked anything up on the internet, Lou?'

'Not yet,' Louisa admitted. 'I wanted to talk to you, first. But I have to admit I'm gutted that I've been lied to all these years. That you knew who I really was and didn't say a word.'

'You're Louisa Veronica Gallet—named after your father and your grandmother—and you're gorgeous from the inside out. That was true this morning, and it's still true now,' Veronica said. 'Love, we kept your mum's secret because she asked us to. We never intended to hurt you. We wanted to keep you safe.'

Louisa bit her lip. 'Sorry, Nan. I know. It just feels...' She paused, trying to find the right word. 'Odd, to think I'm somebody different.'

'You're not different. You're still who you've always been. You're still just as brilliant with a needle, whether it's the bridal and prom stuff or your heritage work. You, my darling,' Veronica said firmly, 'can walk with your head held high.'

'But if Sébastien Moreau is right and I'm actually a princess and heir to the throne of Charlmoux...what happens now?'

'That's something you have to decide, love,' Veronica said.

'My life's *here*,' Louisa said. 'I love my job. I love my life. I don't want to give it all up and go and live in some country I've never even heard of, surrounded by people who really weren't very nice to my mum and will probably be just as vile to me.'

'It might not come to that. Let's start by looking up a few things,' Veronica said. She fetched her tablet from the living room, opened a search engine and looked up at Louisa. 'We'll start with your dad. Louis Gallet.'

She flicked to the image on an encyclopaedia site. 'There he is, poor lad. I wish he'd had enough time to meet you.'

'Me, too.' There was a huge lump in Louisa's throat.

The written entry that went with the picture was very brief, telling them that Louis was born fifty-three years ago in the capital of Charlmoux to King Henri IV and Queen Marguerite, and died in London twenty-eight years ago. There was nothing about him marrying Catherine Wilson, and nothing about them having a daughter together.

'But they were definitely married,' Louisa said. 'Apart from the photographs, I've got their marriage certificate. The wedding happened.'

'Of course it happened. All her legal documents were in her married name. Including her passport and your birth certificate,' Veronica said.

Louisa clicked on the link to Louis' parents. 'They look really cold,' she said.

'Official portraits often do,' Veronica reminded her.

'But it's who they really are,' Louisa said quietly. 'Look how they treated Mum. What makes you think they'll behave any differently towards me, even though I share their blood?' She wrinkled her nose. 'They've sent their lawyer to make me take a DNA test.' She tapped Sébastien's name into the search engine, wondering just how senior a lawyer he was, and sucked in a breath as the page came up. 'I don't believe this, Nan.'

'What?'

'Sébastien Moreau isn't their lawyer at all. He's the heir to the throne.' She shook her head, cross that he'd lied to her about something as simple as that. What else had he lied about—deliberately or by omission? 'Apparently he was chosen by the King's advisors and it's all been sorted through an Act of Parliament.'

Veronica frowned. 'I don't understand. If he's the heir, why is he insisting that you take a DNA test to prove that *you're* the heir? Surely it's in his interests to pretend you don't exist, or to get you to sign some papers renouncing your claim?'

'Maybe that's why I have to take the test first, to prove who I am,' Louisa said. 'He said something about not being able to renounce the throne unless I could prove I was Louis' daughter.' She looked at her grand-mother. 'He suggested meeting for dinner tonight, to discuss it. I'm certainly not going to his hotel suite, so I think we'll bring the meeting forward and have it in a public place.'

'Good idea,' Veronica agreed.

'Can I borrow your scrapbook, Nan?'

'Yes, of course.' Veronica looked slightly worried. 'Though you're not going to lend it to him, are you?'

'Absolutely not. If he wants to take photos of anything on his phone, that's fine, but the original stays here with you. I just want to show him who Mum was. Where I really come from. And…' she lifted her chin '… I want him to apologise for the way they treated her.'

'I'll get the scrapbook,' Veronica said, pushing her chair back.

Meanwhile, Louisa took Sébastien's card from her bag and called the number on it.

He answered within two rings. 'Moreau.'

If he hadn't been the lying snake who represented her father's horrible family, that gorgeous accent would've made her weak at the knees. And that tailoring. And the memory of that beautiful mouth.

But he was on the opposite side to her. And he hadn't been honest with her. No weakening, she reminded herself. Sébastien Moreau might be gorgeous, but no way in hell did she want to get involved with a man like him. 'Louisa Gallet speaking,' she said coolly. 'Change of plan. I'll meet you at three o'clock, in the café at the Drury Lane Ballet Company's theatre.' The one where her mother had danced. Their meeting would be in public, and it would be on her territory rather than his.

'I have a meeting then,' he said. 'Can we make it four?'

'Compromise. Three-thirty,' she said. 'I'll book a table.'

Was it her imagination, or was there a slight trace of amusement in his voice as he agreed to the new time? Heir to the throne or not, by the time she'd finished with him, he'd be grovelling.

'I'll see you then,' she said crisply, and ended the call.

'Was that him?' Veronica asked, returning with the scrapbook under her arm.

'Yes. He's meeting me at the café at Mum's theatre.'

'Your territory? Good plan,' Veronica said with a grin. 'Do you want me to come with you?'

'Bits of me do,' Louisa admitted, 'but I don't want him to think I'm a child who needs someone to bolster her.'

'You're not a child,' Veronica said. 'But this isn't exactly a normal situation. If you change your mind, just say, and I'll be there.'

'Thanks, Nan. But I'll manage. And you look forward to your Wednesday afternoons. I'm not going to make you miss that, just because I'm having a bit of a wobble.' Louisa hugged her. 'Right. Better sort out all my documents. Thank you for the tea and scones.' She held her grandmother a little bit closer. 'And especially thank you for helping me sort things out in my head.'

'That's what I'm here for, love.' Veronica kissed her. 'Good luck. Let me know how everything goes.'

'I'll bring the scrapbook back here on my way home and fill you in,' Louisa promised.

Back at her flat, she booked a table for two at the café, then put the scrapbook in her work bag along with her birth certificate, her parents' wedding certificate and her passport.

This was the kind of business meeting where she needed to dress up. Even though she would rather have worn a summery dress in the June heat, she chose a lightweight navy suit, teamed it with a silky navy vest top and kitten-heeled court shoes, and took out the rope of pearls her father had given her mother on their wedding day. She didn't usually wear make-up during the day, not wanting to risk any smudges of cosmetics accidentally getting on the fabric she was working with, but this was far from a usual day. She took the pins out of her hair, brushed it and put it up in a formal chignon, then did her make-up. Neutral eyes and strong red lipstick, she decided; then added a pair of dark glasses and headed out to Drury Lane.

Séb managed to finish his meeting early enough to be at the café five minutes before he was due to meet Louisa. He was pretty sure that she'd chosen this place because it had a link to her mother, so it was somewhere she knew well; but he'd wanted the advantage of being here first, so he was able to choose the seat where he'd see her walk in.

Though in some respects he knew this behaviour was ridiculous, treating each other almost as if it were civil war. They weren't on opposing sides. She didn't want to be the heir, and he did. They needed to work together to find a mutually agreeable solution that would be best for Charlmoux.

She was three minutes early. In that suit and pearls, she was breathtaking; she reminded him of photos he'd seen of a young Audrey Hepburn, all grace and beauty. And he was shocked to realise that his heart was actually beating faster. He couldn't remember the last time he'd reacted to anyone like that, and it made him antsy.

This wasn't appropriate. This meeting was meant to be about his duty. About doing the right thing.

As she reached their table, he stood up. 'Thank you for coming to meet me, Ms Gallet.'

She inclined her head in acknowledgement, rather than reaching out to shake his hand, and slid into the seat opposite him. 'Nice manners, Mr Moreau. Then again, I'd expect nothing less from the heir to the throne of Charlmoux.'

Uh-oh. He hadn't told her that. Of *course* she would've looked him up on the internet. He should've anticipated that and told her up front.

'Not my father's family lawyer,' she added coolly, 'which you led me to believe you were.'

OK, so he'd omitted some details; but he hadn't lied to her outright. She'd been the one to suggest he was a lawyer; he merely hadn't corrected her assumption. 'Actually,' he said, 'I didn't tell you I was their lawyer. I said I worked for them—which, at the moment, I do. And, for the record, my degree was in law.'

'You're splitting hairs,' she said.

He could argue further and win this particular argument on a technicality, but it wasn't worth it. He needed her to feel that they were on the same team. Time for a strategic retreat. 'I apologise for misleading you, Miss Gallet.'

That took some of the fight out of her, to his relief—that, and the arrival of the waitress to take their order.

'I suppose it puts you in a bit of an odd position,' she said, once they'd ordered coffee. 'My existence, once it's officially confirmed, means that you won't be the heir to the throne any more. Why aren't you just trying to bury the story?'

'Because that would be morally wrong,' he said. 'I

can't rule Charlmoux starting out with a huge lie. I need to know the truth.'

'That's very noble of you,' she said, sounding as if she didn't think he was noble in the slightest. 'But that still doesn't tell me *why.*'

He couldn't tell her the full details. That wouldn't be fair to Marcel. But maybe if he told her some of it she'd understand. 'Something happened to my best friend's family, when we were fourteen. A miscarriage of justice. It ripped his family apart and the fallout was...' He grimaced. 'I don't want to betray a confidence, but it was pretty bad. Since then, all I've ever wanted was to make our country a place where that sort of thing couldn't happen again.'

She frowned. 'But how could you do that?'

'Because I discovered I was good with words. With law. So I planned to qualify as a lawyer and work my way up the justice system until I was in a position where I could start working with the constitution and put in extra safeguards. It wouldn't fix things for my best friend's family, but at least it might stop it happening to someone else's. And in the meantime, as a lawyer, I could help people who were in trouble.'

She inclined her head in acknowledgement. 'But, if the truth is so important to you, why did you lie to me?'

'I omitted a few details,' he said, 'because I was trying to be diplomatic. This isn't an easy situation for either of us. I wanted to establish some common ground between us before we discussed the issues.' He looked at her. 'This might not be the most discreet place to do that.' Or to tell her that the King's health wasn't great and he was planning to abdicate at the end of the summer. Séb planned to pick his moment to tell her that particular piece of information, because he'd already worked out that Louisa Gallet had a stubborn streak a mile wide. One which she might well have inherited from her grandfather.

'All right. Let's try to talk obliquely,' she said. 'If the DNA test proves the identity of your client's grand-daughter, then she can renounce the throne and the heir can carry on?'

'Honest answer? I don't actually know,' he said. 'There isn't a precedent.'

'I don't understand why there wasn't an heir after your client's son died,' she said. 'Surely there's some distant cousin who can inherit?'

Séb shook his head. 'He came from a long line of only children. We'd have to go back so far that any rela-tive would be incredibly distant. The constitution says that if the next in line to the throne isn't within three degrees of kinship, Parliament can appoint an heir.'

'Did the appointed heir know about me when he was appointed?' Louisa asked.

'No. He didn't even know that my client's son was married,' Séb said, 'let alone that a child existed.'

'So how did you find out?' Louisa asked.

'There was a leaking pipe in the archives, a couple of weeks ago. When the archivists moved things from the shelves, they uncovered a box; I presume it had been brought back from London and then somehow forgot-ten about,' Séb explained. 'They've been working their way through the contents of the box, and they found wedding photographs. My PA checked some details and traced things forward.'

'None of the online encyclopaedias mention the mar-riage—or the child,' Louisa said.

'Indeed,' Séb said. If Henri knew about the wedding or Louisa's existence, and Séb still wasn't entirely sure whether the King did or not, then he'd done a very good job of keeping it quiet.

The waitress brought their coffee, and he waited until she'd gone before taking an envelope from his briefcase. 'I had copies of the photographs made for you.'

'Thank you. That's kind.' She leafed through them, and he saw the sheen of tears in her eyes. 'I haven't seen these ones before. They're lovely. My parents look so happy.'

Then he noticed something. 'Those pearls you're wearing. Are they the ones in the photograph?'

'Yes. My dad gave them to my mum as a wedding present.' She lifted her chin. 'She left them to me.'

Did she really think he'd demand them back, when they'd clearly been given to her mother with love? Whatever their financial value, their sentimental value to Louisa Gallet was clearly much higher. In Séb's view, Charlmoux could manage perfectly well without them—and he'd argue that with the King and Queen, if he had to. 'I'm glad you're wearing them,' he said. 'It's important to keep memories alive.'

'I brought photographs, too. Not copies, though,' she said. 'You're welcome to photograph anything you want, or let me know and I'll make copies.'

That was a concession he hadn't expected. 'Thank you,' he said.

She moved their coffee cups. 'They're in Nan's scrapbook, and I don't want to risk anything spilling on it,' she said by way of explanation. Then she took the scrapbook from her work bag and placed it on the table in front of him.

Séb leafed through the scrapbook carefully. There were photographs of Catherine Wilson dancing on stage, and newspaper cuttings about her being made the prima ballerina here at the Drury Lane Ballet Company.

So he'd been right about the link. 'This is where your mum danced.'

She nodded. 'She switched to teaching after she had me—a baby and a touring schedule don't go together very well. They persuaded her to come back for a gala performance in aid of the roof repairs here, so I did actually get to see her dance on stage. I must've been about eight, at the time. It was so special—the kind of thing you always remember. Check out the gallery before you go.' She indicated a wall of photographs on the other side of the room. 'Mum's there. More than once. Make sure you find the *Firebird* picture. She looks amazing.'

For a mad moment, he wanted to scoot over to her side of the table, wrap his arms round Louisa Gallet and hug her. But they were near strangers, definitely not on hugging terms; besides, it had been drilled into him that the heir to the throne didn't act on impulse. He was to remain cool, calm and collected at all times.

'I've never actually been to a ballet,' he said.

'Start with *The Nutcracker* or *Swan Lake*,' she advised. 'They're the most accessible, because everyone knows the story and at least some of the music. I would say try to get tickets for a performance here, while you're in London, because *Swan Lake* is on at the moment; but I know they're sold out for the next month and returns are like gold dust.'

'Maybe I'll get tickets, next time I'm in London,' he said.

And he just about stopped himself suggesting that she joined him.

Not wanting to think too closely about why he might

want to spend an evening at the ballet with Louisa Gallet, he went back to looking through the scrapbook.
There were a couple of candid wedding snaps that he
assumed were from the same set as the ones he'd seen
already, with Louis and Catherine laughing in the sunlight as confetti floated down around them. Pictures of
Louis and Catherine walking in a London park, their
arms wrapped round each other. Of Louis standing with
Catherine, his expression tender and his hands resting protectively round her abdomen: obviously, Séb
thought, Louis had known about the baby.

Then there were pictures of Louisa with her mother
as a baby, a toddler, a teen. He could definitely see both
the Prince and the ballerina in Louisa's features.

'Your mother was very beautiful,' he said.

'It's not just the way she looked,' Louisa said. 'She
was kind and sweet and generous. Her students all
adored her. So did their mums. She was one of those
people who lit up a room—the sort who made the world
a better place just by being in it.'

She didn't have to say the rest. He could see the moment of bleakness in her eyes: she'd loved her mother
dearly and really, really missed her.

He looked back at the wedding photos again. It was
clear that Catherine and Louis had loved each other
very much.

The kind of love his parents shared.

The kind of love his grandparents shared.

The kind of love Séb had almost found with Elodie,
but not quite. And he wouldn't get it because, as the heir
to the throne of Charlmoux, his marriage would have
to be based on what was best for the country.

Now, he was starting to feel the tiniest creeping
doubts. Particularly when he thought about the way his

skin had tingled when he'd shaken Louisa's hand, that morning. He'd never felt that kind of awareness before.

If it turned out—as he rather suspected it would—that she was the rightful heir, she'd have to marry for the country rather than for herself. Would Henri insist that she married royalty? Or would the King think that Louisa needed a consort with experience in a supporting role, someone who could help her rule?

'May I take a couple of snaps?' Even though she'd said earlier that he could, he didn't want her to think that he was taking her for granted.

'Sure.'

'And one of you, as you are now?'

'All right.' She didn't smile, as if she'd guessed that he planned to show the photo to her grandparents and was wary about it.

He took the snaps he wanted, then closed the album and handed it back to her.

'So how does the DNA test work?' Louisa asked.

'The grandchild takes a swab from the inside of the cheek,' he said, 'and the lab compares the sample cells to those of the grandparents. Obviously it's not quite as conclusive as paternity or maternity testing, but the lab can determine if there are shared genetic markers. The experts told me if there's a low number, then the test subjects are unlikely to be related. If there's a higher number, then it's as good a proof as we're going to get.'

'And you already have the grandparents' tests?'

He wasn't going to mislead her again. 'Not yet. I wanted to talk to you, first,' he said.

'*If* I do it—and I haven't agreed yet,' she reminded him, 'what happens next?'

'If the report says there isn't a match, then I don't need to bother you any further.'

'And if there is a match?'

'Then you need to think about what you want to do and what's best for the country,' he said. 'If you're Henri's granddaughter, that means you're his heir.'

'Which means you won't be the heir any more.'

'Your birth would take precedence over the Act of Parliament that named the current heir.'

'What will you do, if it turns out you're not the heir any more?'

Propose to her, so he could still do the job he'd trained for.

Though he still needed a bit of time to think that through. To make sure that it was a logical decision, one that really was best for the country, and not one that was based on the unexpected tingles that had thrown him off balance earlier. 'I haven't had time to consider that properly,' he said. 'Maybe I'd move to an advisory role.'

'How long have you been the heir?'

Séb frowned. 'I thought you'd already looked me up?'

'Yes, but I want to hear the story from you.'

He'd give her the bare bones, because Marcel's story wasn't his to tell. 'All right. I'm the second of four boys. Everyone expected me to join the family business—my family are farmers—but I did well at school, and the headteacher persuaded my parents to let me stay on for sixth form and go to university. I told you that things were tough for my best friend, so I wanted to be a lawyer and change things.'

'So you were the only person in your family to go to university?'

He nodded. 'My brothers are all involved with the farm.' She didn't need to know that he'd bought the farm with the money he'd earned, and transferred the deeds quietly to his family. 'I was in my last year at university when the head of the faculty suggested that I should apply for an advisory post in the royal household.' He smiled. 'I had to sign the Official Secrets Act first, and then I discovered that the role was to be the heir. I did the aptitude tests and had several interviews. They offered me the job.'

'And it's what you wanted?'

'I didn't accept straight away. I thought about it for a few days,' he said. 'I talked it over with my family—as much as I could, within the agreement I'd signed.' Louisa didn't need to know about Elodie, either. 'I knew it would mean a huge change in my life.'

'What made you decide to accept?'

'I think I could make a good king,' he said. 'I've grown up outside of a life of privilege, so I have a good understanding of what it is to be an ordinary person.' Like her, though he wasn't going to dwell on that. 'I think my experiences will help me be a fair and honest ruler. And I want to make my country a better place.' One without miscarriages of justice.

'Do you actually want to be King?' she asked.

'I've spent nearly a third of my life in training for the role, so yes.' He shrugged. 'It would be a waste, otherwise.'

'Doesn't it feel restrictive, having to do your duty all the time and having no real freedom in what you do?'

That was exactly why Elodie hadn't been able to cope with the lifestyle.

'There's a little bit of a clash between freedom and duty,' he admitted, 'but I came to terms with that a long time ago.' Though it sounded as if Louisa saw things the same way as Elodie and would face the same struggles. He'd need to manage that carefully.

'The way I see it, you want to rule and I don't,' she said. 'And you've already been named the heir. So why don't you just pretend I don't exist?'

'Because it wouldn't be honest. Even though I wasn't completely open with you earlier, and I apologise again for that. Dishonesty doesn't sit well with me,' he said. 'I've seen the damage that lies can do.'

'Mr Moreau—' Séb realised that she hadn't once used his first name since he'd first met her, keeping a distance between them '—since you say you value honesty, let me be honest with you. My father's family has never shown any interest in me before. My life's here in London. My family. My friends. I love my grandparents, my aunts and uncles, and my cousins. I love my job; I work with two of my cousins and occasionally with my nan. I love my city. You're suggesting that I might have to give all that up for people who are complete strangers to me. For people who, frankly, weren't very nice to my mum, at a really difficult time of her life.'

Put like that, Séb knew what he was asking of her was completely unreasonable. 'I know it's a lot to ask,' he said. 'But, on the other hand, this is merely a DNA test. It needs to be done under medical supervision, to be legally admissible. It makes sense to do it in Charlmoux, and it will give you a chance to get to know your father's side of your family.'

'Given how they treated my mum, I'm not entirely sure that I want to know them,' she said. 'And I definitely don't want to be Queen. I don't want to spend my life in a goldfish bowl, having to be polite and diplomatic to people I barely know, when I'd rather be working with fabric.'

That was definitely how Elodie had felt. But Elodie

had been able to walk away. He wasn't sure that Louisa would have that same freedom to choose.

'As I said earlier, I'm not completely sure whether you can renounce the crown or what the procedure would be, but if you *can* renounce it then you'll definitely have to prove beyond doubt who you are, first,' he said.

She was silent for a while. Eventually, she nodded. 'If I do the DNA test, there are conditions.'

'Name them.' Was she going to ask for money and privilege? he wondered.

'I want to visit my dad's grave,' she said. 'I know he's in the private chapel in the cathedral, because they wouldn't even unlock the gate for my mum to visit him—Nan told me this morning. She was there.'

Séb hadn't known about that. And he didn't approve of it, either. When people were grieving, they needed kindness, not to be turned away. 'I'll make sure that happens,' he said. Even if it meant having a fight with palace officials, or the King himself, Séb would support her in this.

'I want to plant a cutting of the lavender from my mum's grave in a private bit of the cathedral garden, so at least they'll have *something* shared near each other.'

That seemed reasonable to him, too.

'And I want his gravestone or memorial slab or whatever there is amended to say "beloved husband of Catherine and father of Louisa".'

She didn't want money or privilege: she wanted her mum to have recognition. Something whose cost would be measured in pride rather than money. Would it be a price that the royal family of Charlmoux would be prepared to pay? Right then, Séb didn't have the answer. If it were left to just him, he'd do it. The best that he could do was try to persuade Henri IV to have some common humanity—though what he'd learned from Louisa today made him wonder whether the King's formality and distant manner covered something darker. If the King had known about the marriage and about Louisa, then perhaps Henri's humanity had been buried with his son.

'And finally,' she said, 'I want a copy of a photograph of my dad when he was younger. Not the formal ones you can find on official websites. I want to choose a private one, which will stay private, and I'm happy to sign a legal agreement to confirm that nobody will see the photograph other than me and my closest family.'

Séb was pretty sure that Louisa Gallet wasn't the type to sell a story and a photograph to the media. And she clearly wasn't fussed about all the trappings of royalty. She could've asked for land, for money, for priceless jewellery and works of art. Instead, she simply wanted her mother acknowledged as part of her father's life, and a personal memento for herself.

What she'd asked for had very little price, but enormous personal value to her. Séb could see that it was a test: if her grandparents weren't prepared to acknowledge her for herself, then she didn't want to get involved with them. He'd need every bit of the negotiating skills he'd learned over the last few years to make this happen.

'All right,' he said, 'I'll talk to your grandparents.'

'Not my "alleged" grandparents?' she asked wryly.

'Legally, "alleged" would be correct,' he agreed. But he was pretty sure that the DNA test would show a biological relationship between Louisa and Henri IV. Regardless of genes, she was definitely a chip off the old block. 'I'll call you when I've spoken to them, and we can discuss where we go next.'

'Thank you, Mr Moreau.' She stood up. 'I need to be somewhere. Excuse me.'

'I'll pay for the coffee,' he said.

'It's already paid for,' she said, completely wrong-footing him. 'I gave them my credit card details when I booked the table.'

Before he could say another word, she turned round and sashayed away.

And Séb felt as if he'd just been run over by a steam-roller.

CHAPTER THREE

BACK AT THE HOTEL, Séb checked his watch. Charlmoux was an hour ahead of English time; although it was later than the usual palace office hours, the King and Queen wouldn't be sitting down to dine yet, so he had time to call them.

This was going to be tricky, and he'd need to be extremely diplomatic.

He called Pascal, who promised to arrange an urgent video call with the King and Queen. Ten minutes later, the call came through to Séb's laptop.

'Sébastien? Pascal tells us you're in London. Is this about the trade deal?' Henri asked.

'Not completely, *sire*. I'm also following up on some leads.'

'What sort of leads?' the King demanded.

He sounded irritable; Séb reminded himself that the King was probably feeling unwell, and the older man wasn't being snappy on purpose. 'I'm sorry. I know I should really have this conversation with you in person, *sire*, *madame*, but this is the best I can do right now,' Séb said. 'The archivist found some wedding photographs. Of Louis.'

'But Louis wasn't married,' Marguerite said.

His mother clearly didn't know about the wedding, then; but what about his father? After what Louisa had told him, Séb was pretty sure Henri had known everything. 'I'm sorry to be the one to break it to you both, *madame*,' he said. 'Our research shows that Louis married Catherine Wilson, twenty-eight years ago, in New York. A month before he was killed.'

Marguerite frowned. 'Married? Are you sure?'

'Yes, *madame*.'

'But—but—why didn't we know about this?'

'She was a dancer. A gold-digger. I was working on an annulment,' Henri said tightly.

Marguerite rounded on her husband. 'You *knew*?' In the brief moments before the Queen regained her composure, she sounded shocked and angry. Because her son had married a commoner, or because she hadn't been there to share the joy of the wedding? Was she angry with the King for keeping it from her? Would she have reached out to Catherine?

But her mask was quickly back in place, and Séb could hardly ask her.

Right at that moment, he really didn't like Henri, either as his boss or as his king. Nothing he'd learned about Catherine Wilson so far had suggested that she was anything other than genuinely in love with Louis. 'The marriage was legal and it's valid in Charlmoux,' Séb said. 'And I need you both to prepare yourselves for something else. Catherine had a daughter.'

The Queen's serenity slipped again and Séb could see longing in her expression, and the slight sheen of tears in her eyes. 'We have a grandchild?'

'Rubbish,' Henri said. 'How do we even know Louis was the father?'

'We need to do a DNA test to prove things either way, *sire*,' Séb said carefully. 'She's agreed to do the test, but there are conditions.'

'Don't tell me. Money. Land. Influence,' Henri sneered.

'None of those, *sire*,' Séb said, holding on to his own temper with difficulty. 'She wants to visit Louis' grave, and she wants a copy of a photograph of him when he was young—a family portrait, not an official one. And she's happy to sign documents agreeing that it will not be reproduced elsewhere.'

The King scoffed. 'And the rest?'

This was the bit Séb knew was going to be sticky. Not the financial things the King was clearly expecting, but something personal. And Séb was pretty sure the King would refuse flatly. 'She wants her mother acknowledged on his grave.'

'No,' the King said, just as Séb had expected. 'And she's not my heir. You are. There's an Act of Parliament stating that.'

'It's my duty, *sire*, to point out that if Louisa is Louis' daughter, then that takes precedence over the Act,' Séb said. 'She's within the three degrees of kinship.'

'Do you think she's genuine?' Marguerite asked.

'Yes, *madame*, I do.' He flicked into the photo app on his phone, called up the photo he'd taken in the café, and showed it to them on the screen.

Marguerite swallowed hard. 'I can see my son in her.'

'I can't,' the King said, pursing his lips.

The Queen's eyes glittered as if she wanted to shake her husband. Séb wanted to shake him, too. Violence didn't solve anything, but he wanted to snap the King out of his tunnel vision attitude and make him do the right thing by Louisa.

'Her mother died just over a decade ago,' Séb said. 'She has photographs of her mother with Louis, and not just at the wedding. I've snapped them on my phone and I'll send them over to you shortly. And, as I said, she doesn't want anything financial. She just wants her mother recognised.' He paused. 'She says there were difficulties when her mother entered the country which meant that Catherine was unable to attend Louis' funeral.'

'He was *my son*,' Henri said tightly.

The obstinate expression on the King's face told Séb the thing he'd dreaded having confirmed: Henri had known about the marriage and had ensured that the visa difficulties existed, deliberately keeping Catherine away from the funeral.

'He was my son, too,' Marguerite snapped at him.

It was clear to Séb that, if she'd known, things would have been very different. Hopefully the Queen would help him soften the King towards Louisa. It was the best chance he had of an ally.

'Louis was Catherine's legal husband, *sire*,' Séb said quietly. 'I have copies of the documentation.'

'He should've married someone of my choice,' Henri said, 'and then he wouldn't have been anywhere near London and he wouldn't have been killed. It's *her* fault he's dead.'

Séb reminded himself what he'd told Louisa: that grief could make people act in unexpected ways. 'It was an accident, *sire*,' he said, keeping his voice measured, 'which could have happened anywhere, not just London.'

'Her name's Louisa, so she's obviously named after Louis,' Marguerite said. 'Does she want to meet us?' Her eyes were bright with hope.

'She simply wants to visit his grave and to choose a photograph, *madame*,' Séb said gently. 'Should you wish to be there…'

'No,' Henri said, at the same time that Marguerite said, 'Yes.'

Henri's expression tightened. 'I forbid it.'

'I lost my son,' Marguerite said. 'If we've been blessed with a granddaughter, then I want to meet her, Henri. I want to get to know her. We've already lost too many years. We missed her growing up.'

'We don't know that she's really Louis' daughter,' Henri said again. 'She could be an impostor.'

Marguerite shook her head. 'Look at her photograph, Henri. *Really* look. She has Louis' eyes.'

'No,' Henri said. 'Leave this alone. I don't want anything to do with her.' He stalked out of the room and Séb heard a door slam loudly.

'I'm sorry, *madame*,' Séb said. 'I really didn't intend to cause trouble between you and the King.'

'It isn't your fault.' Marguerite sighed. 'Henri never used to be this…' Then she stopped, as if realising how indiscreet she was being. 'I want to meet her, whatever the test says. My husband doesn't have to know.'

'It's not my place to be involved in any disagreement between you and the King,' Séb said. 'But I was planning to bring Louisa to Charlmoux to do the test. Maybe your paths can cross while she's there.'

'I hope so. Tell Emil what you need from us,' she said. 'We can get the tests organised for the King and myself.'

'Will the King do the test?'

'I'll talk him round. At least, I'll try to talk him round. If I can't, we'll have to manage with just me,' Marguerite said. 'I'll sort out some photographs. Perhaps we can look through them together. And I'll make sure the cathedral officials know that Louisa has my permission to visit Louis' grave.' She paused. 'I could escort her myself, if she'd like me to be there.'

Just what Séb had hoped for. And he was glad to know that at least one of Louisa's paternal family would welcome her. 'Thank you, *madame*. I'm so sorry that this has been a shock for you. I had been wondering…' How could he put this without being offensive? 'If you already knew some of the facts,' he finished awkwardly.

'No. Not at all. But clearly my husband did, and chose not to inform me,' she said dryly. 'It's been a shock, yes.' She shook her head. 'Sébastien, I know I can rely on your discretion. Right now, I'm so angry with him. He kept all this from me, out of stupid, stubborn pride. We could've met the girl our son loved, made sure…' Her voice cracked. 'If Louisa really is my granddaughter, then I want to get to know her.' She swallowed hard. 'I miss my son. I miss him terribly.'

In all the years Séb had known Queen Marguerite, she'd never been so open about her feelings. It surprised him to the point where he didn't know what to say—or how to comfort her, over a video call from the country where her son had died.

'Obviously you've met her,' the Queen continued. 'What's she like?'

'Bright. Articulate.' *Beautiful.* He shook himself. The Queen didn't need to know he found Louisa attractive. And he didn't need to let his libido distract him. The situation was already tricky enough. He smiled. 'I think she might be a little stubborn.'

'Like her grandfather, then.' She gave him a watery smile.

'Potentially,' he agreed.

'Do you like her?'

He liked a lot of things about Louisa. Which probably wasn't a good idea. He couldn't mix things up between his head and his heart. He was committed to the best for Charlmoux.

'Sébastien?'

'Yes,' he said finally. 'I like her.'

'Good. I trust your judgement. Leave my husband to me,' Marguerite said.

'Thank you, *madame*.'

'Sébastien,' she said quietly, 'you're a good man. My son would have approved of you.'

'Even though I just picked a fight with his father?' Séb asked wryly.

'I think,' she said, 'Louis would have picked that very same fight.'

Maybe Louis already had, and Séb had simply taken it up again. 'Perhaps, *madame*,' he said.

'Ever the diplomat, Sébastien.' She smiled at him. 'Let me know when you're coming back.'

'I will, *madame*,' he promised.

Once she'd ended the call, he rang Pascal to fill him in regarding the tests and asked him to arrange the King and Queen's DNA test via Emil; then he glanced at his watch. Would Louisa be in a meeting, or on the Tube? She'd been vague in the café, merely saying that she needed to be somewhere. Maybe a text would be the best way to contact her.

Queen Marguerite has agreed to you visiting the grave, and to photographs. Suggest we do the test in Charlmoux; then you can visit the grave and see a bit of the country while we wait for the results. It should take three days. Let me know when's doable for you. Perhaps we can meet tomorrow evening to discuss? Thanks, SM

Louisa was in her grandmother's kitchen, having returned the scrapbook and filled her in on the meeting with Sébastien, when her phone beeped.

Out of habit, she glanced at the screen. 'It's from

Sébastien Moreau. The Queen says I can visit Dad's grave and see his baby photographs.'

'That's wonderful,' Veronica said.

Though she noticed that Sébastien had only mentioned the Queen, not the King. Did that mean the King didn't want anything to do with her?

Not that it mattered. The Queen had agreed to two of the things she'd asked for, and of course they'd need to wait for the DNA test results before they could agree on the lavender and the wording on Louis' grave. 'He wants me to do the test in Charlmoux. Apparently it takes three days to get the results.'

'When does he want you to go? I'm sure Vicky will be flexible with you at the Heritage Centre, given the number of times you've worked silly hours to meet a deadline for her, and Sam and Milly can help with your clients at the studio,' Veronica said.

'I'm guessing they'll want the test done sooner rather than later,' Louisa said. 'Before the media gets a chance to find out. Excuse me, I'll just make a couple of calls.'

She contacted her cousins first, sending them a group message to explain she needed to take a confidential trip to do with her dad's family, and asking if they'd be able to help with her clients.

Sam replied instantly.

Course we can. Any time. This trip—do you want one of us to go with you? Or we can ask our dads to go with you if you need backup? Or Nan?

Her cousins or her uncles. They'd have her back. Her whole family would. And not just because she was the baby of the family: they all looked out for each other. Louisa blinked back the sudden tears.

Thanks, but I'll be fine.

Milly chipped in.

You can change your mind any time. We'll be there. And if you need to go on Monday then do it. We've got your back.

She messaged back.

Thanks. Love you lots. xx

Although it was strictly gone office hours, Louisa knew her boss often worked late, so she tried Vicky's number. It felt cheeky to ask for time off at short notice, especially as she'd already arranged to go in early and leave early the next day, but to her relief Vicky was happy to be flexible about the time Louisa needed.

'That's all sorted, then,' she said. 'Sébastien Moreau wants to discuss it tomorrow evening, but…' She wrinkled her nose. 'I'm not missing *Swan Lake* with you just for him, Nan. I've been looking forward to that.'

'You don't have to miss the ballet, love,' Veronica said. 'But you told me earlier that he'd never been to the ballet, so why don't you suggest he goes with you, instead of me? Then he can see for himself. It might help him understand a bit more about Louis and your mum.'

'But it's not fair to make you miss out.'

'I've seen *Swan Lake* plenty of times over the years. And we can always get tickets to go together, later in the run.' Veronica smiled. 'We can still have dinner together beforehand, like we planned. Rico won't mind putting in an extra chair at our table. Remember, your granddad and I knew Louis. We might be able to answer questions.'

'And ask some yourself?' Louisa smiled at her grandmother. 'All right. I'll ask him, Nan.'

She sent Sébastien a quick text.

Checked with my cousins and my boss. Can have time off next week. Does that work for you? LG

A few minutes later, he texted back.

Probably quicker to discuss than send screeds of texts. Are you busy now, or when's a good time to call you? Thanks, SM

She called him. 'I assumed from your message that now works for you?' she checked when he answered.

'Yes. Thank you for calling. Your timescale works for me. For the test, you'll need your birth certificate, one official form of photo ID and two passport-type photographs that the person collecting the sample can endorse as a true likeness of you.'

He was polite, but businesslike and to the point. For a moment, she wondered what he'd be like when he was all rumpled and passionate, so carried away that he forgot about formality. Every nerve-end tingled at the idea; but then she shook herself. This was already complicated enough. She needed to be businesslike, too. 'I've got a couple of spare photos from when I updated my ID card last year for the Heritage Centre,' she said, 'so I can do all that.'

'Excellent. Pierre—my security detail—and I will

pick you up from the Heritage Centre on Friday evening, when you finish work. We'll charter a flight to
Charlmoux from London City Airport.'

She hadn't quite expected that. Then again, Sébastien was the heir to the kingdom, so of course he'd have
access to a private plane rather than catch a scheduled
flight. 'All right. Do I need a visa or anything?'

'Just your passport—and that's more for the DNA
test. We'll fly you out and back on a chartered flight.'

'Thank you.'

'And perhaps,' he said, 'we could discuss things a
bit more over dinner, tomorrow evening. If you're not
comfortable coming to my hotel, I'm happy to book
somewhere else.'

'Actually,' she said, 'I already have a dinner reserva-
tion tomorrow, with my grandparents.' She took a deep
breath. 'I have tickets for *Swan Lake*. I was going with
Nan but, as you've never been to the ballet, we thought
perhaps you'd like to have dinner with us first, and then
come with me to the show. And you'll get the chance to
ask them anything you want about my parents.'

There was silence on the other end.

'Mr Moreau?'

'Perhaps, as we might have to work together for a
while, we could use first names?' he suggested.

'All right… Sébastien.' Weird. Why were her lips
suddenly tingling when she said his name?

'Thank you, Louisa.'

Her name sounded very different, the way he said
it, with that very slight French accent. And the tingling
in her lips increased. Weirder and weirder. She'd never
reacted to anyone like this before. They barely knew
each other. And yet…

'And I accept your kind offer,' he said. 'Except I

will pay for the tickets and for dinner. That's non-ne-gotiable.'

'You can argue that one with Nan,' she said. 'But I don't rate your chances.'

There was a hint of amusement in his voice when he asked, 'Are you trying to tell me your maternal grand-mother is scarier than your paternal grandfather?'

'She can hold her own,' Louisa said. 'Oh, she's ask-ing me to check that you like Italian food.'

'I like Italian food very much,' he said.

'Good, because we always go to Rico's before a show. Nan and Granddad have been going there for ever.' She paused. 'Um…would your security guy like to join us?'

'For dinner? He'd usually stand guard near the exit and he'll wait in the foyer during the ballet,' he said.

'He can join us for dinner, at least. We'll sort out a bigger table. I'll text you the address and time.'

'Thank you. What's the dress code?'

'My family's been involved with the stage for years and we always dress up, out of respect for the perform-ers,' she said. 'So it's up to you. A suit is fine. Or if you want to dress down, that's fine, too.' Not that she could imagine Sébastien Moreau wearing jeans. Though, now she'd thought it, a picture slid into her head that made her feel hot all over. Sébastien, in faded jeans and bare feet, walking hand in hand with her along a beach, the sea swishing over their toes…

'Louisa?'

Oh, help. 'Sorry. I missed what you just said.' And she certainly wasn't explaining why. Fantasising about him was just going to complicate a situation that was already like a piece of metallic thread that had tied it-self into unmanageable knots. She needed to get a grip.

'I said I'll wait for your text and I'll see you tomorrow, Louisa,' he repeated.

'All right. See you tomorrow.'

Once she'd changed the arrangements at Rico's and told her grandmother what was happening, Louisa headed for home. Although she'd planned to do some work that evening, to catch up with what she hadn't done during the afternoon, her head wasn't in the right place; she didn't want to make a mistake and ruin the dress while she was distracted. Instead, she spent a while researching Charlmoux. It was still hard to get her head round the idea that she could be the next in line to rule a country.

Sébastien had already told her that the country lay between Italy and France, bordering the Mediterranean Sea. When she looked at the articles online, they told her that the lavender fields apparently rivalled those just a few miles away in Provence. There were pictures of wide sandy beaches with turquoise seas that reminded her of that crazy moment when she'd fantasised about Sébastien. She shook herself and scrolled on through photos of gorgeous countryside and ancient castles that made her itch to explore them and look at the textiles inside. Charlmoux looked like the sort of place where she'd love to go for a holiday—but there was a huge difference between going somewhere for a few days' break, and going to live there permanently, just as there was a huge difference between being a project manager and ruling a country.

Although Sébastien had said that the Queen had given her permission to visit Louis' grave and see the family photographs, she remembered now that he'd said nothing about the King. She had no idea whether she'd be met with chilly formality by the Queen, or even open dislike by the King. Would they see her father in her? Or did they blame her mother for her father's death? She'd need to quiz Sébastien much more closely on the subject.

The internet couldn't tell her much more about Sébastien himself. He rarely seemed to date; then again, as the heir to the throne, he'd probably have to be careful that his girlfriends didn't get the wrong idea. Or maybe he really was just a workaholic who focused on his duties rather than on his personal life. She could hardly criticise him there, given that she rarely dated, either. All her relationships had fizzled out after a few dates, because the men never lived up to her expectations. She wasn't prepared to settle for anything less than her mother had had with her father. True love. The sweep-you-off-your-feet and till-death-us-do-part kind.

The next day, Louisa managed to pretend that everything was just fine while she was at the Heritage Centre; concentrating on her work meant that she could push all the worries out of her head. But all the worries came back as she walked back to her flat from the Tube station. She had no doubt that the DNA test would prove the truth of her parentage; but what would happen then? Would the royal family of Charlmoux just let her walk away from a life she hadn't chosen and didn't want? Or would she end up hounded by the media, as Sébastien had hinted, and be forced to change her life completely, living hundreds of miles away from the people she loved most?

She shivered. There was still a way to go before she had to make that kind of choice. Tonight was all about giving Sébastien a different perspective. Showing him what Louis had seen in her mother.

She showered, brushed her hair and left it down, and changed into a turquoise shift dress, teaming it with a chunky necklace and mid-heel shoes. She met her grandparents at the station, as they'd arranged, and they headed for the little trattoria just off Drury Lane.

Sébastien was already there, seated at their table with a man who she assumed was his security detail. He smiled and lifted his hand in acknowledgement, and her heart gave a little skip.

She couldn't possibly follow in her mum's footsteps and fall for the heir to the throne of Charlmoux. Her life and Sébastien's were too far apart, so how could it work between them? He was handsome and he dressed beautifully, admittedly: but admiring his looks was as far as she could go. She needed to think of him as a model in a bridalwear catalogue. Keep him at a distance.

And yet her pulse was practically tap-dancing as she walked over to the table and he stood up. She'd never felt this fizzy sort of attraction to anyone before and it made her nervous. 'Mr Moreau—Sébastien,' she corrected herself quickly, 'I'd like to introduce you to my grandmother, Veronica Wilson, and my grandfather, Jack Wilson. Nan, Granddad, this is Sébastien Moreau, the heir to the throne of Charlmoux.'

'I'm delighted to meet you,' Sébastien said. He shook her grandfather's hand and kissed the back of her grandmother's hand. 'Mr and Mrs Wilson, Louisa, I'd like to introduce you to my bodyguard, Pierre,' he said.

'Call us Ronnie and Jack,' Jack said. 'We don't stand on ceremony.'

Once all the introductions had been made, they sat down, and somehow Louisa ended up sitting opposite Sébastien.

'Jack, Louisa tells me your family's been coming here for ever,' he said.

'Since it first opened,' Jack said, 'when I was building sets at the theatre down the road.'

'The Wardrobe Department used to come here, too,' Veronica added.

'So you both met through the theatre?' Sébastien asked.

Louisa couldn't fault his manners as he chatted with her grandparents about their work and their family, the arrival of the twin boys that had stopped them both touring and made them take jobs where they could share the care of the children, and then Catherine's arrival. Taking a back seat in the conversation meant she had a chance to study Sébastien. He was polite and showed interest without being overbearing; she would've said it was practised diplomacy, but for the fact that his smile genuinely reached his gorgeous dark eyes.

She also noticed just how unfairly long his eyelashes were. And she was pretty sure that his dark hair would curl when wet, if he let it grow a little longer. She could just imagine him, laughing as he ran hand in hand with her in the street through the rain, trying to protect her from the deluge with his jacket as she unlocked the door to her flat…

Oh, help. Where had *that* come from?

She was going to have to be really careful. Falling for Sébastien Moreau would be a huge mistake.

'Our Cathy loved coming backstage and looking at all the dresses—well, all the girls in the family did,' Veronica said. 'One day, one of the cast was having a fitting. She took Cathy onto the stage and taught her a couple of dance steps. Our Cathy took to it like a duck to water. She ended up joining the cast when they needed some kiddies as extras for the panto. I took her to tap and ballet lessons, and it was obvious right from the start that she had something special.' She blinked back a tear and smiled. 'Lit the stage up when she danced, our girl did.'

'Did you ever think about following your mother onto the stage, Louisa?' Sébastien asked.

Louisa was glad he hadn't caught her wool-gathering and fantasising about him—and even more glad that he'd asked a question she could answer easily. She shook her head. 'Obviously Mum taught me the basics of ballet, and I loved the music she played when I was tiny. I loved it when she used to dance for me, too, but I didn't love dancing enough to put in the kind of work you need to do to make a proper career out of it.' She smiled. 'I followed in Nan's footsteps instead. She used to make clothes for my dolls from the scraps from prom and wedding dresses. Just like she did for my cousins, Milly and Sam. She made our clothes, too. We all fell in love with fabric and we get on well, so we joined Nan in the business.'

'Though our Louisa's always liked the antique stuff. She came with Cathy and me to the Victoria and Albert Museum when she was tiny, to see an exhibition of theatre costumes that included some of the ones I designed. She fell in love with the dresses, the shoes and the fans,' Veronica said. 'And even now, if we go there, she makes a beeline for the costume section and I have to practically prise her away from the displays.'

That tied in with what Séb had seen on Louisa's social media, and he stored that away for future reference. He'd ask Pascal to check whether there were any special textile collections in the National Museum, or even in the palace itself, so he could at least show her something in Charlmoux that she'd enjoy.

'Lou tells me it'll be your first time at the ballet tonight,' Veronica said.

'It is, Ronnie,' Sébastien agreed. 'She says *Swan Lake* is one of the best ones to see, first.'

'That or *The Nutcracker*. You'll recognise a bit of the music,' Veronica said. 'Our Cathy was stunning as Odette and the Sugar Plum Fairy.'

Séb could see the warmth of love and affection in the older woman's smile as she looked at her granddaughter. Louisa clearly came from a really close family. And this reminded him of summer evenings and Sunday lunches with his own family: everyone talking and laughing, plenty of good food, everyone helping with the chores afterwards. For a moment, he felt a pang of homesickness. He hadn't seen enough of his family, recently, and that needed to change.

The Wilsons talked to him about Louis, too: and over the course of dinner he learned more about the Prince than he had in all the years he'd worked at the palace. The Louis they'd known had been sweet and kind and funny, deeply in love with Catherine, and from the sound of it would've make an excellent king because he had the personal touch rather than being super-formal and distant, the way his father was. A prince who'd learned to cook, under his wife's direction, and had thoroughly enjoyed making a roast dinner for his new in-laws. Even though his Yorkshire puddings had been a disaster, they'd all loved it because he'd made the effort. They'd loved *him*, because they'd obviously seen the man and not the Prince.

For a moment, it unsettled him. Since Elodie, Séb had rarely dated, concentrating on his job. He'd forgotten what it felt like for a woman to see him for who he really was. And what kind of woman would he be prepared to let behind the screens he'd learned to put up as part of his job?

Every nerve in his body screamed the answer: the woman who was sitting opposite him. The woman who'd clearly dressed up for tonight, to pay a compliment to the performers, but there wasn't the slightest bit of artifice about her. The woman who'd loosened her hair and it made him think of how it might look spread over his sofa before he kissed her...

His common sense warned him that he needed to back off. Now. This could get way, way too complicated. He couldn't let his heart get involved. This was about doing the best for his country. Doing the right thing. Making a difference. Emotions didn't come into it.

'So do you go to the theatre in Charlmoux?' Louisa asked.

He was glad that his job had taught him to be able to focus on questions, because he didn't want her to guess how much she distracted him. 'Not often,' he admitted.

'Because you don't like it or because you don't have time?' she asked.

'A bit of both,' he said, wanting to be honest.

'That's a shame. I go to the theatre on the first Friday of the month with my best friend,' Louisa said. 'We don't mind what we see—anything from drama to musicals to stand-up.' She grinned. 'Though I can't quite get her into opera.'

He blinked. 'You like opera?'

'Mainly because I love the costumes,' she said. 'I normally go with Nan. Mozart's our favourite. He has a few good tunes.'

He could tell that she was teasing him, and he found

himself really liking this side of Louisa Gallet. That fun, carefree grin made him feel as if the sun had just come out.

Again, the solution to all the problems slid into his mind.

He could suggest it, but he had a feeling he'd meet with a flat refusal because she didn't know him. Somehow, over the next few days, he needed to get to know her better. Find out what they had in common. Make friends with her. And *then* he'd suggest it as a sensible option. Louisa Gallet was a sensible woman, so surely she'd see it was the best solution—for Charlmoux, as well as for both of them?

'What do you do at the Heritage Centre?' he asked.

'Restoration—and that could be anything from dresses to upholstery to wall-hangings,' she said. 'At the moment, I'm working on some bed- hangings that were once a canopy of state.'

'Canopy of state?' he asked.

She took a pad and paper out of her bag and deftly sketched a chair on a dais with curtains above it. 'Like this,' she said. 'Any British ambassador representing the King abroad was given a canopy and a chair of state, among other things. The bed-hangings I'm working on were made from a red and gold silk state canopy from George III's time. The canopy had been cut down to fit the bed, and I'm in charge of the project to clean and repair them.' She smiled. 'When they took the bed apart, you wouldn't *believe* how much dust was on top of the tester—that's the top bit of the bed.'

She glowed when she talked about her work, Séb thought. Clearly she loved what she did. How could it be fair for him to take her away from all this?

Then again, if she agreed to the plan that was rapidly forming in his head, she wouldn't have to leave it all. She could leave the day-to-day State things to him, and continue working with the fabric she loved; and he would get to rule Charlmoux in her name. The title wasn't important to him, but the chance to make Charlmoux a better place was.

The more he thought about it, the more he was convinced that his idea was the perfect solution, because it meant they'd both get what they wanted. He just needed to pick the right time to suggest it and show her that everyone would benefit.

Dinner was fabulous; the menu was on a chalk board, with only a couple of choices per course, because the chef cooked whatever took his fancy at the market in the morning. Bruschetta, gnocchi with sage butter, a *secondi* of salmon fillet wrapped in courgette ribbons and served with side dishes of tiny new potatoes and garlicky spinach, and the sweetest strawberries Séb had ever eaten in his life, served with vanilla ice cream.

'We need to skip coffee,' Louisa said, glancing at her watch, 'or we'll be late.'

'We'll have coffee at the bar in the theatre with you, Pierre,' Veronica said. 'Then you won't have to wait on your own all evening.'

'I'll get the bill,' Jack said.

'It's already sorted,' Séb said. He held Louisa's gaze for a moment when he explained, 'I gave them my credit card details before you arrived.'

Touché, she mouthed.

'Then, next time, dinner is on us,' Veronica said.

'Thank you. That would be very kind,' he said.

They walked down the street to the theatre together, and left Jack, Veronica and Pierre in the bar.

'I meant to tell you,' he said to Louisa as they took their seats, 'you look lovely tonight.'

She smiled at him, clearly surprised but pleased by the compliment. 'Thank you.'

'Is your dress a Louisa Gallet original?' he asked.

She nodded. 'I make most of my own clothes.'

'It's a lovely colour,' he said. 'It really suits you.'

'My favourite. I've always loved turquoise,' she said.

'Like the colour of the sea,' he said, surprising himself. He wasn't usually one for flowery language. What was it about Louisa Gallet that made him say and do things outside his comfort zone?

Then the lights dimmed and the curtain came up. Séb had expected to be a little bored, but he found himself spellbound by the music and movement. And if Catherine had been anything like her daughter, no wonder the Prince had seen beyond the graceful movements and beauty and fallen completely in love with her.

Not that Sébastien was starting to fall in love with Louisa Gallet. This was purely a business relationship. If they could be friends as well, that would make things easier; but the heir to the throne, whether that turned out to be Louisa or himself, couldn't put their duty aside for emotion. There was too much at stake.

At the interval, Louisa checked her phone. 'My grandparents have left,' she said, 'but do you want to go and have a drink at the bar with Pierre?'

'Not unless you do.'

'I'm quite happy sitting here, looking through the programme,' she said with a smile.

'I'll just check in with Pierre.' He tapped a quick message into his phone and was satisfied with the reply.

'So what do you think of the show so far?' she asked.

'It never occurred to me to go to a ballet before, but

I understand why you like it so much. The dancers are very good.'

'So you feel how trapped the Prince is?'

Yes. Being with Louisa and meeting her family had made him realise how constricted the royal world was. Though it had been his choice. He hadn't been born into it and had it forced onto him, the way Louis had. The Prince had clearly tried to change the conventions, but he hadn't had time to really make enough changes before he'd died.

Just like the Prince in the ballet.

He looked at her. 'The Prince has to get married to someone suitable, not the swan girl.'

'That's a tiny bit close to home,' she said, as if picking up on the thoughts in his head, 'as is the fact that there isn't a happy ending.'

'Just as well I read the plot before I came here to-night,' he said dryly.

'That wasn't a real spoiler.' She rolled her eyes. 'Everyone knows *Swan Lake* is a tragedy.'

Louis and Catherine had been a tragedy, too.

She seemed to realise that they were heading towards very shaky ground, because she said lightly, 'I'm just warning you now, I always cry at the end of the performance.'

'I'll make sure I pass you a handkerchief,' he said.

'Monogrammed and starched?'

Was that what she thought of him? Then again, he'd moved a long way from his childhood on the farm. Even from his time at university. Perhaps he *had* become monogrammed and starched, over the years, to fit in with the protocols that surrounded him.

'Just plain,' he said, feeling suddenly antsy. He was starting to see the world in a different way, when he was with Louisa, and he wasn't sure that he was completely happy with what he saw. Had he wasted nearly a third of his life, trying to fit in to court circles when he was really still a bit of a fish out of water? But he didn't belong back at the farm any more, either. Or at university. If he wasn't at the palace, he had no idea where he belonged.

Louisa flicked through the programme, seemingly unaware of the unexpected turmoil in his head, and pointed out bits that she thought he'd find interesting. But he found himself being distracted—by her. Her hair looked so soft and silky. How would it feel, threaded through his fingers? And her arm was resting against his, because the seats were narrow. He could feel the warmth of her skin through his shirt. It would be oh, so easy to move his hand and twine his fingers with hers…

He'd managed to get the unfamiliar feelings back under control by the time the lights went down again, but he was shocked to find himself so moved by the performance. Just as she'd warned him, Louisa was wiping at her eyes; he passed her his handkerchief. Not starched or monogrammed. Just as he wasn't starched…was he?

No, because the skin on his fingers felt as if it were fizzing when it touched hers.

'That was wonderful,' she said, dabbing at her eyes. 'I'll wash this and give it back to you tomorrow.'

'It's fine. I'll put it in with the rest of my laundry.'

'I insist,' she said.

He decided to pick his battles carefully. 'OK. But I insist on giving you a lift back.'

'I've lived in London my entire life. I feel perfectly safe on the Tube,' she said.

'My mother probably shares a lot of views with your

grandmother,' he said. 'They'd both skin me for not seeing you home safely. So no arguments, OK?'

Louisa knew he had a point. 'All right,' she said. 'And
thank you.'

Pierre was waiting for them in the foyer, and escorted
them to the waiting car. She didn't think anything of the
flash she half saw as she got into the car; plenty of people took group photographs on their phone after a show.

Sébastien was quiet in the car, and Pierre didn't seem
inclined to talk either. She gave the driver her address;
when he pulled up outside, she looked at Sébastien.
'Would you both like to come in for coffee?'

'Thank you, but I have work to do,' Sébastien said.

At this time of night?

Then again, he'd probably had meetings all day. He
would hardly have come to London just to see her, and
then waited around for a couple of days while she came
to a decision. He could've done this whole thing over
the phone. 'Well, thank you for the lift home,' she said.

'No problem. We'll collect you tomorrow at five,'
he said.

She remembered then what she'd meant to ask him
earlier. 'What's the dress code? Do I need a ballgown
or anything?'

'Business dress is fine,' he said. 'Though bring
something casual, because we'll go incognito when I
show you round.'

'All right. I'll see you tomorrow.' She tried out some
of the schoolgirl French she'd been trying to remember.
'Bonne nuit, Sébastien et Pierre.'

Sébastien looked surprised, before blanking his expression and giving a courtly inclination of his head.
'Bonsoir, mademoiselle.'

Had she used the wrong word? Most of the French she could remember was from her mother's use of ballet terms. She'd grill Sébastien tomorrow to make sure she used the right terms to the King and Queen, if she actually ended up meeting them.

Back in her flat, she put her dress and his handkerchief in the washing machine on a quick cycle so they'd be dry for tomorrow and she could take the dress with her to Charlmoux, then chose the rest of her clothes for her trip carefully and hung them up so she'd be able to pack quickly in the morning. She set her alarm for half an hour earlier than usual, filled with a mixture of trepidation and excitement. Tomorrow, she'd be seeing her father's country for the first time. Visiting his grave and paying respects on behalf of her mother as well as herself. Maybe she'd meet the family who'd had nothing to do with her for a generation.

Was she doing the right thing? Or would it be more sensible to call the whole thing off? The only people she'd know in Charlmoux would be Sébastien and Pierre. Although Sébastien had been perfectly pleasant to her, the fact remained that her existence and the results of the DNA test were likely to mean he'd lose the job he'd spent almost a decade training for.

If she managed to stay on good terms with him, there was a chance he'd help them both out of this mess by sorting out an Act of Parliament: one which meant she could renounce her claim to the throne and he could rule as he'd planned. And then she could come back to London and life would carry on as usual.

But.

There was that weird tingling business. The way she felt more aware of him than she had of any of her previous boyfriends. There was something about Sébastien that drew her: his quietness, the way he kept everything so private. She'd worked out that he was a man of honour. A man who clearly cared about people close to him. A man who'd given up his freedom of choice so he could change his country for the better. But who was he, underneath all those layers? He intrigued her. What made him tick? How could she persuade him to open up to her?

The questions spun round and round in her head, and she still had no answers by the time she finally fell asleep.

CHAPTER FOUR

THE FOLLOWING DAY, Louisa left the Heritage Centre at five; Sébastien had texted her to arrange meeting her in the car park with Pierre. Just as he'd said, the sleek, anonymous grey car was waiting for them and drove them to the airport.

She couldn't help feeling slightly nervous about this. The DNA test was being done for the benefit of his country, not hers, and she had no idea what kind of reception she'd have in Charlmoux. Hostile? Neutral? Welcoming? Did anyone know about her, other than the royal family?

She was about to ask him more when his phone pinged. He glanced at it and grimaced. 'I'm sorry, Louisa. I need to deal with something. I'm afraid it might take a while.'

State business, she assumed. One of the duties of the heir was clearly to be as economical with information as possible.

She fished in her work bag for the box with the embroidery she'd been working on earlier, and concentrated on that; being busy was much better for her peace of mind than sitting worrying. Just as well she'd brought a distraction with her, she thought, because Sébastien was busy on his laptop until they got to the airport.

'Sorry about that,' he said.

'It's fine,' she fibbed, though adrenalin prickled through her. Was she doing the right thing, going to Charlmoux?

Because it was a private flight, there was none of the queuing Louisa was used to at the airport. And the plane itself was nothing like the ones she'd travelled on before; the seats were wide and plush and comfortable, with a table between them. It was more like a board room than an aeroplane. The whole thing felt unreal.

'It should take us about two hours to get to Charlmoux,' Sébastien told her. 'We'll eat in about half an hour. I thought you might enjoy trying some traditional Charlmoux cuisine; it's very similar to Provençal cooking.'

'Thank you,' she said. 'That sounds good.'

'If you need to charge your phone or laptop, feel free.' He gestured to a bank of sockets.

She plugged in both. 'Sébastien, I know you're really busy and you probably need to catch up with paperwork or what have you, but would you have time to answer a few questions for me, please?'

'Of course,' he said. 'May I offer you a hot drink, or something cold?'

'Coffee would be wonderful, thanks,' she said.

He asked the stewardess for coffee; Pierre opened a newspaper very noisily, signalling that he considered their conversation to be private.

'So what did you want to know?' he asked.

'Obviously I've read up on Charlmoux, but there's a big difference between reading up on something and talking to someone who actually lives there.' She took a deep breath. 'What are the King and Queen really like?'

Séb didn't have a clue where to start answering. 'How do you mean?' he asked carefully.

'When they're off duty, are they anything like my mother's parents?'

'No,' he said. 'They're more formal. Though I suppose that goes with the territory.'

'Do you see much of them, outside state functions?'

'I have a daily briefing meeting with the King.' He could see from her expression that it sounded cold to her. Strange, even. 'If you mean do I socialise with them, it'd be like socialising with your boss.'

'Actually, we have team nights out at the Heritage Centre, and I like my boss very much. I'd enjoy going out to dinner or for a drink with her,' she said. 'But I take your point. Do you actually live at the palace?'

'I have an apartment in the palace. There are guest apartments there, too. You'll be staying in the one nearest to mine.' He gave her a small smile. 'So at least you'll have a familiar face close by.'

'Right.' She was silent for a moment, as if absorbing his replies. 'Apart from the King and Queen, is there anyone else at the palace who knew my father and could tell me anything about him?'

'Some of the senior staff, and some of the retired staff,' he said. 'I can ask the Queen for you if she'd mind you talking to them about him.'

'Oh. It didn't occur to me that protocol might get in the way.' She bit her lip, anxiety clear in her expression. 'Is there anything I need to know about protocol? Anything in particular I need to say or do?'

She'd be a guest of the royal family during her stay; but the King didn't want her there. 'I'd advise just be polite and be yourself.'

'Right.'

She looked slightly forlorn. 'I'll be with you when

you see the King and Queen,' he said, 'so I'll support you as much as I can. Do you speak much French?'

'I learned French at school. Though I'm rusty on everything except ballet terms.' Her smile faded. 'Will the King and Queen expect me to speak French?'

'No. They both speak very good English. But using a little bit of French might help break the ice.'

'What do I call them? *Votre Majesté?*'

'No. You address the King as *sire*—' he slowed his words and exaggerated the pronunciation for her slightly as *seer* '—and the Queen as *madame.*'

'*Madame?* That seems a bit plain.'

He shrugged. 'It is what it is.'

'Should I be addressing you as *sire*?'

He smiled. 'No. I'm not a king.' Yet.

'Prince, then,' she said.

'I'm not a prince, either,' he reminded her. 'Just plain Monsieur Moreau. But, if it helps, I would have addressed Louis as *Monseigneur.*'

'Is there any other etiquette I need to know?'

'Can you curtsey?' he asked.

She laughed, and how strange that it made his heart feel as if it had done a backflip.

'My mother taught me ballet,' she said. 'Of course I can curtsey.'

'You don't actually have to curtsey when you meet the King and Queen,' he said, 'but they'd see it as polite. Or you can shake their hand, but wait for them to extend a hand to you, first. Speak only after you're spoken to, and wait for them to sit or eat before you do.'

'Got it,' she said. 'They take the lead in everything.'

'If anyone else asked me how to behave in the presence of the King or Queen,' he said, 'I'd suggest avoiding personal questions.'

'Except the whole reason why I'm going is personal, so it can hardly be avoided,' she said. 'Is it rude to ask the heir to the throne personal questions?'

He smiled. 'You haven't breached any protocol with me. I'm happy to answer anything you ask—as far as I can, that is.'

She inclined her head in acknowledgement. 'Do the King and Queen want to meet me, or am I your guest?'

'You're my guest,' he said. 'But the Queen will see you this evening.'

He wasn't surprised that she picked up immediately on what he hadn't said. 'And the King won't?'

'He's nearly eighty, and he's not in the best of health,' Séb said. He wasn't breaking a confidence; this was all in the public domain.

'Will he use that as an excuse not to see me?' she asked.

'Possibly. Or he might not actually be well enough to see you. Don't take it personally,' he said.

She glanced at her clothes. 'We tend to dress down at the Heritage Centre. If I'd worn a business suit today, everyone would've asked awkward questions. But I do have business clothes in my case. Will I have time to change before I meet the Queen?'

'Yes.'

'Thank you.' She paused. 'What does the heir to the monarchy do?'

He knew what she was really asking. What would she be expected to do, if she was the heir? 'The heir needs to understand the political and the legal system to deputise for the monarch and ratify Acts of Parliament,' he said. 'There's a diplomatic element as well. I'm involved in trade negotiations—that's part of what

I've been doing in London, this week. And I'm the patron of several charities.'

'I assume you have advisors to help you?'

'I do, but if the decision stops with me then I make sure I'm very aware of all the ramifications,' he said. 'I guess it'd be like the way you and your cousins are your grandmother's representatives for different parts of the business.'

'She's pretty much retired and trusts us to get on with it. So, apart from meeting clients and designing the dress they want, we go to trade shows, negotiate with wholesalers, handle the social media and we're involved with trade associations,' she explained.

So she already had some of the skills she'd need as the heir. Which was a good thing.

'We've all got different strengths and we try to share things fairly between us in the business,' she finished. 'But I'm guessing you can't delegate anything from your job.'

'To some extent, I can,' he said. 'But mostly you do your duty with a smile and you don't count the hours you spend working. The job is your life, and your life is the job.'

'Do you mind that?'

No, but Elodie had. 'It's fine,' he said.

He answered more of her questions over dinner, about the country and its people.

'What do you do in your free time?' she asked.

'I don't exactly have a lot of free time.' Then he remembered he was trying to sell the job to her, so if she did become Queen she'd make him her consort. That meant selling himself, too. 'I've always been a bit of a workaholic.' That sounded bad, too. He was making a mess of this. Usually he was unruffled and sorted things out with the minimum of fuss. What was it about Louisa that made everything feel so upside down?

'What do you do to relax?' she asked.

'I walk in the palace gardens, and I swim,' he said. 'When I've got a problem I need untangling, swimming means I have to concentrate on the strokes and the breaths, so the problem goes into the back of my head and sorts itself out.'

She nodded. 'That's why I do embroidery. I know it's kind of linked to my job, but at the same time it isn't. I'm concentrating on the stitches and the pattern, so I don't have space in my head to worry.'

What made her worry? he wondered, surprised by the sudden surge of protectiveness he felt towards her.

'Where do you swim?' she asked.

'There's a pool and a gym in the palace compound,' he said. 'Though, if I get the chance, I like to swim in the sea.'

'I love the sea,' she said. 'Growing up in London, I didn't really get to the seaside much.'

'Maybe I can take you to the coast while we're waiting for the test results,' he said.

'I'd like that. Though I didn't pack a swimming costume.'

'I can arrange something for you,' he said.

'Thank you.'

That smile was genuine and sweet, and it made him want to throw caution to the winds, scoop her up and kiss her until they were both dizzy.

Which would be a huge, huge mistake.

He needed her to feel safe with him. To get to know him and relax with him. Because this wasn't about attraction; it was about making sure that Charlmoux would be in safe hands, with someone who'd make a difference.

Relax. That was what they'd been talking about. 'What do you do to relax?' he asked.

'I do a dance fitness class every Monday with my best friend, and I go to the theatre,' she said. 'And you probably gathered from Nan that I love museums. Put me in one with textiles, and I'll be happy for hours.'

Little by little, Séb was building up a picture of Louisa Gallet. The more he saw, the more he liked. The more he thought they might be compatible. The more he thought that marriage could be the best solution for both of them—and, more importantly, for Charlmoux.

He just needed to convince her.

Louisa changed into her favourite business suit and tamed her hair into a more formal updo. Wanting something of her mother close, she decided to add the pearls. Sébastien made no comment when she emerged, though his eyes narrowed slightly. Did he think wearing the pearls was a combative move? But asking him might open up a discussion she really didn't want to have. Not when she was already feeling nervous. Besides, he'd already told her to be herself. This was who she was: her mother's daughter.

It didn't take long to get from the airport to the palace. The nearer they got, the more Louisa's nerves jangled. Part of her would've liked to take Sébastien's hand, for comfort; but he was so self-possessed that she didn't think he'd understand why she wanted the support.

The ends of her fingers tingled with adrenalin as Pierre opened the car door for her. But she straightened her back and held her head high as she walked with Sébastien up the steps to the palace. The three-storeyed building was beautiful, the pale stone pierced by tall, narrow windows and topped by a grey slate roof; to her delight, there were turrets at the corners. In other circumstances, she would've loved visiting a place like this. It was bound to contain gorgeous examples of tapestry and needlepoint.

Once they'd walked through the huge front door, she saw a sweeping double staircase with a magnificent balustrade, and portraits that lined the walls. Her ancestors, she presumed, dressed in opulent robes and golden crowns. Yet she didn't feel any connection to them. She didn't belong here.

'What happens now?' she asked Sébastien.

'One of the footmen will take your luggage to your apartment,' he said. 'We have an audience with the Queen.' He indicated the staircase in front of them.

'Before we go—I wait for her to speak to me first, and then I say *bonjour*?'

'*Bonsoir*—it's a greeting as well as a farewell,' he said. 'Though it's fine if you'd prefer to use solely English when you speak with her.'

These were the people who'd been against her parents marrying and who hadn't even let her mother visit her father's grave. She owed them nothing.

On the other hand, the Queen had given Louisa permission to visit the grave. It was the first step in breaking the ice between them. Ice? More like permafrost, she thought. But if the Queen could make the effort, Louisa would try to do the same. *'Bonsoir,'* she said.

Sébastien's smile on hearing his language from her lips bolstered her no end.

'Come with me,' he said, and this time he tucked her hand into his elbow.

Her skin tingled where his fingers touched her

briefly, and she tried to damp it down. He was escorting her formally, as a stranger in this palace. Though she thought that this was also his way of trying to reassure her. And it worked, because with him by her side she felt as if she could cope with anything.

Was this how her mother had felt about her father?

She pushed the thought away. Not now. She was about to meet her grandmother for the very first time, and mooning over a gorgeous man she barely knew really wasn't a sensible idea.

He knocked on the door at the top of the stairs. 'This is the Queen's reception room,' he told her. 'It's known formally as the Cream Drawing Room.'

A footman in navy and gold livery came to the door and had a conversation with Sébastien in rapid French that Louisa couldn't follow.

'He's going to tell the Queen that we're here,' Sébastien said. 'Once I've introduced you, I'm going to leave the majority of the conversation to you and the Queen. I'm there to support you, not to take over. If you need my help, just look at me and widen your eyes, and I'll step in.'

'Thank you,' she said. He'd just made her feel much less antsy about the meeting. And she was glad that he wasn't the type who'd take over and ignore her views.

A few moments later, the footman opened the door fully and allowed them in.

Louisa could see instantly how the room had got its name: the walls were all painted cream and gold, with lots of pictures hanging in wide gilded frames. There was a huge mirror over the fireplace, reflecting the light from the tall window opposite and the enormous crystal and gold chandelier in the centre of the room, and a thick Aubusson rug sat on the polished oak floors.

The sofas and chairs were beautifully upholstered in gold and cream; there was a matching folding screen nearby, as well as a tapestry fireguard that made her itch to take a closer look.

But first she needed to meet the woman who sat on one of the sofas, wearing a plain cream dress with a matching edge-to-edge jacket. The Queen's make-up and coiffure were both immaculate, and she could've walked out of a Parisian high society fashion plate. Her back was straight, and she looked at least ten years younger than she really was. Her hands were resting loosely in her lap, as if she was completely at ease—which wasn't surprising, given how many years she must've lived in this place and how used she must be to meeting foreign dignitaries, Louisa thought, let alone ordinary people like her.

Sébastien gave a deep bow, though he said nothing.

Louisa was really glad she'd changed into her navy suit, though even that didn't feel quite formal enough in these surroundings. She remembered what Sébastien had said about curtseying, and sank into a curtsey.

Though, at the same time, this felt utterly wrong. This was her *grandmother*. Her father's mother. The only time she'd curtseyed to her mother's mother was when Veronica had come to watch a ballet class and Louisa had curtseyed to the audience along with the rest of her class. Veronica always greeted her with the warmest, warmest hug. A curtsey felt much too cold.

Louisa was relieved that etiquette demanded that she waited for the Queen to speak first, because right at that moment she didn't have a clue what to say.

'*Madame*, I'd like to present Louisa Gallet,' Sébastien said.

'Louisa.'

There was no emotion whatsoever on the Queen's

face. But Louisa thought she saw a tiny, tiny flicker in her eye, as if the Queen were blinking back a tear and putting on a brave face.

Maybe this was what it was like to be a royal: hiding your feelings all the time. Had that been part of Sébastien's training, too? Was that why he was so self-contained and starchy? What had he been like before he'd become the heir? What was his family like?

Though it was none of her business.

'Louisa, this is Her Majesty Queen Marguerite,' he said.

'Bonsoir, madame,' she said.

There was no change in the Queen's expression, but she spoke in rapid French. Louisa could barely pick out one word in ten. She dredged up her schoolgirl vocabulary when the Queen stopped speaking. *'Pardonnez-moi, madame.* I haven't spoken French since I was sixteen. I'm afraid I didn't follow most of what you said.' She'd tried to be polite, but it had backfired. Her only option now was honesty.

'Then we will speak in English,' Marguerite said, in perfect English. 'Please, take a seat.' She gestured to the sofa opposite hers.

Louisa did so, glad that Sébastien sat next to her.

'Did you have a pleasant journey to Charlmoux?'

'Oui, merci,' Louisa said, determined that she was going to wrestle *some* French words into her side of the conversation, to prove that she wasn't completely flummoxed by the situation.

'The King is indisposed, this evening,' Marguerite said.

Just as Sébastien had predicted: and he'd told her not to take it personally. She glanced at him, and his dark eyes held encouragement.

'I see, *madame.'* How different this was from the

way Veronica would've greeted a long-lost grandchild. Maybe the Queen was waiting for the official test results before she switched into grandmother mode; or maybe she'd always be stiff and remote.

The formality made Louisa feel more and more tense, even though she knew Sébastien had done his best beforehand to try to bridge the gap between them.

Maybe it was time to stop ignoring the big issue. Not looking at Sébastien, so she could pretend she had no idea that she was breaking protocol, she said, '*Merci, madame,* for your permission to visit my father's grave.' She was absolutely *not* going to call him Louis, as if he was a stranger. Regardless of the DNA test, she knew the truth. Louis was her father. 'And for allowing me to choose a photograph of my father. I brought some photographs for you, in return.'

Marguerite looked surprised. 'Thank you.' She paused. 'I believe you are to take the DNA test tomorrow morning.'

'*Oui, madame,*' Louisa said. 'But, if I may speak frankly. I think we both know what the results will show.'

'That Louis is your father,' Marguerite said very quietly.

Louisa hadn't expected the Queen to agree with her, and she was shocked into silence.

'I can see my son in you. Your eyes. You look like the photographs of your mother. You smile like her.'

Louisa noted the Queen's careful wording. *You look like the photographs.* 'You never met my mother?'

'No. I had no idea my son was even dating Catherine Wilson, let alone planning to marry her. Or that you existed. But, once I'd learned about your existence, I looked up your mother on the internet. There are videos of her performances.' There was the tiniest, tiniest movement of the Queen's hands. 'Catherine was very talented.'

The praise was genuine rather than polite, and it warmed Louisa. 'Yes, she was.'

'Had I known,' Marguerite said quietly, 'things would have been different.'

Known what? About her mother? About the wedding? About *her*? Louisa's eyes prickled and she blinked the tears away. 'You can't change the past.'

'But you can learn from it,' Marguerite said. 'All these years when I could have known you.' Her voice was filled with regret. 'I miss my son.'

'I'm sorry that I never knew him. My mum told me about him—obviously not that he was a prince, but that he was a good man. She loved him very much.'

'Perhaps we can talk about him tomorrow. I can tell you about Louis as a little boy, show you the family photographs.'

'I'd like that very much,' Louisa said. 'And I will give you copies of the photographs of him in London.'

'I look forward to that,' Marguerite said. 'And I would like to know more about you. More about your mother.' She looked at Louisa. 'Those were my mother's pearls. She gave them to Louis.'

Louisa had worn the pearls to give her courage. Was the Queen going to ask her to return them?

'I'm glad,' Marguerite said, 'that you wear them. Pearls need to be worn often, or they grow dull.'

Was this acceptance? Louisa could barely breathe.

The Queen stood up. 'But you've had a long journey, and I should let you rest.'

It hadn't been that long a journey. In other words, Louisa thought, the Queen needed a rest. Though it must be difficult, in your late seventies, years after your only child's death, suddenly discovering that you had a grandchild. All the regrets and the what-ifs must be swirling about inside the Queen's head. 'Thank you for meeting me,' Louisa said politely, standing up.

What happened now?

She glanced at Sébastien, who mouthed, *Curtsey*.

Except…that wasn't what she wanted.

They'd already broken protocol. Maybe it needed a little bit more breaking. She stepped forward, and put her arms round the Queen, hugging her the way she would've hugged Veronica.

There was the tiniest, tiniest resistance: and then Marguerite wrapped her arms round Louisa.

'*À demain*, Louisa. I will see you tomorrow,' Marguerite said.

It was a dismissal, but not the snooty one Louisa had expected before coming here. It was a promise that tomorrow they'd talk further. Learn to understand each other. '*À demain, madame,*' she said.

Sébastien tucked her hand through the crook of his elbow again—an old-fashioned gesture, but one that she really liked—and guided her to the door. 'I'll show you to your apartment,' he said when they'd left the room, and led her through a maze of corridors.

'Here you are,' he said, stopping outside a door. 'I'm literally just across the corridor.' He indicated the door opposite hers.

An apartment.

Where she'd be a stranger in a strange house—well, palace—and a strange land.

'Let me see you in,' he said gently, 'or you're welcome to come and have a drink in my apartment.'

'I…'

'Tell you what,' he said, 'I'll grab a bottle of wine

from my kitchen and come over. Would you prefer red or white?'

'What I'd really like, right now,' she admitted, 'is a cup of tea.'

'In which case, you'll already have supplies in your kitchen. Shall we?'

She swallowed hard and opened the door.

The sitting room was gorgeous; like the Queen's sitting room, the floors were polished oak and there was a thick rug. The Louis XIV chairs and sofa had gilt frames and were upholstered in blue velvet, and there was a table with a chair that she could use as a desk for her laptop or to work on the embroidery she'd brought with her.

The bathroom was sumptuous marble, the bedroom was all floral chintz with a four-poster bed, and the kitchen was compact but well fitted and very modern. As Sébastien had predicted, it was well stocked; there were four different kinds of tea in the cupboard, a range of soft drinks, and a bottle of white wine in the fridge along with milk and a lemon.

'I'll bring the tea through in a moment—if you'd like to join me?'

'Of course,' he said.

Boiling the kettle and preparing a pot of tea for two made her feel slightly more normal, and Louisa was glad that Sébastien hadn't pressed her to talk about what had just happened, because she hadn't quite processed it yet.

'The English answer to everything?' Sébastien asked with a wry smile when Louisa brought the tray containing a teapot, milk jug, sugar basin and two cups and saucers into the sitting room.

'Most of the time, it works,' she said. 'And thank you.'

'For what?'

'For giving me a bit of space, just now—and also for not leaving me completely on my own.'

'You have a lot to think about, so you need space; and I'm the only person you know here, even though we've known each other only for a couple of days, so of course I'm not going to abandon you,' he said gently.

Her smile made him feel as if she'd just turned the lights on full overhead. She poured the tea. 'Help yourself to milk and sugar,' she said.

'Thank you.' Milk and sugar weren't what he wanted. What he really wanted was…

No.

He needed to remember why she was here.

And that didn't include fantasising about how soft her mouth might feel against his. This weird pull towards her needed to stop. Now. Before it distracted him too much.

'Tomorrow,' he said, 'the plan is to do the DNA test first thing, before breakfast.'

'The lab will work over the weekend?'

'For this, yes. What time shall I call for you?'

'I…' She shook her head, looking slightly helpless. 'What time do you normally have breakfast on a Saturday?'

This time, he smiled. 'Early, so you tell me when would suit you.'

'How long does it take to do the test?'

'With all the admin, maybe a quarter of an hour,' he said. 'You're very welcome to have breakfast with me afterwards. Then we'll join Queen Marguerite to visit the cathedral before it opens to the public.'

He could see the longing in her face. Then again, he

knew how much she wanted to visit her father's grave, on her mother's behalf as well as her own. 'Seven-thirty?' she suggested.

'That's fine. Come over when you're ready. You'll need your passport, birth certificate and photographs.'

'They're all in a folder in my work bag.' She sipped her tea. 'You were right when you said the King wouldn't be there this evening.'

'Because he's not well. I also said not to take it personally,' he reminded her.

'What's actually wrong with him?'

It was public knowledge, so Séb knew he wasn't betraying a confidence. 'He has a heart condition.'

'How, when he doesn't have a heart?' she scoffed. 'I can't believe he kept so much from the Queen. That's terrible. Louis was her son. She had a right to know what was going on.'

'Palace diplomacy,' Séb said, even though privately he agreed with her.

'Dishonesty, more like. And you really want to be a king?' She shook her head. 'I certainly don't want to be Queen, not if that's the price. You're welcome to the throne.'

Which would have been music to his ears, but for the conversation he'd had with Pascal earlier that day. He set his cup and saucer back on the tray. 'It's not quite as simple as that.'

'You said you were good with words—with the law.' Her eyes narrowed slightly. 'Can't you pass an Act of Parliament so you can just circumvent me and carry on as before?'

'Technically, I could draft the wording for one.'

'Does that mean you won't actually do it?' she

asked. At his nod, she frowned at him. 'I don't understand. Why?'

'Because the bill preceding the Act wouldn't get through Parliament. Louis was very popular. It's one of the reasons why the King left it so long to organise an heir.' He'd planned to get to know Louisa better and give her the opportunity to know him better, before he made the suggestion. Doing it now might be rushing things. On the other hand, it might be a good idea to plant the idea in her head now. If he gave her a little time to think about it, he was sure she'd come to see the sense of it.

'There is a solution,' he said carefully. 'One that would allow me to rule, and you to do whatever you wish.'

'We already know that.' She rolled her eyes. 'You just have to pass an Act of Parliament.'

'Or there's a simpler, easier way,' he said.

'What?'

'You could marry me.'

CHAPTER FIVE

MARRY HIM?

Louisa stared at Sébastien. She couldn't possibly have heard him right. The man in the elegant suit seated opposite her on the royal sofa looked completely at his ease. As if he'd suggested a business arrangement, instead of what she regarded as something incredibly personal.

He hadn't even *asked* her to marry him. He'd just suggested it as a mutually beneficial arrangement. She'd never heard anything so cold-blooded in her entire life.

Unless, of course, this was a parallel universe. Or she was having a peculiar dream: one that felt real, but it couldn't possibly be because his suggestion was so out of left field.

Or he might have said something else entirely, and her subconscious had replaced it with something ridiculous, simply because—if she was honest with herself—she was more attracted to Sébastien Moreau than to anyone else she'd ever met.

'Did you just suggest that I should marry you?' she checked, trying to keep her voice as even and calm as possible.

He didn't look remotely perturbed. She didn't have the faintest clue what was going on in his head. He was completely inscrutable as he told her, 'As the heir to the throne, you'd need to marry for dynastic reasons. You couldn't just choose to marry whoever you like.'

But her father had. Prince Louis had married the woman he'd chosen—the woman he'd loved. Her mother. Was Sébastien trying to tell her that she wouldn't get that choice?

'That's outrageous,' she said.

'It's simply how things are,' Sébastien said. 'If you marry someone who's not used to this kind of life or not suited to it, believe me, you'll both be extremely unhappy.'

That wasn't true. Her parents had been blissfully happy in the short time they'd been together, and her mum hadn't been brought up in a posh family, let alone royal circles. 'No,' she said. 'When—*if*—I marry someone, it'll be because I love him, the way my mum and dad loved each other. The way my grandparents love each other. The way my cousins and my uncles love their partners.'

He spread his hands. 'I'm merely giving you an option to consider, Louisa.'

Louisa couldn't believe he could be so cool and calm and collected about it. This was the first time anyone had proposed to her: and, instead of the hearts and flowers and sparkles she'd always assumed went with a proposal of marriage, he'd offered her cold, hard reasons. He'd made it feel like an everyday business transaction instead of something special.

'No,' she said.

'You don't have to give me an answer now.'

'My answer will be the same tomorrow, and the next day, and the next,' she said. 'The only reason I'll ever get married is for love.'

That slight incline of the head told her how naive he thought she was. Well, tough. Instead of making ridiculous suggestions, maybe he could put that formidable intellect of his to better use and sort out the Act of Parliament that would release her from any obligation and clear his way to acceding the throne.

'As you wish,' he said, his expression completely unreadable. 'I'll give you some space. You know where I am if you need anything.'

After he'd closed the door behind him, Louisa stayed exactly where she was. Right at that moment, she felt like a fish out of water, miles away from anyone who loved her. She slid to the floor and drew her knees up, wrapping her arms round her legs. It had been a huge mistake to come here. She should've insisted on doing the DNA test in London.

On the other hand, tomorrow she would actually be able to visit her father's grave.

'Oh, Mum. I wish you were here,' she whispered. 'I wish I knew what to do.'

Even though Charlmoux time was an hour ahead of London, Louisa knew it was still too late to call her grandparents. She could call Sam and Milly, but she didn't want them to worry about her. She settled for sending them all a brief text, reassuring them that she was fine and making a joke about managing not to be thrown into the dungeons so far. Then she unpacked, showered, and set her alarm for the morning.

Although the bed was sumptuous, with comfortable pillows and the perfect mattress, Louisa couldn't sleep. The situation rolled round and round her head. She still couldn't believe that Sébastien had asked her to marry him, purely so he could rule the country in her stead. It was ridiculous. Impossibly cold. And to think she'd started to like him. To think she'd wondered what it would be like to kiss that beautiful mouth.

Tomorrow, she thought, was going to be awkward in the extreme.

The next morning, Louisa woke to her alarm. Her eyes were sore and her head was pounding from a night spent tossing and turning. A shower and washing her hair made her feel a bit better, though she could see in the mirror that her poor night's sleep really showed in the shadows under her eyes. Cross with herself, she used the lightest make-up possible and pulled her hair into a severe bun. Presumably this counted as a business meeting, she thought, and put on a dark grey business suit. Dressed, ready to face him and carrying the documentation she needed, she walked across the corridor to Sébastien's apartment at precisely seven-thirty.

Even though it was a Saturday, he was wearing a formal suit, so she knew she'd made the right call. But again she wondered whether he actually owned a pair of jeans and a T-shirt. Looking at him, she simply couldn't imagine him growing up on a farm, with muddy pawprints from the farm dogs on his jeans or hair from the farm cats smeared across his sweater. He was a smooth, urbane machine. Part of the palace.

She shook herself. 'Good morning.'

'Good morning. Did you sleep well?'

'Very,' she fibbed, not wanting to admit to just how much his proposal had rattled her. 'Is the doctor here?'

'No. We're meeting her in my office,' he said.

This time, he didn't take her arm as he shepherded her through the endless corridors; Louisa wasn't sure whether she felt more relieved or disappointed, and that in turn made her feel even antsier. How could she possibly want closer physical contact with someone who'd asked her to marry him as a business deal?

In his office, Sébastien introduced her to Pascal, his PA, and to the doctor who was conducting the test.

Louisa handed over the photographs and documentation, and the doctor signed the back of photographs to confirm they were a true likeness of the person whose documents she'd seen and whose DNA she was collecting. She also signed a form from the lab, stating that she'd seen the birth certificate and passport of Louisa Gallet.

The swab took seconds and was completely painless.

The doctor smiled at her. 'All done.' She sealed the swab in a container, which she placed in a sample bag and sealed it; in turn, the sample bag was placed in an envelope with the form. She sealed the envelope and signed along the join where the flap of the envelope met the back. Sébastien and Louisa added their signatures next to hers.

'The lab will be in touch with the results,' she said with a smile, and left.

'Is there anything you need, Mademoiselle Gallet?' Pascal asked, his tone kind.

'Thank you, but I'm fine,' she said.

'I've arranged that access you asked for, Séb,' Pascal said.

It was the first time Louisa had ever heard Sébastien called anything other than his full first name or the more formal 'Mr Moreau'. Was that what his family and friends called him? she wondered. Was he different with them—more relaxed and carefree, a Séb rather than a Sébastien?

'Thanks, Pascal. Can you text me the details, please?'

Sébastien asked. 'Louisa and I are with the Queen this morning.'

'Ah. Visiting the cathedral.' Pascal looked slightly awkward. 'I'm sorry that the circumstances of your visit are bittersweet, Mademoiselle Gallet. But I hope you enjoy your stay in our country as much as you can.'

'Thank you, *monsieur*,' she said.

She walked back to the apartment with Sébastien.

'I promised you breakfast,' he said. 'Just to reassure you, there are no strings.'

'Good, because my answer on *that* subject is still no,' she said, glad that he'd been the one to refer obliquely to his proposal.

His apartment seemed similar to hers, though she noticed that his sitting room had bookcases as well as comfortable sofas; she found herself wondering what he read. His kitchen was much larger, and there were what looked like children's drawings attached with magnets to the outside of his fridge. Obviously she couldn't be rude enough to go and inspect them, but it was a fair guess that they'd been drawn by younger family members. It was heartening to see that he was clearly as close to his family as she was to hers.

For just a moment, she could imagine him hefting a laughing toddler onto his shoulders, or sitting on the floor to play a game or read a story to a bunch of children who idolised him and hung on every word; it made her feel all gooey inside. Which, given his proposal, was dangerous. Marriage, for him, wasn't about love and family. It was about duty. That wasn't anywhere near enough for her.

'I thought we'd eat here,' he said, indicating the small table by the window that was already set for two. 'I usually eat breakfast here because it has an excellent view of the palace gardens, and it catches the sun in the morning. Have a seat and I'll make breakfast.'

'Don't you have someone to make breakfast for you?' she asked.

'For coffee and toast? Hardly,' he said. 'Anyway, I've always made my own breakfast. It grounds me for the day.'

Sébastien hadn't forgotten that he came from an ordinary background, then, and didn't expect to be waited on hand and foot. She liked that.

'But I can arrange for the palace kitchens to bring you an English breakfast, should you prefer,' he added. 'And I can make tea if you'd prefer that to coffee.'

'Coffee and toast is fine by me,' she said. Then her manners kicked in. 'Can I do anything to help?'

'No.' He gave her a brief, unexpected smile that made her heart do a backflip. 'It won't take me a second.'

He put bread in the toaster, placed butter and a dish of apricot jam on the table while the coffee brewed, then brought over the coffee, a plate of toast and a jug of hot milk. 'Help yourself. There's plenty more.'

It felt oddly intimate to be having breakfast with him in his kitchen. She couldn't even remember the last time she'd had breakfast on her own with a man who wasn't related to her. And again she thought of his suggestion: *You could marry me.*

No. Of course not. It was ridiculous.

And it was even more ridiculous that she suddenly felt shy with him.

Although Séb had planned not to mention his proposal, giving Louisa the space to think about it and mull it over in her own way, he could see that she looked awkward and miserable. He really couldn't stand by and let her suffer.

'Are you worried about this morning?' he asked, wondering if she'd be defensive and hide the truth.

'No. I think we broke the ice last night, and the Queen and I will come to some kind of an understanding,' she said.

'Are you worried about meeting the King?'

'Yes and no,' she said. 'I'm guessing that his health will be an excuse for him not to see me until the DNA results are back.'

'That's possible,' Séb admitted, 'but, as I said last night, he does have a problem with his heart. He's planning to step down at the end of the summer.'

Her gorgeous brown eyes widened. 'Is that why the DNA test had to be done as soon as possible?'

'Decisions need to be made,' he said. 'Once we know all the facts.'

'You mean, we need the test results,' she said. 'Just to be clear, I have no intention of ruling the country, and I have no intention of marrying you.'

'Is that what kept you awake, last night?' he asked.

She looked away. 'No.'

He knew she wasn't quite telling the truth. It made him feel guilty; yet, at the same time, it was a good sign. She'd been thinking about it. Thinking about him. Just as he'd been thinking about her. But now wasn't the time to push her about it. He needed her to feel comfortable with him; then maybe she'd be more inclined to look at his proposal more realistically instead of giving a knee-jerk refusal. 'It's only one of the options—one of the easier ones, I think, but you have choices.'

'Do I?'

She looked trapped, and it made him feel guilty. He

wanted her to feel more at ease. 'Yes. We'll make time to discuss them. But for now let's concentrate on this morning.'

'What's the dress code for today?' she asked.

'What you're wearing now is fine for this morning with the Queen,' he said. 'But, as I said back in London, we need to be incognito while I'm showing you round. I'd suggest changing into something more casual, so you look like a tourist.'

'I *am* a tourist,' she pointed out. 'What are you planning for this afternoon?'

'Something I hope you'll like,' he said. 'Pascal's been talking to a couple of the curators at the National Museum. They've arranged to let you see some things that aren't usually on show.'

She looked surprised, then pleased.

'It's not all bad in Charlmoux, you know,' he said.

She wrinkled her nose, and Séb was shocked to realised how cute he found it. How cute he found *her*. He reminded himself that he needed to concentrate on what was right for Charlmoux and not let himself get distracted.

'I looked up Charlmoux on the internet,' she said. 'I thought it was the kind of country I'd love to visit on holiday—to see the chateaux, walk on the beaches and visit all the museums in the capital.'

'You can at least see some of the museums and the palace while you're here,' he said, 'though I can't promise we'll have time to visit the beach or the lavender fields.'

'What sort of farm does your family have?' she asked, surprising him by switching to something personal.

'Mixed,' he said. 'My brother André deals with the

dairy side—we produce organic cheese—Jacques handles the wheat and barley, and Luc works with my best friend in the vineyard.'

'Do you ever feel left out?' she asked.

It was a question nobody ever asked him; and, in a way, he did feel left out. Though it had been his free choice to take the palace opportunity, so he had no grounds to complain about anything. 'We have regular video calls,' he said. 'They send me photos so I can see my nieces and nephews growing up, and I have a supply of drawings for the front of my fridge.'

'But you don't see them as often as you'd like to?'

No, but he wasn't going to admit it. 'Probably not as much as you see your family,' he said. He didn't want to think about his family and how much he'd neglected them for his job. He wanted to concentrate on sorting out the accession to the throne. 'More coffee?'

After breakfast, they met the Queen and her security detail and headed for the cathedral. The building was magnificent, with soaring architecture and beautiful stained glass. The family chapel was behind a locked grille, just as Veronica had described; but the gate was opened for her.

'We'll leave you alone for a while,' Marguerite said.

Louisa looked at the dark grey marble slab with its gold lettering. There was plenty of space to add the words she wanted. She'd brought a white silk rose with her, like the ones in her mother's wedding bouquet, and placed it on a corner of the slab. 'Hey, Dad. So I finally get to visit you,' she said. 'I'm glad I've met your mother. We've started to break the ice. Your father might be another matter, but I'll make the effort—if he'll let me.' She took a deep breath. 'I don't know if you were trying to escape the palace and join a normal family, or if you wanted to bring Mum back here to be your queen. She never talked about it to me and it's too late to ask her, now.' She paused. 'I'm really not sure I'm cut out to be a queen. I love what I do and I love working with my family. Even if you'd lived and you'd brought me up here, I think I would still have loved fabric and wanted to work with Nan.' And she might have had younger brothers or sisters who were much more suited to the role of ruler; she wouldn't have minded stepping aside for them.

She laid her hand over his name. 'I wish we'd had the chance to know each other, Dad. But maybe I'll get to know you more through your mum.'

The Queen.

Who was waiting for Louisa in the cathedral…with Sébastien. The man who'd suggested that she could marry him. Not 'should', but 'could'. Suggesting, rather than ordering. It still rankled that he'd said it. But Sébastien Moreau was the kind of person who thought deeply about things before he spoke. The kind of person it was worth listening to.

Just…marriage?

'I'm sticking to my decision, Dad,' she said softly. 'Doing what you did. Marrying for love, or not at all.'

She took a photograph of the grave for her grandmother, then headed out to where the Queen and Sébastien were sitting.

'Are you all right, Louisa?' Sébastien asked gently.

Although he hadn't touched her or even moved towards her, weirdly it felt as if he'd just given her a hug. Even more weirdly, she was tempted to walk into his arms, rest her head on his shoulder, and take strength from his nearness.

So not appropriate, given that he'd proposed a marriage of convenience.

She dragged her mind back to her present situation. 'I'm fine, thanks.' She turned to the Queen. 'Thank you for letting me see the grave and put a rose there.' Even if it was tidied away again by the cathedral staff in a few minutes' time, at least she'd been able to put the rose on his grave for her mum.

'I wish he'd had the chance to meet you,' Marguerite said. 'And I'm sorry your mother didn't...' Her words tailed off, but Louisa was pretty sure she knew what the Queen meant.

Breaking protocol, she took Marguerite's hand and squeezed it. 'I understand.'

Back at the palace, Sébastien excused himself to catch up on paperwork and Louisa thoroughly enjoyed spending the rest of the morning with her grandmother, looking through photographs of her father as a child and listening to Marguerite's stories. Though she also found herself wondering what Sébastien had been like as a child: had he been quiet and serious, as he was now? As the second of four boys, had he grown up in a big, noisy family full of laughter—the way she had, even though she was an only child?

Not that it was any of her business.

She showed the Queen photographs of herself as a small child and gave her copies of the wedding photographs.

'New York.' Marguerite looked at the photographs and took a deep breath. 'I always thought he'd marry here, in the cathedral where all the Princes of Charlmoux were christened and married. I thought I'd see him get married.'

'Nan always regretted not being able to make Mum's wedding dress,' Louisa said. 'She made the wedding dresses for all my aunts and cousins. And she'll definitely make mine.'

'So you have a young man back in London?'

'No.' Louisa smiled ruefully. 'Nobody's ever made me feel the way my dad made my mum feel. I'll know when I meet the right one.'

'Hmm,' the Queen said.

'It's all right,' Louisa reassured her. 'Sébastien will find a way to work this out so nothing will change here. He'll step up to the throne at the end of the summer, as planned, and I'll be back in London.'

'Maybe,' Marguerite said. 'The DNA test might change everything.'

Louisa shook her head. 'My father was a prince—though I still can't quite get my head round that. But I'm not a princess or a queen, and I belong in London. Though I hope,' she said, 'that you and I will stay in touch.'

'We will,' the Queen said warmly.

Marguerite persuaded Louisa to stay for lunch with her, and asked Sébastien to join them. 'Perhaps you could show Louisa round the palace, this afternoon,' she suggested.

'That's kind, but we have an appointment with the curators at the Museum of Charlmoux, *madame*,' Sébastien said. 'They're letting us see exhibits that aren't often on show that I think Louisa might be interested in—a wedding dress from the eighteenth century, and some things called *marquettes*.'

'Samplers,' Louisa said. 'Although they're decorative nowadays, back then they were functional. They taught girls their alphabet and how to embroider for their trousseau.' She smiled. 'You might regret this, Sébastien. I can talk for hours about fabric and needlecraft technique. You'll probably have to tell me to shut up.'

'Indeed,' he said dryly. But there was a flicker of amusement in his eyes. She realised that he was laughing with her rather than at her, and it warmed her.

Once they'd left the Queen, they both changed into casual clothes.

Seeing Sébastien Moreau in jeans for the first time made her catch her breath; he looked even more gorgeous than he did in a suit. For the first time, he looked accessible. *Touchable.* His plain blue T-shirt hinted at a perfect six-pack beneath; he'd teamed it with faded denims and plain black trainers.

'I didn't expect you to wear jeans,' she said. 'I didn't think you'd even own any.'

He smiled. 'The idea is to blend in with the rest of the tourists. And of course I have jeans. Do you really think I'd go grape-picking in a suit?'

'You go grape-picking?' she asked, surprised.

'The whole family joins in at harvest time,' he said. 'I always take a fortnight off to help.'

She could just imagine it: his family, working together, chattering and laughing, then eating together at a long table spread with a red-and-white-checked cloth in the evening. So very different from the starched, formal life at the palace.

But this was his choice—and she had no right to judge him, she reminded herself.

Pierre joined them, also in casual clothing, strolling just far enough away to give them privacy yet near enough to make sure that Sébastien was safe. Louisa didn't think she'd ever get used to the idea of having personal security.

The museum was a pale stone building with tall windows and a slate roof; next to the river, it looked very pretty indeed, and she took a few snaps to send to her family later. If he'd asked her beforehand about her idea of the perfect afternoon, it would've been this: in a museum, with a private viewing of historical textiles and talking to a curator who knew her subject inside-out. The eighteenth-century wedding dress, the *marquettes* and the Regency era shoes all fascinated her.

Louisa loved the fact that Sébastien had made the effort to find something she'd enjoy. He was quietly thoughtful, a quality she appreciated.

But then again, he'd also suggested a marriage of convenience. She still couldn't quite believe he'd done that, and she was cross with herself for letting it stick in her head. They'd known each other for less than a week. Marriage was completely out of the question.

Even if she did think he was gorgeous.

Even if he did pay attention to what she said.

Even if he did intrigue her.

He was really patient in the museum, translating when either Louisa or the curator got stuck; even though it clearly wasn't something that interested him, he didn't press them to rush and didn't seem to mind that their appointment overran by quite a big margin.

Once they'd finished at the museum, he bought them both iced coffees and showed her the pretty tourist spots round the city, everything from an iconic bridge with love locks clasped to it through to pretty squares, a gorgeous glass arcade, and the fountain outside the city hall.

Charlmoux was a beautiful country, but it was odd to think that her father had grown up here—that, had the accident not happened, she might have grown up here. Yet it didn't feel like home; it felt so very far away from London.

There had been no communication from the Queen, so Séb was pretty sure that there wouldn't be a summons to join the royal table for dinner. But that gave him the chance to show Louisa a side of the palace he liked, and maybe change her view of life as a royal. 'Perhaps you'd like to have dinner with me this evening, and then I can show you the palace gardens?'

'That would be nice.'

Polite mode. Well, he could change that. Surprise her. 'Good. We'll stop at the supermarket on the way back.'

She frowned. 'Don't you have to eat whatever the palace kitchens cook?'

'Only if it's a formal dinner and I'm attending,' he said. 'Otherwise, it's my choice. And, actually, cooking relaxes me.'

'Then I hope you'll let me help.'

Working with her would be a way of showing her that they could be a good team. 'Sure.' It had been a while since he'd shopped for himself—with his timetable, it was easier to have groceries delivered—and he was surprised by how much he enjoyed the domesticity of it. Back at his flat, between them they prepared Parmentier potatoes, salmon baked with a pesto crust, greens that he was going to wilt in garlic butter, and apple crumble made the way her grandmother had taught her, with cinnamon and oats.

'And a glass of wine while it's all cooking,' he said, taking a bottle of rosé from the fridge. 'This is from my family's vineyard. I hope you don't mind your rosé on the dry side.'

'Perfect for a summer evening,' she said.

He poured them both a glass and handed one to her, then raised his in a toast. 'Welcome to Charlmoux.'

'Thank you.' She took a sip. 'This is seriously nice.'

'Thank you. I'll pass your comments back to Luc.'

'He's your brother in charge of the vineyard?'

Séb nodded. 'He has twin girls who currently spend their days dressed as fairies, complete with wings and magic wands.'

She laughed. 'I remember going through that phase. Nan had this amazing shimmery material, all ice blue and silver. She made me the perfect dress and gauzy wings.'

He could imagine it. And all of a sudden he could see Louisa with her own daughter on her lap, reading fairy stories together. A daughter—*their* daughter—in a fairy dress, waving a magic wand...

He shook himself, and brought the conversation back to something much less dangerous for his peace of mind.

Dinner was perfect. Louisa insisted on sharing the washing up; her bare arm brushed accidentally against Séb's and his blood felt as if it was fizzing through his veins. He needed to be careful here. If he lost his head and gave in to the crazy impulse to wrap her in his arms and kiss her, he'd make a mess of this. Her time here had nothing to do with attraction; it was about doing the right thing for Charlmoux. As Louis' daughter, she was the rightful heir. Blocking her accession to the throne would be a huge miscarriage of justice.

'Come and see the gardens,' he said.

They walked together in the dappled evening sunlight. The rose garden was in full bloom, richly scented, and the herbaceous borders were a riot of colour and shapes.

'This is gorgeous,' she said. 'Is it open to the public?'

'No,' he said, 'but that might be a consideration for the future.'

'Beauty like this needs to be shared,' she said. 'Even

if it's only a couple of days a week. It's too lovely to be kept to just a few people.'

He liked the generosity of her spirit. 'You're right,' he agreed. The security team would raise a few objections, but they wouldn't be insurmountable. 'Is that what you'd do? Open it a couple of days a week?'

She nodded. 'Either with no admission charge, or a small one that would go to an appropriate charity. Granddad's involved with a scheme that helps disabled people visit gardens. He's talked a few people into opening their private gardens a couple of times a year to help. My cousins and I—and Nan and my aunts—bake the cakes for afternoon tea to raise more funds.'

Given how excellent her apple crumble had been, he wasn't surprised that she could bake. 'What's your speciality?' he asked.

'Lemon drizzle,' she said. 'I always used to make it with Nan's recipe, but when my best friend went vegan I found a good recipe with no eggs or dairy so she didn't miss out. We make sure there's a gluten-free option among the cakes, too, so everyone's included.'

The way she'd been brought up sounded very much like the way he'd been brought up. 'My mum always baked for school fundraisers,' he said. 'Madeleines and lemon tarts.' His mother would adore Louisa. Not that it should matter: he'd made it clear to his family that when he eventually got married it would be a dynastic match, not for love. To someone who could cope with living in the public eye. Now, Séb was starting to wonder whether he'd made the right decision. He'd planned to marry for duty; Louisa was adamant that she'd only marry for the kind of love her parents had shared. But could there be a middle way?

The walled kitchen garden was next, and he showed

her the heritage varieties they'd gathered over the last five years.

'Granddad would love this,' she said. 'He adores his allotment. If he was here he'd make a beeline for the head gardener and ask if they could swap some seeds.'

'I can arrange that, if you know what he'd like,' he said.

'Can I take some photographs for him and talk to him about it?'

'Sure,' he said. 'Though obviously I'd ask you to bear in mind security issues.' He wasn't going to be heavy-handed about it; Louisa was bright enough to see the issues for herself.

'Of course. Maybe you'd like to check the photographs before I send them,' she said. 'Do you walk here much?'

'Every evening, if I'm here and there isn't a function,' he said. 'I like walking here first thing in the morning, too, when it's just me and the birds singing their heads off. It reminds me of home.' He hadn't intended to let that slip out. In future, he'd need to be more careful; this wasn't about opening his own heart.

'It's hard to believe we're in the middle of a huge city,' she said. 'This feels like the middle of the countryside.'

He took her through a side gate to the formal knot garden with the fountain at its centre.

'I love this,' she said. She bent to sniff the lavender, then glanced up at him and smiled. 'I might ask the Queen if I can take a cutting.'

Séb wondered if she had any idea just how beautiful she was. Then he caught his thoughts; this wasn't about attraction, it was about a sensible business arrangement. About joining forces with the woman who was the biological heir to the throne, so his last decade's work wasn't wasted and the country would be guided safely.

Living in a flat meant having no garden. Even Louisa's grandparents' garden, although full of flowers, was tiny; her grandfather grew all the veg at his allotment. Having a garden like this to walk through every day, winding down from work, must be utter bliss, she thought. The colours, the shapes, the birdsong, the splash of water in the fountain…just *bliss*.

Walking here with Sébastien, she could imagine this was their own private paradise: from the formal knot garden with its neat hedges of box and lavender, through to the lushness of the rose garden and then the bursts of colour in the borders.

It was incredibly romantic, filling all her senses.

Her hand accidentally brushed against his, and a tingle shot straight up her arm. It would be oh, so easy to let her fingers tangle with Sébastien's and walk hand in hand with him in the peace of the palace gardens. Maybe kiss him in one of the rose arbours…

But they weren't dating. They weren't falling in love with each other. Sébastien might be gorgeous, and thoughtful, and have all the qualities she'd want in a partner: but they weren't really on the same side. He'd suggested marriage as a business arrangement, and Louisa refused to marry for any reason other than love.

The tiny personal bits he'd let slip—about his nieces and his mother's baking—made her think that Sébastien was the kind of man she could fall in love with. But there was a crown in the way, and she needed to keep that in mind.

Once they were back in the corridor outside their apartments, she smiled at him. 'Thank you for today. I really enjoyed the museum. Showing me round must've put you very behind with your admin, so I won't take up any more of your time today.'

He gave a formal half-bow. 'I'm glad you enjoyed it. And you must be tired.'

They both knew she wasn't.

But she could see in his eyes that he, too, thought it would be safer to spend the rest of the evening apart—putting themselves out of reach of a temptation that would seriously complicate things.

'*À demain,*' she said.

'*À demain,*' he echoed. 'I'll see you for breakfast, and then we can plan what you'd like to do for the rest of the day.'

'All right. Would you mind just checking my photographs, first, to make sure there aren't any security issues?'

'Of course.' He took her phone and skimmed through the photos she'd taken of the garden. 'They're all fine.'

Back in her apartment, she sent texts to her family to show them the *marquettes* and the wedding dress, and the bits of the palace gardens she thought they'd love. Then she soaked in the bath and thought about Sébastien. He was still almost as much of an enigma now as he'd been the first day she'd met him in London. She knew a little about his family, and she knew he had integrity.

But did a man so schooled to duty have any room in his heart for love? Because, without love, there was no way she could consider marrying him.

CHAPTER SIX

ON SUNDAY MORNING, after breakfast, Sébastien showed Louisa round the palace.

'The Queen has requested that we have lunch with her,' he said, 'and maybe this afternoon I can drive you out to see some of the countryside. Maybe I can show you the lavender fields.'

'Thank you. I'd like that,' she said.

She was just taking a closer look at a wall-hanging in one of the large reception rooms when she heard Sébastien give a sharp intake of breath. 'Good morning, *sire*.'

Seer. There was only one person he could possibly be addressing. A person with a slow, measured tread interspersed by a tap.

Her grandfather.

Adrenalin shivered through her.

'*Madame* has given me permission to show Miss Gallet some of the rooms in the palace,' Sébastien continued. '*Sire*, may I present Miss Louisa Gallet?'

She turned round to face him, glad that Sébastien was standing right next to her.

'Miss Gallet,' the King said, his voice cool.

'Louisa, this is King Henri IV of Charlmoux.'

Curtsey. Louisa knew she ought to curtsey. But the

contempt in the King's expression made her fold her arms and glare straight back at him. *'Sire.'*

'The dancer's daughter,' the King mused, a sneer on his lip.

'Prima ballerina,' she corrected, just about managing to keep her voice cool and collected. How dare this man disparage her mother? 'A position which I'm sure you realise only comes through talent and a lot of hard work. My mother was amazing, both as a ballerina and as a person, and I'm very proud of her. I'm proud of where I come from.' But she couldn't help adding waspishly, 'I know you come from a privileged background, but surely you can appreciate the value of determination and effort? Or are you just as snobbish with Sébastien because he doesn't come from a background like yours?'

'Leave it there, Louisa,' Sébastien murmured to her. 'Confrontation isn't going to help.'

She knew that, and she would've managed to keep her temper under control had the King not curled his lip at her. 'It seems you are an insubordinate child.'

'Child?' She scoffed. 'You're almost a decade away from teenage me, and you're fifteen years away from the lippy twelve-year-old I once was.'

The King frowned. 'Lippy?'

'Insolente,' Sébastien translated.

'But then, I didn't know you existed,' she said. She lifted her chin. 'Whereas I rather think you knew about me.'

The King fixed her with a steely glare. She glared back, standing her ground; and the King was the first to look away.

Then she noticed that the hand leaning on the stick was trembling. She remembered what Sébastien had said about the King being ill. And maybe, just maybe, the King's confrontational manner was because he couldn't bear to admit to what he saw as weakness and anyone else would see as understandable: grief and loss.

She'd been at that place where you'd just lost the person you loved most in the world, and everything felt as if it had caved in on top of you.

Even though she was still angry about the way he'd behaved towards her mother, she could empathise with his loss. Having a fight with him now wasn't going to make a scrap of difference to the past. They needed to find a point of agreement rather than stoke the discord between them.

She could feel Sébastien move beside her; he was clearly about to try mediating, but she wanted to do this herself. She held up one hand as a signal to him.

Still looking at the King, she said, '*Sire*, it must be as hard for you and the Queen, losing your only child, as it was for my grandparents to lose their only daughter. As it was for me to lose the only parent I knew. And I'm sorry I didn't get the chance to know your son. Everything my mother and my grandparents told me about him, everything the Queen told me yesterday, makes me know I would have loved him. Just as I know he would have loved me.'

The King looked back at her; he didn't say a word, and she knew he was giving her the chance to put her side of things.

'I haven't come here to tarnish your son's memory, *sire*,' she said quietly. 'Far from it. I'm here to do the DNA test and to learn more about the side of my life I didn't know about before. And maybe it's a chance for you to learn more about the side of his life that you—' She stopped. The King *had* known about his son's marriage. And she wasn't prepared to pretend that the King had been left in the dark. She finished with the nearest she could get to a compromise. 'That you weren't as familiar with. I have given the Queen some photographs, and I'd be happy to answer any questions you might have.'

The King looked at her some more. Then he inclined his head. 'We will speak later.' With that he turned away and walked out of the room, leaning on his cane but keeping his back straight.

Louisa blew out a breath. 'That was…' She had no words to describe it.

'It could've been a lot worse,' Sébastien said. 'Shouting—'

'—doesn't make things better,' she cut in. 'I know. I'm sorry. I didn't mean to start a fight.'

'Sure you're really fifteen years away from being a lippy twelve-year-old?' His smile took the sting out of his words; and he was right. They did need to laugh about it and break the strain.

'I might've regressed a bit.' She rolled her eyes. 'Which is atrocious of me. I'm usually really good with Mumzillas.'

'Mumzillas?' He tilted his head to one side, his dark eyes holding hers.

'Difficult mothers of the bride—the sort who micro-manage and go over the top,' she said. 'I can normally talk them round. Perhaps I should try to see the King as a Mumzilla.' She spread her hands. 'A Kingzilla, maybe.'

Sébastien burst out laughing. 'Just don't ever tell him that's what you think of him.'

'Now I've said it, it's going to be very hard not to,' she said.

'What you said to him—that was kind,' Sébastien said.

'I was trying to empathise with him. It doesn't stop me being angry about his behaviour,' she said, 'but understanding is the first step to finding compromise. I'm not here to fight.'

'I'm glad to hear it,' he said dryly. 'So—on with the tour?'

'On with the tour,' she said. It was strange how relaxed she felt in Sébastien's company. As if she'd always known him. She felt *settled* when she was with him; and, considering they'd only known each other for a few days, that was strange.

At lunch, the King was notable by his absence, but Louisa chattered happily to the Queen about her visit to the museum and what she thought of the palace tapestries. She wasn't sure whether the Queen knew she'd clashed with the King or whether Marguerite was being tactful and not discussing it, but she was starting to really like her other grandmother.

Sébastien took her out to see the lavender fields after lunch.

'You're allowed to drive?' she asked, surprised, when he opened the front passenger door for her and then climbed in behind the wheel while Pierre sat in the back.

'Provided I have security with me, yes,' he said.

'Even when you visit your family?'

'Pierre's an honorary Moreau,' he said. 'He's getting very good at picking grapes; though he's not as good as me at backing up a tractor and trailer.'

She laughed. 'Right.'

The lavender fields were stunning against the bright blue Mediterranean sky, swathes of purple bordered by bright yellow cornfields and tall dark green cypress trees. Sébastien parked the car so they could walk along the edge of one of the fields, and Louisa took plenty of photographs to send home, knowing how much her grandparents would enjoy them. Her mother would've loved visiting here; Louisa could just imagine her mother dancing between the rows of lavender bushes while her father watched, smiling.

'OK?' Sébastien asked.

'Just thinking about my parents and imagining them here,' she said.

He took her hand and squeezed it briefly. 'I'm sorry. I didn't mean to make you sad.'

'I'm not sad, exactly.'

'Douce-amère,' he said. 'Bittersweet.'

'Yes. It's the things you didn't get a chance to do that you miss,' she said softly.

He didn't release her hand as they continued walking, and it made her feel cherished. She'd remember this moment for ever: walking in the warmth of the sun, with the scent of lavender surrounding them, birds singing, and Sébastien holding her hand.

Sébastien was the kind of man who noticed little things, and knew what to do to make things feel better. And he did it quietly, without making a fuss: she appreciated that. More than that, it made her think again about his proposal. He'd made it sound like a business deal; but holding someone's hand to comfort them wasn't businesslike. It was personal.

Was it the right solution to their dilemma?

Could he grow to love her? Were these weird feelings bubbling through her the beginning of falling in love with him?

She had no answers, and she wasn't ready to discuss it. But Sébastien was just there, holding her hand, not demanding or pushing. Just *there*. And, right at that moment, she was glad.

Séb had meant to hold Louisa's hand simply to give her a moment of comfort. But, for the life of him, he couldn't release her hand. Not when the lavender bloomed in front of them, scenting the air. Not when the birds were singing. Not when the sun kissed their skin.

He'd never felt like this before, and it worried him. He needed to keep a clear head to sort out the accession to the throne. But being with Louisa made him feel giddy. He needed to pay attention and focus on his duty.

Just as they got back to the car, Pascal called. Séb sighed at the news. 'Pierre, would you mind driving us back?'

'Of course,' the security detail said with a smile.

'What's happened?' Louisa asked, climbing into the back of the car with him.

He brought one of the press websites up on his phone and passed it to her so she could see the headline: *Who's That Girl?* The photograph was of them together after the ballet, and below that was another of them at the museum.

She blanched. 'Does that mean they'll find out who I am and start talking about the throne?'

'Apologies for sounding arrogant, but they're probably focused on me,' Sébastien said, 'and the story will be about whether you're a candidate for a future bride.' He sighed. 'They do this whenever they spot me with anyone female. It's one of the reasons I don't date very much, because it puts too much pressure on my girlfriend.' Pressure that had shattered his relationship with Elodie beyond any hope of repair.

'But I'm not your girlfriend,' she pointed out.

The air suddenly felt as tight as a coiled spring. She wasn't his girlfriend. *But what if...?*

'No,' he said, 'you're not. Don't worry. It'll die down.' He hoped. And he hoped these weird, unexpected feelings would die down, too. There was no place for feelings where the throne was concerned.

There was no summons from the King when they returned to the palace, and the Queen was conspicuous by her absence, too. Séb made a few enquiries. 'The King isn't well,' he told Louisa.

'Is it my fault?' she asked.

'No.' Although the tension earlier probably hadn't helped matters with the King's health, he wasn't going to dump that particular burden on her. 'I'm afraid you're stuck with me or your own company, this evening.'

'Do you need to work?'

'No.' Which wasn't strictly true, but he could catch up later. 'We could walk in the gardens again.'

'I'd like that,' she said.

Although Séb kept the conversation light between them, he was still thinking of how he'd felt in the lavender fields. He felt it here, too; he could imagine her barefoot on the lawn, teaching two children to throw a tennis ball for the dogs—just as his own mother had taught him.

Oh, help.

Fantasising about a future with Louisa wasn't a good idea. He didn't want her to feel forced into marrying him. Suddenly, he wanted her to want to be with him. And his plans for a marriage of convenience simply imploded.

Clearly the media had been doing some digging overnight, because Monday's newspapers had a new headline—*Our Secret Princess!*—and she learned from Sébastien that the staff at the palace press office were kept busy firefighting.

'Can I leave you to your own devices?' Sébastien

asked. 'You're welcome to sit in my office with a book or what have you, but there are going to be a lot of phone calls.'

'All in French, using vocab I didn't have to start with, and at a speed where I can't pick out the words,' she said. 'I think I'd rather stay here in the quiet and sew.'

'All right. If there's anything you need, text me,' he said.

Louisa lost herself in her embroidery, but late that morning there was a knock on her door. When she answered, it was one of the liveried footmen; he spoke excellent English which put her French to shame. 'Mademoiselle Gallet, *madame* requests your company. Would you come with me?'

She left her sewing where it was and followed him to the Queen's drawing room. He had a rapid conversation with the liveried footman at the door, who announced her. But when she walked in, she discovered the King and Sébastien waiting with the Queen.

'Thank you for coming, Louisa,' Marguerite said. 'Please sit down.'

Heart thumping, Louisa took a seat on the sofa next to Sébastien, opposite the King and Queen. She caught Sébastien's eye and he mouthed something at her; it took her a moment to work out that it was *Kingzilla*. She managed to stop herself bursting into laughter, but he'd made her relax in the best possible way.

'The lab results are back,' Sébastien said.

'Already?' She frowned. 'I thought you said it would take three days?'

'They've been working intensely to speed things up a bit,' he said. 'Which is just as well, given the press at the moment.'

'And?' For pity's sake, this wasn't like some televised

awards do where the presenter had been briefed to give a massive dramatic pause before announcing the winner. She needed to know the truth. *Now.*

'There are enough points of similarity between your test and those of *madame* and *sire* to say with certainty that you are Louis' daughter.'

She glanced at the King, who had gone puce but was silent.

Unexpectedly, Marguerite stood up and walked over to her. 'I knew when I met you on Friday that you were my granddaughter. Now we have the scientific proof.'

Louisa stood up and hugged her.

'And now I can welcome you to Charlmoux properly, *ma petite-fille.*'

'Isn't that "little girl"?' Louisa asked.

'*Fille* is daughter, *petite-fille* is granddaughter,' Marguerite explained. 'And maybe one day you'll come to call me *mémère.*'

'I assume that's French for "grandma"?'

Marguerite nodded. 'Or *mémé*, for a pet name, but I know I need to earn that.' She hugged Louisa again. 'I am so glad. I miss your father very much and now I will get to see him again in you.' She glanced at the King. 'And when Henri steps down at the end of the summer, you will be Queen.'

'Forgive me for being blunt, but I'm *not* a queen,' Louisa said. 'I know what I've read about Charlmoux and what Sébastien has told me, but I'm English. My life is in London—my family, my friends, my job. I'm not pushing you away, and I'm very glad to have my father's family as part of my life, but there's no way I can be Queen of Charlmoux. Sébastien is the heir. There's the Act of Parliament in place.'

'That's superseded by your existence,' Marguerite said. 'Isn't it, Sébastien?'

'I think,' Sébastien said, 'I need to take Louisa somewhere out of the way of the press until we're absolutely clear about the situation.'

'Where will you take her? To your family?' the Queen asked.

'I was thinking perhaps the summer palace,' Sébastien said, 'but obviously that would be with your permission and provided schedules allow.'

'That's a good idea. I'll get Emil onto it and he can move anything necessary,' Marguerite said.

'Who's Emil?' Louisa asked.

'The King's PA, like Pascal is mine,' Sébastien explained.

'Do I get any say in this?' Louisa asked. 'My vote would be to put me on a plane back to London.'

'And abandon you to the media?' Séb asked. 'No. Being doorstepped can feel overwhelming. We need to protect you, work out what we'll say to the press, and look at what additional skills you need.'

Louisa looked at the King, who had been silent throughout and clearly wasn't happy about the results of the DNA test at all. 'I don't think you would like me to be Queen, either, *sire*. Which puts us on the same side.'

'It's a shambles,' he said, shaking his head. 'You can't stay here, because the press will be at the gates. And you can't go back to London, because they'll hound you. Sébastien is right.' He pursed his lips. 'Go to the summer palace.'

'But won't the press follow us there?'

'The press are very used to anonymous cars with darkened windows coming and going from the palace,' Sébastien said. 'They'll assume that I'm going somewhere, or that we're sending a car to pick someone up for a meeting here. They won't know you're in the car, and we won't be tailed. Pierre will act as your security detail as well as mine. If you pack your things now, we'll leave before lunch. Anything else you need, we can order on the way.'

'But—'

'No buts, *ma petite-fille*,' Marguerite said. 'We'll look after you.'

'Don't worry about work back in London,' Sébastien said. 'You told me last week that you could make any time this week—your cousins are handling your clients at the bridal workshop, and your boss gave you time off from the Heritage Centre. We should have this all sorted by the end of the week.'

That long? she thought, dismayed.

'Bridal workshop,' the King muttered, and rolled his eyes.

Louisa narrowed her eyes at him. 'I'm very good at my job, as you'd know if you'd actually bothered to take an interest.'

'Henri, stop it,' Marguerite said firmly. 'And, Louisa, just because your grandfather snipes at you, it doesn't mean you have to snipe back. Be the better person.'

Louisa had never seen a king being told off before—or been told off herself by a queen. And she knew that Marguerite was right. This was exactly how Veronica would've handled the same kind of situation if Jack had clashed with any of his children or grandchildren. 'Sorry, *madame*,' she said. At Marguerite's piercing gaze, she added, 'I apologise, *sire*.'

'Henri?' Marguerite looked at the King.

'Pardon,' he muttered, then rolled his eyes and added, 'Louisa.'

'*Bien.*' Marguerite gave a sharp nod. 'Now, Sébastien. You were saying?'

'Louisa,' he continued, 'you can stay for another week, if need be. That will give us enough time to work out how we're going to handle the situation and for me to assess what skills you have already and what I need to teach you.'

'But I don't want to be qu...' Her voice tailed off as she registered the grimness of his expression.

'It isn't a matter of choice any more, I'm afraid,' he said.

'If the King can stand down, why can't I?' she asked. 'Surely now we've proved who I am, I can renounce the crown.'

'I'm working on it,' he said, 'but we need to be prepared for all eventualities.'

All eventualities. Did that include marrying him? If he raised the issue now, in front of the King and Queen...

To her relief, instead he asked, 'How long will it take you to pack?'

'Ten minutes,' Louisa said.

'Good organisation skills. That's an excellent start,' he said. 'I'll show you back to your apartment.'

By the time she'd packed and knocked on his apartment door, he'd packed, too. They returned to the drawing room so she could say goodbye to the Queen.

'Stay in touch, *ma petite*,' Marguerite said.

'*Oui, madame.*'

Louisa was about to curtsey when Marguerite added, 'And don't you dare curtsey to me. You're my granddaughter.'

Louisa smiled and gave her a hug instead.

'You curtsey to me. I'm the King,' Henri said, his chin jutting out obstinately.

'Yes, you are,' Louisa said. 'But you're also my grandfather. Tell me, *sire*, do you plan on being the same kind of grandparent that you were a father-in-law?'

'*Insolente,*' the King said, scowling.

'I'll hold my tongue,' Louisa said. 'Solely for my grandmother's sake.'

He scowled even harder.

She didn't curtsey to him; but he didn't hug her. Stalemate it was, then.

'*Au revoir,*' she said.

'*Bonne journée,*' the Queen said. 'Look after her, Sébastien.'

She insisted on carrying her own luggage to the car, and noticed that he did the same. He held the door to let her into the back seat of the car first, then joined her.

'So what now? Do I hide my face as we go out of the gates?' she asked as Pierre took the wheel.

'There's no need,' Sébastien reassured her. 'The car has privacy glass, so they won't be able to see in.'

'It feels as if we're rushing down a rollercoaster slope and I can't stop the car,' she said.

'I understand,' he said. 'I felt the same, the first time the paparazzi looked for me, but you get used to it.'

'I don't want to get used to it, Sébastien,' she said. 'I'm not a princess.'

'Technically,' he said, 'you are, and I should be calling you *madame.*'

'Oh, *puh-lease,*' she said, rolling her eyes. 'You first knew me as plain Louisa Gallet. That's not going to change just because…' She closed her eyes for a moment.

'Everything's changed,' he said softly. And there was nothing plain about her. Nothing at all. She glowed from the inside out.

She opened her eyes again. 'Technically, do you have to bow to me?'

He stifled his amusement. Just. 'Yes.'

'Well, *don't*,' she said. 'I'm not a princess.'

Yes, she was, but she clearly needed time to get used to it. 'All right, plain Mademoiselle Louisa. Let's get to work,' he said. 'I'm going to make notes as we talk, if that's all right.' He smiled at her. 'Talk me through what happens between someone making an appointment and you giving them the finished dress.'

'How much detail do you want?' she asked.

'As much as you want to give,' he said.

'OK. I ask them to bring their ideas to the appointment—any pictures they've seen of dresses they like, the sort of colour scheme they're thinking about, the sort of hairstyle and veil and bouquet they want. We talk about what she likes, and we have gowns she can try on to see how it looks.' She ticked off the steps on her fingers. 'That's the point where I might guide her towards a different-shaped gown, one that'll flatter her shape better and will make her feel fabulous. Then we'll go through the material samples so she chooses the type of material and colour. I'll make a trial dress in very light cotton, and we'll agree any changes in hemline or shape or decoration. Then I cut out the real material and pin it together, do a fitting, sew it and add the decoration, do another fitting with the shoes and underwear she'll wear on the day to make sure it all works, pin up any final alterations, and then it's the final fitting where she takes the dress away.'

'In business terms, you break the task into steps, you know which order each step has to be done in, and you work your way through it.'

She nodded.

'And all the time you deal with your clients—and their families—you need to take their feelings into account.'

'Yes.'

'It's exactly the same with being a royal,' he said. 'Just your projects might be a bit different. So you're not actually as under-prepared as you think. You already have some skills—organisation and diplomacy for a start. What media experience do you have?'

'I've been interviewed a couple of times,' she said, 'mainly by the local paper and specialist bridal magazines and websites. I've also talked to specialist heritage websites about my restoration work.'

'Then you already know some of the media skills,' he said. 'It'll be just a matter of practising and polishing.'

'I don't want to do this at all,' she said.

He took her hand and squeezed it. 'I'm trying to find an escape route for you, Louisa, but you need to understand that it might not be possible.'

'Can't I be like a...like a sleeping partner?' she asked plaintively.

Oh, the picture that put in his head. Of waking in the morning with her in his arms, her head pillowed on his shoulder. Of her smiling at him when she opened her eyes. Of her reaching up to kiss him good morning, and kissing would turn to touching...

Louisa saw the deep slash of colour across Sébastien's cheekbones and realised how her comment must have sounded to him.

'I meant in business terms,' she mumbled.

But it was too late; there was a picture in her head, too. Of Sébastien sprawled across her bed. He clearly had a similar picture in his head, because his fingers tightened round hers for a moment.

'Business terms,' he said, obviously making an effort. 'Business. OK. There is a way, but you've already said no to that.'

She grimaced. 'I can't marry you just to get out of ruling the country.'

'We both win, that way,' he said.

'What if you fall in love with someone? What if I fall in love with someone?'

'Then you'd have to suppress it. To be royal is to put the country first,' he said.

She shook her head in exasperation. 'That's so cold-blooded.'

'It's the way it is,' he said. 'The country needs stability.' His phone beeped; he glanced at the screen, then showed her the latest message from Pascal. 'The press have traced the same paper trail that I did. They've posted photographs of you and Louis, showing the similarity between you.'

'But they don't know the results of the DNA test.' And then a nasty thought hit her. 'Unless someone leaked it?'

'They don't need to know the results,' he said. 'Those headlines tell us they've already made up their minds. As far as they're concerned, you're the legitimate Princess of Charlmoux, and I'm no longer the legitimate heir. It's only a matter of time before they find out that's absolutely true.'

'But that's not fair on you. You've worked for the royal family for years, training to be a future king.' She bit her lip. 'I can't learn all that in a week.'

'No,' he agreed, 'but you can learn a lot.'

'I'm not going to be Queen.'

'If you step down, and I take over as Regent,' he said, 'what happens if you fall in love with someone, get married and have children? They'll still be next in line to the throne.'

'Not if you were King.'

'We're in uncharted territory,' he said gently. 'There is no precedent. Very few monarchs have abdicated, and only on the grounds of ill health. I might still be able to rule as your regent—if Parliament agrees—but *your* children would still be the heirs, not mine. So all you'd be doing is shifting the burden to them. Is that what you want?'

She simply stared at him.

'We can waste time arguing,' he said, 'or we can be practical. And you strike me as a practical woman.'

She narrowed her eyes at him. 'Are you trying to push me into marrying you?'

No. He was seeing everything he'd worked for about to go up in flames. Every sacrifice he'd made—losing his relationship with Elodie, not seeing enough of his family—would all be for nothing. And all his years of training, of looking at things calmly and dispassionately, had deserted him. He could feel the panic seeping through him like cold, stagnant water. What the hell was he going to do? How could he fix this?

He took a deep breath. 'No. I'm not trying to push you into marrying me. I'm telling you what your choices are.'

And only one of them included him. He pushed the thought away before it overwhelmed him. There was so much at stake here. 'Either you step up and rule the country—in which case I need to start getting you up to speed with things—or you marry me and let me rule, in which case I'll still need to teach you a few things because you'll still have to do at least some of the PR stuff.'

'I've already told you. The only reason I'll ever marry is the same as my parents. Love. Nothing less,' she said.

Even if you ignored the scientific proof, Séb thought, Louisa was Henri's granddaughter. She had the same obstinacy.

She wanted a fairy tale. True love.

The problem was, love *was* a fairy tale when it came to his world. There was no real room for love in a royal marriage. Mutual liking and respect would be a bonus, but the important thing was the ability to put the country first.

He couldn't give her any sweeteners. Maybe she'd feel better about the idea of getting married to him if she thought he was in love with her, or if she fell in love with him. But that would mean a combination of lying to her and manipulating her—neither of which sat well with him.

She was the heir, and he thought she had the makings of a good ruler. He just needed to teach her to see it, too.

'Let's get on with the business,' he said. 'There are royal duties. The diplomatic stuff: hosting foreign dignitaries and the like. The Queen will help with that, and the palace staff know what they're doing, but you still need to host people. And some of them can be difficult.' He smiled at her. 'Which is where your Mumzilla experience comes in.'

'Got it.'

'There's some legal work, but you'll be supported by the palace officials.'

She made another note on her phone.

'Then there are the charity patronships. Your grandfather might want to keep some of them; your grandmother might want to keep others.'

'Are you a charity patron?' she asked.

He nodded. 'Mine are mainly to do with mental health and justice.'

'Because of what happened to your best friend?'

She'd remembered? Part of him felt warmed. 'Yes. The thing about a charity is to pick the ones you've got a personal connection with, either in your interests or your experience. I think you'd be particularly strong with heritage and the arts, because of your work and your mum. Plus bereavement—especially for children who've lost a parent.'

'Yes. And women's health and cancer, because of my mum,' she said. 'So what exactly does a charity patron do?'

'Your endorsement helps support awareness of the charity and raise their profile, which in turn helps them with fundraising. They might ask you to have your photograph on a leaflet, or help front an appeal,' he explained. 'You might be a keynote speaker, or turn up at an event as a VIP, or give out awards, or write something personal they can use in the press. It depends on what sort of involvement you want to have, and the palace press team can help you polish anything you're not sure about.'

'This all sounds quite daunting,' she said. 'I don't want to be Queen—and if it was a job I'd say that I wasn't a suitable candidate. I don't have the experience or the skills.'

'You're being too hard on yourself,' he said. 'Supposing someone joined the bridal workshop yesterday morning, you were assigned to be their mentor, and they told you at the end of their first day that they were rubbish at their job.'

She frowned. 'But that's ridiculous. Nobody can be perfect on day one. There's a lot to learn in the job, plus you need time to settle in.'

'Exactly.' Sébastien looked at her. 'You're not going to be the perfect princess right this very second. But you already have some of the skills from your job, and I can teach you the rest.'

'I'm not a princess,' she insisted. 'My life's in London.'

He spread his hands. 'Give me this week. See if it changes how you view things.'

'A week?' She bit her lip. 'I'll give you until Friday.'

He only had until Friday morning to teach her how to be a princess and step up to do the right thing.

But Sébastien had never shied away from a challenge, and he wasn't going to start now.

CHAPTER SEVEN

WHEN THEY ARRIVED at the royal summer palace, Sébastien showed Louisa to her room.

'I can see the sea!' she said, looking delighted. 'And it's actually turquoise, like the photographs. It's amazing.'

'We'll go for a walk on the beach, later,' he said. 'It's a private beach, and the locals are really protective of our privacy, so you don't have to worry about press intrusion.'

'That's good,' she said.

He showed her round, then introduced her to Hortense, the middle-aged housekeeper, who'd brewed coffee for them and had a tray with mugs, a cafetière and a jug of milk. 'We're going to take over the conservatory for our office, Hortense, if that doesn't get in your way?'

The housekeeper smiled. 'You never get in my way, Séb. Just let me know when you want more coffee.'

'We will.'

Louisa made the effort to thank Hortense in French, and the housekeeper patted her arm. *'De rien, ma petite.'* She smiled. 'I knew your *papa*. My mother was the housekeeper here before me, and your papa was very kind to a lonely little girl. He showed me how to make sandcastles on the beach, and make a bridge over the moat from razor shells.'

Séb could see the glint of tears in Louisa's eyes as she thanked Hortense.

'Everyone speaks well of your father,' he said gently as he ushered her to the conservatory. 'Louis was a good man.' And he rather thought that the people of Charlmoux would take Louisa to their hearts, too.

'The Queen showed me photographs of him at the beach. Would it have been here?' she asked.

'Very probably,' he said. 'OK. Time to make our game plan. I don't mean to scare you, but we need to be practical. Even if you can step down from royal duties—' and he was pretty sure that wasn't an option '—you'll still be of interest to the press and you'll need to be careful in public: what you do, what you say, and your expression.'

'Is that why you're always so starchy?'

It was the second time she'd accused him of that. 'I'm not starchy,' he said, stung.

'It's how you come across to me,' she said. 'I have no idea what makes you tick. What makes you laugh, what makes you want to weep, what drives you.'

'In public,' he said, 'I've spent the last few years being the heir to the throne. The country needs me to be stable and serene—or, as you put it, starchy. I smile, I keep my shoulders relaxed and my head held high, and I smile some more.'

She frowned. 'It sounds like living in a goldfish bowl.'

'Yes,' he said. 'I'm afraid it goes with the territory. You get used to it.'

'I don't think I'd ever get used to it.' She grimaced.

'It was different for Mum; she was a performer. I'm more of a back room person.'

'The best performers are nervous before a show. Adrenalin keeps them sharp,' he said. 'Let's start with interviews. We'll role-play it, with me as the journalist, and film it on my laptop so we can review it together.'

'Like television, you mean?' Her eyes went wide. 'I've never done that.'

'I know,' he said, as gently as he could. 'We need to establish a baseline so we can see how you're coming across and what you need to work on.'

'Do you get questions in advance?'

'To some extent,' he said. 'The palace PR team will be well-briefed enough to come up with a list of the most likely questions in any given situation, so you'll be pretty much prepared. But you'll always get something you're not expecting.'

'Right.'

He patted her hand. 'This is a practice. A safe space, and there are no wrong answers,' he said. 'Go and sit on the sofa.' He started to set up his laptop. 'Most of this is obvious, but I'll give you a few tips while I'm getting the angle of the screen right. Smile and maintain eye contact—with your interviewer if it's in person, or with the camera if it's an online session.'

'Got it.'

'They'll want a good quote they can use, so keep your answer concise, clear and jargon-free; but also make sure you answer the question in full, because they might edit out the question if it's not a live broadcast. Focus on your key message. If you don't understand the question, ask for clarification. If you don't know the answer, say so, and say why—you might not have read a report, and it's better to say that rather than try to bluff your way through it. Speak slowly, keep it positive, and keep your speech to less than a minute at a time.'

'A minute's a very long time to talk,' she said.

'Exactly,' he said. 'Short and sweet is the way to go.'

'What if they ask me something I don't want to answer?'

'Use the ABC approach,' he said. 'Acknowledge the question, bridge your response, and contribute your key message.'

Louisa was glad that Sébastien was being brisk and businesslike with her. Of course the press were going to be interested in her, even if she did manage not to be on the throne, and it made sense to prepare herself as much as possible, to learn these new skills, she simply needed to pay attention and practise. 'ABC,' she repeated. 'Acknowledge, bridge, contribute.'

He came to sit next to her on the sofa. 'We're live now. Good afternoon, Your Highness. Thank you for joining me today.'

Highness? What? Then she remembered to smile and make eye contact. 'Thank you for inviting me, Mr Moreau.'

He gave her a predatory smile. 'How do you feel about becoming Queen?'

He wasn't even going to ask a soft question first, to let her warm up? Though maybe it was more realistic, because a journalist would go straight for the big one. ABC, she reminded herself. 'I can't really answer that properly at the moment, Mr Moreau,' she said, 'because that depends on whether there's someone more suitable to rule. But I'm very much looking forward to seeing more of Charlmoux and its people, including my father's parents.'

Sébastien gave her an approving wink, and whipped through his list of questions.

Louisa stumbled over a couple of the answers. 'Can we backtrack so you ask me the question again?' she asked.

'No. What would your mum have said to her students in a dress rehearsal?'

'Keep going and pick up your place as soon as you can,' she said.

'This is exactly the same thing. Ignore the mistakes and keep going,' he said. 'Smile. Make eye contact. Remember your key points. And we're back in role in three, two, one.'

The 'interview' only lasted for ten minutes, but it felt like much longer. By the end of it, Louisa felt as if someone had flattened her.

'Time to review it,' he said, and played back the recording.

Louisa was very aware of the way she'd messed up some of the answers. 'That really wasn't good,' she said when the recording stopped.

'It's a good *start*,' he corrected. 'Remember, this is our baseline and it'll get better from here on. What would you change for the next round?'

'I'd prepare the answers better, so I don't look as if I'm making things up off the top of my head,' she said.

'That isn't being fair to yourself,' he said, 'because we didn't prepare in the first place. Don't change the goalposts.'

She knew he had a point; but seeing herself on screen, so gauche and hopeless, had rattled her. 'With your experience of giving interviews, what do you think I need to change first?' she asked.

'Your body language,' he said. 'You fidget with your hands, and fidgeting makes you look less confident.'

'How do I stop doing that?'

'When you're talking, use your hands,' he said.

She frowned. 'You just said I need to stop fidgeting with my hands. Doesn't using them mean I'm fidgeting?'

'No. When people talk normally,' he said, 'they tend to use their hands to emphasise points. Do that in an interview. Even if the camera's trained solely on your face, the gestures will make your face look more animated.'

She nodded. 'And when I'm not talking? How do I stop fidgeting?'

'Nest your hands together—one within the other—and keep them on your lap,' he said. 'It'll make you look relaxed, even if you're not feeling it.'

Louisa definitely wasn't feeling relaxed right then, but she followed his directions.

'And your posture,' he said. 'When you sit, lean forward slightly, with both feet on the floor; it's a more active position. If you're standing, put one foot slightly in front of the other and then you won't sway.'

'Is this better?' she asked, sitting in the way he'd suggested.

'Much,' he said. 'Last thing—shoulders relaxed and head high.'

She smiled. 'Mum used to tell me to pretend there's a string pulling me up from the top of my head. Long neck, shoulders down.'

'Perfect,' he said. 'That's probably why you walk like a dancer.'

He'd noticed that? It made her feel hot all over. Especially as she'd noticed how he moved, too, with economy and grace.

'Now we've done the physical stuff, let's go through your answers. You're doing most of the talking, and I'll make notes.'

He took her through each question, making her analyse her answers and consider where she thought they needed changing. By the time they'd finished, Louisa felt a lot more confident.

'Thank you. That was really useful,' she said. 'Let's repeat the interview and see how I'm doing.'

'We'll take a break, first,' Sébastien said. 'We've been focusing on this all afternoon. You need time to recharge and let this stuff sink into your brain. Let's go and walk by the sea. I'll just tell Pierre where we are.' He sent a message to his security detail, then shrugged off his jacket and removed his tie, and led her through the garden.

They left their shoes by the garden gate—the beach was sandy, studded every so often with shells and smooth pebbles—and headed down to the shoreline.

'I can't believe the colour of that water,' she said. 'Can I paddle, or do I have to be careful of jellyfish or what have you?'

'It's very safe,' he said. 'There might be the odd sharp shell, but that's it.' He rolled his trousers up to his knees. 'Come on.' He took her hand and drew her to the edge of the sea.

'Oh! It's colder than I expected,' she said. 'Do you come here often?'

'Not as often as I'd like,' he said. 'When I get time off, I tend to go and see my family. But the beach is a treat.'

'We sometimes went to Cornwall in the summer—Mum had some friends who moved there when they retired from dancing. I loved walking along the sea like this,' she said.

'Just you and the waves swishing onto the shore. It's the best thing ever for clearing your head,' he said.

And then she realised that he was still holding her hand.

Suddenly this didn't feel like a break from business. It felt like a date. If she stood still and closed her eyes, would he kiss her? Would she taste the salt air on his lips? Would his kiss be sweet and offering, or hot and demanding?

She shook herself. This was ridiculous. And she couldn't let herself forget that he'd suggested a marriage of convenience. He only wanted to marry her for political reasons; letting herself get carried away by emotions would be very stupid. Even if it was the most beautiful summer day by the sea, and she was walking hand in hand with the most beautiful man.

She thought he was starchy. She didn't know what made him laugh, what made him weep, what drove him.

Séb had been so focused on wanting to change the world that he hadn't stopped to share his dreams with anyone. After Elodie, he'd thought that the kind of relationships the rest of his family had were out of his reach—that his eventual marriage would be a political match.

But was Louisa right? Could their match be more than just political?

If so, then she'd need him to open up to her; and he didn't even know how to start. He didn't open up to anyone nowadays—not even to his family and Marcel. He'd thought it was a strength, being self-contained; now, he wondered if it was a weakness.

Open up.

She'd told him what she didn't know about him. Maybe that would be the best place to start. 'Bad puns,' he said.

'What?'

'You asked what made me laugh. Bad puns,' he said.

'Uh-huh.' She looked wary, but intrigued as well.

'And my family. I laugh with my family. Especially my nieces, when they tell me a joke and get the punchline wrong. It's adorable.'

She smiled. 'Yeah. I'm dying for my cousins to start having babies, so I can read them the stories my mum read to me.'

Did she want babies of her own? The question caught in his throat and he couldn't ask her. 'Injustice,' he said instead. 'That's what makes me weep.'

'What actually happened to your best friend's family?' she asked.

He grimaced. 'It feels as if I'm betraying a confidence.'

'It's not going anywhere,' she said, tightening her fingers round his.

He knew he could trust her. So he told her.

'That's terrible,' she said when he'd finished. 'I was the same age as Marcel when I lost my mum. But she didn't want to die. It must be so much harder if you keep wondering why your dad would want to leave you—or if you could've said or done something to make a difference and stop him taking his own life, even when it's obvious that nobody could've changed what happened.'

'It's why I studied law,' he said. 'I wanted to help people who'd been through something like that. And I wanted to be able to change the law so there were more safeguards.'

'You said Marcel works with your brother Luc at the vineyard, now?'

He nodded. 'It was my suggestion. I felt bad about not being able to support him properly when it all happened. My parents were a bit wary at first. I mean, was a vineyard really the best place for someone who had a problem with alcohol? But I thought it would help because he'd be with people who valued him, and I hoped the job would make him focus on something physical and help stop things spinning round in his head. I couldn't help him as a teen, but I could help him when we were older, give him the chance to get his life back on track.' He shrugged. 'He's settled, now. He's getting married after harvest, and I'm going to be his best man.'

'I'm glad things have worked out for him,' she said.

'So am I,' he said.

He found himself holding her hand until they were back at the garden gate. And then, unable to help himself, he drew her hand up to his lips, pressed a kiss into her palm, then folded her fingers round it. 'Thank you for listening,' he said.

Her eyes had gone wide and colour had bloomed in her cheeks.

Not that he was going to draw attention to it, because his own face felt hot and his mouth was tingling where it had touched her skin.

'Let's take five minutes' break,' he said gruffly, 'because I need to check in with Pascal, and no doubt you want to tell your family where you are.' And five minutes would be enough to get himself back under strict control. He'd make sure of it.

After Louisa had spoken to her grandmother in London and her cousins to let them know she was staying in

Charlmoux until Friday, she spent a while with Sébastien looking at the constitution and the legal system in the country. Hortense cooked them a wonderful dish of sole meunière for dinner, which they ate on the patio while they watched the sun set over the sea. They sat sipping a glass of wine as the sky gradually darkened and the stars started to come out.

'So what drives *you*?' Sébastien asked. 'Why do you love fabric so much?'

'I think it's the way it makes me feel,' she said. 'I've always been fascinated by the heritage stuff, so that's why I'm a bit greedy and I work at the Heritage Centre two days a week, and the rest of the time at the studio. It's the best of both worlds, the old and the new.' She smiled. 'Watching Nan make dresses and seeing how people just glowed when they put the dresses on: I wanted to do that for people, too. And I like giving brides and teenagers the dress of their dreams.' She spread her hands. 'I know the dress isn't the most important part of the wedding—marriage itself is the important bit—but a dress makes a difference. Whether it's a wedding or a prom, it's a day when all eyes are going to be on you. It's a lot of pressure, especially if your confidence isn't great to start with. A dress can help you feel confident.'

'Like when you wear your mother's pearls?' he asked.

She nodded. 'Which I now know were my great-grandmother's.'

'I would've stood up for you if Henri had demanded them back,' he said.

'Even if he went Kingzilla on you?'

Sébastien laughed. 'Yes. I'm not scared of him. I respect him—even though I know he's behaved badly where you're concerned—because he's been progressive during his reign and he's trying to make the country as modern as he can. But I think he has a blind spot about his son.'

Louisa sighed. 'He blames my mum for the accident—even though she wasn't there.'

'It's unfair,' Sébastien said, 'though I can understand his thinking. If your dad hadn't married your mum, he wouldn't have been in London that day and the car wouldn't have hit him. Except,' he added, 'your dad might have been in London on business for Charlmoux. But grief makes people act in strange ways.'

'I guess.' She paused. 'Sébastien, thank you for helping me. I'm sorry this is taking up so much of your time.'

'It's not your fault,' he said. 'And it's a pleasure.'

Scarily, it was. She'd seen a different side of him, here—the non-starchy Séb that she thought he might be with his family. And he was starting to let her in. She'd been moved by what he'd told her about his best friend, how he'd felt guilty about not being able to give Marcel enough support; and she'd seen a moment of wistfulness in his face when he'd said how Marcel was settled now. She rather thought that Sébastien was a man who felt deeply, but had taught himself not to show it.

And that changed his suggestion of marriage. Maybe it wouldn't be a business arrangement, after all. Maybe, if she managed to unlock the layers, she'd find a man who'd make her feel the way her mother had felt about her father. The thought was exhilarating and scary at the same time. Could she get to know him properly? Would he let her?

To her surprise, she found herself yawning. 'Sorry. I don't mean to be rude.'

'You're not. It's the sea air making you sleepy,' he said.

'I think I'm going to head for bed,' she said.

'I'll stay out for a bit,' he said. 'The stars are amazing out here, where there's no light from the city to dim them.' Though he stood up politely when she rose from her chair.

On impulse, she walked over towards him, intending to kiss him on the cheek. That sweet kiss on her palm on the way back from the beach had changed things between them, made them easier with each other. But either she'd misjudged or he moved, because she ended up kissing the corner of his mouth instead.

He froze. She was about to apologise and back away when he cupped her face in his hands, and his mouth brushed hers in the softest, sweetest kiss.

'*Bonsoir*, Louisa,' he whispered. 'See you tomorrow.'

She had no idea how she managed to walk into the house and up to her room, because that kiss seemed to have scrambled her brain. And she was still thinking about kissing him when she finally drifted off to sleep.

CHAPTER EIGHT

THURSDAY WAS THEIR last day at the beach house. How had these few days gone by so quickly? Louisa wondered.

'I think we've covered everything major,' Sébastien said at last. 'The only other thing I can think of: did your mum teach you any ballroom dancing as well as ballet?'

'No. Why?' Louisa asked.

'You might have to dance at a charity ball,' he said. 'You should be OK, because you've had some dance training and most of the men will be able to lead you. Or…' He paused. 'I could teach you the basics of the waltz and the foxtrot.'

Her pulse leapt at the idea of dancing with him. 'I'd like that. I've got my turquoise dress with me, and shoes I can dance in.'

'Great. We'll run through it tonight, after dinner.'

It was Hortense's evening off; she'd left them cold poached salmon and salad in the fridge, along with a bowl of strawberries, plus home-made ice cream in the freezer. Sébastien had changed into a suit and Louisa into her turquoise dress. It felt weirdly like a date. Dressed up, dinner and dancing…

Would he kiss her tonight? Or would he remember

that tomorrow they were going back to the palace, and keep his distance from her?

As the stars began to shimmer in the darkening sky, Sébastien flicked into a music streaming app on his phone. 'I've found a playlist for the foxtrot. That's a good one to start with.'

The lawn was smooth and flat, feeling like velvet underneath her feet, and it made the perfect dance floor. She concentrated on Sébastien's instructions and learning the steps, though being in his arms was seriously disrupting her ability to think of anything except how it felt to be close to him.

'I think you've got the hang of the foxtrot,' he said. 'Now the waltz.' He flicked into a different song: Louis Armstrong's 'What a Wonderful World'.

''The waltz is easy: just six steps, and you can break them down into two sets of three,' he said. 'What we're going to do is make a kind of box.' He demonstrated. 'Back, side, close, forward, side, close. One-two-three, one-two-three, and you're using alternate legs. Nice and simple.' He grinned. 'It's way easier than anything you do in a dance fitness class.'

'Maybe.' And maybe she could teach him a few moves from her class. Get hot and sweaty with him…

Oh, help. She needed to concentrate, or instead she'd be standing on his toes.

'Now we need to get into ballroom hold. Put your left hand on my shoulder,' he directed, 'and hold my left hand with your right—we're holding our arms out to give us balance.'

It was a formal hold, but when his right hand was resting on her waist and his left hand was curled with hers, it felt incredibly intimate. If she leaned forward slightly, he'd be in kissing distance. When they started to move to the music, even though all Sébastien was doing was talking her through the steps in the simplest possible terms, Louisa couldn't concentrate. She was too aware of the way their legs were practically sliding between each other's as they moved. This was like making love with their clothes on. And she couldn't shake the idea of making love with Sébastien. Kissing him. Touching him. The final intimacy.

She couldn't think straight, and she couldn't dance straight, either; she stumbled, and he kept her upright. And that made it even worse.

Think of something unsexy, she told herself. Listen to him. Follow the steps.

Except she couldn't think of anything except Sébastien. The warmth of his skin. His clean, masculine scent. How much she wanted to kiss him.

'We're going to turn, though it's not going to be like a ballet pirouette,' he said. 'Just keep going with the steps, and trust me not to steer you wrong.'

Sébastien Moreau was a man of integrity. Over the last week, she'd learned to trust him.

But this was something else. Holding him close, not knowing quite where she was going because she couldn't see behind her—and, when he started turning them, it felt as if she were floating. Swept off her feet. Dancing on air. Every cliché rolled into one, yet making it something new and special and wonderful.

Did he feel it, too?

He'd stopped talking her through the steps, but she didn't need the instructions any more. She was dancing instinctively, following his lead and letting him guide her as they glided round their makeshift dance floor. And how good it felt to be close to him, dancing, together, swooping and swaying and swirling.

At the end of the song, he dropped out of the ball-room hold and cupped her face in his hands.

She opened her eyes and looked at him. His eyes were huge and dark, full of longing.

For her?

She didn't dare ask.

But then she found herself looking at his mouth. The sensual curve of his lower lip. The perfect Cupid's bow of his top lip. And she ached to taste him.

Maybe he could read her feelings in her expression; maybe she'd accidentally said it aloud; or maybe he felt exactly the same way that she did, his body humming with the same need, because he dipped his head and brushed his lips against hers, light as a butterfly's wing. Her mouth tingled where he'd touched her; and it wasn't enough. It wasn't anywhere near enough. She wanted more: she wanted all of him.

'Sébastien,' she whispered, and slid her arms round his neck.

Somehow his hands had moved down to her waist, and he'd drawn her close against him.

All she had to do was rise up on tiptoe and brush her mouth against his, just as tentatively as he'd kissed her. Asking. Offering. Promising.

His arms tightened round her, hers tightened round him, and then they were really kissing. And it felt like the warmth of a spring sun unfurling round her after a long, dark winter. As if she'd finally found where she really belonged.

He broke the kiss. 'Louisa.' His voice was husky, cracked with need. 'The timing's all wrong. We have to go back to the palace tomorrow,' he said.

'But we have tonight,' she said. 'Here and now. Just you and me.'

His eyes darkened and he kissed her again. 'Tell me to stop,' he said, when he'd dragged his mouth from hers.

That was the last thing she intended to do. Instead, she took his hand and pressed a kiss into his palm, the same way that he'd done that first day by the garden gate and put her senses all in a spin. 'I have a question for you. Do you have a condom?'

His breath hitched. 'Louisa, my self-control's hanging by a thread.'

Good. She wanted it to snap. She wanted *him*. All of him. For tonight.

So, instead of being sensible and walking away, she reached up to kiss him.

He kissed her back, his mouth hot and demanding, and she felt as if she were burning up with need and desire.

'Last chance to be sensible,' he said when he dragged his mouth away from hers.

She shook her head. 'I want you, Sébastien. Tonight, you're mine and I'm yours.' They could deal with all the complications tomorrow.

In response, he scooped her up in his arms and carried her into the house. Louisa had never seen him in caveman mode before, and it sent a thrill of desire through her. He kissed her at the foot of the stairs, then carried her up the stairs to his room. He closed the door behind them with his foot, then let her slide down his body until her feet touched the floor again, leaving her in no doubt about just how much he wanted her.

'I've wanted this all week,' he said, his voice husky. 'Maybe even since the first day I met you and you made me feel as if I'd been steamrollered.'

'That's how you made me feel, too,' she admitted. 'And I want you so badly.'

He kissed her until she was breathless. 'Hold that thought,' he said, and went to close his curtains before switching on his bedside light.

In the dim light, she felt ridiculously shy. Sébastien clearly noticed, because he kissed her lightly. 'If you want to change your mind, Louisa, we can stop now.'

She shook her head. 'I'm not changing my mind. I want you, Sébastien. It's…' She hesitated, unable to find the right words.

'It's scary,' he said. 'There's a risk that doing this might wreck everything.'

'I don't understand why I'm feeling shy with you,' she said.

'It's the getting naked bit,' he said. 'I can turn the light off, if that would help.'

'But then I won't be able to s—' She felt the colour storm into her face as she realised what she was about to confess.

He laughed. 'That goes both ways, Louisa.'

He wanted to see her naked, just as much as she wanted to see him. And the knowledge made her pulse rate leap up a notch.

'I have another idea,' he said. 'You take off a piece of my clothing, and I take off a piece of yours. We'll take it in turns.'

He wanted her to undress him.

To let him undress her.

The idea made her knees go weak and the ends of her fingers started to tingle with adrenalin. 'Except that's not quite fair. You're wearing more than I am,' she pointed out.

He opened his arms. 'Let's not count my jacket and tie. I'm all yours. Do with me what you will,' he invited.

She took his jacket off, then his tie. And then she

looked him in the eye as she undid the buttons on his shirt, one by one, the tips of her fingers tingling as they brushed his skin. When she pushed the soft cotton from his shoulders, she caught her breath. He was beautiful. Muscular without being a gym gorilla, with a light sprinkling of hair on his chest, the kind of olive-toned skin that loved the sun, and the most perfect abs.

She wanted to paint him. She wanted to sculpt him. But most of all she wanted to explore every millimetre of him.

'My turn,' he said.

She could feel his hands shaking as he unzipped her dress, stroking down her spine and kissing the nape of her neck. She could see them shaking as she stepped out of her dress and he hung it over the back of a chair; and it made her feel better to know that he was just as nervous about this as she was.

'You're so beautiful,' he said as he turned back to her, the top of his forefinger tracing the lacy edge of her bra. 'I want to touch you, Louisa. Kiss you.' He dragged in a breath. 'All over.'

She wanted it, too. So much that her mouth had gone dry and she couldn't utter a single word. Her fingers just weren't working properly, because she couldn't undo the button of his trousers. The backs of her fingers brushed against the skin of his abdomen, and every nerve end felt as if it was fizzing. In the end, she looked at him. 'Sébastien. I've turned into this incapable mess. And I…' She shook her head. She couldn't even find the right words, now. How pathetic was that?

He kissed her lightly. 'Me, too. I can't think straight when I'm with you.'

'I'm used to sketching dresses—but I want to sketch you. Just like you are now, all rumpled and sexy as hell.'

She trailed a finger down his chest; his breath hissed with need and pleasure, sending a thrill through her. She reached up to kiss him again.

Time seemed to stop, and she had no idea which of them had finished undressing the other; all she was aware of was the way Sébastien almost ripped the top sheet off his bed, picked her up and laid her back against the pillows.

They really were going to do this.

Make love.

But she hadn't been prepared for how it felt to be skin to skin with him.

How it felt when his mouth tracked a path down her body, when he licked and nibbled and teased her with the tip of his tongue, making her wriggle impatiently.

How it felt when he touched her, his fingers teasing and caressing, finding out exactly where and how she liked being touched, what made her gasp and hold on to him.

It was as if he was trying to memorise her with his hands and his mouth and his body, the same way she was trying to memorise him. And she wanted to remember every nanosecond of tonight.

Finally he slipped on the condom. 'OK?' he asked.

'Yes,' she said, and he eased into her. He was gentle, giving her time to adjust to him and then he began to move.

This wasn't just satisfying a physical urge, it was a connection deeper than she'd expected; and she really wasn't prepared for how it felt to climax with him buried deep inside her, waves of pleasure that spiralled and bound them closer together. She cried out his name and heard him groan her name in return, shuddering as he reached his own climax. He collapsed next to her, their arms still wound round each other, their breathing rapid.

'I'll be right back,' he whispered, a few moments later. 'But please don't go back to your own room. Stay with me tonight, Louisa. I want to fall asleep with you in my arms. To wake up with you.'

Spend the night with him. Fall asleep in his arms. Wake up and he'd be the first thing she saw.

How could she resist?

'I'll stay,' she said.

She felt as if she was smiling from the inside out when he came back. This felt so right, so perfect. He slid into bed beside her and drew the sheet over them before shifting so she was cuddled into him. He pressed a kiss against the top of her head, warm and affection- ate. And it felt as if this was the real Sébastien, the one he kept hidden behind the starchy exterior. He'd let her close. Trusted her with himself.

Yes, things were a bit complicated in their lives right now, and she had no idea how this was going to work out—but she was sure that they'd find a way. Together.

Sébastien knew when Louisa had finally fallen asleep; her breathing had slowed and deepened. Having her curled in his arms, her head pillowed on his shoulder and her arm wrapped round his waist, was just what he wanted.

He'd known it would be good between them. But he hadn't guessed how perfect it would be.

Tomorrow, before they went back to the palace, he'd ask her to be his queen again. It was the practical solu- tion to the problem for both of them. Sort of. He knew that Louisa wanted love—the kind of passionate, in- tense love she'd seen in the ballet and heard of between her parents; right now, he couldn't offer her exactly what she wanted. But, with time, he thought that love would grow between them. They could have everything: the duty and compatibility Charlmoux needed, and then over the years the kind of love she wanted.

He just hoped she'd give him a chance.

The next morning, Louisa woke in Sébastien's arms, warm and comfortable. Even though they were going back to the palace today, it was going to be fine—because they'd be together.

Then she realised that Sébastien wasn't asleep. His breathing was shallow and not quite even. Was he simply being kind and letting her sleep in, or had he changed his mind since last night and was lying there, working out how he could back out of this?

Doubts seeped up her spine, turning her cold.

Last night had been perfect. Last night, she'd thought that maybe he felt the same way as she did. That he wanted to be with her for her own sake—that he, too, thought they could find a way through all the political stuff together. But had she been kidding herself? Had she just seen what she'd wanted to see? Was she expecting too much from him? Was he even capable of giving her the love she wanted?

Time to be brave. 'Good morning,' she said.

'Good morning.' His voice was neutral, cool and calm. There was none of the passion she'd seen last night. None of the love. He was obviously back in royal mode.

His next words confirmed it. 'I've been thinking. These last few days, we've got on really well. We're compatible, in lots of ways. I think our marriage would be a happy one.'

She sagged with disappointment. So he was still seeing it as a business decision, nothing to do with love. Worse still, it sounded as if he assumed she was just going to go along with the idea of marrying him.

And she couldn't.

Not when he viewed it as logical, not emotional. If she married him for the country's sake, she'd always want something he couldn't give her. In the end, they'd make each other miserable.

'Compatibility isn't enough, Sébastien,' she said, as gently as she could. 'I want the kind of love my parents had. It's not negotiable.'

Love.

Séb had told himself last night that love would come, in time. But what if it didn't? He'd loved Elodie, but he'd neglected her for his work. He'd neglected his family. What if he neglected Louisa, too? What if she ended up resenting him because of that?

And even if she did find this amazing, all-consuming love she seemed to want, what then? She'd still have her duty to the country. Maybe the man of her dreams—he forced himself to ignore the thousand paper cuts of jealousy at the thought that it might not be him—wouldn't be able to cope with the pressure of Louisa's job. And love wouldn't be enough to bolster either of them.

Louisa might want love, but duty would serve her far better. The practical stuff, the stuff she seemed to be ignoring, would protect her far more than love would.

He could tell her he loved her. But her idea of love was something he knew was impractical and fragile—something that would be crushed under the weight of the throne. And what did he know of this all-consuming passion? How could he promise her something he might not be able to give, something he knew he couldn't live up to, even if he tried his best? That wouldn't be fair to either of them.

'I'm sorry, Sébastien. I can't marry you,' she said quietly.

Because she was chasing after rainbows that would vanish and leave her stranded. How could he make her see that what he was offering was something stronger, something that would last? 'Louisa. What you want— it doesn't exist,' he said.

'My parents had it,' she said, her chin tilting at a stubborn angle.

'If your father hadn't died, would it have been enough?'

Her eyes narrowed. 'So you're saying you don't believe my parents loved each other.'

'No. What I'm saying is that love isn't something that stays like that for ever. All the frothy, hearts-and-flowers stuff eventually fades over time. It isn't real. It isn't permanent. It…' He shook his head in frustration. Right now, all he seemed to be doing was pushing her further away. 'You can't ignore the practical stuff. The job's the thing that's all-consuming, not love. You need someone who can cope with that. Someone who will support you properly. Someone who understands the job.' Someone who'd protect her.

'Marriage isn't a job, Sébastien. *Love* isn't a job. And it does exist, even though you're trying to deny it.'

'But feelings change,' he said. 'When the grand passion goes, how do you know that you'll stay together? Once all the sex and the attraction and the excitement has faded, there won't be anything left to support your marriage—or the throne. Whereas if you start with compatibility and understanding, maybe friendship, that's something you can build on.'

'It's not enough,' she said. 'Without love, it's never going to be enough. I can't marry you.'

She'd rejected him. He wasn't enough for her. And he couldn't tell her he loved her. Not the kind of love she was looking for, because it didn't exist. He could offer her loyalty, affection, honour, support—things that would always stay true, and for him added up to a lot more than love—but he couldn't offer her the rainbows she dreamed of.

She dragged in a breath. 'I know it's ridiculous, given last night, but would you mind closing your eyes?'

She was walking out on him?

Well, of course she was. Because he couldn't say what she wanted to hear. And he wouldn't offer her empty promises.

He was an honourable man who always did the right thing, so he did exactly what she'd asked.

He could hear rustling sounds as she dressed. 'I'll see you later. I need to pack,' she said.

When the door closed behind her, he sat up, drawing his legs up and wrapping his arms round his shins, and rested his head on his knees.

He'd taken a gamble.

And lost.

CHAPTER NINE

THE JOURNEY BACK to the palace was hideous. Louisa wore her business suit as if it were armour. When she climbed into the back of the car with Séb, she said, 'You don't mind if I sew, do you?'—and then jammed in her earbuds before waiting for his answer.

He retreated to his laptop, but kept glancing at her in the hope that he could catch her eye and she'd talk to him. But her attention was resolutely fixed on her embroidery.

Back at the palace, she was forced to take out the earbuds.

'The Queen wishes to see you,' he said.

'Of course,' she said, all cool and calm and as starchy as she'd accused him of being.

He'd taught her well. He ought to be proud, instead of feeling as if she'd just eviscerated him.

The footmen took their luggage; he showed her to the drawing room. 'I'll be in my office, if you need anything.'

She looked surprised. 'You're not coming with me?'

'They didn't ask for me,' he said, and gave her his courtliest bow. *À la prochaine.* Maybe his absence might make her heart grow fonder. Or maybe not.

'You wished to see me, *madame*?' Louisa asked.

Marguerite gave her a hug. 'Welcome back.'

The King was sitting on the sofa. He looked at her and folded his arms. 'It's public knowledge now. You're the heir.'

Louisa mirrored his body language. 'My life is in London. My family, my job, my friends. I can't rule Charlmoux from London, and I don't want to give everything up and move here. Just give me the paperwork to say I renounce all claim, and I'll sign it.'

'You can't,' he said, not looking particularly pleased about it.

'It's true, *ma petite*,' Marguerite said.

Louisa stared at the King. 'Explain to me how you can step down and I can't.'

'The constitution is clear,' Henri said. 'Ill health is the only grounds for standing down from the throne.'

'Can't you just install Sébastien as your regent?'

'No,' Henri said. 'Because you are my granddaughter. You are the heir.'

On the one hand, it was nice to know that he'd come to some kind of acceptance of her. On the other, she was trapped. 'There has to be a way out of this,' Louisa said. 'I don't want to rule. You don't want me to rule. Sébastien has spent years training to take over from you, and he'll do a great job. Can't we tell everyone there's been a mistake and I'm not related to you at all?'

'No,' Marguerite said, 'because that would be tarnishing your father's memory.'

'So I'm stuck,' she said.

'You have family here,' Marguerite said. 'You have a job. You have friends—Sébastien, for a start.'

Louisa willed herself not to blush, thinking about last night. She and Sébastien weren't friends. They'd been lovers, but they weren't friends. Not any more.

'Your father is buried here,' Henri added.

'My mother is buried in London,' she countered.

'The press is full of speculation,' Henri said. 'If you go back to London, they'll follow you. Do you really wish your brides to have to fight their way through your front door? Will your cousins mind being followed down the street with a camera in their faces?'

'That,' she said, 'sounds like blackmail.'

'No. It's how some of the press behave,' he said. 'Stay for a little longer. Please. We can work out where we go from here. And,' he added, 'your grandmother and Sébastien have shown me the error of my ways.'

She stared at him. 'Meaning?'

'Meaning,' he said, uncrossing his arms, 'that I owe you an apology. I owe your mother an apology.'

The thing she'd wanted and thought he'd never give.

'Louis loved your mother. I should have supported him better. I should have allowed them to marry,' Henri said, 'and I should have let her attend his funeral. But I was angry, and I was grieving. I didn't behave well.' He paused. 'But I want you to be clear that I didn't know about you.'

Would it have made any difference? She wasn't sure. 'You evicted Mum from the flat.'

'I shouldn't have done that, either,' he said.

'She was scared you'd take me from her.'

He flinched. 'I can understand her fears, given how I treated her. I apologise. I...' He blew out a breath. 'I don't know what I would have done. And I can't change the past,' he said. 'But I can learn from it. And I have something to show you.' He patted the seat beside him.

Feeling slightly antsy, she sat down.

He took a folder from the table next to him and handed it to her.

She opened it to discover a plan by a monumental mason, showing a new carving for the slab of Louis' memorial.

Beloved husband of Catherine and father of Louisa

'I—I don't know what to say,' she whispered. There was a huge lump in her throat.

'Sébastien told me what you wanted. I trust this is correct?'

She nodded. 'Thank you.'

'Perhaps,' he said, 'we can have a truce. Start again.'

She smiled. 'I'd like that.'

'*Bien.* Now, I assume you wish to freshen up after your journey.'

It was a dismissal, but a much kinder one than she'd ever expected from him. 'We'll talk later,' she promised.

In return, he patted her hand. Given that he didn't seem the kind of person to give hugs, she knew that was a huge gesture.

'Will you walk with me, *ma petite*?' her grandmother asked.

Louisa nodded, and walked with the Queen through the long gallery.

'Right now,' Marguerite said, 'I would say you're feeling trapped. But I hope that will change, in time. You are the heir, and we can't pretend that you don't exist.'

'I'm not a queen,' Louisa said.

'But you will be, and you'll be a good one.' Marguerite paused. 'Looking back, I think your father felt trapped, too. But, having met you, I think your mother would have supported him so he would have been a good king. You have my support, you have the King's support, and I believe your family in London will support you, too. You can make this work, Louisa.'

'Can I? I'll have to give up so much,' Louisa said. 'I'll hardly see my family. I'll have to leave London. And I love my job.'

'It's about finding a workable compromise,' the Queen said. 'Your family will always be welcome here, and video calls will help in between. You can still visit London. And you don't have to give up all of the textile work you love—you can make time in your schedule for yourself. The pleasure will be all the sweeter when time is so precious.'

Something about the Queen's tone and those last few words made Louisa wonder. 'Just how ill is the King?'

'Sicker than he will admit,' Marguerite said. 'But if you need him to stay on for another year, until you're ready, then he'll do it.'

'He needs to step down,' Louisa said, 'and you all need me to step up.'

'Talk to Veronica,' Marguerite said. 'You can perhaps say things to her that you wouldn't feel comfortable saying to me. Talk to Sébastien.'

Ironic: the Queen expected her to open up to a man who wouldn't open up to her. Though she did need to see Sébastien, to thank him for persuading her grandfather to change the wording on her father's grave.

'Take your time,' Marguerite said, squeezing her hand. 'And I'm here if you need me.'

'Thank you,' Louisa said, and went to find Sébastien. She got slightly lost on the way to his office, but a footman stepped in to help.

He looked up from his desk when she knocked on the door. 'Was there something you needed?'

'To thank you,' she said. 'The King showed me the monumental mason's plan for the new wording.'

He shrugged. 'It was the right thing.'

Which was what drove him, she knew. 'How did you persuade him?'

'We talked,' Sébastien said—as always, giving none of his feelings away.

'I...um—' She glanced at Pascal.

'You can say anything in front of Pascal. He's discreet,' Sébastien said.

'The King says I can't step down. That the only reason for stepping down is ill health.'

'I did warn you,' he said quietly.

Sébastien had also offered her a way out. But she'd already turned him down, so it was no longer an option. 'I'm staying for a bit longer,' she said. 'Until we work out where we go from here.'

'I'd say that would be a press conference, shadowing the King for a while, and then a coronation after the King steps down at the end of the summer—or maybe he'll delay it until you're ready,' he said.

'What about you?'

He shrugged. 'I'll resign at a suitable point.'

Resign? Leave the palace? But this was everything he'd worked for. He was losing just as much as she was. Changing his life because of her. 'That's—'

'It is what it is,' he cut in. 'Was there anything else?'

It wasn't a discussion she wanted to have with him in front of anyone else, but it was pretty clear Sébastien had no intention of being alone with her. 'No. It's fine. But thank you.'

'De rien.'

And he was in full starch mode, because his smile didn't reach his eyes.

Right now, he was more distant than she'd ever known him; and he clearly wanted her to go. 'I, um... I'll catch you later.'

She spent the next hour talking things through with her grandparents in London. Another hour walking in the palace gardens and thinking about it. Another hour sewing, concentrating on the stitches while she worked things through in the back of her head.

And then she went to see the King and Queen.

'I've talked to Nan and Granddad,' she said. 'And I've thought about it. If my dad had still been alive, he would've been the heir and I would've followed in his footsteps. I chose to join my family's firm in London; and now it's time I chose to join the family firm here.'

'You're sure about this, *ma petite*?' the Queen asked.

Louisa nodded. 'You said about finding a workable compromise. That's what we'll do. And we'll make it the best for everyone.'

Sébastien had taught her that.

He'd also taught her that she had to choose between love and duty. She still didn't agree. But until he was prepared to see there was an alternative, there was nothing she could do but wait.

'You look—' Pascal began.

Séb shook his head. 'Don't even go there, please.'

'She doesn't really want to do the job. You do. There has to be a way round it.'

There was. But Louisa had rejected it. Rejected *him*. And Emil had tipped him off that Louisa had agreed to step up and be the heir. Between them, perhaps he and Emil could advise Louisa to appoint Pascal as her private secretary; he'd do an excellent job of supporting her.

But her life wouldn't include Sébastien himself.

'No,' Séb said.

He didn't eat with her, that evening; as far as he knew, she ate with the King and Queen.

He spent the weekend catching up with paperwork; hers was spent in a press conference, as he'd predicted. He watched it at his desk, and she completely charmed her audience. The preparation he'd coached her through had paid off. Which was a good thing, he reminded himself. He wanted her to do well. To be reconciled with her grandparents. For the country to be stable.

Just…he wished it had been different. That he'd been by her side.

Despite the fact that she lived in the apartment opposite his, he managed to avoid her for the next couple of days. But he missed her. He missed her with a visceral ache he hadn't expected. Walking in the garden made him miserable, because he remembered walking there with her; and it brought back memories of the way they'd danced together in the gardens of the beach house. How they'd waltzed. How they'd kissed. How they'd ended up making love.

He'd intended to teach her how to be a princess, but somewhere along the way he'd fallen in love with her.

And he really didn't know what to do about it.

She wanted love. He knew that. But had he left it too late to offer her love? Would she believe him, if he told her how he felt? Or would she think he was just trying to talk her into a marriage for the country's sake?

After another poor night's sleep, he was pacing the palace gardens when he rounded a corner and almost bumped into her.

'Sorry,' he said.

'No harm done,' she replied. Then her eyes narrowed. 'Are you all right?'

He lifted his chin. 'Yes, of course.' And then he sighed. Maybe he should tell her the truth. 'No. I'm as miserable as hell.'

'Why?'

'Because,' he said, 'something happened when we were at the beach house.'

Colour stormed her cheeks.

He shook his head. 'Not that,' he said. 'Though that, as well.'

'I'm not following.'

'According to Pascal, I'm not making a lot of sense to anyone, nowadays,' he said dryly. 'Can we talk?'

She nodded, and he walked with her towards the wildflower meadow.

'Something I never told you: when I agreed to be the heir, I was dating someone seriously,' he said. 'Her name was Elodie. We'd been law students together. I loved her, and I hoped we had a future together. But she really, really hated life at the palace. The press were always in her face. It got in the way of her work. And she didn't see enough of me, because I was too busy trying to learn everything I needed for my new role and I neglected her. In the end, she told me she couldn't do it any more. She didn't actually give me the ultimatum, but the choice was obvious: love or duty. I chose duty. And maybe I made the wrong choice.'

Louisa wasn't sure what surprised her more: that Sébastien had been serious about someone, or that he was admitting to being wrong. But what had happened with Elodie explained why he didn't believe in love, and why he'd insisted that love had no place in a royal marriage.

In his experience, love had been versus duty rather than supporting it.

'Do you still love her?' Because, if he did, he should never have made love with Louisa.

'No. In any case, she's happily married, and she has two children and a flourishing career as a family law-yer—the life she wanted and the life she deserves. I don't mean…' He sighed. 'Why is this so difficult to explain?'

Probably because he was talking about his feelings. But if he was actually going to open up to her, she didn't want him to stop. 'Keep talking. It doesn't matter if it's muddled. Just talk,' she said.

He nodded. 'When I say the wrong choice, I mean I was wrong about love. I thought I could manage with-out it. And I've discovered that I can't.' He stopped at the edge of the flower meadow. 'Shall we sit?'

'Sure.' She sat down opposite him.

'The last few days have been unbearable,' he said.

'Because you're no longer the heir?'

'It's not that,' he said. 'It's you. You were just the other side of the corridor, but you might as well have been at the edge of the universe.' He paused. 'I discov-ered that I miss you. And duty isn't enough, any more. I want…'

She held her breath.

'I want you,' he said finally, and looked her in the eye.

His feelings blazed from his eyes: but she needed to hear him say it. Needed him to open up to her. So she simply waited for him to go on.

'I didn't expect,' he said, 'to fall in love with you.' He broke off a few stems of flowers, and began to weave them together. 'And it was everything about you. In

London, when you told me off in the café. When you showed me the magic of ballet and made me realise how your father had seen your mother. Here, when you brought the sunshine back into the Queen's face and you were kind to the King, even though you were justifiably angry with him. When you cooked with me, and it felt like being a family.'

Just how it had felt for her.

'At the beach house, when you were determined to learn and make things work. On the beach, when you held my hand. And that last night, when we waltzed together under the stars... I wanted to fall asleep in your arms. I wanted you to be the first thing I saw when I woke. Except the wrong words came out.' He blew out a breath. 'I want to marry you. But it's got nothing to do with us being compatible and being able to rule the country together, and everything to do with the fact that I love you and I can't function without you. Without you, it's like a bit of me's missing. The better part of me.'

Sébastien loved her.

He really loved her.

'And this is all too little, and too late, and too hopeless. I know that. You're going to be busy, just as I was. You don't have time for any of this. I'll do the right thing: I'll resign from my office at the palace and disappear quietly,' he said. 'But I didn't want to go without telling you how I feel about you. And telling you to your face that you're right. Without love, marriage is worth nothing.'

'So what do you want, Sébastien?'

'Really?'

'Really.'

'I want you,' he said. 'And I don't mean *la Princesse*

Louisa. I mean I want Louisa Gallet. I'd like to start again. Ask you to date me. Walk through the lavender fields with me at sunset. Watch the sun rise over the sea. Maybe come to the farm and help with the harvest, even if you can only spare a couple of hours.'

'Is that what you're going to do? Go back to the farm?' she asked.

'For a bit,' he said. 'While I work out what to do next. If I want to practise law, I'll need more training.'

'What about all the work you've done here?'

'It's not the right sort of work for me to be a barrister or solicitor,' he said. 'But in the meantime I can make myself useful to my family.'

'Duty,' she said.

He shook his head. 'Love. I love my family. I've neglected them, too.' He blew out a breath. 'So now I've told you the truth. I neglected the woman I intended to marry, and I neglected my family. I was worried I would neglect you, too, and you'd end up resenting me.'

'Or maybe,' she said, 'you just need to learn that love and duty can work together. I've talked to my grandparents about compromise.'

'Is that why you're staying?'

'Even the brightest lawyer I know can't get me out of taking over from my grandfather,' she said. 'I worked for my mum's family firm in London. Now it's time to work for my dad's family firm.'

He looked down at the flowers he'd plaited into a crown. 'As the Queen.'

'From the end of the summer,' she said. 'Though I could do with a consort.' She tipped her head to one side. 'If you know anyone who might be interested in the job?'

'That depends,' he said. 'Because I've learned something over the last few days. I've learned that, without love, nothing is enough.' He looked at her. 'So where do we go from here? Do you think you could learn to love me?'

He'd been honest with her. It was her turn to be honest with him. 'I already do,' she said. 'I think I did right from the start. Even when I thought we were on opposite sides, you made me tingle. And here in Charlmoux you always made me feel you were on my side, supporting me instead of taking over.'

'Good, because that's what I was trying to do.'

'And you made things happen—things I couldn't do for myself. You got my grandfather to apologise and change the wording on my father's memorial. You introduced me to my grandmother.'

'And I screwed up,' he reminded her. 'I hurt you, and I'm so sorry.'

'We all screw up,' she said. 'As my grandfather told me, you can't change the past, but you can learn from it. And you're bright enough to be a quick learner.'

'Right now,' he said, 'I think you have more confidence in me than I do.'

'I do,' she said, 'because you're a good man. You have integrity. You try to do the right thing, and you want to make the world a better place. But that isn't why I love you.'

'Why do you love me?' he asked.

'That's the thing,' she said. 'Some things you can't explain. You just feel. Like when you watch someone dance *Swan Lake*. You can dissect the techniques, the choreography, the costumes—but none of that can explain how it makes you *feel*. You don't need to explain feelings. They don't have to be neat and tidy and packaged away. They just *are*.'

'And you make me feel, Louisa. You really do.' He paused. 'I thought I had to choose between love and duty. You showed me that I'd got it completely wrong.'

'So now you want it all?'

'I want you,' he said. 'Which is the same thing. So will you consider dating me?'

He wanted to date her.

He'd asked her for herself, not for the crown.

Finally, finally, he was opening up to her. 'What if,' she said, 'I want more than that?'

'If I could, I'd give you the sun, the moon and the stars,' he said.

'That isn't what I want,' she said. 'I want something a lot more precious than that. A lot bigger than that.' She met his gaze. 'I want your heart, Sébastien Moreau.'

'You have my heart,' he said. 'And my love.' He shifted so he was on one knee. 'And you want more than dating? So do I. Louisa Gallet, you make me want to be a better man, and I'll love you to the end of our days. I haven't got a ring to offer you—but I'd want you to choose it with me anyway, because you're my partner and I'll always listen to what you want. Will you marry me, Louisa? Not for duty, not for convenience, but for love?'

'Did you ask the King's permission to propose to me?' she asked.

'No, because your hand isn't his to give. It's *yours*.'

'Yes,' she said.

'Yes, it's your choice, or yes, you'll marry me?' he asked.

'Both.'

She saw the moment realisation hit, and it was as if the sun lit him up from the inside.

'I love you,' he said softly, and he kissed her.

Then he picked up the crown he'd plaited. 'Marguerites and cornflowers.'

'My grandmother's name, and my mother's eyes,' she said.

He placed the crown on her head. 'These flowers will fade, but you'll always be my princess. My queen.'

'And you,' she said, 'will always be my Sébastien.' She kissed him, and stood up. 'Come on. We have news to share.'

He got to his feet and took her hand. 'One day I'll buy you a proper tiara.'

'I don't need diamonds. I'm keeping this one,' she said. 'I'll press it. And one day we'll show our children how their father proposed to me—with a crown of cornflowers and marguerites.'

EPILOGUE

Two years later

VERONICA MADE A last adjustment to Louisa's veil. 'You look beautiful,' she said. 'Every inch a queen, wearing your mum's pearls.'

'I look like a queen because I have the very best dressmaker,' Louisa said. 'The one my mum would've chosen, if she'd been getting married in the cathedral.' The same cathedral where Louisa had been crowned Queen of Charlmoux two summers ago.

'Your mum and dad would've been so proud of you,' Veronica said, her voice thick with emotion. 'I love you.'

'Love you, too,' Louisa said. 'And I'm so glad we have video calls, so at least I get to see you whenever I want, even if Granddad has to give you the hugs for me.'

'Last check,' Sam said. 'Something old?'

'Mum's pearls,' Louisa said.

'New?' Milly asked.

'Dress.'

'Borrowed?' Nina, Louisa's best friend and the third bridesmaid, asked.

'Mémére's tiara.' The one Marguerite had worn on her own wedding day. Louisa looked at her other grand-mother and smiled.

'And blue's your bouquet,' Veronica finished.

Louisa had chosen white roses, like the ones in her mother's bouquet, combined with the cornflowers and marguerites that Sébastien had made into a crown for her, the day he'd asked her to marry him for love.

'Check: fairy flower girls?' Sam asked.

'Oui!' Sébastien's nieces chorused, beaming their heads off and making their fairy wings—made for them personally by Louisa—shimmer.

'Your grandfathers are waiting downstairs,' Veronica said. 'Time to go.'

Between them, the bridesmaids managed the train of Louisa's dress down the sweeping staircase. The dress was a simple silk sheath with a three-metre detachable train, overlaid with lace that matched the foliage curls of her tiara and formed the high neck and sleeves.

Jack and Henri were waiting for them at the bottom of the stairs.

'It's how I thought your mum would look,' Jack said, his voice hoarse.

'My Louis would be proud of you,' Henri added, not to be outdone. *'Ma petite-fille.'*

Sam and Milly helped her into the golden carriage drawn by four white horses, while Nina shepherded the flower girls to one of the limos and Jack and Henri climbed into the other side of the carriage. Then the grandmothers of the bride and the bridesmaids climbed into the other limo to follow the carriage to the cathedral.

'Wave out of the window,' Henri said to Jack. 'You're her grandfather, too, and they want to see you.'

Louisa hid a smile and waved out of the carriage windows at the people lining the streets. People were waving madly, cheering and clapping as the carriage went past; there were banners bearing her initial with Sébastien's in hearts.

When they arrived at the cathedral, there was a barrage of media photographers waiting for her. Although all she wanted to do was to walk down the aisle to Sébastien, she also knew the people of Charlmoux wanted to share these moments, so she posed patiently.

Finally her grandmothers went into the cathedral; Nina checked her train, and then Louisa tucked a hand into the crook of each grandfather's arm and the usher held the door for them to enter.

As they walked down the carpet, the pianist and cellist started playing Einaudi's 'Le Onde', which always reminded her of walking on the beach hand in hand with Sébastien at the edge of the sea; the sun was streaming through the clerestory windows, and the whole thing felt magical.

He was waiting for her at the altar, and her heart skipped a beat.

He turned to look at her and smiled, and she knew that everything was going to be just fine.

Jack stopped and lifted her veil. 'I love you. Be happy,' he whispered.

'I love you, too,' Henri added. 'Be happy.'

Louisa smiled, and stepped forward to join Sébastien at the altar.

The archbishop welcomed them, and delivered a sermon all about love. Sébastien held her hand as Jack read Shakespeare's *Sonnet 116*, and then Henri read an excerpt from Thomas à Kempis's *De Imitatio Christi*.

They said their vows, exchanged rings, and finally the archbishop declared them husband and wife, saying, 'You may now kiss the bride.'

Sébastien smiled, mouthed, 'I love you,' and leaned in to kiss her.

After they'd signed the register and a last blessing from the archbishop, they walked down the aisle together and posed for the press on the cathedral steps. To the cheers of the crowd, Sébastien kissed his bride. The rest of the wedding guests lined up on either side, then threw dried cornflower and marguerite petals as confetti while Sébastien and Louisa walked down to the waiting carriage.

On the short journey back to the palace, Louisa and Sébastien held hands and waved with their free hands.

'Well, now, *la Reine* Louisa of Charlmoux,' Sébastien said at the reception, after the food and speeches. 'Are you ready for our first dance?'

'Our first married dance, *le Prince* Sébastien.' Her grandfather, before stepping down, had made his granddaughter's future consort an official prince. She smiled. 'Now the train's detached from my dress, yes. I don't think I could have danced with the train.'

'You look amazing. You *are* amazing,' he said.

When they walked onto the dance floor, the band started playing 'What a Wonderful World'—the song he'd first taught her to waltz to.

'It doesn't get any better than this,' Sébastien said.

'Oh, but it does.' Louisa smiled. 'I have some very hot-off-the-press news for you.'

'What?'

'I seem to have followed in my mother's footsteps. Falling in love with a prince of Charlmoux, and...'

His eyes widened. 'Are you telling me...?'

She whispered in his ear, 'Yup. I discovered this morning, in seven and a half months' time, you'll be meeting someone who's the second in line to the throne of Charlmoux. It's why I had my very own bottle of champagne—or, as our waiter is sworn to keep secret, sparkling elderflower.' Then she pulled back slightly, so she could see his reaction.

In answer, he gave her the widest, widest smile, picked her up and spun her round. 'I love you,' he said. 'Both of you. My queen, and our prince or princess baby...'

* * * * *

COMING SOON!

MILLS & BOON®

Coming next month

FORBIDDEN KISSES WITH HER
MILLIONAIRE BOSS
Hana Sheik

Karl said, "Show your grandfather what he can't see. The talent and hard work that brought you this far."

"I'll try." She didn't say it with much conviction though.

He heard it and shook his head. "Make me believe that you mean it."

She breathed slowly and thoughtfully through her nose and then gave it another go.

"I can do it."

"A little better. But it won't cut it because I don't believe it."

Her frustration had been simmering for nearly a day now. All of her flight she'd been wringing her hands, oscillating between being angry at her grandfather to wanting to please him and giving in to his demands. He'd sacrificed for her. Wasn't it time for her to do the same for him, even if it meant her happiness was on the line?

"Make me believe you," he stressed, those dark eyes of his cutting through her.

A switch flipped in her and when she opened her mouth, she didn't recognize the words coming out or the emotion thrumming through her.

"Damn it, I can do this! I'm the only one who can do this, and that should be enough."

Lin hadn't felt the quiver in her hands until the bouquet trembled slightly. Somehow Karl dragged out the fear of losing her grandfather's love and of being abandoned by him and channeled into strength. She burned with the power of belief in herself. Her head rushed with the sensation and her heart was fuller for it.

She needn't look to Karl to see his approval.

Though his face barely dropped its cool guard, he was smiling and nodding, and she didn't think that anything else could have made her feel better in the moment. The swooping in her stomach and the breathless tightening in her chest were just products of the outburst she'd just had…or so she told herself. It wasn't because Karl looked sexier smiling, or that she suddenly noticed how close he was to her, his cologne in the air she breathed and his body heat so enticingly near.

She just had to remember that he was now technically her boss…

Making him very forbidden fruit.

Continue reading
**FORBIDDEN KISSES WITH HER
MILLIONAIRE BOSS**
Hana Sheik

Available next month
www.millsandboon.co.uk

Copyright © 2022 Hana Sheik

MILLS & BOON

THE HEART OF ROMANCE

A ROMANCE FOR EVERY READER

MODERN

Prepare to be swept off your feet by sophisticated, sexy and seductive heroes, in some of the world's most glamourous and romantic locations, where power and passion collide.

HISTORICAL

Escape with historical heroes from time gone by. Whether your passion is for wicked Regency Rakes, muscled Vikings or rugged Highlanders, awaken the romance of the past.

MEDICAL

Set your pulse racing with dedicated, delectable doctors in the high-pressure world of medicine, where emotions run high and passion, comfort and love are the best medicine.

True Love

Celebrate true love with tender stories of heartfelt romance, from the rush of falling in love to the joy a new baby can bring, and a focus on the emotional heart of a relationship.

Desire

Indulge in secrets and scandal, intense drama and plenty of sizzling hot action with powerful and passionate heroes who have it all: wealth, status, good looks…everything but the right woman.

HEROES

Experience all the excitement of a gripping thriller, with an intense romance at its heart. Resourceful, true-to-life women and strong, fearless men face danger and desire - a killer combination!

To see which titles are coming soon, please visit

millsandboon.co.uk/nextmonth